SCIENCE AND TECHNOLOGY EDUCATIC
AND FUTURE HUMAN NEEDS

Volume 8

The Environment and Science and Technology Education

Science and Technology Education and Future Human Needs

General Editor: JOHN LEWIS
Malvern College, United Kingdom

Related Pergamon Journal

INTERNATIONAL JOURNAL OF EDUCATIONAL
DEVELOPMENT

Editor: PHILIP TAYLOR

Throughout the world educational developments are taking place: developments in literacy, programmes in vocational education, in curriculum and teaching, in the economics of education and in educational administration.

It is the purpose of the *International Journal of Educational Development* to bring these developments to the attention of professionals in the field of education, with particular focus upon issues and problems of concern to those in the Third World. Concrete information, of interest to planners, practitioners and researchers, is presented in the form of articles, case studies and research reports.

The Environment and Science and Technology Education

Edited by

A. V. BAEZ
Chairman Emeritus, Education Commission of the International Union for the Conservation of Nature and Natural Resources

G. W. KNAMILLER
University of Leeds, Leeds

J. C. SMYTH
Paisley College, Scotland

Published for the

ICSU PRESS

by

PERGAMON PRESS

OXFORD · NEW YORK · BEIJING · FRANKFURT
SÃO PAULO · SYDNEY · TOKYO · TORONTO

U.K.	Pergamon Press, Headington Hill Hall, Oxford OX3 0BW, England
U.S.A.	Pergamon Press, Maxwell House, Fairview Park, Elmsford, New York 10523, U.S.A.
PEOPLE'S REPUBLIC OF CHINA	Pergamon Press, Room 4037, Qianmen Hotel, Beijing, People's Republic of China
FEDERAL REPUBLIC OF GERMANY	Pergamon Press, Hammerweg 6, D-6242 Kronberg, Federal Republic of Germany
BRAZIL	Pergamon Editora, Rua Eça de Queiros, 346, CEP 04011, Paraiso, São Paulo, Brazil
AUSTRALIA	Pergamon Press Australia, P.O. Box 544, Potts Point, N.S.W. 2011, Australia
JAPAN	Pergamon Press, 8th Floor, Matsuoka Central Building, 1-7-1 Nishishinjuku, Shinjuku-ku, Tokyo 160, Japan
CANADA	Pergamon Press Canada, Suite No. 271, 253 College Street, Toronto, Ontario, Canada M5T 1R5

First edition 1987

Library of Congress Cataloging in Publication Data
The Environment and science and technology education.
(Science and technology education and future human needs; vol. 8)
Papers from the Bangalore Conference on Science and Technology Education and Future Human Needs, held in Bangalore, India, Aug. 6–14, 1985, which was organized by the Committee on the Teaching of Science of the International Council of Scientific Unions.
1. Environmental protection—Study and teaching—Congresses.
2. Science—Study and teaching—Congresses. 3. Engineering—Study and teaching—Congresses.
I. Baez, A. V.   II. Knamiller, G. W.   III. Smyth, J. C.
IV. Bangalore Conference on Science and Technology Education and Future Human Needs (1985)   V. International Council of Scientific Unions. Committee on the Teaching of Science.
VI. Series.
TD170.6.E58   1987   333.7'07   86-25239

British Library Cataloguing in Publication Data
The environment and science and technology education. — (Science and technology education and future human needs; v. 8)
1. Environmental education
I. Baez, A. V. II. Knamiller, G. W.
III. Smyth, J. C. IV. Series
333.7'07   GF26

ISBN 0-08-033952-2 Hardcover
ISBN 0-08-033953-0 Flexicover

Printed in Great Britain by A. Wheaton & Co. Ltd. Exeter

Foreword

In recent years at numerous conferences at international, regional and national levels, eco-development experts have stressed the urgency of spreading the concept of sustainable development. Nevertheless, problems of environmental degradation are becoming more serious day by day in developing countries. It is now apparent that ecologically sound environmental management practices will be able to gather a self-propelling momentum only if these will help ensure the secure livelihood of the rural and urban poor and provide them with food, fodder, fuel, fibre, water and shelter. We therefore need a structured mechanism to enable rural families to discuss problems relating to their livelihood security in the context of the management of basic life support systems. I believe that we need for this purpose a global grid of conservation clubs organized by educational institutions such as village schools, as well as colleges and universities. The pleas for people's participation in programmes designed to foster development without destruction will continue to remain a mere slogan unless there are mechanisms for enabling people to discuss their environmental problems and develop their own solutions. The African food crisis underlines the urgency of harmonizing ecological and agricultural rehabilitation plans. Unless this happens the quality of life in rural areas will deteriorate further in many developing countries, leading to an increased influx of "environmental refugees" in cities. It is in this context that the Bangalore Conference has been a significant milestone in our efforts to spread, through education, the message that conservation *is* development.

M. S. SWAMINATHAN

Preface

The Bangalore Conference on "Science and Technology Education and Future Human Needs" was the result of extensive work over several years by the Committee on the Teaching of Science of the International Council of Scientific Unions. The Committee received considerable support from Unesco and the United Nations University, as well as a number of generous funding agencies.

Educational conferences have often concentrated on particular disciplines. The starting point at this Conference was those topics already identified as the most significant for development, namely Health; Food and Agriculture; Energy; Land, Water and Mineral Resources; Industry and Technology; the Environment; Science Education and Information Transfer. Teams worked on each of these, examining the implications for education at all levels (primary, secondary, tertiary, adult and community education). The emphasis was on identifying techniques and resource material to give practical help to teachers in all countries in order to raise standards of education in those topics essential for development. As well as the topics listed above, there is also one concerned with the educational aspects of Ethics and Social Responsibility. The outcome of the Conference is this series of books, which can be used for follow-up meetings in each of the regions of the world and which can provide the basis for further development.

JOHN L. LEWIS
Secretary, ICSU–CTS

Acknowledgements

Many people have been involved in the assembly of material for this volume, which stems from the Environment Topic of the International Conference on "Science and Technology Education and Future Human Needs", held at Bangalore, India from 8 to 15 August 1985, organized by the Committee on the Teaching of Science of the International Council of Scientific Unions (ICSU) and hosted by the Indian National Science Academy.

The pre-conference preparation of activities for the Environment theme was directed by A. V. Baez and Julia Marton-Lefèvre of ICSU. For the purpose of gathering material the topic was divided into four sub-themes:

(1) the Science curriculum: co-ordinators G. W. Knamiller and J. C. Smyth;
(2) the Technology curriculum: co-ordinator Conrado Bauer;
(3) the Social Sciences and Arts curriculum: co-ordinator Enikö Szalay-Marzsó;
(4) Non-formal Education: co-ordinator M. A. Partha Sarathy.

M. A. Partha Sarathy also maintained links between the topic planning team and the conference planners in India. The co-ordinators assembled papers relating to their own sub-themes which were either circulated in advance of the conference or made available to participants at its commencement.

At the conference the Topic Group was led by A. V. Baez and T. N. Khoshoo. The conference papers, which were augmented by others brought by participants, were discussed in twelve workshops, whose leaders and rapporteurs were members of the planning and editorial teams, with the addition of Sálvano Briceño. The papers and workshop discussions provide the material for this book, which is divided into five parts as follows, with the names of those responsible for preparing them:

  I. Introduction and Key Issues – A. V. Baez;
 II. School-based Primary and Secondary Education – G. W. Knamiller and J. C. Smyth;
III. Community-based Environmental Education and Links with Other Conference Themes – S. Jakowska;

ix

IV. Tertiary, Professional and Vocational Environmental Education – C. Bauer, assisted by G. R. Francis and M. K. Wali;

V. Non-formal Public Environmental Education – L. Wayburn.

The final editing has been carried out by A. V. Baez, G. W. Knamiller and J. C. Smyth.

In order to include as wide a range as possible of the materials and discussions, papers have been condensed to varying degrees with the omission of much detail together with many references to other relevant literature. Readers who wish to follow them up may do so by consulting the authors, whose addresses are listed at the end.* The editors hope that what is included here will, however, give a reasonable review of the proceedings of an exciting conference.

For an occasion like this the credit must be evenly spread among all of the participants, including many who are not listed contributors. Among these are the local schoolchildren and their teachers who took so memorable a part. Especially we thank our Indian hosts, who could not have done more to provide an environment conducive to success. The support and enthusiasm thus generated can never be adequately represented between the covers of a book.

*A figure in brackets following a name in the text, e.g. Baez (4), refers to the numbered entry in the list at the end (pp. 417 et seq.).

Contents

Part II

School-based Primary and Secondary Environmental Education

Part III
Community-based Environmental Education and Links with Other Conference Themes
S. JAKOWSKA

Part V
Non-formal Public Environmental Education

I Introduction and Key Issues in Environmental Education

1

The Environment Theme at the Bangalore Conference

A. V. BAEZ

**THE ACTIVITIES OF THE ENVIRONMENT GROUP AT
THE BANGALORE CONFERENCE**

The Bangalore Conference was attended by 310 persons from 64 countries; 48 persons from 27 countries were registered in the Environment topic, of whom 10 were from India, but these numbers do not reflect the total number of people who participated because there was some cross-linking of activities among members of the eight conference topics. Thirty-five Environment papers were printed up before the conference and 15 others were submitted at the conference.

The Environment topic is unique in that the themes of all the other topics are actually key issues in environmental education, in particular those dealing with food, agriculture, resources and health. For this reason the Environment topic was, perhaps, the broadest and possibly the most difficult one to organize.

Since the seat of the conference was in India, we were particularly pleased that so many Indians who have been active in environmental activities participated in the Environment topic, including such distinguished personalities as Dr M. S. Swaminathan, Director of the International Rice Research Institute, who delivered the plenary lecture for the Environment topic, and Dr T. N. Khoshoo, former Secretary of the Department of Environment of the Government of India. Mr M. A. Partha Sarathy, Deputy Chairman of the Commission on Education of the International Union for Conservation of Nature and Natural Resources, was particularly helpful in making local arrangements.

All the Environment participants attended the plenary sessions as well as the joint workshops with the groups on Health and on Ethics and Social Responsibility, but they broke up into sub-groups to participate in workshops dealing broadly with formal environmental education at the primary and secondary levels, on the one hand, and, separately, at the

3

tertiary level, where special emphasis was placed on the education of professionals in engineering and technology. Several workshops were devoted to non-formal education both in and out of school. Some of these emphasized the use of visual and dramatic arts in generating an environmental ethic.

Two of our participants, Sophie Jakowska of the Dominican Republic and Bernt Hauge of Norway, came to Bangalore a week early to work with the teachers and children of a local school to put on a play with an environmental message before the entire Environment group. Since the title of the conference stresses "future human needs" they wanted to dramatize the fact that children represent the future and should be allowed to participate in the activities of the conference.

Two other workshops are worthy of note because they illustrate how departure from the procedure of reading papers livened up the workshops and promoted active participation. Professor Blum of Israel, who was a participant in the Food topic, and Professor Fensham of Australia, who was participating in the Industry topic, collaborated with us in running a workshop illustrating how games can be used as an educational tool in environmental education.

A very special treat was the excursion involving an overnight stay at the Bandipur Wildlife Sanctuary, where we saw at first hand how environmental education activities are carried out in the field with the help of a permanent professional staff and student volunteers. It also gave us a chance to see the agricultural landscape and the city of Mysore.

A chairman and a rapporteur were appointed for each workshop. Resource persons were chosen on the basis of the subjects of papers they had submitted before the conference. The chairman then structured his or her workshop period allowing the resource persons to elaborate their topic on the basis of their papers and/or their experience, without actually reading the paper. In this way time was found for discussions, which were summarized by the rapporteur. Participants were urged to describe case studies of activities that had actually produced results.

THE PAPERS

The material for this book comes, in part, from the papers which were submitted to the conference. Most are not reproduced in their entirety but their titles, and a list of names and addresses of authors, appear in Annex I. Readers interested in obtaining the full papers may correspond directly with the authors, some of whom were not able to attend the conference.

The final output of the entire conference is not a single volume but nine separate volumes dealing with its eight topics, plus one dealing with organizational details and giving an integrative overview. Our volume deals with the topic *environment*, but the emphasis is on how to introduce an environmental component into science and technology education both in and out of the classroom.

TARGET AUDIENCE

The Environment volume is addressed to three target groups. The first consists of all the participants – not just the members of the Environment group – who would like to know what went on in the Environment discussions.

The second target group consists of those people who would have liked to attend the conference but who, for whatever reason, were unable to do so.

The third target group consists of that large audience of science and technology educators who are just beginning to become aware of the importance of including environmental issues in their teaching.

It is also important that the volume convey some of the excitement and spirit of the conference, and we felt that this could not be done through the customary conventional proceedings.

SOURCES OF CONTENT

Not only the papers written for the conference, but the activities and discussions that took place in the workshops and plenary sessions are the two sources of this book. We had stressed all along to the authors and participants that we did not want philosophical discussions or definitions of environmental education. These have already been adequately covered in several international conferences. What we wanted were case studies and reports about environmental education projects so that others might try these approaches. In other words we wanted answers to the question: *What have you done that actually worked?*

Recognizing that environmental education is something that cannot be confined to the classroom, we requested inputs dealing with both formal and non-formal education; and because the conference dealt with science and technology we asked authors to describe their experiences of infusing environmental concepts into the syllabuses and curricula of existing science and technology courses. We sought inputs as well from the realm of the social sciences and the liberal arts. We also sought inputs from the non-formal sector where games, outdoor activities and the mass media are useful in reaching a large audience for the purpose of raising the level of awareness of conservation and environmental issues.

2

Science, Technology and the Environment

A. V. BAEZ

THE BASIC HUMAN NEEDS

Any list of basic human needs, past, present or future, would include food, shelter, health and safety as survival needs; education, employment and possibly some form of industrialization as development needs; wealth, security and growth as perceived needs.

Of course, man does not live by bread alone. Human needs go beyond the purely physical and are immersed in social and economic environments as well. Humans need meaningful employment, leisure time, and the human qualities of respect, care and affection. Deprived of these a person may languish just as surely as if deprived of food and water.

Most of our physical needs demand access to natural resources such as land, water, and air, which, with the aid of radiant energy from the sun, generate plants and animals – the so-called renewable living resources. Non-renewable resources such as minerals and fossil fuels are, of course, also needed for human survival and development. All these resources are to be found on a thin layer of the earth's surface known as the biosphere. It is the physical environment in which we live. The link between the environment and human needs is therefore clear. Now we must consider the links between science, technology and the environment.

SCIENCE AND TECHNOLOGY

One must recognize a basic difference between science and technology. Technology, unlike science, deliberately sets out to create things that satisfy human needs. It has been said that science explains what *is* and technology creates *what never existed before*. Technology has always generated devices and procedures, often exhibiting great creativity, to do things which serve useful ends.

How about science? What does it have to do with the satisfaction of

7

human needs? After all, science is concerned primarily with the search for knowledge and understanding of the physical world. As such science was, in the past, considered objective and value-free. The scientific observer was supposed to be able to stand to one side and record events impartially, and without affecting their course. But we now know that, at least at the atomic level, the mere act of observing events affects them. At the macroscopic level also, the concepts of cybernetics suggest that feedback links the observer with the object of his observations. In the study of the environment, in particular, we now recognize that "holistic" and "systems" ways of perceiving reality are needed, and these invariably involve the observer as part of the observation. People, partly because of their sheer numbers, have affected the environment in devastating ways.

The understanding that arises from scientific investigation does satisfy a "need to know" which is uniquely human, but it is mainly through technology that scientific knowledge has been able to produce dramatic improvements in the provision of food, shelter, health and safety – the survival needs – during the past 200 years, at least in certain parts of the world.

Besides the basic sciences of physics, chemistry and biology a new science – ecology – has arisen recently out of the biological study of species, but it is now much broader than biology and is, in effect, an interdisciplinary science which considers the interconnectedness of many phenomena previously considered independent. Ecology shows how all living things on the earth – plants and animals – depend upon one another and upon the chemical elements which are in the biosphere as well as on the energy which comes from the sun.

Another thing that is recent, in historical terms, is the tremendous power which human beings have achieved, through technology, to alter the physical and chemical composition of the surface of the earth. As W. S. Fyfe says in his book *Global Change*, "We live in a special period of history of our planet. Man, because of his intelligence and science, is changing the environment, and has become the major force in the transport of solid earth materials, and his chemical by-products are changing the hydro-sphere and the atmosphere."

Still another idea, which for the moment is simply an interesting hypothesis, is that the earth behaves like a homeostatic entity – that is, a self-regulating and self-healing body analogous to an animal, which has built-in devices to ensure the continuity of life, for example by regulating its temperature and the chemical composition of its atmosphere. These are like the complex mechanisms that generate healing after a wound.

J. E. Lovelock, in his book *Gaia – A New Look at Life on Earth*, defends a hypothesis that "the entire range of living matter on Earth, from whales to viruses, and from oaks to algae, could be regarded as consisting of a single living entity, capable of manipulating the Earth's atmosphere to suit its own needs and endowed with faculties and powers far beyond those of its constituent parts".

But human beings, although part of this living organism, have, through the use of science and technology, so altered its life support systems that all living things are threatened with disaster or extinction – if present trends continue – either through the relentless impact of an exponentially increasing human population – already beyond the 4000 million mark – or as a result of a man-made nuclear holocaust. There is need, therefore, for an ecologically oriented science and technology education to contribute its share to a reversal of these trends while there is still time.

ENVIRONMENTAL CONCERN AND SUSTAINABLE DEVELOPMENT

Consideration of human needs presumes that we must actively seek ways to improve the quality of people's lives. This implies dealing with values in our education, even in science and technology education.

Improvements in social and economic conditions are needed. Development must continue to be promoted in both industrialized and less developed countries but we must find a way of creating a balance between the utilization of natural resources and economic growth. A desirable goal, it would seem, would be to generate economic development which does not exhaust renewable and non-renewable resources. This, incidentally, is the theme of IUCN's World Conservation Strategy, a document to which we shall refer later.

One of the aims of the Bangalore Conference was to promote social and economic development through the proper kind of science and technology education. In environmental terms this means an education that leads to a rational utilization of the earth's resources. Since this is linked with the concept of sustainable development we can now state one of the major objectives of the environment theme as follows: *to demonstrate how a concern for environmental improvement can be articulated through a science and technology education which promotes sustainable development*. The word sustainable is important, because science and technology have, unfortunately, often been used to foster development which leads to the exhaustion of natural resources, the deterioration of the environment and the extinction of species.

ENVIRONMENTAL EDUCATION

Public awareness of these issues was raised world-wide by the United Nations Conference on Human Environment held in Stockholm in 1972. An important outcome of this conference was the creation of a new agency called the United Nations Environment Programme (UNEP). In response to, or in support of, its Declaration some governments created or gave increased support to environmental protection agencies to reverse the trends that were leading to ecological disaster.

In the process a discipline called environmental education has evolved. Its main characteristics as outlined in Unesco's Tbilisi Conference on Environmental Education are: (a) a problem-solving approach, (b) an interdisciplinary educational approach, (c) the integration of education into the community, and (d) a life-long, forward-looking education. UNEP has supported environmental education work in several United Nations agencies such as Unesco and FAO, as well as in the International Union for Conservation of Nature and Natural Resources (IUCN).

There is no specific mention of science and technology in Unesco's outline, but no other specific disciplines are mentioned either. *It is, therefore, the task of the exponents of science and technology education, such as those who participated in the Bangalore Conference, to invent new ways in which the concepts of ecology, which lie at the heart of environmental education, can be infused into education as a whole and into science and technology education in particular.* Surely science should constitute the foundation on which proper ecological value-judgements are based, and technology should provide the practical means of solving the ecological problems posed by industrial and other societies.

In an outline paper prepared at the early planning stage Mrs Enikö Szalay-Marzso commented on the heterogeneity of the case studies that were being collected. She stressed the need for all teachers to be aware of the holistic nature of the natural order, including mankind, its intricately linked pattern the product of millions of years of development, maintained in order by a high use of energy; it is "a series of unique events, i.e. any intervention is irreversible and any attempts to restore order once disturbed creates more disorder". The first objective, therefore, is "to develop the knowledge, skills and attitudes leading to a new system of order, values and a conservation ethic, which will enable people to contribute to the wiser management of nature". The complicated task of the social sciences and arts is "to build up the same image in youngsters of how to reach the same goal as resulted from the natural sciences".

We have the task of persuading decision-makers of the need for a new type of in-service training for teachers to help them relate together the natural and social environment. We have to find the best formulae for environmental education at every level, and encourage people to think horizontally as well as vertically. "Environmental education = communal/public education, a matter of the whole society. It is necessary to orient in time and space . . . The classical place of public education: everywhere; the classical time: always; the classical medium: everybody."

What follows represents some of the approaches to this goal.

3

Environment and Education – an Indian Perspective

The problems of environmental education in the developing countries were a recurring theme at the Bangalore Conference. Because India was the host country it is appropriate to begin by looking at these problems through the eyes of three Indian participants. M. S. Swaminathan in his plenary address took a global view of the problem. T. N. Khoshoo considered the Indian experience, and M. Wali, now teaching in the United States, noted that an environmental ethic, the need for which is at last being recognized globally, has strong historical roots in India. Contributions from several other Indians will appear in subsequent Parts.

Dr M. S. Swaminathan has had a long and distinguished career in research, education and administration. He is presently the Director General of the International Rice Research Institute in the Philippines and President of the International Union for Conservation of Nature and Natural Resources. His plenary address for the Environment theme follows.

Education, Environment and Livelihood Security

M. S. SWAMINATHAN

The year 1985 marked the 40th anniversary of the use of the atom bomb as a war weapon. It also marked the 40th anniversary of the United Nations, established to promote peace on earth and goodwill among all its inhabitants. The potential impact of a nuclear war on the environment is a subject which has aroused considerable debate. Similarly there are predictions on the likely impact on global weather as a result of changes in carbon dioxide concentration caused by the expanded use of coal and fossil fuels on the one hand, and destruction of forests on the other.

In spite of many conferences, symposia, and discussions at the national, regional, and international levels, we find that ecological rehabilitation is almost a lost cause in most developing countries. An important reason for this is the growth in population and the consequent pressure on basic life support systems. A projection of population growth during the period 1980–2100 undertaken by the World Bank is given in Table 1. As will be seen from the data, the population of India is likely to exceed that of China from about AD 2050 onwards. When population growth is accompanied by the neglect of rural areas, the pace of environmental degradation gets accelerated due to the unplanned expansion of urban areas on the one hand, and the struggle for basic human needs in villages on the other.

The recent food crises in many African countries have underlined the interrelationship between ecological deterioration and economic decline. Africa's population is projected to triple by 2025, reaching 1.5 billion. *Over 40 per cent of Africa's people now live in countries where grain yields are lower than they were a generation ago*. The loss of tree cover, both in closed forests and in savanna settings, is extensive. A few countries such as Mauritania and Rwanda are badly affected. In many countries wood collection for fuel and other uses exceeds the sustainable yield of remaining accessible forests. In Kenya demand is 5 times the sustainable level. In Ethiopia, Tanzania and Nigeria demand is 2.5 times the sustainable yield.

13

TABLE 1   *Population Projections: 1980 to 2100 (Population in Millions)*

	1950	1980	2000	2025	2050	2100	Total fertility rate – 1982	Year in which NRR = 1
Selected countries								
China	603	980	1196	1408	1450	1462	2.3	2000
India	362	687	994	1309	1513	1632	4.8	2010
Indonesia	77	146	212	283	330	356	4.3	2010
Brazil	53	121	181	243	279	299	3.9	2010
Bangladesh	44	89	157	266	357	435	6.3	2035
Nigeria	41	85	169	329	471	594	6.9	2035
Pakistan	37	82	140	229	302	361	5.8	2035
Mexico	27	69	109	154	182	196	4.6	2010
Egypt	20	42	63	86	102	111	4.6	2015
Kenya	6	17	40	83	120	149	8.0	2030
Regions								
Developing countries:								
Africa	223	479	903	1646	2297	2802	6.4	2050
East Asia	587	1061	1312	1542	1573	1596	2.3	2020
South Asia	695	1387	2164	3125	3810	4172	4.9	2045
Latin America	164	356	535	732	856	921	4.1	2035
Sub-total[a]	1670	3298	4884	6941	8400	9463	4.2	2050
Developed countries	834	1137	1263	1357	1380	1407	1.9	2005
Total world	2504	4435	6147	8298	9780	10,870	3.6	

[a]Regional figures do not add to "Developing countries sub-total" due to rounding.
Source: 1950: UN estimates; other years: 1984 World Bank estimates and projections.

In Sudan it is roughly double. Restoring African woodland and forests is thus essential to the restoration of the hydrological cycle, and to the recovery of agriculture (see the Worldwatch paper No. 65 by Brown and Wolf, 1985).

The dimensions of the tree plantation programme needed are vast. If fuelwood consumption continues to rise by 3 per cent a year Africa will need an additional 20 million hectares of fuelwood plantations by the year 2000 to cater for the increased demand without further denuding the remaining forests. In a similar calculation, which a fuelwood committee of the Government of India made in 1982, it was concluded that a minimum of 3 million hectares will have to be planted under quick-yielding fuelwood trees each year up to AD 2000 to meet the growing needs. Since over 40 per cent of the total area is already under agriculture, the only way this can be done in India is the planting of all wasted lands (often misnamed "waste lands") with leguminous shrubs and trees and other appropriate tree species which can provide to the people of the area fuel, fodder, feed and fertilizer through biological nitrogen fixation. A non-governmental Society for the Promotion of Wasteland Development was organized in 1982 for this purpose, and early in 1986 the Government of India set up a National Wasteland Development Board for the purpose of planting trees in 5 million hectares of wasted lands every year.

At the UN Conference on Desertification (UNCOD) held in 1977 in Nairobi, a Plan of Action to Combat Desertification by AD 2000 was developed. A recent assessment of the implementation of this plan of action by the United Nations Environment Programme (UNEP) has revealed that the goal set up by UNCOD to stop desertification by the year 2000 is no longer feasible, since efforts undertaken to control desertification so far have been inadequate. The direct impact of desertification is on food-producing lands. UNEP estimates the annual losses to be 6 million hectares transformed into desert land. Further, every year the productivity of 20 million hectares is reduced to no economic return.

It is not in Africa alone that we face a serious threat to long-term *nutrition security* as a result of the disappearance of the tree cover and the consequent damage to land, water, flora and fauna. Food security has been defined by the FAO as the "economic and physical access to food to all people at all times". Nutrition security is a wider concept including the availability of food of adequate quantity and quality as well as safe drinking water. Lack of clean drinking water in many villages in developing countries is an important cause of poor health both in children and adults. In addition, some essential vitamins and minerals may have to be supplied, particularly to pre-school children. Here again, social forestry programmes can help to provide simple botanical remedies to some of the specific nutritional disorders of an area, through the incorporation of appropriate horticultural plants in the choice of the species to be planted.

Let me cite two other examples of what is happening in continents other than Africa. Over 40 million people now live in the Himalayas. Most of them are very poor in spite of the vast natural endowments of the Himalayas. Early in this century it was estimated that the forest cover of the Himalayas amounted to about 60 per cent of land area. Some experts calculate that it has now dwindled to only one-quarter as much. Nepal's forest cover is believed to have declined from 57 to 23 per cent between 1947 and 1980. In India the Himalayan sector accounts for one-quarter of the country's forest cover. Yet it is being so rapidly reduced that several parts of the Himalayas may become barren by the beginning of the next century, unless steps are taken to provide the people with water, food, fodder, fuel, fibre and fertilizer. The local population, particularly the women, are very conscious of the threat to their future and this resulted in the launching of the "Chipko" (hug the tree) movement, largely by women. A very large proportion of the cattle population is maintained by the people just for meeting the manurial requirements of crops. Because of heavy animal pressure, only plants which are non-edible survive. Even these are cut for fuelwood. Not only floods, droughts and soil erosion threaten the livelihood security of the people living in the mountains, but the future of the agriculture of the plains of North India is also in jeopardy. Rising water tables resulting in the spread of soil salinity and alkalinity, and frequent incidence of flash floods in periods of heavy rainfall, are causing damage to agriculture and misery to the population.

The greed of the rich, the genuine needs of the poor for fuel and fodder, careless technology in road construction, mining and other "development" activities, and the absence of a systems approach in the design and implementation of agricultural and industrial projects in ecologically fragile areas, have all contributed to the rapid decline of Himalayan forests during the past 50 years. For example the rapid progress in the planting of apple orchards in the states of Himachal Pradesh and Jammu and Kashmir of India not only resulted in clearing forest lands for horticulture but took a heavy toll on forest trees, since several million tons of apples and other fruit had to be packed in wooden boxes for being sent to the plains. Later calculations by a Planning Commission Task Force showed that to meet the wood requirements for packing apples from 1 ha, about 10 ha of properly managed forests will be needed, if the wood is to be provided on a sustainable basis.

A long-term threat to food production as a result of forest denudation comes from the coincident extinction of genetic resources of plants and animals along with forest canopies. The tropical moist forests are veritable mines of valuable genes. In several important food crops, genes for resistance to important pests and diseases come from wild species and primitive cultivars occurring in forest areas. Some of the tropical forests have been described as pharmaceutical factories, since they contain many medicinal plants and herbs. We cannot really estimate the harm that will be done to the future of agriculture if we do not preserve for posterity the fruits of thousands of years of natural evolution and human selection.

An international undertaking for the conservation and exchange of plant genetic resources, as well as a FAO Commission on Plant Genetic Resources, have come into existence in recent years. These developments, together with the activities of the International Board for Plant Genetic Resources (IBPGR), provide a more organized framework for genetic conservation activities in economic plants.

One more example of current trends in human settlements is a result of the growth in the population of "ecological refugees", a term used by Norman Myers to indicate the people who have no option except to leave their original homes because of desertification and a collapse of the basic life support systems. Western Amazonia has large wetlands, which are in several instances not suitable for conventional agriculture. Yet in those parts of the region which lie in Colombia, Peru and Ecuador, landless labour families are moving in. In Peruvian Amazonia such population is expected to reach about 5 million by the turn of the century. Extensive damage to forest ecosystems is being caused by the slash-and-burn system of cultivation. At the same time there is immense scope for promoting sustainable agriculture and thriving rural communities through scientific land and water use planning. Amazonia is very rich in freshwater fish fauna: one calculation reveals that the introduction of aquaculture practices would help to generate far more good-quality animal protein than 40,000 square kilometres of cattle ranches. I could cite many more examples of this kind. What is clear is the urgent need for scientific land and water use practices based on sound principles of ecology, economics, energy conservation and employment generation. How can we initiate an *economic ecology movement* in the Third World where there is urgent need for symbiotic relationships among forestry, food production and human happiness to be nurtured and strengthened in every village?

How can we reverse these trends and make sustainable development a reality? This is where education holds the key. Without awareness there is no analysis of problems. Without analysis there can be no action which can have an enduring impact. Also, we have to avoid the temptation to make erudite analysis of ecological problems by scholars an end in itself. Paralysis by analysis is then the end-result. I believe that the time is ripe for educational institutions to take the lead in launching and guiding the management of natural resources. This has to begin from the basic unit of a village and move upwards, rather than through the development of plans at a national or global level for local implementation. Such a suggestion by itself is neither original nor new. It has been made many times by many experts in many places. What is important is to develop an economically and socially feasible and replicable mechanism for achieving the goal of eco-development which can trigger a self-propelling movement.

I propose for your consideration the following four ideas. In proposing them I wish to stress that there is need for considerable flexibility based on local needs and possibilities while converting these ideas into concrete action plans.

1. SCIENTIFIC LAND USE

Agricultural advances in recent years have been triggered by the development of high-yielding breeds of crops and livestock. The breeding of strains possessing a broad spectrum of resistance to pests and diseases and to diverse soil stresses involves extensive hybridization followed by rigorous selection. Coupled with good management, these breeds help to raise crop and animal productivity to high levels, as is clear from the agricultural scene in most developed countries and some developing countries.

The large-scale cultivation of improved genetic strains, together with good soil fertility and water management, helps to increase production through higher yields per hectare. Land is a shrinking resource for agriculture. The opportunities now open for increasing agricultural production through a vertical pathway of higher yields per hectare and greater intensity of cropping, through multiple and inter-cropping, make rational land-use planning possible. By taking advantage of such opportunities, lands prone to erosion, and which are marginal to crop husbandry, can be placed under silvi-horticultural or silvi-pastoral or fuelwood farming systems.

The FAO study on "Agriculture Toward 2000" estimates that even if crop yields on land already cultivated were to increase by 72 per cent, another 200 million hectares will have to be cleared in the next 20 years for meeting the food requirements of the estimated population of over 6 billion people at that time. Fortunately, the untapped yield reservoir in many farming systems in most developing countries is quite high. Hence every country will have to accord high priority to bridging the gap between potential and actual yields in farmers' fields by identifying and removing the constraints responsible for the yield gap.

Even if farmers in some parts of a country achieve high productivity levels, farmers living in remote areas, and in mountainous or desert regions, lacking roads and communication facilities, will still grow only annual food crops in lands which should ideally be under tree cover or tree farming, since meeting their home needs for food and other essential commodities determines their priorities in land use. If the farming families in such areas are to be persuaded to adopt ecologically sound land-use practices it will be essential that they are assured of the supply of the staple grains they need. Governments will have to build visible stocks of the food grains needed by the people living in remote and ecologically endangered habitats so that the local population will have confidence that their food needs will be met. Unless such confidence is built up, it will be futile to preach to them the harmful effects of shifting cultivation, soil erosion and loss of tree cover.

Where governments have built their own national food reserves, they should build grain stores in all areas where there is need for shifting the land use from annual to perennial crops or to agro-forestry and mixed farming systems. Before the normal sowing season, every family should be assured of the adequate supply of their staple. Where governments do not have such stocks of their own, a special "Food for Scientific Land Use" or "Food for Forest Development" or any appropriately named programme should be initiated by national governments with appropriate assistance from the international community. The World Food Programme, for example, can provide food grains for a programme designed strictly for bringing about desirable changes in land use, in addition to its regular programmes based on humanitarian considerations. In global terms there is abundance of food stocks today. According to the FAO these stocks are expected to reach nearly 300 million tons by the end of 1985. A beginning of the Food for Forest Development programme can be made if all nations having these stocks will pledge 5 per cent of their stocks for such a programme. Depending on needs and circumstances, some of this food grain stock can go to Food for Work programmes in the forestry sector.

In all chronically drought-prone areas there is need for a "Good Weather Code", indicating the steps that should be taken in the occasional seasons when rainfall is good. This will call for anticipatory planning and advanced preparations for extensive tree planting, if soil moisture levels prove adequate for seedling establishment. Normally both national and international funds are scarce when the rainfall is good. However, it is precisely during such seasons that much valuable work on afforestation, and anti-erosion measures can be undertaken. Thus we see today a paradox. When there is drought, food and funds become readily available. But when the soil moisture conditions for tree and grass establishment are excellent, no special support becomes available. A "Good Weather Code", indicating the steps that should be taken in normal rainfall seasons, will hence help to optimize the benefits from good rainfall for eco-development.

2. ESTABLISHMENT OF A GRID OF LOCAL LEVEL "CONSERVATION CLUBS" FOR SUSTAINABLE DEVELOPMENT

Today we see in several parts of the world chain activities and groups such as Rotary and Lions Clubs. Members of these groups meet on prescribed dates at prescribed places and discuss programmes which interest them. Developing countries are making large investments in the educational sector, and even in poor countries there are now few villages without a primary school. Can we develop a mechanism by which educational institutions, whether they are schools, colleges, or universities, can serve as catalysts in organizing at the local level a forum for the generation of awareness of the environmental problems of the area, and in promoting community action to meet the basic needs of people for food, fuel, fodder, feed, fibre, and fertilizer through the optimum use of the land, water, and labour resources available in the area? I believe that organizations such as the International Council of Scientific Unions (ICSU), the International Union for the Conservation of Nature and Natural Resources (IUCN), and the World Wildlife Fund (WWF) should take a lead in launching such a movement, spearheaded by academic institutions, resulting in the establishment of Conservation Clubs everywhere.

3. ECODEVELOPMENT CORPS OF PROFESSIONALS

(a)   Preparation of Action Plans

The first step is the preparation in each country of a National Conservation for Development Programme, consisting of detailed action plans at the local level for eco-development. Where such plans exist or can be prepared soon, the kinds of professional expertise needed for implementing the plan could be articulated in fairly precise terms. Where they do not exist, one of the early tasks of the Members of the Eco-Development Corps will be the preparation of detailed action plans in consultation with the local population and authorities. Thus, the corps could help in the preparation of eco-development plans as well as in the conversion of plans into accomplishments.

(b)   Organization of a Global Grid of Back-up Institutions

A very important prerequisite for the successful implementation of this programme is the availability of a global grid of outstanding support institutions. Depending on the nature of the job to be done, as for example, anti-desertification measures, production of food, fodder, fuel and fertilizer (through biological or organic sources), control of animal and human diseases, irrigation and drinking-water supply, biomass utilization, improved natural resources management, the support of advanced institutions located both in developed and developing countries should be enlisted for providing technical help when needed throughout the duration of the project and for training members of the corps. The back-up institutions will serve as an umbilical cord supporting the project until the work reaches a self-reliant and self-propelling state. The organization of such a consortium of scientific and technical institutions for supporting the Eco-Development Corps will not only help to harness the best available know-how, but will also generate a sense of participation among large numbers of academic and research institutions, scientists and technologists in a programme of great human significance.

(c)   Selection and Deployment of Members of the Corps

This is the key element of this programme. Once the precise tasks to be performed under the National Eco-development plan are articulated, the nature of the expertise needed will be clear. There has to be a proper match between the nature of the expertise and skills needed for successful task implementation and the nature of the skills possessed by the candidate. Interest in *do-how* is more important than just *know-how*.

Once the candidates have been chosen carefully according to the needs of each action plan, they should be given suitable predeployment training and orientation in appropriate institutions belonging to the back-up consortium, as well as in a suitable institution in the country where they are to work.

Deployment of members of the corps will be in clusters. For example, for a project aiming at agricultural and ecological rehabilitation there will be need for a group consisting of an agronomist, a forester, a veterinary expert, and a social scientist. In addition, every cluster should preferably have a medical graduate who can attend to human health problems. Whenever the members of the corps are unable to find solutions to some of the field problems (such as new soil health and plant health problems), they should seek the assistance of the appropriate back-up institution. In the initial stages, members of the corps could help in optimizing the benefits from the Food for Development programmes for unskilled labour, like the National Rural Employment Programme of India, Food for Work programmes, and Employment Guarantee Scheme of Maharashtra.

(d)   Duration of the Project

In order to achieve some tangible results, such a programme should be planned until AD 2000. Obviously, many of the young professionals agreeing to give a part of their early life for this emotionally satisfying and intellectually challenging work may not be prepared to stay for more than 3 years. In addition to young professionals in the age group 20 to 30, the services of retired persons possessing the requisite health, expertise, and enthusiasm can also be enlisted. Each person who is leaving the project should be replaced with a person with similar expertise so that the continuity of the work is maintained. In work designed to achieve ecological rehabilitation a 15-year period is the minimum before visible and lasting impact is achieved.

(e)   Remuneration

The monthly honorarium paid to the volunteers should not exceed the amount which a national doing similar work may receive in his/her country. However, suitable dormitory and other arrangements which will help to provide free lodging and boarding and recreational facilities will be needed.

(f)   Composition

In developing countries such as India, China, Bangladesh, and the Philippines where large numbers of trained people are available, the Eco-development Corps may consist predominantly of nationals of the country. Even where expatriate expertise is needed, each eco-development cluster should include a minimum of 50 per cent of local youth.

4. ROLE OF MASS MEDIA

The first human form is believed to have evolved in East Africa some 25 million or more years ago. Human beings may have existed as a species for about 2 million years. Yet it was only about 10,000 years ago that human beings started growing food, rather than merely gathering it from the wild state and hunting wildlife. Thus, if the existence of human beings as an independent species is equated to a 24-hour day, we have been farmers for only about 7 minutes. Even during these 7 minutes we have practised market-oriented agriculture only for a few seconds. Within these few seconds we have been confronted with numerous problems including changing consumer preferences. We do not know what new pests and soil and atmospheric constraints (including temperature changes from higher CO_2 content) we will have to face in the future. We do not know what physiological and morphological traits will be needed for plants to perform well in a post-nuclear war era, if unfortunately such a calamity befalls our planet. Future generations of scientists and farmers will not have the tools with which they can solve such problems if we do not make genetic resources conservation, evaluation, and utilization a common cause, and accord it the highest priority.

How can the above message become part of the daily life of every citizen in every country? How can we generate widespread awareness of the economic and biological necessity of conservation measures? There is no single or simple method of involving people in conserving their own environmental assets. The message has to start from the primary school and will have to become, over a period of time, a way of life.

In the past, rural communities replenished soil fertility through organic recycling. Women selected the best cobs or panicles to be used as seed during the next growing season. They unconsciously selected in this process genotypes possessing resistance or tolerance to the major pests in the particular region. Similarly, selection was practised among animals so that adaptation to local conditions is the major characteristic of indigenous breeds of farm animals.

With the onset of modernization, conservation agriculture gave way to exploitative farming. With specialist agencies taking over the responsibility for seed production and fertilizer and pesticide distribution, the involvement of the local people, particularly illiterate women, has diminished or vanished. Consequently, conservation is now regarded as a Government responsibility rather than a joint sector activity between the people and public agencies.

In modern mass media such as television, radio, and the press, we have powerful tools for education and awareness generation. Where there is no awareness, there is little or no action. I would like to suggest that every television and radio station, and every newspaper, should carry at least one item on genetic conservation each day. Just as reporting on weather has become an integral part of daily news reporting, reporting on genetic conservation and eco-development should also become a daily feature.

Ecological security is the foundation for enduring nutrition security. If the soil is hungry and thirsty, plants wither, animals have little to eat, and people either migrate to swell the ranks of ecological refugees or perish. The challenge before us is vast. Time is running out in many areas to prevent the damage being done to basic ecological assets becoming irreversible. It is obvious that we have so far failed to identify methods by which we can convert our resolutions into reality. Sharp rhetoric at conferences will not reduce the need for hard and sustained work by every member of the community. The conservation and enrichment of the environment is everybody's business. Unless we learn to promote and adopt, in agriculture, industry and daily life, practices which are ecologically and economically sustainable, we will destroy the prospects for a happy life both for ourselves and for the generations yet to be born. The role of education in creating consciousness and ensuring action is vividly brought out by the old Chinese saying:

If you are planning one year ahead,
   plant rice.
If you are planning ten years ahead,
   plant trees.
If you are planning a hundred years ahead,
   educate the people.

Environmental Education: the Indian Experience

T. N. KHOSHOO

Dr T. N. Khoshoo was Secretary of the Department of Environment of the Government of India under Prime Minister Indira Gandhi, and had served as Director of the National Botanical Research Institute. The range of target populations in India is so great that Khoshoo's paper contains ideas applicable to many other countries. Extracts from this wide-ranging paper are quoted here, and also in Part III (p. 235) and Part V (p. 401).

One of the important aspects of environmental education in India is its link with an historical tradition of long duration. Thus, concerning the shortcomings of the treatment given to the environment by the modern media, Khoshoo writes:

> Environmental ethics have been ignored. I would illustrate this with some thoughts given in one stanza of *Isho Upanishad* which says: "This universe is the creation of the supreme power and is meant for the benefit of all; individual species must therefore learn to enjoy its benefits by regarding themselves as a part of the system in close relationship with other species; let not any one species encroach upon the rights of others".
>
> These thoughts represent ideal concepts of ecological harmony and are not different from the underlying message of the World Conservation Strategy. Being in Sanskrit, these thoughts have remained away from us not only on account of the language barrier, but also because of lack of good environmental communicators among those who know Sanskrit.

The tenor of Khoshoo's approach is illustrated by the following quotations.

> The chief objective of environmental education is that individual and social groups should acquire awareness and knowledge, develop attitudes, skills and abilities, and participate in solving real-life environmental problems. The perspective should be integrated, interdisciplinary and holistic in character.

25

Obviously, the approach has to be both top-downward (from planners/decision makers) and bottom-upward. The important objective in environmental education and awareness therefore is not to introduce a *new subject, but a new approach to education* which cuts across various subjects.

Essentially, Environmental Science is not a single subject, but a conglomerate of both basic and applied sciences as well as engineering, socio-economics, ethics and law. Rather, the idea should be to bring in environmental concern in all subject areas so that an environmental bias permeates all facets of one's life and does not get compartmentalized in one place.

In any environmental education and awareness programme, there is need for realism. In India, over 70% of its population lives in the villages, and nearly 40% is below the poverty line. Thus the villagers can be the protectors as well as the destroyers of the environment. Therefore, their perception is of vital importance and it is necessary to have identity in perceptions of the people at the grassroot level and those who plan and devise policies regarding environment.

Khoshoo considers in detail first formal education under headings of school, college and university education and then non-formal education under such headings as adult education, activities for children, eco-development camps, development of educational material and teaching aids, and many others. He concludes:

The aim of formal and non-formal education is to widen the base of awareness in India, a country where centuries co-exist and which is diverse in almost everything. Such mass awareness will lead to location-specific action programmes which must be well thought out and based on scientific and technical knowledge.

A Holistic View of Human Ethics

MOHAN K. WALI

If there is one lesson that is to be learned from global environmental issues today it is this: ethics and social responsibility will have to be viewed for humanity as a whole. It is time to remind ourselves of Socrates' dictum: "I am a citizen of the world." Forty years ago, when the first experiment on the atom bomb succeeded, Robert Oppenheimer visualized the potential of immense human destruction in the mushroom cloud and reflected through the lines of the Bhaghavad Gita:

> I am become death, the shatterer of worlds;
> Waiting that hour that ripens to their doom.

The words of Arthur Koestler admirably summed up the practical lesson:

> If I were asked to name the most important date in the history and prehistory of the human race I would answer without hesitation, 6 August 1945. The reason is simple. From the dawn of consciousness until 6 August 1945 man had to live with the prospect of death as an *individual*; since the day when the first atomic bomb outshone the sun over Hiroshima, mankind as a whole has had to live with the prospect of its extinction as a *species*.

In the most recent past millions of bison were shot on the North American prairies; tigers and elephants were indiscriminately hunted in unprecedented numbers in Asia and Africa – some to the point of extinction – and the jungles of the Amazon were destroyed. In the western world it is only recently that we have seen a realization of the imperative need to conserve the world's ecosystems and maintain biological diversity. Yet the sacredness of living things was a basic tenet of Hindu philosophy thousands of years ago.

Webster's *New International Dictionary*, 1936, defines ethics as "the science of moral duty, or more broadly, the science of ideal human character and the ideal ends of human action". This age-old view of ethics for humanity as a whole was heightened by the venue of the ICSU meeting – India – Mark Twain's "cradle of human race, birthplace of human speech, . . . great grandmother of tradition". Over two millennia and four centuries ago, when concern for environmental issues was perhaps not so prevalent elsewhere, the wise sages of India coined the weighty phrase "ahimsa permo-darma", "non-cruelty to animals, the supreme religion". This codification as "supreme religion" of the sacredness of all life derives from the ancient Hindu philosophy.

4

Key Issues in Environmental Education

E. RUGUMAYO

The quotations in this section are from the paper entitled "Key Issues in Environmental Education", by Edward Rugumayo, an African biologist and educator.

> Environmental problems arise as a result of activities in various fields of human endeavour, especially in scientific and technological fields. Others arise as a result of natural forces at work. Since these problems are the result of multi-faceted activities, both man's and nature's, their solution must be based on an inter-disciplinary approach. In this approach biology has an important role to play.

Concerning the key issues in environmental education Rugumayo says:

> Third World countries have more or less similar problems, but priorities can only be determined by each country after it has assessed concretely the problems as they express themselves in real life. Generally, after a survey of various countries' environmental issues, the key issues fall under six headings: *conservation, food, family planning, water-related and pest-vectored diseases, pollution* and *energy*. It should be quite apparent that these issues can be dealt with by other scientific disciplines, but then only partially. In other words, the problems require an inter-disciplinary approach, with the degree of involvement of biology depending on the nature of the particular problems which have been identified and defined for study.

ECOLOGY AND ENVIRONMENT

The importance of biology becomes clear when one considers that the subject of ecology, which now plays a central role in environmental education, had its origins in biological studies.

29

The science of ecology began with simple studies of individual species within their surroundings. These studies were largely descriptive. Later, ecological studies went beyond this stage and included several species, sometimes associated ones, in a given community. The concept of ecosystem did not emerge until the 20th Century, although Darwin in his studies on evolution had already described interdependence and the struggle for survival among living organisms.

The second half of this century, which was preceded by two devastating world wars that saw the deployment on a massive scale of the most lethal weapons, including the use of the atomic bomb, aroused scientists to the realization that unless nuclear energy was put to peaceful use, the likelihood of man destroying himself was not the result of someone's runaway imagination. It could happen.

At about the same time, with stepped up industrialization all over the globe, it became apparent that the unprecedented rate of industrial growth, and the unchecked exploitation of natural resources, could lead to their *depletion*, with disastrous consequences not only to the environment, but to man as well. Or, to put it more bluntly, by destroying the environment man would automatically also destroy himself. Concurrent with this view was the other aspect of industrialization which was brought to the attention of the general public by Rachel Carson in her now celebrated book, *Silent Spring*. This book brought out sharply the serious damage caused by the indiscriminate use of chemical sprays (pesticides, herbicides and fungicides) and the effluents from industries, on the fauna and flora in the environment. In a word – the dangers of *pollution*.

The concept of a total global environment is a product of the convergence of many forces – *industrialization* (giving rise to the depletion of natural resources and pollution of the environment), the effects and dangers of weapons of mass destruction, the overall global technological advancement which makes *communications* between nations, organizations and individuals an easy affair, and *ecological studies* of the natural as well as man-made environment. In addition to these forces, there is an even more compelling factor. This is the prevailing *international economic order* in which there is an ever-widening gap between the rich and poor nations, as well as between the rich and poor within individual nations.

Thus the concept of total global environment is derived directly from ecological studies of the outcome of the convergence of the above forces. These studies base their work on the basic principles of ecology which may be summed up in three simple "laws". These "laws" are the following:

1. All forms of life are *interdependent*. The prey is dependent on the predator for the control of its population, and the predator on the

prey for the supply of food. These forms of life interact and have a reciprocal relationship with the non-living environment.

2. The stability of ecosystems is dependent on their diversity and complexity. A tropical forest of 150 plant species is more stable than a man-made forest with two or three plant species. This is the *law of stability*.

3. *All resources* – food, water, air, minerals, energy – are *finite*. In other words, there are limits to growth of all living systems. These limits are ultimately dictated by the finite size of the earth, and the finite input of energy from the sun.

The key issues in environmental education mentioned at the start of this paper appear in the third block of Fig. 1, where they are preceded by a block outlining the procedural steps taken to arrive at them. Rugumayo suggests that any country wishing to establish its own list of key issues in environmental education should follow the procedural steps listed in the second block, and elaborated on overpage.

These, then, are the procedural steps recommended for identifying and defining key issues in environmental education for which biology has a special significance:

1. *Reviewing existing data and literature*: It is necessary to review the existing literature and data before any serious work begins. The tendency for experts to ignore this step and begin from their own hurriedly-formed premises can be costly in time and money. This step is economical both in terms of finance and time.

2. Arising out of the review of existing literature and data, it would be possible to draw up an *inventory* and *ranking of major environmental problems*. At this stage the key issues which are particularly relevant to biology would be defined and researched by teams of biologists and educators.

3. Designing case studies of environmental education programmes related to particular objectives. The topics of the case studies would be taken from the inventory of environmental problems above.

4. Any research programme worthy of the name must carry out a *cost-effective analysis* of its activities; and the public must be informed if they are getting their money's worth for investing in research and education. This is a painful but necessary step.

5. Every education and research programme should have a built-in *evaluation component*. This enables both the researchers and the donors of funds to assess the effectiveness of the research programme. At the same time, and side by side with evaluation, each country should set up a *monitoring system* to keep watch on the state of the environment.

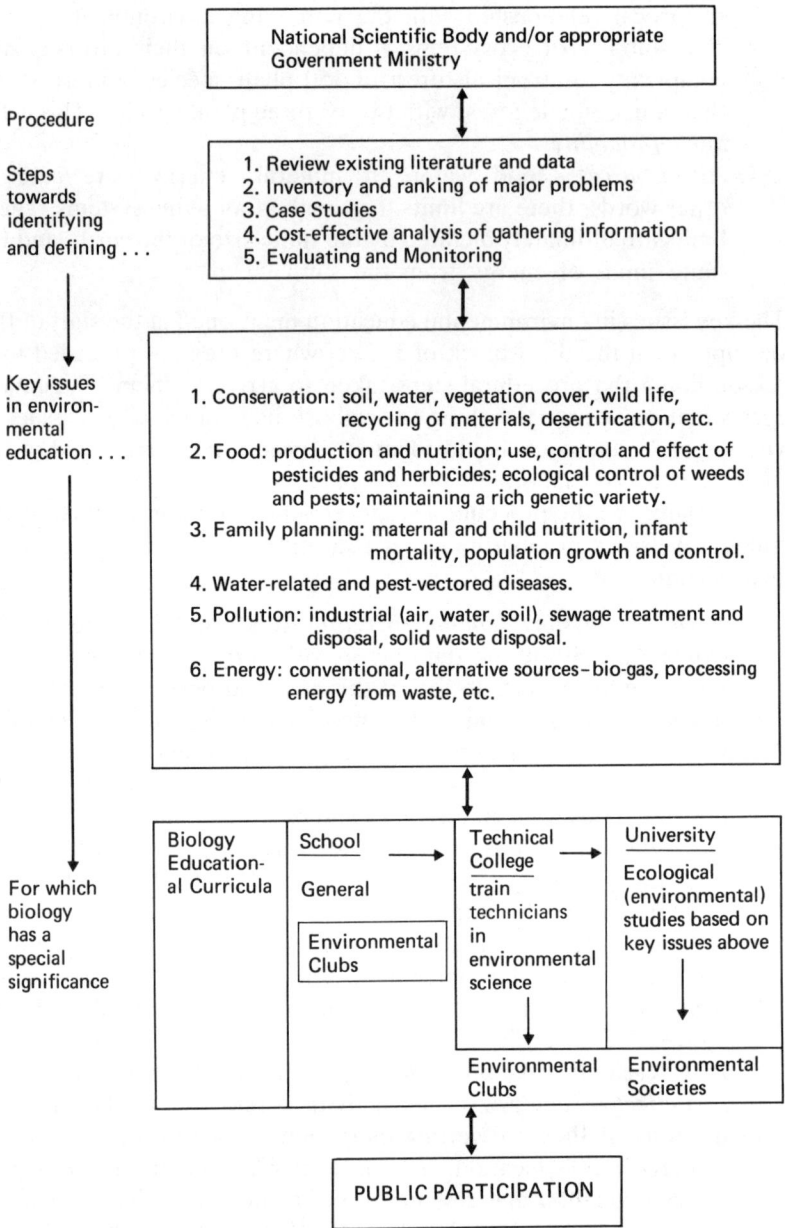

FIG 1 Diagram showing the procedure necessary in identifying key issues in environmental education and how these may be integrated into a national environmental education programme.

It is interesting to note that several of the key issues listed in Fig. 1, such as food and energy, and others by implication, are among the eight areas of concern discussed at the Bangalore Conference, which demonstrates how the Environment theme encompasses, to a large extent, all the other themes.

The topic of conservation, which heads the list, will receive special consideration in the next section. All the other themes fall within the purview of the other Conference themes. Rugumayo argues – and in this he is probably reflecting an African experience – that a national body such as a national science/technology research council should play a co-ordinating role in the allocation of topics to different educational and research institutions dealing with the environment.

Included in this overall programme there should be a *national programme for training personnel to work in areas of environmental education*. This should include the training of technicians in environmental science techniques, and university graduates in ecological/environmental studies. The latter's programme would be based on general principles of ecology, with special emphasis on the key issues mentioned above.

The environmental education programme should encourage the formation of *nature conservation/environmental clubs and societies in all educational institutions* – from primary through university. Furthermore, the *community at large* must be educated and made aware of the programme on environmental education. The community should spear-head the campaign for a better environment by keeping watch over changes being brought about in the environment through the activities of various agencies, both public and private. For instance, in Kenya there have been national campaigns for conservation – afforestation, building of small dams and gabions, and an overall attempt at the national level to conserve fuel, water and trees, in which the public have taken a part. There are efforts to protect the rhino, fight desertification, increase arable land and control a high population growth rate through family planning methods. There are active wild life and conservation clubs in schools. UNEP's influence in Kenya is quite evident judging by the amount of space in the national press devoted to environmental issues. At one time, public outcry prevented what could have amounted to environmental disaster. This was in connection with a sugar factory company which had been granted permission to build a sugar factory by cutting down the only forest in the area. The local member of parliament and the residents protested vehemently until a government directive was issued to stop the construction of the factory. *The forest was saved by the vigilance of the community*.

On the other hand, there have been environmental disasters as in the case of Haiti. Just over a generation ago, in the 1950s, forests covered over 80% of Haiti's land surface. By the end of the 1970s *only* 9% of the forest remained. In the wake of this drastic deforestation which destroyed vegetation cover, Haiti experienced four consecutive years (1973–77) of severe drought. A process of soil erosion and desertification as a result of the interruption of the natural water cycle has set in. Haiti can solve this problem through a coordinated programme of afforestation and conservation in which the government, educational institutions and the community would each play its appropriate role. Madagascar has the same tale of woe as Haiti's.

Another example of environmental neglect is that of Uganda where over a decade of political maladministration has led to the near-destruction of the once-famous national parks of Ruwenzori and Kabalega. In the latter game park, the rhino is extinct. The case of Uganda shows that the absence of positive governmental policy in the area of environmental education and conservation inevitably leads to the destruction of the environment.

The other cases above – Haiti and Madagascar – go to show what happens when there is rapid urbanization without a corresponding increase in the supply of public utilities, i.e., electricity and/or gas, or other alternative sources for fuel. The result is that the new urban dwellers depend on the rural forests for their fuel requirements, with disastrous results. In the absence of cheap sources of energy for the urban poor, alternative sources of energy must be found. China (People's Republic) on the other hand, has come to grips with the problem of cheap fuel, with a conservation element built in, by using an alternative source of energy, that of *bio-gas*. In China, it is estimated that a $10m^3$ digester produces fuel gas equivalent to 7 tons of coal. By 1974, one county, Miyang in the Szechuan Province, had about 100,000 digesters, producing fuel for more than 76% of the population. Raw materials for bio-gas exist in China, but perhaps not in such abundance in other Third World countries. *Each country, therefore, has to take inventory of its potential in this area*, and come out with novel solutions to its problems. Here biology plays an important role.

The production of bio-gas is a good example of how a novel solution, using ecological methods, may lead to the solution of other related problems. The bio-gas digester furnishes cooking gas as its primary product, and removes a disease vector at the same time. Human waste containing parasite eggs of *Schistosoma* is channelled into a water-seal, odourless latrine with a three-chamber sedimentation tank. In the absence of snails, eggs die within a month. The sediment is afterwards used as *fertilizer*. Thus bio-gas production simultaneously deals with a number of environmental problems, and resolves them. At the *energy level, it produces fuel gas; the issue of water-related and pest-vectored diseases* is resolved by destroying the eggs of *Schistosoma* while producing fertilizer from the sediment; *increased food production is assured*, and by proper disposal of plant, animal and human waste the *danger of pollution* is minimized.

All of these examples reinforce the idea that the study of biology is important, but that an interdisciplinary approach is needed for the solution of environmental problems and in the selection of activities in environmental education.

5

Education and Conservation Strategy

A. V. BAEZ

Of all the key issues in environmental education mentioned in Rugumayo's paper, conservation was put at the head of the list. Rugumayo quite properly gave precedence to the conservation of non-renewable resources such as the fossil fuels: oil, coal, natural gas, etc. More efficient and cost-effective methods of extraction and utilization of these limited resources could obviously extend their useful lifetimes.

But the goal of sustainable economic development can, in the long run, only be achieved if the *renewable* resources, such as plants and animals which derive their energy from the sun, are used in a way that ensures the sustainable utilization of species and ecosystems. This is one of the themes of IUCN's World Conservation Strategy.

The following presentation is based upon an address given in Ontario by Albert Baez to the Man–Environment Impact Conference 1982 on the subject of the implications of the Strategy on Environmental Education.

A TURNING POINT

Conservation and sustainable development can, and indeed must, work hand in hand to avoid the destruction of the living resources which sustain life. This presents an educational challenge because it will never be implemented unless a majority of people understand the problem of living resources and are motivated to conserve them.

Some progress has been made through environmental education as illustrated by the following incident. Graham Kelleher and I were walking along the shore at Cairns in Australia facing the Pacific Ocean. We were talking about the importance of raising the level of public awareness of environmental issues when a large pelican swooped down gently and started to walk gracefully at the water's edge. Several people, including some children, stopped to look at this extraordinary bird. No one disturbed him. All seemed to enjoy just watching this elegant creature who obviously belonged there. Kelleher said:

> I think we have made some progress. If this bird had landed here twenty years ago a boy might have picked up a stone and thrown it at him just for fun. It wasn't cruelty. He didn't mean any harm. In those days it was just considered sport to try and hit a moving target. Birds were considered much lower on the scale of living things than people. There were lots of them. They were expendable and it was our right to deal with these lower forms of life as if they had no feelings and didn't matter very much anyway.
>
> Things have changed. Without articulating the thought, the children and their parents today obviously feel differently about the bird. The message of the ecologists has at last seeped through. But it has taken time!
>
> I think people today have different feelings towards the earth and its inhabitants. They seem to have a greater respect for living things whether they be plants or animals. I sense a new respect for life, and a new appreciation for the beauty of living things.

I begin on that positive note because I am an optimist. But I also realize that we are in a period of crisis and that environmental education must take some bold new steps and accelerate its pace, otherwise the forces of destruction will gain the upper hand.

Some progress has been made toward conservation and environmental sanity, otherwise we might be overwhelmed by gloom as we consider the global trends. The Global 2000 Report to the President of the United States says "If present trends continue, the world in 2000 will be more crowded, more polluted, less stable ecologically and more vulnerable to disruption than the world we live in now." Other documents, including "North–South: A Program for Survival", "Limits to Growth", "100 Pages for the Future" and "Down to Earth", document the destructive impact of man on the environment and the degradation of the biosphere.

Other books such as *Extinction* and *Fate of the Earth* develop the theme with alarming statistics that not only humanity but all life on earth is doomed either to an accelerated destruction of nature and natural resources or the sudden destruction of all forms of life should a holocaust result from a full-scale nuclear exchange between the two superpowers.

The key phrase, however, is "if present trends continue". People everywhere, and especially those who have the slightest grain of optimism, should now dedicate themselves to ensure that present trends do *not* continue. The adage "if you are not part of the solution you are part of the problem" was seldom more appropriate.

Until very recently all the curves of the consumption of fossil fuels rose exponentially. But it is clear that, because the earth and its resources are finite, they cannot continue to do so for ever. At the present rate of consumption known oil reserves will be depleted in two or three decades, and there is no solace in hoping that a huge new source equivalent to the sum of all previous oil consumption will be found, because even if it were *it would last only about a decade*. This is the conclusion one reaches from the law of exponential growth with a doubling time of 10 years – the present figure applicable to global oil consumption.

Population growth follows a similar curve with an average doubling time of 35 years. A decrease in the birth rates will cause the increase to be slower, but the significant fact is that the increment alone in the world population will be 4000 million, if not in 35 years, then in 40 or 50 years. In other words we are headed toward a world population of 8000 million somewhere between AD 2017 and AD 2032 at a time when our grand-children will still be alive.

If we do not make an effort to turn things around in a controlled way they will turn around in disastrous ways, simply because the world and its resources are finite. In the process the quality of life will decrease and life will become unbearable for some people. We are at a crucial turning point in history. Some point to inevitable trends, while others express the hope that through our own active participation we can effect changes for the better. Roszak, in his book *Person/Planet*, speaks of "the creative disintegration of industrialised society which will bring about the transition from an industrial to an ecological society". Bybee notes that the change will require a shift from competition to cooperation. He points out that whereas aggressiveness was adequate for a society in which resources seemed to be unlimited and were apparently there to be exploited for gain, a willingness to share might be more conducive to survival in a world where all the resources are known to be limited.

Whether a trend exists or not, there is certainly a need to change from habits of waste to those of conservation of resources. Conservation, therefore, has an important role to play in bringing about a new era. A document which gives us hope for implementing conservation and at the same time permitting economic development to take place is the World Conservation Strategy whose educational implications I wish to explore.

THE WORLD CONSERVATION STRATEGY

Ecology, which is the science that deals with the interrelationships of all living things is at the heart of the World Conservation Strategy – a guide for living and surviving on the planet. It shows the way for nations to conserve their portion of the earth even as they go forward with much-needed developments. It also points the way to greater collaboration among nations to protect the great commons of the earth; the oceans and the seas, the atmosphere, international river systems, migratory wildlife and Antarctica.

It represents the combined ideas of hundreds of scientists and other thinkers associated with three international organizations: the International Union for Conservation of Nature and Natural Resources, the United Nations Environment Programme and the World Wildlife Fund. It describes what must be done if we are to create a planet which we can enjoy ourselves, and which we can pass on to the next generations in good conscience.

The Strategy reconciles the human need to develop the earth in order to live with the human need to conserve the earth in order to survive. It argues that conservation and development can be mutually re-enforcing, and sets the scene for conservation-minded people and development-minded people to unite in a common effort toward survival. It is a guide for the use of the earth's living resources based firmly on the logic of conservation. We have to face the fact that the biosphere that sustains us – the earth's thin layer of air, water, soil and living things – is deteriorating rapidly because of the burden our species puts on it. If the deterioration due to the man–environment impact continues, we face a dismal future.

The Strategy identifies the most urgent environmental problems the world faces. It then goes on to describe in detail how governments and other organizations can solve these problems. The goal of the strategy is a *sustainable world society*. It calls for a community of nations, each maintaining its own part of the earth, all cooperating to protect the biosphere that sustains life.

It is not intended to save a particular species nor to remake the human character. It is intended to convince people in government, commerce, industry, labour unions and the professions that conservation must be in the forefront of our endeavours if the human enterprise is to be successful.

The first priority is *to see that the essential ecological processes and life-support systems of the earth are in good functioning order*. Examples of essential ecological processes include: the regeneration of soils helped along by micro-organisms, the recycling of nutrients such as carbon and nitrogen in plants, the purification of air and water by forests and the pollination of flowering plants by insects. Such processes are essential because all life depends on them.

Examples of life-support systems include the agricultural and forest systems, the coastal wetlands and the freshwater systems. Because of the widespread destruction and pollution of these systems, they are losing their productivity at ever-increasing rates. Management programmes are necessary to stop such destruction.

The second priority for keeping the earth habitable is *preservation of genetic diversity*. That means managing our use of living resources so that the maximum number of different species of plants and animals are allowed to remain alive and are not made extinct. Programmes for the sound management of land and water uses and the preservation of habitats are essential, as are procedures to prevent over-fishing and over-hunting, to stop the illegal trade in wild plants and animals, to prevent the introduction of exotic species into habitats where they will, in all probability, devastate the native species. There is a need for cooperation among all nations to protect the species before it is too late to do so.

There are, of course, other reasons for preserving the species. Simple human compassion is one. The extraordinary beauty of natural forms is another. Perhaps most important, we are morally obliged to our descendants not to leave the earth less alive, less interesting and less wondrous because we have been here.

The third main objective is the *sustainable utilization of species and ecosystems*. In simplest terms this means setting aside portions of the earth as untouched reserves and using the remainder wisely so that it remains for ever productive. Sustainable utilization is somewhat analogous to spending the interest while keeping the capital intact. The ultimate goal, a sustainable world society, would benefit everyone. Conservation and increased yields might, to cite just one example that applies in some parts of the world, "put fish back on the working man's table".

It has been suggested that the Strategy does not give sufficient emphasis to the problem of human overpopulation and its relentless growth. My own list of major global concerns: population, pollution, poverty and proliferation of nuclear weapons – the four Ps – has always put population first. There is no question but that man has had the most devastating impact on the biosphere of any species, and that this will continue to get worse as long as population growth continues to outstrip all indices of economic growth and development.

EDUCATIONAL PROBLEMS

The magnitude of the educational task can be gauged if we consider the totality of the target groups that must be addressed: legislators and administrators; development practitioners in industry, commerce and trade unions; professional bodies and special interest groups; communities most affected by conservation projects; school children and students; teachers and teacher trainers; youth group leaders; the general public.

It is my opinion that while some progress has been made in putting the environmental message across to school and university populations, not enough effort has been expended in educating policy-makers in government and industry. If they were convinced of the importance of a conservation strategy they could make important decisions and implement some drastic changes in a relatively short time to prevent the destruction of species and ecosystems which sustain life and make economic development possible.

The first educational problem therefore stems from the fact that so many target groups must be served. The second problem is how to apply our modern ideas of learning to a task that is so demanding in terms of new knowledge and of profound changes in the affective domain.

Let us review the essence of the teaching–learning process in order to assess the magnitude of the educational task ahead. What do we mean by teaching and learning?

1. To teach is to create situations where learning can take place.
2. Learning manifests itself in behavioural changes.

The first of these statements implies that the learner can make discoveries for himself. The second implies that if you have really learned something you are capable of generating self-induced behavioural changes. If learning does not take place, teaching has been futile. The Strategy explains why this is very important:

> Lack of awareness of the benefits of conservation and its relevance to everyday concerns prevents policy makers, development practitioners and the general public from seeing the urgent need to achieve conservation objectives. Ultimately, ecosystems and species are being destroyed because people do not see that it is in their interests not to destroy them. The benefits from natural ecosystems and their component plants and animals are regarded by all but a few as trivial and dispensable compared with the benefits from those activities that entail their destruction or degradation.

The behavioural changes proposed in the Strategy are so sweeping that they amount to a new environmental ethic. It says:

> Ultimately the behaviour of entire societies towards the biosphere must be transformed if the achievement of conservation objectives is to be assured. A new ethic, embracing plants and animals as well as people, is required for human societies to live in harmony with the natural world on which they depend for survival and well being. The long-term task of environmental education is to foster or reinforce attitudes and behaviour compatible with this new ethic.

The element of time is an important consideration. To stop the destruction of some endangered species, for example, requires immediate action. Administrators and decision-makers in government and industry could possibly do something about this. Raising the level of public awareness and creating an environmental ethic, on the other hand, are long-range goals for which the target group includes the general public as well as pupils and students in schools and universities.

TOWARD A WORLD ENVIRONMENTAL EDUCATION STRATEGY

Several strategies are needed to solve the global crisis: a strategy for peace and a strategy for population control, as well as a strategy for conservation. I think the time has also come to consider the need for a world environmental education strategy.

Individual action should not be discounted. Having recognized that the greatest possible environmental devastation would occur in a nuclear holocaust, it behoves all environmentalists and lovers of life to participate in activities which would minimize the probability that a holocaust will occur. Since this is still subject to different interpretations, no clear-cut recommendation is given here, but certainly men and women of good will everywhere *should act in such a way as to reduce the probability that a nuclear exchange takes place.* Proliferation of nuclear weapons is, in my estimation, "a holocaust looking for a place to happen".

Individuals can start by living their daily lives following an environment ethic. This would include taking steps to conserve natural resources and to minimize the extinction of plant and animal species. They can then expand the boundary conditions of their environmental thinking so that they broaden daily to the point where they are thinking about the global implications of what were once conceived as merely local environmental problems.

I have written elsewhere that, to improve the quality of life, education must generate curiosity, creativity, competence and compassion – the four Cs. As time goes on the importance of compassion has, in my judgement, increased. It is needed more than ever at this turning point in history. When I first wrote about compassion I had only fellow-feeling and social responsibility in mind. I now believe that a feeling of compassion, and even affection, must be extended to all living things and to the entire biosphere which teems with life, if we are to animate an environmental ethic. The fifth C – conservation – can be a direct consequence of compassion.

I would like to make a special plea for the role of science in environmental education. Although the generation of humane attitudes toward living things is of utmost importance, these attitudes must rest on accurate knowledge – the firm scientific foundation of ecology. The subject of ecology upon which many arguments are based is a science which, in turn, leans heavily on biology, chemistry and physics. The concepts of ecosystems, species and genetic diversity, for example, require a thorough understanding of genetics. The concept of the biosphere which links the laws of thermodynamics with the requirements of living things also illustrates the interdisciplinary nature of the scientific base which underlies environmental studies.

Since both ecology and environmental education are interdisciplinary activities it is only natural that the environment has already been chosen as the integrating concept in many integrated science courses. This was recognized a decade or so ago in the science education sector of Unesco even before a formal environmental education programme was started there. Throughout the decade of the 1970s many integrated science courses were generated round the world in which the environment was used as the integrating factor. We need to strengthen the scientific basis of environmental education.

John Smyth has suggested that any educational response to the World Conservation Strategy should identify those deficiencies in the public concept of man's relation with the environment which lead to failure to support conservation measures, as well as the characteristics of the educational system which perpetuate these conceptual deficiencies in the general public. He says the aims and objectives of a re-oriented education strategy should be defined. It is at this point that the task becomes one of incipient revolution, since whole attitudes are involved and no element of education is left unaffected.

There have been many attempts to define the nature of environmental education in its more formal education context, but no agreed solution. The whole enterprise is weakened in the eyes of unconvinced administrators by this deficiency, which is made worse by woolliness and by the diversity of incompatible proposals. A high-powered effort is needed to be definitive in the eyes of society.

It is certainly necessary to define carefully the connections within man/environment systems which it is necessary to understand in order to subsume the practical measures needed to achieve the objectives of the Strategy. Then there is a need for a more detailed statement of behavioural objectives for the different target groups. Since formal school education is often the pace-setter in these matters, more specific sets of objectives should be devised, covering knowledge of facts and concepts, skills to be attained, and attitudes to be fostered.

CONCLUSION

In conclusion let us consider why man–environment impact is the key educational issue in the 1980s.

Man prides himself in being the only intelligent animal on the earth. Yet he is the only one that has caused vast devastation on the biosphere.

In less than a thousand years, which is the blink of an eye in geological time, he has consumed most of the fossil fuels which took nature millons of years to produce. The air we breathe is full of noxious fumes and radioactive particles of his making.

He has placed millions of tons of concrete and cement on roads and cities where there were once forests and wildlife. At least 3000 square kilometres of prime farm land is disappearing each year under buildings and roads in developing countries alone.

Thousands of millions of tons of soil are being lost each year as a result of deforestation and poor land management.

Hundreds of millions of rural people in developing countries are forced to strip their land of vegetation in order to find wood for cooking and heat.

Each year 4000 million tons of dung and crop residues are burned for fuel, which could otherwise regenerate soils.

And now man has the capability of generating a nuclear holocaust which could devastate the biosphere and make life on earth extinct.

A new sense of humility must be born in mankind. We should realize that if human beings could be removed from the earth, the earth could probably heal itself and become once again a planet where the oceans were clean, the air pure and the forests green and full of wildlife. Remember, the earth, its plants and animals can survive without us, *but we cannot survive without them!*

There are those who believe that a world environmental education strategy is too grandiose a scheme. But what, short of that, is going to reverse the trends that are driving us to damage the planet even further?

I believe man is intelligent enough to generate an environmental ethic, through education, which can point the way to achievement of the goal of *sustainable development for mankind.*

6

Key Environmental Issues and Formal Education

J. C. SMYTH

Part of what follows is based on a paper, originally published in *The Environmentalist*, **3** (1983), which was circulated as a pre-conference paper. Other parts of it are referred to later (p. 56).

The earlier papers, by Rugumayo and Baez, illustrate well the escalating environmental problems which education now has to tackle. The problems could be attributed to maladaptations between man and environment resulting from the vast differences in both scale and speed which now separate human cultural change from biological change.

Rugumayo's key issues (some of which have been the subject of other volumes in this series) are the consequences of rapidly growing and dangerously shifting human populations, making increasing demands on diminishing resources of space and materials, suffering from declining quality in exchange for quantity and from the unhealthy concentration of wastes. The changes have been associated with rapid developments in science (including medical science) and technology, but these have mostly taken place in northern temperate countries and have not always been suitable for transfer nor directed towards relief of the most urgent needs of other countries. Indeed they are closely bound up with gross imbalances in the distribution of wealth and power which may have made the developments possible but which must now be re-directed before disaster becomes irreversible. Although education starts most easily from local issues it must therefore reach out eventually to a global environment. Science educators must collaborate with those of other disciplines to provide better understanding of the needs of people. The call for a concerted effort to give education a more specific environmental dimension has been widely recognized. Education systems are, however, among the most conservative of human institutions and matching the rate at which they can be changed to the human and environmental need is not easy. The task is complicated by the difficulty of defining environmental education and what it aims to achieve. Most people agree that it embraces elements from virtually all the traditional fields of knowledge, and the word "holistic" has come into use to emphasize that understanding the whole environment is more than understanding a sum of its parts; but of course the result is unwieldy. It is simplified for many by adopting a viewpoint associated with some particular concern – public health, wildlife conservation, urban planning – but these may result in conflicting ideas rather than a comprehensive outlook. For some it is a guide to the technologies of environmental management, but all too often these overlook inconvenient elements and long-term trends. For others it is an emotive response to threats of impending doom, to be pursued as a crusade, religious or political, rather than as a sober search for truth. To resolve difficulties of this sort we need some kind of agreed structural model, adaptable enough to suit the wide range of target audiences and the different forms of education through which they may be approached. It must also be adaptable to locality, since learning will generally be most effective where it relates to an environment familiar to and valued by the student.

> The environmental educator thus has the task of constructing a conceptual model of the human environment as something whole and continuous, extending far beyond the limits of familiar surroundings, yet exhibiting internal structure and processes of which detailed appreciation may be vital. The framework must be capable of receiving all kinds of issues, relating them to other components of the environmental system, and providing ways of evaluating and managing them. It needs to be founded in a real world of experience, where skills may be practised and attitudes developed, even although the starting points may be environments sadly impoverished. This demanding programme will be limited to widely varying degrees by the circumstances in which it is mounted, but even restricted progress in the right direction will be worthwhile. Although deeply dependent on the insights and methods of long-established academic disciplines, environmental education has been established and has survived as a new entity, aimed to integrate the talents of all who can contribute to realisation of its objectives.

Although there are many routes into education, as these pages will show, formal education has a special significance, not just because it provides the only access to a whole population (while at school) but because of the seal of importance which it attaches to the subjects with which it deals, a quality that has its effects far beyond the bounds of education. There are various ways, many discussed below, by which environmental teaching can penetrate formal education. To obtain this seal of approval, however, it must compete successfully with the long-established philosophies and methodologies of traditional curricula. This means that it must be demonstrably excellent, both in the quality of its subject content and in its success as a discipline for educating the young. This calls for well-tested material support and teachers trained in methods appropriate to its range and variability. Thereafter it must be given real value in whatever certificate its students obtain that will carry them on to employment or educational advancement. The tertiary sector of education has a special responsibility here.

No area of education is more bound up with environmental issues than science and technology. Many of the world's problems are the results of science and technology misapplied, and their control will be equally dependent on our advancing knowledge of how they can be applied better. Many past mistakes might have been avoided, however, by a clearer appreciation of the intricate linkages between different environmental components – ecological, social and cultural – within a whole system. In this field more than any other the scientist must work with exponents of other disciplines, and this should also be reflected in his education. The benefits of cross-fertilization between scientists, social scientists and artists are well illustrated in the papers which follow.

Environmental education implies a balanced growth in appreciation and understanding of the environment in all its dimensions: the spatial environment, the social environment, the temporal environment both past and future; and also of the subject's own internal environment which so much influences his behaviour – of physiological and psychological needs, of memory, imagination and creativity. All of them are recognizable and definable to some degree in scientific terms, but these will rarely be enough to explain the behaviour of a subject in relation to his environment, and therefore to modify it. At the heart of environmental education lies recognition of the identity of subject and environment as the two inseparable and interdependent parts of a single system. If education can lead people to see their environment as something to be cared for as they care for themselves, then progress is being made.

The knowledge required to solve environmental issues is bound to vary so much that it can only be defined by the circumstances in which teaching takes place. Care is needed to avoid over-simplistic treatments of issues for which the scientific foundation is too complex or under-researched. More important than detailed knowledge, therefore, are the concepts which can be derived from a particular study and which may be transferable, the skills required to investigate it and the attitudes which may be fostered thereby.

What, in summary, can education, especially science and technology education, offer in response to the issues set out in the preceding chapters? Among other things the following seem important:

Develop a systemic approach to man–environment studies, from the level of the individual in his home territory to that of the species in the biosphere;

Seek to balance as well as to extend, the growth of experience between all aspects of the environment, external and internal, spatial, temporal and social;

Relate the approaches and methods of the sciences more explicitly to those of the humanities and the arts, for a more rounded understanding of man–environment interrelations;

Foster a progressive development of awareness, understanding, evaluation and creative guidance of change, backed by the knowledge and concepts, skills and attitudes appropriate initially to surroundings which are familiar, thereafter expanding outwards;

Practise the formulation of questions in open situations, even if this is more difficult than the solution of problems on fixed assumptions;

Explore the nature of value systems, relating them to ecological and behavioural as well as to economic and political standards;

Be outward and forward-looking, preparing a healthy future as well as healing past injuries;

Prepare for the likelihood that the effects of applying science and technology, however expertly, will be as good as the outlooks and intentions of those who apply them and the quality of their own integration with their environment. Education always has responsibilities for both.

7

Environmental Studies in Pakistan

S. M. A. and N. M. TIRMIZI

In their paper the authors give an interesting case study of the relationship between environmental conditions and curriculum design. They point out that

> In Pakistan the environmental problems fall broadly into three categories:
>
> (a) those arising out of a phenomenal increase in population;
> (b) those arising out of the processes of development;
> (c) those arising out of poverty, ignorance and lack of resources.

It is interesting to note the emphasis on the three Ps: population, pollution and poverty. They also make an earlier implicit reference to the fourth P: proliferation of nuclear weapons.

The paper discusses the environmental studies curriculum produced by the Population Welfare Division in collaboration with the Ministry of Education and ends with this summary:

> In short, there is a great urgency that environmental education be imparted at all levels of education and full use be made of mass media. The following main objectives are to be kept in view while formulating policies for the purpose.
>
> 1. *Awareness*: to help individuals and social groups acquire an awareness of and sensitivity to the total environment and its problems.
> 2. *Knowledge*: to help individuals and social groups acquire basic understanding of the total environment, its associated problems and humankind's responsible role and presence in it.
> 3. *Attitude*: to help individuals and social groups acquire social values, strong feelings, commitment for the environment and the motivations for actively participating in its protection and improvement.

4. *Skills*: to help individuals and social groups acquire the skills for solving environmental problems.
5. *Evaluation ability*: to help individuals and social groups develop a sense of responsibility and urgency regarding environmental problems to ensure appropriate participation which will ensure individual and collective action for the solution of these problems.

Lastly it has to be fully realized that along with social progress and the advances in production, science and technology, the capability of man to improve the environment is also increasing with each passing day. To achieve the desired environmental goal, the world as one nation has to think how to get a thorough insight of the problems so that necessary steps are taken to leave a better environment for future generations.

This demands the acceptance of responsibility by citizens and communities and by enterprises and institutions at every level, all sharing equitably in common efforts.

The paper includes a 5-page annex giving a tabular analysis of curricular concepts in environmental education. Throughout the conference the curriculum group was constantly reminded of the need for science and technology education to work along with the social sciences and the arts to achieve a rounded perception of man and environment.

II School-based Primary and Secondary Environmental Education

1

Environmental Education in Schools

G. W. KNAMILLER

Part II is about environmental education in primary and secondary schools and about participants' attempts to work within the formal structures of which they are a part. As our central aim was to focus on the implementation of education programmes relevant to human needs, the workshop, in one way and another, constantly addressed the problem of how to get environmental education into schools as a living, dynamic component of the curriculum. To a large extent the rationale for environmental education in schools was assumed: children as future decision-makers represent the long-term hope for the sustainable use of natural resources, and schools offer a world-wide institutional base for mass transmission of this environmental principle.

Here we attempt an overview of the papers and workshop discussions relating to school-based environmental education. We go beneath the rationale to the tangle of practical issues with which the workshop struggled. To establish a base-line we start with a brief summary of environmental education objectives. The two sections that follow – The Content and The Place of Environmental Education in the Curriculum – are considered from the point of view of implementation. In a sense they set the stage for the final section, Constraints and Opportunities, which highlights the work of "top-down" and "bottom-up" strategists. Throughout the whole discussion runs an underlying theme – the interaction between the school and the community in the cause of achieving a viable balance between conservation and development. We conclude the section with a selection of the papers referred to in the review.

OBJECTIVES

The general aims of environmental education have been stated and restated many times. Our purpose here, as it was in the workshop, is not to

55

invent new aims but to develop what we have. What follows is gleaned mostly from Professor John Smyth's paper.

For children to develop an environmental ethic we must redefine the objectives of formal education. Schooling has been, and to a great extent still is, for the purpose of enabling the individual (or by extension the tribe, ethnic group, social class or nation) to extract the maximum advantage from the natural and social environment in which he operates. This perhaps was reasonable when there were not so many of us, and when we could move away from local ecological crises. With our growing awareness of the finite capacity of the biosphere, however, and man's ability to alter its life-support systems drastically and permanently, we realize that the central objective of education must shift. Man and environment must now be presented in school as a single system in which the activities of the individual must be adjusted to the capacities of the environment. Only in this way can both man and environment be maintained in a healthy state. We must help children, as Hass says, "to perceive themselves as part of their environment: the 'object' environment is taken over as a personal responsibility – a prerequisite for self-determination". Or, as Badasconyi puts it, "personality grows into and irradiates the environment".

With this overall objective in mind the main ideas to be developed in schools are:

1. The complementarity of organism and environment;
2. The selectivity of the individual to input and output;
3. The extent of interconnections from an individual outwards;
4. The enabling and constraining properties of energy and material resources;
5. The significance of short-term and long-term change;
6. The consequences on individual, society and environment of human life-styles;
7. The choice of criteria and the procedures available for guiding and managing change.

To achieve these objectives skills must be developed for realizing them. They will include:

1. Skills of data-acquisition, handling and presentation;
2. The formulation and testing of hypotheses;
3. Skills of prediction and evaluation;
4. Skills of imagination and creativity to complement those of science;
5. Behavioural skills needed to achieve objectives as a member of society.

Attitudes to be fostered might include:

1. A sense of identity with one's environment, enjoyment of it, and respect for the processes upon which it depends;

2. A critical attitude to received information;
3. A sense of community with other people and with other living things;
4. Respect for oneself and for the unique human capacity to overcome biological and other environmental constraints;
5. A sense of continuity with the past and with the future;
6. A sense of responsibility for making choices of action consistent with caring for the future as well as the present;
7. A commitment to contribute personal talents to participation in the improvement of environmental quality.

These concepts, skills and attitudes, expressed in a form suited to the prevailing circumstances, can provide a basis for the construction of a checklist of objectives against which a programme of studies may be arranged and assessed.

THE CONTENT

Identifying the content of environmental education for schools is a very challenging task. The difficulty is due, as Smyth says, "to the all-embracing nature of its subject-matter and the diversity of approaches and attitudes among those who promote environmental education". Amazingly, however, there is little disagreement among practising educators about the specific environmental knowledge to be included in particular disciplines. Most biology educators, for instance, tend to agree on topics to be included in secondary biology courses. Chemistry educators likewise tend to agree among themselves, as do geography, history and arts educators. Also, there is a great deal of cross-disciplinary empathy among subject specialists when reviewing the environmental content of other subjects. The material that Horvath describes in her paper (26), and Badacsonyi in her paper (3), rings very sound to me, a biologist. If such agreement exists, where then does the debate over environmental education content become heated? Three major areas of controversy emerged in the workshop. Although they are considered separately here, in practice they overlap and interlock.

Localization

The first point has to do with localization, that is how locally placed should and can the content be? Elstgeest (17) goes so far as to say, "only within the concrete environment of each child can we offer environmental education, because the child grows up in it, learns from it, belongs to it, depends on it, contributes to it, and even has his own influence on it". Many environmental educators would agree with him, in principle if not always in practice. A vast majority would certainly say that content must be related to the local environment and cultural context of the community surrounding the school. Indeed, most agree with Smyth that "environmental education can be seen as a progression through a concentric series of environment zones of decreasing familiarity, defined in terms of spatial, social and temporal characteristics, and taking into account the internal (physical and mental) environment, as well as the external environment". Environmental studies at the primary level commonly begin in the classroom, the school compound and the immediate community. As one progresses through the school grades more distant environments and more abstract environmental concerns become the foci of study. One problem with this is that as children become more able to cope with the intricacies of real environmental problems the curriculum takes them away from local issues. Thus, at the secondary level in Western countries one tends to find, for example, more material on population growth in the Third World than on personal consumption habits of Europeans and Americans, and more time devoted to forest depletion in Brazil than to the loss of plant species from English hedgerows. One is likewise frequently shocked to find in Third World countries rural children studying industrial air pollution rather than the effects of open fires in houses, and studying electricity and gas as energy sources instead of firewood and cow dung. For some reason – perhaps the general feeling that secondary education should be academic and abstract – it seems more appropriate to study someone else's problem. While we would not wish to imply in this day of international communication and global environmental concerns that studying the other person's problem is necessarily a bad thing, doing so often draws us away from our own local environment and our own everyday behaviours which influence it. "Think globally and act locally" is not sufficiently applied in secondary environmental education programmes.

Much of the Third World has a particular problem in localizing environmental education content because of its colonial legacy, which continues to mirror the educational practices and qualifications of the "North". Krasilchik (34) summarizes the point: "Due to mechanisms of cultural dissemination, there is a tendency in underdeveloped countries to study and worry more about problems typical of regions in an advanced stage of industrialization, than about those themes which to them are more typical and more urgent. Thus, topics related to the different types of industrial pollution and the inappropriate use of natural resources are very popular, while problems of nutrition, basic sanitation, housing, agriculture and employment do not receive the attention that they deserve in studies dealing with environmental education." Atchia (1) makes the point that the Third World must not make the same mistakes with environmental education as when they imported, wholesale, science and mathematics curricula from Europe and America: "Communities and governments (in the Third World) have been slowly dropping the traditional colonial curricula in order to introduce more development-oriented subjects. Those of us educators and educational developers concerned with the environment are trying, in parallel with these changes, to infuse an environmental dimension into these subjects."

The concern for localization of environmental education content is felt not only in the international context but also within countries. Great environmental, economic and cultural differences exist here as well. Nationally devised environmental education programmes tend to homogenize content, much of it with an urban industrial bias, in an attempt to achieve a common core of academic knowledge for all children. Vongchusiri (53) lists 13 learning units recently developed for secondary schools in Thailand. Among the titles are "Electricity is Valuable", "The Land We Live On", "Food Additives", "I Love Trees", and "Air Pollution". These suggest exciting environmental topics, but particular units are perhaps more locally relevant to some areas in Thailand than to others (see p. 107).

This begs the question whether specific regions or even schools within a country have a choice of learning units. What is implied here is a "shopping list" approach to localization. If local educators, say district environmental education committees or perhaps even individual schools, were able to select learning units from a range on offer which they thought were relevant to their own area, it would go a long way toward helping to localize environmental education content. Prefabricated and packaged learning units can come from many quarters. The most common and acceptable supplier, of course, is the Ministry of Education, either through its own curriculum development department or its designates, normally in universities and institutes of higher learning. Other agencies have arrived on the scene in recent years, however, and are developing environment curriculum materials for schools. Most of them are produced by non-governmental organizations such as wildlife foundations, or by business corporations. British Petroleum, for example, has been developing and distributing environmental education materials for schools for a long time. Much of the material is intended for school youth clubs and societies within an extracurricular programme, but some of it is useful for classroom teaching.

One of the participants in the Workshop at Bangalore, Jim Connor, described what can only be called "extracurricular" work from his job as Director of the Science Education Department at New York University, in helping particular developing countries produce the *Pied Crow's Environment Special* magazine (see p. 350). This kind of material is beginning to emerge in many countries, and offers teachers another set of materials to help them develop their own locally based learning units.

Going a step beyond allowing individual schools to choose environmental learning units from a central store, is to provide schools with a model or template to guide local educators in writing their own curriculum. Crawford (then a staff tutor in science with Strathclyde Regional Education Authority) offers such a model (13) developed by the Strathclyde

Environmental Education Group, and discusses how it has influenced the construction of science courses currently taught in Scottish schools. Hass also offers a curriculum model which he calls "a structural framework for action-based environmental education". Smyth has developed "a matrix for the construction of course content", and Knamiller (33) suggests an "issue-based curriculum model" (see p. 157).

One international initiative of this sort has recently been attempted in Europe, and has been very fully described in the set of papers by Gravenberch, van Trommel (22) and Wals (56). Gravenberch introduces it in *The European Community Network and the Dutch Pilot School Work*.

In 1973 the Council of European Community Ministers approved an action programme for the Community, which enabled activities aimed to emphasize environmental education as an important part of general education in schools in the various member states of the European Community. In 1977 the Commission of the European Community allocated financial means which enabled the establishment of a network of primary schools, the so-called European Community Environmental Education Primary Network (ECEEN). Thanks to a subsequent allocation of means in February 1983, secondary schools in the member states now also have a network of pilot schools.

The ECEEN aims at:
1. an improvement of the quality of environmental education in the schools involved, by means of mutual co-operation and learning from each others' experiences;
2. gathering, try-out and dissemination of teaching materials on environmental education.

From the very beginning of the Network activities in European schools, the coordination of project activities has been the responsibility of a coordinating team consisting of staff members of the Curriculum Development Unit of the University of Dublin, under the guidance of Mr A. Trant.

Members of the Coordinating Team travel over the year through Europe, and stimulate teachers in the pilot schools to contribute to the educational aims. In a general seminar in Aberdeen (Scotland) in 1983 it was decided to have the secondary pilot schools clustered in groups, each group being expected to concentrate on a specific environmental topic. Topics chosen were: Land Use, Urban Studies (two groups), Water, School and Community, and Air.

Mutual reporting of the topic-work in the groups is done during the general seminars, along with the planning for the coming year.

Each topic-group, furthermore, meets in a mid-year seminar, together with their specific theme leader and specialists who are placed at the groups' disposal by the Coordinating Team.

As an example of how things work out we describe in short the activities in one theme group, the air group. The group decided to concentrate on monitoring air quality in their local areas in order to obtain an overview of the "all-over-Europe" situation during a specific time span.

During their mid-year seminar the teachers of the schools familiarized themselves with the experimental techniques they would like to use, together with their pupils, during the actual international survey of air quality in summer and autumn 1985. On the advice of the specialists, monitoring of the lichen and leaf-yeast populations in the local areas, were used as indicators of air quality. This was done in combination with the monitoring of local geographical conditions and local climatic conditions during the lichen and leaf-yeast survey. All data were sent to the Irish specialists, who processed them into an overview of air quality all over Europe, by computerized data-handling. The theme group on air is now planning an additional activity, to do with the fact that the Council of EC Ministers is expected to have a special meeting in Brussels on air quality and control of air pollution in the EC. The pilot schools in the air group now plan to gather articles on this topic from local newspapers, both shortly before and after the Ministers' meeting. The idea of course, is to monitor public reaction in the various countries in the EC for the gathering of Ministers on an important environmental issue, and to report the results on a European scale.

Although offering curriculum models to regional educators and school teachers is another way of localizing environmental education content, the idea carries with it the assumption that not only are local educators capable of writing a curriculum but that they are free to do so. It also carries with it the obvious need for pre- and in-service training of teachers in how to use the model for developing locally based learning units. Kanhasuwan and Webb (31) outline such in-service workshops at the primary level in Thailand (see p. 111). Gwata (23) describes how a district education office in Zimbabwe organized local teachers to prepare syllabuses and learning activities in environmental mathematics. Young and Maggs (60) offer some wonderfully descriptive case studies of their work in Indian primary schools to help teachers make use of their local environment across the curriculum (see p. 119). In regard to pre-service teacher education, Trommer (50) describes his work with student teachers in Germany, on a project related to a particular gravel lake close to the campus. This was a starting point for training teachers in how to develop their own materials on local environmental issues when they begin teaching. In one of the workshop sessions at Bangalore, Myriam Krasilchik gave a most interesting account of her project with student teachers in Brazil in the development of an environmental course for the gardeners who worked on the grounds of the university. The students, with Krasilchik's help, organized the course, wrote the materials and taught the sessions. The environmental work with the university gardeners certainly was localization-personified, and it gave the students skills and confidence in constructing their own local environmental education learning units.

The crucial point in both the "shopping list" and the "modular framework" approaches to localizing environmental education content in schools is that a degree of teacher independence in curriculum development must be allowed and indeed encouraged. Also, teachers must be educated in how to do it. Curricular freedom and teacher capability, however, exist only sparingly in many countries.

The environmental educator's aim of localization is often bedevilled by centralized education systems with their common syllabuses and examinations, a topic that we shall return to later. It must be said here, however, that the tendency of teachers and students in centralized systems is to concentrate on the nationally devised curriculum materials and to pay less attention to the local environment. Local studies may be viewed as irrelevant, or even as a cultural barrier to school-based learning. The pay-off of schooling is passing the national examination. It is not being able to assess and respond to local environment/development issues. And this brings us back to Smyth's concern about the central objective of formal schooling: that it must shift from an emphasis on individual advancement if we are to help children develop an environmental ethic that is practised locally.

Knowledge or Skills

The second point of controversy about environmental education content in schools has to do with the balance between knowledge and skill learning. Putting the debate in terms of polar opposites: do the concepts and principles of environmental education really matter, or is the heart of environmental education to be found in the skills of critical observation, analysis of information, clarification of values, decision-making and social action? No-one disagrees that both knowledge and skills are important. It is the mix between the two that is argued about.

The interpreted opinion of the workshop is that at the primary level the emphasis should be on the skills. Hass implies that environmental education at this level is mainly about skill or "process" learning. Indeed his model of an environmental education curriculum is itself a "process" model. Mishra (40) says that the environmental studies programme in Indian primary schools offers a strategy for "learning how to learn". Elstgeest (17) too implies an emphasis on skills:

Children learn best by being immersed fully in their own work: by seeing themselves, by doing themselves, by thinking themselves, by puzzling themselves, by verifying their own suppositions themselves, by experimenting themselves, by drawing conclusions themselves on the strength of evidence which they have collected themselves. They should also make mistakes themselves which they then should rectify themselves in the light of new information and evidence which they have uncovered themselves.

The European Community Environmental Education Network Project, reported by Gravenberch and van Trommel (22) and in Joke Wals' paper (56), also tips the balance toward skills. This is made evident by the way that the Project allows participating schools to evolve their own environmental studies, and does not dictate particular topics or a common set of specific concepts and principles to be learned. Young and Maggs (60), reflecting on their work over a long period of time in Indian primary schools, firmly emphasize the skills, particularly the role of environmental education in language and mathematical development. Achieving the skills of literacy and numeracy is the central core of primary education everywhere in the world, and any attempt to introduce environmental education at this level must take note of this concern.

The balance between knowledge and skills at the secondary level, as gleaned from the Workshop, however, tends to shift in favour of knowledge content. Atreya (2), Glasgow (20), and Reeves (42), all reporting on attempts to inject environmental education content into various science disciplines in secondary schools, reveal a knowledge bias. Again the requirement of common syllabuses and examinations, and also the reliance on textbooks, almost force a knowledge content approach. The Papua New Guinea Secondary Schools Extension Project, described by Vulliamy (54), is particularly relevant here because it consciously integrates skill learning within a core academic programme, through its school and community projects in out-stations. Crawford's Strathclyde curriculum model also represents a blend of environmental concepts and skills. The Agriculture as Environmental Science Project, reported by Blum, is another example of a conscious attempt to balance knowledge and skills. It does this by carefully selecting a limited number of topics. By doing so it allows teachers and children to work with skills in some depth. An important factor in determining a knowledge or skills bias is how many principles and concepts are to be taught. The more knowledge to be taught the less time there is to exercise the skills (see p. 151).

To summarize, statements of the aims of environmental education always include a basic set of knowledge and skills to be learned. But few curriculum materials are helpful in guiding the teacher and children to choose the proper proportion of each. The primary level seems more open to skill learning than the secondary level, albeit that skills are more commonly related to the development of language and mathematics. What might be called the higher skills of environmental education, such as in-depth analysis, valuing and decision-making, are not commonly dealt with at primary level. This is not always the case, however. Young and Maggs give some excellent case studies of these higher skills being attempted in some Indian primary schools. Nevertheless, from a child development point of view, these higher skills are perhaps more properly placed in the secondary school. Yet it is at this level that the balance shifts to knowledge content at the expense of environmentally related skills. Certainly in practice this is so because of pressure on the teacher to get through syllabuses which are knowledge-based. Also in many countries there is no tradition of project work in schools, at either primary or secondary levels. Studying a local environment/development issue as a class project necessarily places an emphasis on skill learning. But the time it takes to do project work means that only a limited amount of knowledge content can be considered. Also, subject-trained teachers at secondary schools are traditionally more concerned with the knowledge and skills of their own disciplines than with the hard-to-handle environmental education skills of cross-disciplinary projects.

Participation

This brings us to the third and perhaps most controversial point about the content of environmental education in schools, which in a sense encompasses the first two. Should education for *participation* be an integral part of environmental education content in schools? By this we mean helping students evolve behaviours for restoring and conserving the environment, by engaging them in real environmental issues. It means not only education in the higher-order environmental education skills mentioned above, but going beyond these to the skills associated with social action: identifying alternatives, predicting consequences, implementing actions, assessing progress and making adjustments to the action programme. Krasilchik again: "It is not enough for environmental education to create a lucid consciousness, it is necessary that this consciousness be translated into coherent behaviours in which collective action finds a fundamental solution for the processes of environmental decay." In practice this means that teachers and children go beyond simulations and gaming in the classroom, useful as these methods may be, to actively engaging in environmental issues in the community. Only in this way can the skills associated with solving environmental problems be learnt.

It must be emphasized that to become involved in real issues in the community is one thing: integrating this work into the school curriculum so that children are allowed to reflect on the participation skills they are applying is quite another. The old Chinese proverb "I do and I understand", does not hold for learning participation skills any more than it does for learning technical skills in agriculture by merely having a school garden if the application of fertilizers, spacing and germination rates are not experimented with and considered academically in the classroom. More to the point is the saying, "I understand only when I reflect on what I do."

Issue-based Learning

In this sense *participation* becomes school content, and is closely linked with the debate over knowledge-based versus issue-based learning. Peter Kelly, in the book *Biological Education for Community Development* (Taylor & Francis, 1980), summarizes the difference between the two

TABLE 2

Knowledge studies	Issue studies
Emphasis on knowing and understanding	Emphasis on problem solving and decision making
Unknowns tend to be known	Unknowns not necessarily known
Reflective	Motivation derived from social and/or individual action
Low moral load	High moral load
Precise terminology	Confused terminology
Unitary integration	Eclectic integration
Mainly invariable, possibly hierarchical, arrangement of concepts	Variable arrangement of concepts

(Table 2). Knamiller attempts to interpret these differences in terms of environmental education in the context of rural schools in developing countries (Table 3).

An issue-based approach in environmental education is most conveniently described as a project where subject content and skills are learned in light of real, local environmental concerns. At the core is a field study that involves learners in systematically gathering, analysing, evaluating and expressing information and values for the purpose of identifying local environment/development problems and making decisions about relevant social action. Issue-based learning becomes the vehicle for the participation skills.

There are many examples in environmental education where studies of local interest are taken to the analysis stage, and even the decision-making stage, about what could be done: but most stop here. Few go as far as participation. It is striking, for instance, how so many children in Wales

TABLE 3

The emphasis of environmental education is on:	Lesser emphasis is on:
Planting crops on a hillside to minimize erosion	Explaining the structure of soils
Applying oral hydration therapy to infants suffering diarrhoea	Extolling the virtues of boiling water
Growing (catching), preserving and cooking fish	The ecology of fish populations
Building efficient wood burning stoves	The energy cycle
Controlling food crop pests	The interaction of plants and animals
Building economical and pleasant shelters in which to live	The sociology of human behaviour
Developing and maintaining a community organization for protecting local water supplies	Describing systems of human organizations
Identifying a specific local environmental problem	Discussing global environmental issues
Participating in solving a specific local environmental problem	Doing simulations

study castles, and how so few schools become involved in community programmes to preserve them. It is equally striking in Zambia to find tree plantations on school compounds but rarely on family farms. In a rural secondary school in Zimbabwe, Knamiller went as far as having students design firewood cookers more efficient than the three-stone "maphifwa", but failed to launch a programme for testing them in homes. Young and Maggs detail a wonderful example of an issue-based study at Koregaon Primary School in Pune district in India (see p. 122), where the school was so close to participation, and indeed touched it with their report to the village elders. Perhaps it is simply unreasonable to expect schools to be able to engage in participation skills fully.

At one of the school out-stations in the Papua New Guinea Secondary Schools Community Extension Project, mentioned above, the students worked with local people in setting up a village water supply. It is most interesting to note that the students' technical work on the project was assessed. Vulliamy writes: "For part of their assessment, students were rated according to the cleanliness of the water emerging from small filtration drums they had constructed using tin cans, coconut coverings, stones, gravel and sand." This idea that it might be possible to assess students' performance in a skill area in a community project, albeit a technical one and perhaps not as complex to assess as the participation skills, is very heartening indeed. A frequent criticism of a skill approach to environmental education is that it is impossible to measure students' work. The Papua New Guinea programme opens the door ever so slightly in this regard.

Steven Landfried, an American high school teacher visiting the workshop, told us about a class of secondary school children who got involved in a local toxic waste problem (35). They made a videotape relating to the situation, including interviews with various people, and aired it on the local television station. Viewers were invited to respond and they did. Whether or not the participation skills were consciously taught and reflected upon in the classroom, they were certainly exercised. Much of the best teaching in any subject, of course, is intuitional, and there should be no reason to think that environmental education teaching is any different. This does not mean, however, that all inspired environmental advocates make good environmental educators. To teach participation certainly requires environmental knowledge and motivation but also a very cool head, an intimate knowledge of children, knowledge of how the work can be integrated within the school learning programme, and a keen sensitivity to the politics of the school, the community and the forces in action between the two.

These qualities are clearly brought together by Blanchard (8) in her fascinating description of the Marine Bird Conservation Project (MBCP). (This paper appears in Part V, on p. 369). The objectives of her project were to: "teach seabird biology and conservation to youths and adults; promote conservation attitudes and lawful, sportsmanlike behaviours; and establish a locally run support base for conservation." Significantly the project was not initiated by the schools, but rather by an outside agency, the Quebec–Labrador Foundation. The project took youth out of school and into a residential youth programme. Later, leading adult members of the communities were trained to assume many of the teaching responsibilities. School teachers were left out initially because of their rapid turnover rates in this isolated part of Canada. The details of the programme clearly place an emphasis on participation skills, at least for those members of the community who became involved; some of them teachers and children.

For environmental education the logic of linked knowledge compared with fragmented knowledge is compelling. The hope of the subject- or knowledge-based approach is that children, when they leave school, will be capable on their own of "gelling" the content into a structure of thought relevant to a particular life-problem. The hope of linked knowledge, achieved through an issue-based approach, is that children while in school will stay in touch with the world of their parents and communities, and will be better able and more likely to participate in community issues when they leave school.

But, as we have seen, it is difficult to get this type of learning into schools. The argument against using participation skills as content and issue-based learning as its vehicle is twofold. Participation is said to be impractical and politically dangerous. From a practical point of view the time in school to do issue-based projects relative to the academic work required for current syllabuses and examinations is just not available.

Also, participation requires that the curriculum be integrated at times, and that individual schools have the freedom to create their own projects in response to local issues.

Inevitably learning through participation in real environmental issues places the school in the political arena. It is the nature of environmental issues to be political at some level, whether it be trying to get English farmers to preserve wild flowers or to get the village water pump repaired in Ghana, or attending a disarmament rally anywhere in the world. Such a role for schools is not normally acceptable to most parents or politicians. On the positive side, opposition to school children becoming involved in environmental issues is probably less when the issue has a heavy majority backing in the community. The political dimension, however, can place the teacher in a very precarious position. Does he remain neutral or does he take sides, with the possibility of splitting the school and being bombarded by the community? Indeed it takes a very exceptional person to play the role of link-person between school and community on environmental issues.

Reviewing this section on content for schools we find a good deal of agreement between environmental educators about what knowledge should be included in subject disciplines. There is less agreement, particularly in practice, as to the questions of localization, the balance between knowledge and skills, and whether or not to teach participation skills through real environmental issues. Localizing environmental education is a universal goal, at least in principle. The conditions for encouraging localization are that local educators have a degree of freedom in curriculum development and have the capability to use it. Quite rightly there is a difference between primary and secondary levels as to what skills to include and at what depth. Observing, communicating and valuing are emphasized in primary school. These, plus the higher-order skills of analysis, decision-making and participation, are more within the domain of secondary school children. Which of these skills should be included and at what depth, their time allocation and whether or not they should be taught through real experiences in local communities are points of controversy. These areas of controversy do not normally arise as a matter of principle. Most environmental educators agree in principle about localization, skills and participation. The tension exists between theory and what is perceived as practicable. Rigid, nationally defined syllabuses, examination structures and the resulting fall-out make it difficult, but not impossible, to practise what we preach.

Nevertheless, environmental education content is dynamic and continually evolving, of course faster on paper than in practice in school classrooms. A major point to be remembered, however, is that decisions on selection of content are being made all over the world. And another crucial area that concerns the selectors, at international workshops and in classrooms, is where to place environmental education in the current school curriculum. It is to this point that we now turn.

PLACING ENVIRONMENTAL EDUCATION IN THE SCHOOL CURRICULUM

There seems to be little controversy over how and where to place environmental education in the current school curriculum. Of the three basic approaches commonly acknowledged – integration within subject disciplines, creation of separate courses and relegation to the extracurricular, out-of-school programme – most school educators readily opt for integration. Principle and practicability seem to merge more easily here.

In general the Bangalore Workshop was no exception to this rule. Young and Maggs convincingly place environmental education in all areas of the primary curriculum. Elstgeest sees the primary child's interaction with his environment as the starting point for all learning. Jadhao *et al.* (28) and Mishra (40) document how Indian primary schools are emphasizing a "teaching through the environment approach".

At the secondary level there are several case studies that exemplify the integration approach. Glasgow focuses on the injection of environmental content into the natural science subjects in Caribbean Secondary Schools. Similarly Reeves discusses attempts in Bangladesh to squeeze environmental themes into current science courses. The development in Scotland of a general science course for all students who are not already doing a separate science, provided an opening for environmental topics to surface as part of the new package. As Crawford explains, "This [science course] provided the opportunity for the influence of the Strathclyde Environmental Education Group's (an informal group of interested professionals) philosophy and approach to be directed at the centre of the development of the science curriculum."

A most imaginative venture in integration is from Williams (58). In responding to the need for materials that emphasize social implications in integrated science courses in Britain, particularly those associated with cross-cultural understanding, he got together with science educators in Zambia to produce such learning units as "Carrying Loads on Heads", "Charcoal", "Methane Digestors", "Arid Zones and Desertification". (The distribution of these units is being handled by the Centre for World Development Education in London.)

Moving to mathematics, Begg (7) offers some 40 pages of practical activities on how environmental themes are being expressed through mathematics in New Zealand. Equally useful is Begg's "theme analysis", where he demonstrates in a matrix "how a package of [environmental] themes should be analysed to show subject coverage so that other aspects of the [mathematics] syllabus will not be ignored". Tirivavi (48) explores the environmental learning that can be achieved through the study of statistics at the secondary level. Vulliamy describes how an environmental science dimension is being integrated into the whole of the core curriculum of the Secondary Schools Community Extension Project in Papua New Guinea.

The technical subjects are also ripe for the integration of environmental content. In a wonderfully personal paper Gondwe (21) reflects on his own attempts as a secondary agriculture teacher in Malawi to incorporate environmental themes, including aesthetics and ethics, into what might be called a conventional subject (see p. 167). Blum shows how the Agriculture and Environment Sciences Project in Israel managed to inject such topics as "The Rise and Fall of DDT", "Let's Protect Plants", and "Fight Against Hunger" into agriculture education. It is a pity that there were no home economics educators at the workshop. We did, however, have a joint session with the Health theme (see p. 243), and many examples of the integration of environmental concerns in health education were brought forward.

Quite aside from these examples of environmental injection into science, mathematics and technical subjects, the Environment theme, unique among the themes of the Bangalore Conference, included educators from the humanities and the arts. This was done to emphasize the point that environmental education draws on all subject disciplines, and to reflect their complementary roles in producing environmentally competent citizens. Horvath (26) offers excellent examples of "the roots of human behaviours resulting in the ecological crisis of our time". Badacsonyi (3) discusses the importance of an "emotional motivation" for studying the man–environment relation, and for discovering beauty in nature and in ourselves. Her examples of children's work in music, poetry and the visual arts are inspiring indeed. They help us to see ways that environmental education can respond to the internal environment of children. The environmental educator's ultimate goal – behavioural change – is rarely accomplished through logic alone. Imagination, intuition, creativity, concern, all play significant roles in developing a personal environmental ethic. Their stimulation through the arts must be an integral part of environmental education programmes for schools at all levels.

One of the highlights of the Environment Workshop was a children's performance of an "eco-drama" called "The Flight of the Flamingo" (see p. 221). They did a marvellous job, the children performing with grace and confidence. Academically, sensually and emotionally it expressed how well arts and science can combine, and the great potential for integrating environmental education into the schools arts programme.

In short, integration is currently the dominant approach to getting environmental education into schools. Separate courses in environmental education at the school level, although they do exist in some countries, are not at all common.

The Extracurricular Approach

There is, however, considerable interest in placing environmental education in the extracurricular programme of schools. We have seen that the skill content of environmental education, particularly the higher-order skills and more specifically those associated with participation, is very difficult to inject into the academic work of schools. The time factor, the assessment procedures, the authoritarian nature of teaching and the expectations of children, teachers and parents, all militate against engaging in real environmental issues in the community. The school is, nevertheless, a sanctuary of young people who, because of their education, are potentially capable of addressing and helping to solve environment/ development problems. Why not then, the argument goes, find a vehicle that is associated with the school, where children and youth can be more easily organized, but which does not interfere with its intended purpose? This is happening, of course, all over the world. In association with extracurricular programmes in school, wildlife clubs, conservation societies, consumer protection organizations, environmental liaison groups and so on, have sprouted up almost everywhere. Even the more traditional out-of-school organizations such as young farmers' clubs, scouts and science societies are adopting active programmes in environmental awareness and protection.

At the conference we were very fortunate in the Environment Workshop to be able to visit Bandipur National Park in the rain shadow of the Western Ghats, some 50 miles from Mysore (see p. 232). We were even more pleased to be hosted in part by members of the Wildlife Conservation Club of St Joseph College. The knowledge, insights and commitment of these young people and their leaders for environmental concerns in India were inspiring indeed. Aside from guiding us around the Park, the students joined our workshop sessions where they animatedly joined in discussions about environment and development, and about the role of school in these matters.

Going a step beyond the extracurricular programme in schools is the people's science movement in India. Within this movement science education centres are arising from local communities. Although not formally connected to schools, many of their activists are professional educators and many of their clients are teachers and children. Jayshree Mehta (39) describes the structure and activities of the Vikram A. Sarabhai Community Science Centre in Ahmedabad. She reports that some of the questions frequently asked by the community and to which the Centre responds are: "Can we avoid pollution without stopping our textile mills?", "Can rickshaws ply on roads without making a terrible noise?", "Why is our river dry during a major part of the year?", "Why is our river dirty?" (see p. 397). It is not always so easy to ask and respond to such questions in daily lessons in school, particularly if they carry with them the expectation that attempts will be made to do something about such problems.

Perhaps it is here, at the edge between formal and non-formal education, that environmental education might best be able to achieve a holistic approach among school-aged children. But the extracurricular, out-of-school programme has its own drawbacks. Among them is securing and maintaining an effective leadership, by necessity mostly drawn from school teachers. It also requires active national and regional organizations to back up local resources and efforts and to provide continuous stimulation and recognition. Regardless of the potential strength of this sector, one of its characteristics is that it is attended by the most academically able children in the school and those from the higher income groups. It touches few children relative to the mass who inhabit schools daily. This is why we are so concerned about getting viable environmental education programmes into the formal sector in a systematic way. Thus, we finally turn our attention to the ecology of formal education systems in search of innovative ways to get our programmes implemented in schools.

CONSTRAINTS AND OPPORTUNITIES FOR IMPLEMENTATION IN SCHOOLS

Organizing environmental education for school learning is challenging because of the all-embracing nature of the subject matter and the diversity of people's views of what should and should not be included. But a further, and perhaps more difficult, challenge to actually getting environmental education operational in classrooms arises from the nature of school itself and the forces that determine what goes on inside. Without a clear and realistic awareness of what motivates children to learn, teachers to teach, parents to accept and education officials to encourage, innovations in environmental education are unlikely to take root and grow.

In the discussion above we have alluded to some of the forces which affect such issues. These include localization, the skills, the issue-based approach, and how to place the content of environmental education into the school curriculum. For a more comprehensive view, we include here (p. 79) a paper by Dr Graham Vulliamy, an educational sociologist at York University in England. The paper was written after the conference as a summary of the Environment Workshop's discussions about implementation of environmental education in schools. Although the focus is on education systems in Third World countries many of the concerns expressed are universal.

Given this overview of constraints and opportunities embodied in education systems, several case studies presented at the Workshop explicitly and implicitly addressed the implementation problem. Glasgow (20) helped us to build a framework for considering the case studies, in which "top-down" strategies are on one side of the implementation spectrum and "bottom-up" strategies on the other.

Top-down

While acknowledging in the Caribbean the crucial role of science teachers' associations, civic groups and government departments such as health, environment and agriculture in promoting formal school programmes in environmental education, Glasgow (p. 135) sees the officially constituted *subject panels* who design the science syllabuses for the Caribbean Examination Council (CXC) as "the single, most successful agent for integrating environmental information and attitudes into school curricula". She proceeds to spell out the environmental inputs that subject panels have made in secondary biology, chemistry and integrated science syllabuses. Equally important, she discusses how students' acquisition of the new content is to be assessed, through written and practical CXC examinations, and a form of continuous evaluation termed school-based assessment. Included in an appendix are sample CXC examination questions. She makes the point that other examining bodies used in the Caribbean, for example the Cambridge Examination Syndicate, have indeed embodied environmental content in their syllabuses. But it is possible to attain success in their examinations without actually covering the content. "The claim for CXC", says Glasgow, "is that the evaluation strategies leave teachers no alternative but to include environmental aspects in a way that is very relevant to the student. This is the force which gives the desired direction or 'push' from the 'top-down'."

Reeves (42) also takes the "top-down" approach. Although on the surface one would think that Reeves is working in a completely different context, Bangladesh and the English-speaking Caribbean share a common educational heritage, with its legacy of nationally defined syllabuses and public terminal examinations. Bangladesh has, of course, other constraints that affect the implementation of environmental education in schools, which Reeves clearly delineates. He also indicates several positive directions that Bangladesh has taken, and includes examples where environmental education has been recently injected into science disciplines. Reflecting on curriculum change he says that commitment of government and local people, provision of good teaching/learning materials, better teacher education and improved conditions of service for teachers all must be included in the recipe for change. To skimp on one spoils the brew. For the entire package to become operational, leadership must come from the top. In this regard his "Ladder of Influence in the Educational System" in Bangladesh says it all (p. 140).

Other case studies, although not so explicit as Glasgow's and Reeves', imply a "top-down" strategy. Vulliamy (54) describes the Secondary

School and Community Education Extension Project as "the Ministry of Education's highest priority project". It is funded by the government's National Public Expenditure Plan and "developed to test the feasibility of providing a more relevant rural education, whilst avoiding the dangers of a dual curriculum split between academic and vocational streams". Although the project encourages curriculum development at the local level, these efforts are not only guided by a four-person SSCEP headquarters team in Port Moresby, but each school is allocated five extra staff, some of whom are expatriates. Adjustments in the assessment procedures are also worked out to cater for the insertion of more practical work in communities. Nevertheless, the programme is designed so that students will compete favourably with those students from non-project schools. It is felt that academic standards must be maintained or even increased, so the SSCEP schools do not come to be seen by parents and the community as second rate.

In his concluding discussion Vulliamy says that the top-down strategy, which embodies a "gradualistic" or pilot project approach, is very costly. It also "poses critical questions concerning its potential replicability on a wider scale". He continues: "However, if innovations are to be any more than merely 'on-paper' changes, then teachers require extensive support, especially in the early stages. The constraints on effective change . . . are usually far greater than policy-makers recognize."

Kanhasuwan and Webb (31) and Vongchusiri (53) do recognize the problems of innovating in Thai schools. Thailand has a national policy on environmental education for its schools. The Institution for the Promotion of Teaching Science and Technology, a government-funded body for developing science and mathematics curricula for all schools throughout Thailand, launched in 1981 a project entitled "The Development of Materials for Environmental Education". The project organized a workshop of interested and knowledgeable people from various agencies to detail environmental education content for schools. What followed, as mentioned above, was a set of 13 learning units which were finalized in 1983. The top-down task now is to get teachers and children to use them in schools before the project ends in 1987. The time factor is significant, as it points out the long commitment necessary to achieve change. Now it is a matter of teacher education and making sure that assessment procedures are coordinated with the new materials.

Kanhasuwan and Webb address another factor in the "top-down" strategy, which is alluded to in the Papua New Guinea study: that is the bringing in of foreign "experts" to help implement new environmental education programmes. Webb, an Australian, was invited by Pranakorn Teachers' College in Thailand to assist in organizing and conducting in-service training and to prepare written materials. She catalogues some of the problems that arise in response to the foreign expert, from the dependence syndrome on the part of hosts to the felt need of Western experts to take environmental education beyond the level of learning *through* and *about* the environment to learning *for* the environment.

Lieberman (36) implicitly approaches these concerns as well. In this case an outside agency, RARE, Inc., a non-profit conservation organization based in Washington, DC, initiated the programme in several Latin American countries under grants from USAID. In some cases RARE staff, in conjunction with country nationals, launched an entire curriculum development effort from writing materials to piloting and teacher training, while in others it responded mainly to requests to assist in teacher education. Although problems associated with foreign input in the top-down strategy are not mentioned in the paper, a thoughtful discussion on the topic would be most useful.

Bottom-up

At the other end of the implementation spectrum are the case studies which describe individual efforts of teachers striving to make change from the "bottom-up". Prominent among these is Vincent Gondwe's paper (21). When he wrote it Gondwe was an agriculture teacher in a rural secondary school in Malawi. The paper is a personalized account of Gondwe's quite successful attempt to beat the examination system (see p. 167). He says that in the back of his mind was the constant aim that the national syllabus itself has to change. As a teacher, he felt that the only way he could influence the process was to demonstrate the success of the alternatives he had evolved at his school.

Knamiller too, but in a much more modest venture and as a foreign import, set out to see if the general science syllabus in operation in rural day secondary schools in Zimbabwe could easily accommodate environ- mental injections, and if local teachers and students would accept them. Working together with the two science teachers at the school the syllabus topic, energy cycle, was chosen as it conveniently happened to be the next topic in the scheme of work. The topic was localized under the title, "The Cooking Food Energy Cycle" (p. 157).

When, however, this venture in a real school was reported in a seminar attended by Ministry of Education people, science curriculum developers and teacher trainers in Harare, it quickly became apparent that some of the participants had no idea of the conditions that prevail in typical rural day secondary schools. It was also apparent that they were tied to the Cambridge syllabus and examinations. That curriculum development in science could possibly begin by working in the schools and communities that receive it, rather than starting from existing syllabuses and assemblies of experts meeting in the capital, was a novel idea, and not readily acceptable.

One way to achieve potential success for broad base change through the bottom-up strategy is for those individuals working in the classroom to advance to higher positions of decision-making in the education structure. This, in fact, is what Gondwe has done. He is no longer a school teacher but occupies an office in the Malawi Ministry of Education, and now is listened to at this level. Another way is to form a grass-roots power base; that is a group of professional individuals who are knowledgeable and concerned about environmental education, and who also know the politics of the education system. Two case studies are exemplars in this regard.

Crawford (13) has been mentioned above in the context of injecting environmental topics into a new general science course in Scotland. The point to be made here is that "an informal group of interested professionals", calling themselves the Strathclyde Environmental Education Group (having an impressive-sounding title is extremely important) was able, when the opportunity presented itself, to become influential in curriculum design. Indeed the education authorities sought their advice. How the group managed to get themselves into such a position in the tangles of Scottish educational bureaucracy makes fascinating reading. What can be reported here is that the group knew the ins and outs of this bureaucracy. This was extremely important because they knew when the time was ripe to make an input, and also they had curriculum models and approaches ready to offer. But beyond this, when the danger arose "of the complete removal of the environmental issue from the new science course" (due to problems with its piloting in selected schools) the group was in a position to respond positively. And later when, as Crawford says, "The curriculum development process itself had severely distorted the theoretical model (originally developed by the group) the group was able to keep in touch with grass-roots teachers 'who kept faith'."

The great lesson here is that, just as local environmental protection organizations must keep constant watch over possible erosion of their efforts to maintain a conservation effort, so too must environmental educators be constantly alert to maintain environmental education programmes in schools. This is not to say that a rigid stance is called for, but that the informal group must be vigilant, flexible and willing to compromise. This can only be done by keeping the organization active beyond the initial stages of the implementation process for the important maintenance functions of monitoring and further response. A corollary to this lesson is that such groups must maintain their contacts with grass-roots teachers as well.

Crawford gives further advice. When a committed informal group manages to get itself into a position to make curricular suggestions let its members be as true to their theoretical intentions as possible, even if a bit radical. Then "invite" the official curriculum developers to document how the programme is working in schools. Hopefully they will not disregard the entire programme so that some parts of the new approach will surface in future curricula.

There is a concern here, Crawford reminds us, that teachers, having tried and indeed liked the more radical initiative, may continue to employ it even when official guidelines alter the new approach. Nevertheless, the role of "bottom-up" strategists is to present alternatives to education systems, which like other complex systems are notoriously conservative and resistant to change.

For the other case study that exemplifies a grass-roots group's action in initiating and maintaining an environmental education programme we return to Blanchard (see p. 369). This programme was discussed above in relation to the questions surrounding participation as content and the issue-based approach. It must be added here that, like the Strathclyde Environmental Education Group, the Quebec–Labrador Foundation had an impressive-sounding title, was well organized, and carefully researched the politics of the local education system. Unlike Strathclyde it was clearly focused on a very specific environmental concern, the conservation of marine birds, while Strathclyde's brief was much more broadly based. Also the Foundation was a more formally constituted body and had money to seed its project. It was able to launch its own out-of-school education programme for youth and training courses for adults in the community. It also recognized the power of local school parents' committees to influence the curriculum in school. Putting together all of these thrusts – direct contact with youth, the community and the parents' committees – the project was able to inject its philosophy and approach into local schools. It goes without saying that the project has evolved some basic curriculum materials that teachers could use to develop learning activities in school.

Crawford's final suggestion for "bottom-up" strategists is exemplified in Blanchard's work, and is probably a dictum for all environmental educators toiling locally for input into schools: "Above all, one needs patience, stamina and a modicum of contrived interference."

2

Teaching for the Environment in Third World Schools: Some Implementation Constraints

GRAHAM VULLIAMY

There is widespread agreement that environmental concerns should be taught in the schools of developing countries, to provide students with greater knowledge and understanding of conservation and to influence their future behaviour. However, unless educators have some understanding of the context of Third World schooling, attempts at reform are likely to be frustrated. There are four broad categories of potential implementation constraints that should be addressed.

1. THE SOCIO-POLITICAL CONTEXT OF SCHOOLING IN THE THIRD WORLD

In many colonial countries prior to Independence, the educational system was clearly stratified into a European-style academic education for expatriates and schools that the colonizers tried to make relevant to agriculture and local community concerns for the majority of the indigenous peoples. On the one hand, therefore, the route to upward social mobility became clearly identified with a style of academic education that was often totally irrelevant to the countries concerned, being based instead on syllabuses and examinations derived from the metropole. On the other hand, attempts to relate schooling to local community concerns became identified with attempts to keep the colonized in an inferior position. This has resulted in deep-seated attitudes concerning the role of schooling that persist today. Schools tend to be valued extrinsically for their ability to promote mobility out of the subsistence sector to formal sector jobs, via the acquisition of examination certificates, rather than intrinsically for any knowledge or understanding gained within them.

Schools everywhere tend to reproduce the structure of the society of which they are a part. However, it has been convincingly argued that the effects of the "diploma disease" in distorting the style and content of schooling are far greater in developing countries, because the differentials between the lifestyles of the educationally successful and the unsuccessful are so much greater than in industrial countries. Any attempt at curriculum reform in Third World schools must recognize that parents and students are likely to reject any innovations which do not accord with the prevalent routes to high-status examination success.

2. THE EDUCATIONAL SYSTEM

Attempts to innovate must also take account of key features of the educational system as a whole. If, for example, curricula are centralized and assessed by national examinations, then pilot curriculum projects in isolated schools are likely to be rejected because students become disadvantaged *vis-à-vis* those in conventional schools. Similarly, the addition of new school subjects or learning experiences, even if in all schools, are likely to be rejected if they are not given the same examination status as conventional work.

The style of national examinations tends to be a more important determinant of the content and process of teaching than syllabuses. Research indicates that the vast majority of questions asked in school examinations in developing countries test factual recall, rather than comprehension or application skills. This encourages the rote teaching of factual information and places a low premium on the relevance of such teaching to the students' own lives.

Classroom teaching in developing countries therefore tends to be characterized by a formalistic, didactic style. This is reinforced by the fact that most teachers have themselves had very limited education and training. Since teachers are often unsure of the subject matter they teach, they are frightened of deviating from the syllabus or of encouraging the asking of questions by students.

Attempts to innovate within schools must also take account of powerful interest groups within the educational system. The school inspectorate, for example, is likely to prove a more potent influence on teachers' behaviour than the ideals of curriculum developers.

3. THE NATURE OF THE SCHOOL

A combination of the two sets of factors discussed above culminates in an incentive structure for teachers and students that militates against any deviations from inherited concepts of teaching and learning. In such circumstances the lofty ideals of educational reformers are likely to be defused by pressures from within the school itself – from students in the classroom and from teachers in the upper level of the school hierarchy outside the classroom.

Schools in developing countries are also often characterized by very poor resources, by chronic teacher shortages and by organizational problems caused by weak leadership. In such circumstances, suggestions that teachers should adopt more "progressive" teaching styles adopted in the West – project work, discussion groups, drama, games and so on – are both unrealistic and inappropriate. Unless the incentive structure is altered to reward such teaching and learning processes, and unless teachers are provided with adequate in-service facilities to help support such activities, then their attempted adoption will prove counterproductive.

4. SCHOOL–VILLAGE TRANSFER

Even if schools do effectively teach about environmental issues, research suggests that there are likely to be major constraints on the likelihood of such teaching influencing students' behaviour outside the school. Firstly, for the reasons highlighted above, students do not tend to perceive "school" knowledge as having any relevance to their everyday lives. Secondly, where such "school" knowledge is explicitly related to the local environment, it often conflicts with indigenous knowledge and felt needs. For example, many attempts to "improve" local agriculture are based upon Western methods or assumptions that fail to take account of traditional cultures associated with subsistence gardening. Similarly, attempts to teach a more conservational approach to indigenous agriculture (by advising against slash-and-burn techniques of shifting cultivation, for example) are unlikely to succeed unless they are based upon a thorough understanding, both technical and cultural, of why villagers farm the way they do.

CONCLUSION

An elucidation of the above four levels of constraint should help guard against the simplistic assumption that all we need is case studies of successful practice as models for the teaching of environmental issues in Third World schools. Careful attention must be paid to the context in which any innovation is attempted. Thus approaches to environmental education that have been found to be successful either in formal schooling in Western countries or in non-formal, community-oriented projects in the Third World are not likely to be successful in Third World schools because the constraints are very different.

This is not, however, a recipe for pessimism, but rather for a more realistic appraisal of the implementation task. Once constraints are recognized they are more likely to be overcome. The import of the above analysis is that if the teaching of environmental issues is to be encouraged in Third World schools, such work must be given high status in the eyes of students and teachers. In countries with the more conventional centralized curricula and examinations, this requires changes in national syllabuses and examinations, together with teacher training programmes to support such changes. It is also likely to require infiltrating environmental concerns into the higher-status subjects (such as english, maths and science), rather than creating new subjects which would inevitably be accorded lower status.

3

Case Studies on School-based Environmental Education

The papers which follow are a selection of those which were circulated before or during the conference, and have been chosen because of the points which they illustrate. Some are in their original forms but most have been reduced because of constraints on space. Many other very valuable papers were used at the conference, however, and a full list, together with the addresses of the authors, appears at the end of the book. The editors hope that this will enable readers who wish to consult a paper which could not be included here, or any paper in its original form, to make the contacts necessary.

Case Studies on School based Environmental Education

Order and Disorder in Nature: Action-based and Interdisciplinary Environmental Education in the Natural Sciences

HELMUT HASS

INTRODUCTION

In topical discussion the terms "world and environment" are usually the object of pessimistic forecasts and seldom the target of optimistic hope, expectation and meaning. In this situation the burden of responsibility lies with the school. We need today a basic trust in the creative power of man and his ability to preserve and develop the order of our world.

The analysis of scientific programmes and curricula shows, however, that the starting point and motivation for environmental education generally lies in the damage suffered by our world. Environmental awareness has come to mean the "awareness of disorder" in nature and society. The educational concepts thus derived contain a "destruction therapy" of a strongly negative tone. Meaningful action is reduced to a kind of "avoidance strategy" characterized by an attitude of fearful expectation. Technology as an applied science has developed into an "enemy of nature".

In this dilemma we should remind ourselves of the true goal of science: to seek, discover and understand the natural *order* of our world.

SCIENCE, TECHNOLOGY AND ENVIRONMENTAL EDUCATION

Recent developments in the basic science disciplines and a change of course in the concept of technology give grounds for hope that deeper understanding of the complex structure of our Earth will lead to a more thoughtful treatment of our biosphere:

1. Progress in the theoretical understanding of complex open systems combined with comprehensive and rapid electronic data-processing for documentation, simulation and the forecasting of changes in the environment;
2. A wider understanding of order and disorder (entropy), based on new studies of the thermodynamics of irreversible systems;
3. The evolution of non-harmful and adapted "intermediate" technology, e.g. the exploitation of solar energy, the recycling of wastes, ecological methods in agriculture, biotechnology.

Science teaching is seen here as the confrontation of students with the order of nature. Apart from ascertaining data and facts, the chief aim is the search for fundamental laws in order to recognize the patterns on which nature works. In this way, for example, the "principle of minimal entropy production" in living systems in a steady state could serve as model for the development of new technologies.

The Concept of Order (interdisciplinary aims of science)

Four central correlating views (general aims) are conveyed by the natural sciences:

1. Order and disorder are seen to be on the one hand basic properties of biotic and abiotic systems in nature and on the other hand fundamental categories of human perception and the intellect as such.
   (Order as a basic dimension)
2. The natural order prescientifically thought of as "holistic" arises at all levels of description and observation out of the reciprocal influence of the various elements of systems on one another.
   (Order as the property of a system)
3. The natural order prescientifically considered as "stable" is a dynamic process in a steady state accompanied by a supply of energy and the generation of entropy which may be regulated by minor intervention.
   (The maintenance of order)
4. The natural order prescientifically seen as "constant and self-evident" is a unique event in an irreversible process of development which has lasted for millions of years but in which major intervention results in the disintegration of order.
   (The origin and disintegration of order)

These views of the correlation of order and disorder in nature also determine the position and responsibility of man on earth. The uniqueness and sensitivity which characterize the order of complex, dynamic systems require a new mode of thinking in the treatment of the environment:

The classical, monocausal "exclusive" mode of thinking changes to an "inclusive" form of "reticular thinking" in global spheres of reference. The consequence of this assessment may be expressed as follows:

> Awareness of the environment leads to the awareness of order in nature. The discovery that man is part of this order creates confidence, permits interpretation and provides motivation for responsible action under both rational and emotional guidance, towards the maintenance of order.

Teaching Methodology

With some simplification, four phases or aspects of the confrontation with natural order may be recognized:

1. The comprehensive experience of the order of natural systems, e.g. hydrosphere, atmosphere, lithosphere, biosphere.
   (Phenomenological–holistic aspect)
2. The systematic description and classification of natural orders, e.g. the periodic system of elements, the system of natural life, mechanics, optics, acoustics, the thermal laws in classical physics.
   (Descriptive–taxonomic aspect)
3. The systematic analysis of the elements and subsystems in search of invariants (laws); e.g. the law of conservation of matter and energy in physics and the law of conservation of information in genetics and cybernetics.
   (Analytical–functional aspect)
4. Comprehensive (holistic) understanding of the origin and disintegration of order in natural systems, e.g. the theory of relativity, the theory of evolution, the thermodynamics of irreversible processes.
   (Synthetic–ecological aspect)

These four phases or aspects correspond to the historical course followed by the natural sciences, but also contain the typical stages of an ontogenetic process of learning gone through by men following up scientific discoveries: from the comprehensive experience of phenomena via their description and analysis, to an extended comprehensive understanding of the natural order on a higher plane.

Psychological studies suggest that the learning of scientific concepts takes place in a smaller sequence with both adults and children.

> In keeping with the idea of "learning by discovery", the natural sciences become a "discovery of order in Nature". A gradual (step-by-step) process of learning leads through various stages of recognition superimposed upon each other to a growing understanding of the maintenance, origin and disintegration of order.

In science teaching this course suggests itself in the design of curricula as well as the planning of single series of lessons. Even a single period may well contain elements of this "step-by-step" sequence.

The correlation between aims and methods in science is shown diagrammatically in Table 4.

Psychological Implications

The teaching and learning processes develop along three anthropological "lines of power", which in the Western tradition have always been regarded as the goal of all education: the complete development of the personality through equal furthering of *feeling, thought* and *action*. Pestalozzi symbolically called this "the power of the heart, the head and the hand".

The controversy in our society about environmental aims makes it plain that one-sided people (rationalists) are just as dangerous in the present state of the environment as excessively emotional persons or those who demand action at all costs (technocrats). The danger of intolerance and uncritical ideologizing may easily arise as soon as our lives become too specialized, as the present state of affairs in the environment proves. An imbalance between thought, feeling and action may quickly lead to neurotic disturbances with frequently catastrophic results for human society (see Table 4).

TABLE 4   Natural Sciences – the Discovery of Order

Aims of science	1 Order as a basic dimension	2 Order as a property of a system	3 Maintenance of order	4 Origin and disintegration of order
Psychological dimensions				
Thought ("head")	Experience and perception	Contemplation and classification	Elementary analysis	Comprehensive understanding
Feeling ("heart")	Wonder and admiration	Enjoyment and realization	Mastery and autocracy	Cooperative encouragement
Action ("hand")	Reverence and protection	Arrangement and description	Technical manipulation	Tending and conservation
Methods of science				
	Phenomenological– holistic aspect	Descriptive– taxonomic aspect	Analytical– functional aspect	Synthetic– ecological aspect

Learning by discovery

Environmental education through science teaching therefore also means holistic self-experience in the confrontation of order and disorder in nature with the goal of a balanced co-existence between the natural and the man-made environment.

The reorientation of science teaching needs new attitudes, for the teacher himself, and, as a consequence, for teacher training and teacher refresher courses.

Environmental education, as a task and a contribution to the maintenance of order in nature, offers the science teacher an extension of meaning and interpretation which goes far beyond the mere transmission of scientific knowledge and abilities.

This certainly requires greater commitment and effort from teachers in the classroom, but also provides a new motivation and significance.

Action-based Project Strategy

The themes of natural sciences mentioned above fit readily into the traditional scheme of science teaching. Empirical research, however, suggests that special emphasis is placed on description and analysis (2nd and 3rd aspects). The importance of the comprehensive experience and understanding of nature (1st and 4th aspects), which to environmental education are of greater psychological significance, generally comes a poor second.

A further difficulty has become evident in recent years: many people today recognize environmental problems and have some insight into the order, or rather the disorder, of our universe, but what is missing is sufficient motivation to commit themselves actively for the environment.

The step from awareness of the environment to conscious acting for the environment appears to be the most difficult one. A commitment to action presupposes a far-reaching process of identification with the environment.

Just as language can only be perfected by speaking, so autonomy of action can only be acquired through action itself. How is this to be achieved?

Although the projects, case studies and lessons already carried out in European schools are of considerable diversity, they are nevertheless characterized by surprising similarity in teaching pattern, described by the term "action-based environmental education". This description refers to the intensive interplay between the learners and their learning environment. Environment in this case should be seen as the field of action, experience and living conditions in which class work develops in a network of open relationships.

The planning of environmental studies generally takes place in our experience in three phases, which may be called the *context, process* and *output* phases (see Fig. 2).

Learning by action

A simple project strategy	I. CONTEXT phase Education *by* the environment	II. PROCESS phase Education *about* the environment	III. OUTPUT phase Education *for* the environment

FIG. 2   Action-based environmental education.

Many contacts, experiences and phenomena constitute education *by* the environment (context phase). This phase of project work corresponds to the confrontation with order in nature as a basic dimension, which at the same time leads to the awareness of "disorder" (problems of the environment). The problems and questions thus touched on lead to systematic learning *about* the environment (process phase). This is characterized by a systematic description and analysis (*cf.* 2 and 3 in the concept of order), with growing awareness, knowledge and ability to commit oneself *for* this environment (output phase).

(a)   Context Phase

The initial phase of the projects is characterized above all by those taking part in them (pupils, teachers, parents, experts, etc.), by the individual peculiarities of the schools (curriculum, subjects, examination stipulations, etc.), and by the background conditions. The "context" of everyday life motivates the participants, generates themes and creates awareness of problems from which aims may be set down. The familiarity of the surroundings makes a personal appeal and thus induces personal processes of thought. At this point it is important that the initial situation should be open, that actions and decisions should not be predetermined (open learning). The pupils can play a determining role from the beginning, making use of their own interests and previous knowledge. The choice of project should therefore be made with a view to showing the environment as a complex phenomenon and complete experience.

The pupils experience changes of their environment in the field of tension between ecological wishes and economic necessities. This precipitates decisions, gives the aims a sense of urgency and provides a trigger for action. Strategies for the solution of problems and plans of action must be developed.

(b)   Process Phase

In the interests of associating learning with research and discovery, an investigation strategy is developed, basic knowledge is acquired, and various methods are practised. In the first part of this phase the teacher initiates the learning process by organizing material and giving the class the benefit of his wider information. It is, however, already important to encourage the pupils to work independently in small groups, in order to gain experience for larger investigations with group work on open-air sites.

In these small groups the pupils learn co-operative behaviour, the importance of teamwork becomes clear, and the summarizing of results is practised.

The knowledge and methods thus acquired allow the pupils in the second part of the process phase to carry out largely independent investigations in the environment as their field of experience. The teacher can now take a back seat, since he, like his pupils, does not yet know the results of these investigations. This also brings about a change in the attitude of the pupils to their teacher. This in itself leads to a greater autonomy in the learner, and encourages many pupils who tend to be passive in traditional classroom work.

(c) Output Phase

School lessons usually finish in this situation. One is left with the unfortunately rather dubious hope that the pupils, when confronted with decisions in later life, will act with consideration for the environment. Action-based environmental education trains this behaviour. Three main types of possible courses of action may be laid down:

1. Conscious activity on behalf of the environment must start in the pupils' personal sphere (e.g. saving energy in one's own home, rejection of the throw-away mentality).
2. Actions aimed directly at improving and making good damage to the environment (e.g. looking after the school playground, cleaning up the bed of a stream, planning and building a children's playground).
3. Arousing public awareness by passing on acquired knowledge and publishing results (e.g. informing the public of the condition of ponds, streams, parks and gardens, participation in discussions on the environment).

FORESTS, TREES AND MAN

The following is intended as a paradigmatic illustration of a topical environmental subject.

The Concept of Order

1985 was declared the "Year of the Forest" by the United Nations Food and Agriculture Organization, and a world-wide campaign for protection of the standing growth of forests was launched. Not without cause: in addition to the systematic destruction of the forest by felling in the developing countries we now have damage caused by air pollution in the industrial nations of the north. If one accepts the pessimistic forecasts of the scientists, there will be no more forests in Europe by the year 2000.

The damage to forests, i.e. the disorder in nature, may well become the *leitmotiv* of a series of lessons with environmental aims. Nevertheless, in accordance with the previously explained concept of discovery learning, there should follow a gradual approach towards order in nature. The educational effect results from incompatibility between the experienced order at the level of the tree organism, its structure and reciprocal influence on abiotic and biotic elements of the biosphere (forest ecosystem), and the intervention of man in the interlocking structure of order.

Thus the following main points arise (see Table 4).

(a)   Order as a Fundamental Dimension
(phenomenological– holistic aspect)

Associative surveys on the subject "tree" or "forest" indicate that for most people trees are important in many aspects of their lives, even without any special mention in school. The tree/forest is more than just a supply of wood for building purposes, a source of energy (as firewood), producer of oxygen, of fruit, etc. It possesses manifold links with mythology (the tree of the Gods, the tree in Paradise), art (the tree as a symbol), town planning (the formation of "green zones"), and ecology (symbol of the environment), etc., all of which may be represented through various media (slides, films, etc.). Even better are excursions, and field study centres to strike the note of first-hand experience. Activities such as these can really be carried out in any subject of the curriculum. Contacts with the wood industry, agriculture or forestry offer further possibilities.

(b)   Order as the Property of a System
(descriptive–taxonomic aspect)

A single tree in its structure of organs, tissues, cells and molecules shows itself to be a highly complicated system. But forests do not consist only of trees. Forests are ecosystems whose biotic and abiotic elements contain complex geographical–historical structures. The single elements of these often represent partial systems whose reciprocal influence on one another constitutes the functional order of the forest. This offers a wide scope for diverse scientific studies, from getting to know the various species of trees, plants and animals to the assessment of soil and air factors, climate surveys, cartography, in co-operation with the official authorities, and other activities. The observation of forest damage is a natural consequence that follows without any special directive; as an example of "disturbed order" it makes a greater impact than in a survey orientated exclusively on forest destruction.

(c)   The Conservation of Order
(analytical–functional aspect)

The geographical–historical and functional order of the forests, and also of single organisms, depends on the cycling of materials and the flow of energy. All processes of transport take place due to differences in energy levels. In these, the energy is not lost (First Law of Thermodynamics), but is given off in a degraded form as heat (Second Law of Thermodynamics). The principle of temporary storage of energy in "biomass" offers a subject for studies on biological production, with suggestions for possible use by man. At this level almost all the natural sciences can make a contribution. The degree of difficulty depends, of course, on the age of the pupils. Important aspects of the steady state, the self-regulation capacity of ecosystems ("biological balance"), minimal entropy production, the great economy of the metabolic processes, the role of the forests in the hydrology of the landscape, the effects on the climate, offer manifold possibilities of varying degrees of difficulty. Only when seen against this background can the present-day destruction of forests in the industrial nations be meaningfully discussed.

(d)   The Origin and Disintegration of Order
(synthetic–ecological aspect)

Like all living creatures, trees have an individual life history (ontogenesis: origin, growth, maturity, death). The basic biological rhythm is modified by seasonal rhythms (winter–summer, dry and rainy seasons), by which the individual origin and disintegration of order become evident. Phylogenetic adaptation to the respective environment can be interpreted by the theory of evolution. But the forests also have a life-history, which in the course of evolution meant a continuous development of "togetherness". Through this way of thinking, the functional structure of the ecosystem becomes clear. After a single intervention by man the former structure may be renewed in the course of a succession of steps from the pioneer stage to the climax stage: the ecosystem of the forest has a certain capacity for self-regulation, by which, with reasonable usage, a symbiosis between forests, trees and man may be achieved (forestry, shifting cultivation, collecting and hunting, etc.).

Major intervention by man, such as extensive felling and the use of chemicals destroys the delicate steady state, i.e. the structure of order. Since the forest is enmeshed to a high degree in other ecosystems, there may in addition, be unforeseeable changes in the whole biosphere. Man behaves like a parasite, and in doing so destroys his own life-support systems.

Action-based Case Studies

On the theme "Forests, Trees and Man" many action-based projects are possible.

One case study, "Trees in our town" has a general interdisciplinary structure and can be treated in any age group of pupils at varying levels of difficulty. The *leitmotiv* is the healthy tree as a symbol of life and of order in nature.

The starting point for the project may take as an example the trees in the school grounds (or trees near the school, e.g. in public parks), the care of which may at the same time constitute one of the targets of the project. From the example of the trees, a basic understanding of ecosphere may be developed, which includes man as an integrated part of the biosphere.

After dealing with local aspects, a regional or global insight into the relations between trees and man may be cultivated. The disturbance of order in the ecosystem (destruction of trees by felling, pollution of the environment, etc.), provides material for further actions, whose aim is a symbiosis between trees and man.

A second case study, "Forests in danger", is chiefly concerned with the damage to forests in the industrial nations, in a more specialized form in biology for the secondary school.

Here too the tree is a symbol of life, whose "sickness" and "death" becomes a symbol of the disturbed order in nature. The context, process and output phases correspond to the consultation between a "doctor" and a "patient" (symptoms, diagnosis, therapy).

Both case studies are intended to create a strongly emotional experience of the environmental situation through the personification of the tree as a "symbol of the environment".

Both projects convey varied scientific knowledge, basic abilities and attitudes, which lead to goal-directed activity.

CONCLUSION

The primary condition of all forms of action-based environmental education is that those involved (students and teachers) should identify with the purpose of these activities, possess the requisite knowledge, and employ appropriate courses of action. It is superfluous to enquire where this process of development begins. The present-day situation of the global environment offers more than sufficient motivation.

Certainly not all environmental projects lead to tangible results, but in practice the amount of activity within these projects nevertheless indicates a growing readiness to take a spirited stand in discussion and not merely to evade responsibility through resignation or withdrawal.

Conscious action that bases its proceedings on the future becomes a key experience. And that is surely a beginning.

Children and the Environment

JOS ELSTGEEST

> "Environment" is simply: the world around us. It starts with the skin of our body and reaches out in all directions, in ever widening circles, until it embraces even the Universe.

We have departed from the simplicity of this straightforward meaning. We have dressed the word in many guises, particularly those associated with filth and doom. Somebody must do something about it! But what should be done and by whom?

One common sound dominates: "Environmental Education". The cry goes out: the schoolteacher, of course, should raise the warning finger and wag it. Many of us, adults, regard the school as the means to transfer elsewhere our own queasiness – and our guilt – concerning the welfare of the environment, which we prefer to think of as an abstraction instead of as a reality of which we are a part.

Raising an admonishing finger at children is starting at the wrong end. Children do not pollute the environment: they do not spray insecticides, nor weedkillers; they do not fill the air with sulphur dioxide; they do not defile surface waters with phosphates and oil slicks, nor the deep seas with nuclear wastes. The little toffee wrappers or lollipop sticks casually discarded over the shoulder do not pollute the earth.

Earth pollution is a problem for adults, caused by adults, and it should be solved by adults. Besides, this problem leaves the children cold, simply because it is too big to grasp. Neither chanting "green slogans", nor clean-up or tree-planting festivals have any value: children will shove broomsticks into the ground with equal pleasure as long as it happens during class hours. A good habit is not established by a single action.

Even the best textbooks and programmes in environmental education may be doomed because the *real* environment of a child cannot be described in general and abstract terms.

The way each child experiences the environment is unique. Growing up, learning and gaining insight within his/her own environment is most natural for a child, and each child accomplishes it in his/her own way, accommodating to thousands of impressions. This natural quality of children is a good basis, but not the essence, of environmental education.

Environmental education comes into being when this development, which for every child occurs so naturally and as a matter of course, is consciously and positively influenced, secured, encouraged, enriched, and arranged by responsible adults who belong to the child's own environment and who thus become part of the interactions between the child and the environment.

Needless to stress that school teachers assume a very important place among the adults in this education, and that their responsibility is extremely great. The way teachers act can be enriching to the children, or it may have the reverse effect. In either case the effect is lifelong.

Good teaching is a diversified professional activity, meant to help children to discover their own potential, and it must show continuity to permit them to develop it and to build upon it.

In environmental education children must progress in knowledge, organization, discipline, and self-reliance through an active and affective involvement with the world around them. But the object of this cannot be "the whole world". The whole big world is far too large for children to comprehend, but with proper guidance they can learn to care for "their world".

The immediate environment of the school provides seeds and fruit, plants and flowers of various designs; it permits study of the architecture of living wonders and penetrates the panorama of relationships of form, structure, and function. There is a plethora of animals that dig and tunnel, crawl and fly, hide and seek, eat and are eaten, where children can learn to observe how the behaviour of living things patterns into survival and procreation.

The environment in all its complexity presents itself to the child through manageable, comprehensible, and approachable details. Choose a tree or a shrub, and you have an interesting living structure that also shelters, feeds, or otherwise supports a multitude of other living things. Choose any small area and make it a mini-field for study. The complexity of the interrelationships is reduced enough to be comprehensible to a child, and it will invariably lead to new insights. Stretch a string between two points across an area which includes a path, a ditch, a hillside, a brook, a dyke or a garden. The interrelationships of soils, rocks, plants, animals, and the influences such as trampling, exposure, or erosion, come into focus.

By all means extend your focus and attention to other areas within the environment: to the neighbours, to the land and to the community. Shun nothing, but leave also some choice to the children. By all means exhaust the possibilities offered by *your* environment or, at least, make an attempt.

Environmental education should always be evident in a primary school: children busy germinating seeds and growing plants, collecting and plotting the information, arranging collections and exhibits, using instruments or other aids to refine their observations, using reference books and atlases, or audiovisuals, or pondering over questions and problems in a "nature corner".

Children who participate in the changes in their environment and who learn to recognize the relationships of cause and effect, and who begin to understand the interdependence and interactions, including themselves, cannot fail to perceive that they, too, play a role in these interactions. And when their interactions become more conscious, more organized, more scientific, they acquire a growing insight into how the environment, to which they belong, can be profoundly influenced by their actions. They also begin to understand how the environment affects their own actions and lives.

The children whom I saw the other day working on the problem of providing garden snails, which they wanted to keep for further study, with a "comfortable home in which they would feel happy", these children were obviously building a sound foundation of honest environmental awareness.

> Environmental education is not a matter of telling the children *about* it. It is necessary to use the unique environment of every child as a source of information, as a ground for learning, a mine of wisdom. Only then can we expect our younger children to accept responsibility for the earth they share with others. When this feeling of responsibility becomes ingrained in their personality, they will be able to carry it into adult life, when our problems become theirs.

When Froebel called the school a "kindergarten", he was not thinking of toddlers and infants kept out of danger and mischief like cherubs amidst sweet-smelling flowers. The school of all the children belongs in this garden, and the garden itself is the earth on which they grow. They have to care for it, to keep it neat, healthy and productive, sharing the joy of being part of it all – the garden in which we all hope to survive.

Some Problems and Perspectives of Environmental Education in the School

MYRIAM KRASILCHIK

Since the 1960s projects and initiatives have proliferated in many countries to develop environmental education. The causes vary greatly in different regions due to different economic, political and social contexts.

In some countries a vision of development associated with savage and unbridled industrialization leads those working for environmental preservation to act in such a way as to lessen the damage caused, in an attempt to guarantee a life quality acceptable to the majority of the population.

In other situations the outbreak of interest in environmental education stems from a process of political transformation. When authoritarian regimes give way to democratic regimes and social reorganization becomes necessary, the population in general is called upon to exercise its citizenship and discuss various problems, including those relating to environmental conservation. Thus, the necessity to inform and prepare for participation in the decision-making process leads to a broadening of environmental education programmes.

Besides these factors, the normal processes of dissemination of ideas by academic and international institutions strongly influence the creation of environmental education programmes.

Several initiatives (correlated and often derived from the same causes) aimed at transforming the educational process form an intricate and complex system of interrelations, contributing to the intensification of environmental education programmes.

One example is the school–community relations movement which aims to foster concern for the environment. Another example is the analysis of the social implications of science and technology, which nowadays is an integral part of science education programmes and from which also stems consideration of the role of human activities in the deterioration and preservation of the environment. Health education is still another case of a field of knowledge closely related to environmental education as defined by the World Health Organization: "a balanced existence between people and the natural and man-made physical environments in which they live" (*Health Education and Biology Teaching*, Unesco, 1984).

An analysis of the problems and perspectives of environmental education should also take into consideration the differences in development that exist among countries, the actual concept of development adopted and the relations between countries in different stages of development.

In many cases industrialized countries not only export serious environmental problems, but also do not always propose solutions that interest underdeveloped countries. For this reason some of the problems faced by countries of the third world are largely derived from aspects of neo-colonialism and economic domination that raise questions such as those put by Chiappo, who asks: "Can we Latin Americans, Africans and Asians, inhabitants of the needy South accept as valid the way of seeing and interpreting ecological facts adopted by the countries of the super-industrialized, wealthy North?" (in "Environmental education and the Third World", *Prospects*, 3, 1978).

Conciliation between the interests of development and social progress in regions of the third world and preservation of the environment demand a well prepared population and enlightened institutions that could bring about the process of creating new forms of action and economic activities that would respect the necessity of maintaining the ecological balance. Environmental education has a significant contribution to render in this process.

Due to mechanisms of cultural dissemination, there is a tendency in underdeveloped countries to study and worry more about problems typical of regions in an advanced stage of industrialization, to the detriment of themes which to them are more typical and more urgent. Thus, topics related to the different types of industrial pollution and the inappropriate use of natural resources are very popular, while problems of nutrition, basic sanitation, housing, agriculture and employment do not receive the attention that they deserve in studies dealing with environmental education. Besides more appropriate content, it is also necessary to establish objectives which contribute more to the formation of consciousness and individual and collective behaviour, which raise in students a critical and active involvement in the search for better conditions for environmental restoration and preservation.

It is therefore urgent to reconsider environmental education, keeping in mind that society has, as a rule, specific legislation as a defence instrument, but that in the majority of cases of aggression against the environment, legal mechanisms are only put into action when pressure is brought to bear by the population in an effort to resist powerful interests. Today it is simplistic to suppose that preservation of the environment depends only on goodwill and responsible behaviour. Much more is demanded of the population: "Perspectives of environmental education cannot be considered without regard to the continued economic development of the future. As long as the destruction of the environment remains a sanctioned privilege, environmental education is a catchword on paper, devoid of any credibility and effect" (Werner Katzman, "Perspectives of environmental education in Europe" in *Long Term Development of Environmental Policy and Environmental Education in Europe*, Austrian Society for the Protection of Nature and Environment, 1983).

Many frequently adopted postures are aimed at environmental preservation but may actually be self-defeating since they are not always based on analyses that go to the root of the essential problems. One of these positions, very frequent in relation to environmental preservation, is that in which people deal only with superficial aspects, in general due to lack of a critical point of view and also to a lack of capacity for in-depth and detailed analysis. Some movements in defence of the environment, having little impact, end up by actually aggravating the problem, since interested and courageous individuals waste their efforts but are satisfied with the illusion that they are contributing to lessening the effects of attacks on the environment.

Another very frequent type of behaviour consists of verbal denunciations which are not translated into coherent action. Here the individual recognizes the problems but has an ambiguous attitude as to how they can be solved.

It is therefore not enough for environmental education to create consciousness; it is necessary that this consciousness be translated into coherent behaviours in which collective action finds a fundamental solution for the processes of environmental decay.

To this end environmental education programmes must aim not only at providing individuals with a solid basis of knowledge that will allow them to obtain and use information critically; the citizen must be able to analyse complex situations, discuss them, make decisions about problems of values and, going further than the mere expression of ideas and sentiments, assume positions as to these situations through participation in actions aimed at their solution.

Among the various possibilities for the development of environmental education programmes, the formal education system is still that which offers the best conditions, due to its having an institutional basis, the school. However, various aspects of the educational system place obstacles in the path of development of environmental education as it is known today. These are:

1. *School curriculum*. The organization of the school curriculum, divided into hermetic disciplines each the responsibility of one teacher, always occupying the same schedule for one certain class, is a serious obstacle which does not allow school programmes of environmental education to fulfil their broadest objectives. The analysis of environmental problems cannot remain restricted to one segment of the curriculum, but demands an overall and integrated examination of intricate and complex factors. Thus, for full use of the school as the site for environmental education, the curriculum must undergo a process of reflection and reorganization based on centres of interest, general themes, or possibilities which would give greater freedom for a new mapping of knowledge and of the cultural offerings of the school to its students.

2. *Teacher preparation*. Teachers, in order to face the task of curricular reorganization demanded by environmental education, must handle, besides the traditional aspects of the sciences (physics, chemistry and biology), the social, political and cultural aspects as well. To be able to do this their training must be quite different from that which they now receive. Teachers' performance leaves much to be desired in terms of the content of their courses and, above all, in terms of student–teacher interaction. As a general rule, classes are held in a climate that reinforces the authoritarian relationship between students and teachers, in which the latter are seen primarily as transmitters of information and not as orientators and catalysers of debates. Thus there are no conditions for the discussion of controversial topics such as are the majority of environmental problems.

   Insecurity in dealing with controversial issues which involve decision-making and the formation of value-judgements leads many teachers to avoid participation in these programmes. Others, although they may be well prepared, are frightened by the dangers that may be contained in subjects with obvious political connotations. They fear the reaction of the school authorities, of parents, and often of elements of the community itself.

   For the handling of environmental problems, a changed posture in the classroom is necessary. It is impossible to educate a conscientious and active citizen without giving him the opportunity to express and discuss his own ideas with other members of the community of which he is a part.

3. *Teaching material*. Much of the didactic material for teaching was produced at the height of the environmental education fad. Some of these innovated only in content while maintaining a structure equivalent to the material used in other school subjects. They are, in general, very

structured, which is incompatible with the greater objectives of environmental education. Other projects concentrated on the production of games and simulations to bring participants to consider adverse points of view and to revive their capacity for discussion.

However, this material, although it may be useful, has its limitations, since schematic situations do not contain ingredients of real-life situations, the differences in nuances, the unforeseeable human reactions. There is also the fact that argumentation without conviction, used as a purely rhetorical exercise, can cause distortions to which we must remain alert.

Although we recognize the limitations of the school as a space for environmental education, we believe that it is possible to find ways through the formal educational system by which students can become active citizens. This will only be possible with the opening of the school to involvement with real problems of the community to which it belongs, by means of actions linked directly to political and sociocultural activities in the community. It is essential to develop a feeling of respect for popular culture in its diverse manifestations, for the various forms of community organization and for folk wisdom.

For this to come about we must abandon the conventional approaches used in formal education and devote ourselves to the search for didactic processes that lead to immersion in environmental problems. This, however, must be done in such a way as to achieve solidarity, through fellowship and a community of interests, and not in the paternalistic and authoritarian manner which generally prevails in school–community relations.

One of the paths that opens up in the search for familiarity with real life is the use of projects based on participant research conceived as a joint activity of researchers, in this case teachers and students who work jointly on a project aimed at solving an environmental problem. Perfecting the pedagogic processes derived from action research or participant research should benefit and create actual situations for the organization of knowledge and critical consciousness as intended by environmental education.

This type of research has been criticized for its supposed lack of rigour or as interference in the relations between subjects and researchers. However, it is erroneous to suppose that any type of research can be carried out by isolated investigators in a totally objective position. As to the rigour, it is essential that researchers be encouraged to follow new paths, secure in the knowledge that in group work a greater number of alternatives for solution will crop up, which does not imply lack of knowledge about, or abandonment of, basic research techniques.

In conclusion, it seems to me that to carry environmental education to its ultimate consequences, namely action, one must strive for direct contact of the students with the problems and persons involved in an attempt to improve quality of life.

The IPST Environmental Education Project

PRICHA VONGCHUSIRI

The Institution for the Promotion of Teaching Science and Technology (IPST), with its main function the development of science and mathematics curricula for all schools throughout Thailand, has now focused its attention on environmental issues. Since one major objective of the science curricula developed by the IPST is "to develop an understanding of the consequences of science and technology on man, society and environment", it launched in 1981 a project entitled "The Development of Materials for Environmental Education". Its purpose is to inject environmental elements into science curricula for all school students throughout Thailand. The environmental education project was included in the Fifth National Economic and Social Plan (1982–1987).

EXPLORING AND ANALYSING THE SCIENCE CURRICULA

The IPST environmental education team was assigned to explore and analyse the existing school science curricula at all levels, in order to see to what extent topics and contents related to environmental education currently were included. Moreover, a workshop was organized in September 1981 to which over 50 participants from various agencies were invited to present information concerning environmental problems of the country. During the workshop the participants discussed the following topics with regard to the Thailand environment: cause and effect, problem levels, preservation and prevention, how to educate students, dissemination. The meeting also emphasized that materials should contain both positive and negative phases of the environmental problems, and suggest how best to solve them. Moreover, student age and local situation should be also considered.

After the workshop the meeting suggested that characteristics of the environmental materials should include:

1. Knowledge of and understanding about the environment and related problems.
2. An awareness of and an interest in environmental problems.
3. Attitudes to promote and to solve the environmental problems.
4. Skills in decision-making and problem-solving on environmental issues.
5. Student participation to solve the environmental problems.

OUTLINING THE SCHEME AND DEVELOPING PROTOTYPES

Information and ideas gained from these activities provide guidelines for the development of environmental education materials in terms of both the scope of content to be covered and the method of presentation.

After the workshop the continuous activities of the IPST team were as follows:

1. Set up criteria for content selection and media use by
   (a) selecting interesting problems of Thailand;
   (b) selecting interesting and urgent problems of Thailand;
   (c) emphasizing the present situation with respect to the future and the past;
   (d) containing adequate basic knowledge of environmental science;
   (e) giving the good environmental information as well as the bad;
   (f) encouraging student–community participation;
   (g) giving practical environmental experiments in order to understand real situations;
   (h) encouraging creative thinking and decision-making;
   (i) giving real experiences in order to understand real situations;
   (j) using a variety of media.
2. Develop the thirteen learning units for secondary school: each unit consists of a student book, slide–tape and posters.
3. Organize the workshop to consider the developed drafts, comments, suggestions and recommendations from experts, teachers and representatives from various concerned agencies participating in the workshop gathered for the revision of the draft materials.

OUTCOMES

Based on the information and data received from the workshop, the revision of the draft materials was finished in August 1983. The topics and brief descriptions of the thirteen learning units are as follows:

1. *Electricity is valuable*: electricity-saving households will lead to national conservation of electricity and non-renewable resources.
2. *I love trees*: many benefits are obtained from trees, so love and care should be given to them.

3. *Irritating sound*: sources of noise pollution, its harmful effect, and means of protection.
4. *The land we live on*: land use in Thailand, the effects of farming, forestry and mining on the environment and the way in which man may control live environment impact.
5. *Transportation and energy*: means of transportation and the use of energy as well as their effects on the environment.
6. *Population and balance of nature*: population dynamics, population growth and life style, the causes of the problems that impact on the environment and the ways to control population growth.
7. *Food consumer's guide*: how to select the proper kinds of food required to keep healthy, the dangers of certain chemicals that accidentally or intentionally get into the food and are hazardous to health; how to rightfully protect ourselves as consumers.
8. *Food additives*: food additives commonly used in everyday life, the needs for adding them to foods, their long-range effects on our bodies.
9. *Water: a stream of life*: the full value of water from sources on earth, the causes and effects of polluted water and the proper ways to clean polluted water.
10. *Noise in daily life*: loud noise has physical and mental effects on people, the cause, and effects, of noise and how to control it.
11. *Wondering about trees*: what a tree can do, what is obtained from it and how to conserve it.
12. *Air pollution*: the importance of clean air, causes and effects of polluted air and ways we can control it.
13. *Solid waste – our problem*: causes and effects of solid waste on the environment and how to control and manage the problems.

These materials are suggested for use in schools in 1984 and four of these have now been disseminated. This project will go on until 1987.

An Environmental Education Development Project for Elementary and Secondary School Levels

LADDAWAN KANHASUWAN and JOAN WEBB

Thailand has a national policy on environmental education for its schools, but most of its teachers do not have the knowledge or skills to implement that policy. This is an account of the development of one project in Thailand which aimed to give teachers in-service training and prepare written materials for teachers to use. The project under discussion is supplementary to the work being done by the Institute for the Promotion of Science and Technology.

INITIATIVES

Mrs Joan Webb visited Pranakorn Teachers' College in July 1980 with a group of students from Kuring-gai College of Advanced Education, Sydney, Australia, where she is a lecturer in science education. She was invited to talk to the science staff of Pranakorn College on the work she was doing in environmental education in Australia. Following this, Miss Laddawan Kanhasuwan, of the Pranakorn science staff, took the initiative to ask Mrs Webb to conduct a workshop for Thai teachers on how they could use the environment in their teaching. At the time of writing (1985) seven workshops have been held at Pranakorn College, covering methodologies for environmental education at elementary, secondary and tertiary levels. Written materials have been produced in Thai for activities in the field using the school grounds, a national park, rocky shore and zoo.

111

OBJECTIVES OF THE PROJECT

General

The emphasis of the project is to develop social values and a greater awareness about concern for the environment.

Specific

1. Teachers and student teachers should be led to a greater awareness of their own environment.
2. Teachers and student teachers should learn a range of skills to enable them to teach about the environment.
3. Teachers and student teachers should develop skills in writing work-books and teachers' guides for field work in such places as the school grounds, the zoo, a national park, and a rocky shore.
4. Teachers and student teachers should be encouraged to apply the methods of teaching demonstrated at the workshop to their own local environments.

THE INFANT LEVEL WORKSHOP

Why Teach Environmental Education to Infants?

Children in infant school are at an age when important attitudes can be formed and encouraged, attitudes such as curiosity, responsibility, cleanliness, perseverance and co-operation.

Environmental education may be used as one vehicle to help foster these attitudes, not only towards the child's natural environment, but towards the built environment and the social environment. For example, the problem of litter and pollution is a major one in Thailand, especially in the cities, and a start must be made somewhere in educating the whole populace. We believe teachers have a major role to play in this aspect of environmental education, and the process should start at infant level.

Which Environment?

Where should the activities of environmental education be carried out? Particularly for the infant level, activities should focus on the school playground; long and expensive bus excursions to national parks or seashore will not achieve the objectives as efficiently as frequent explorations of the familiar but often not looked-at local environment.

Awareness of one's surroundings can start by careful observation and simple recording of the plants and animals of the playground. The concrete objects of the living and non-living world can help provide tools for the development of skills in verbal communication, measuring, reading, writing and the creative arts. The fundamental characteristic of environmental education, its interdisciplinary nature, is nowhere better able to be expressed than in integrated programmes of the infant school, and, to a lesser degree, the primary grades.

Concepts to be Learned

The concrete objects of the local environment can be used to help teach such concepts as:

1. living and non-living;
2. texture;
3. shape;
4. size;
5. colour;
6. growth;
7. reproduction;
8. variation.

Skills to be Learned

The concrete objects of the local environment can be used to help develop skills in:

1. observation;
2. measuring;
3. verbal communication;
4. reading;
5. classifying;
6. writing;
7. creative work.

Think of the possibilities of a collection of 10–15 leaves from different plants in the playground. First they could be sorted into groups on the basis of size, or shape, or colour or texture. They could be measured; they could form the basis of discussion groups to encourage the use of language; they could be used to make colourful patterns on paper using paint (leaf prints). From leaves it is only a short step to the whole plant.

Infant Workshop Programme

Day 1 1. Outline of project to date (with slide–tape presentation).
       2. Environmental education for infants in Australia.
       3. Environmental activities for infant children

(a) work in the college grounds;

(b) written and creative work in the classroom.

Day 2 1. More environmental activities for infant children (field work and class work).

2. Preparation of a teacher's guide by course participants (in Thai).

3. Visit to a local school playground to make preparation for trials of activities with children.

Day 3 1. Pre-excursion lessons for a visit to the zoo.

2. Visit to the zoo.

3. Writing up activities suitable for infant classes visiting the zoo (in Thai).

Day 4 1. Course participants work with small groups of children at the local school.

2. Writing a short story with an environmental theme, one with a message and suitable for reading by infant children (in Thai).

3. Discussion of workshop.

Responses from course participants and schoolchildren indicated that this workshop was providing interesting and enjoyable experiences which were a long way from traditional methods. More importantly, at the grass roots level, initiatives had been taken to introduce Thai people to the environmental ethic.

WORKSHOP FOR PRIMARY TEACHERS

Programme

Day 1 1. Objectives.

2. Techniques of writing.

3. Study of local primary school grounds.

4. Small group discussion about activities for student workbook and teacher's guide.

Day 2 Writing materials on school grounds.

Day 3 1. Pre-excursion work for a visit to the national park at Sam Lan.

2. Bus trip to national park. Overnight stay.

Day 4 1. Field studies in the national park.

2. Writing student workbooks and teacher's guide for national park studies.

Day 5 Completion of written materials.

Day 6 1. Pre-excursion work for a visit to the zoo.

2. Visit to the zoo.

Day 7 Writing student workbooks and teacher's guide for the zoo.

Day 8 1. Pre-excursion work for a visit to the rocky shore.
        2. Visit to rocky shore at Bang Saen.
Day 9 1. Writing student workbooks and teacher's guide for the rocky shore.
        2. Planning for trials in schools.

The Written Materials

The course participants wrote, in Thai, a student workbook and teacher's guide for each of the four environments, working in a group of five. These were printed and all participants joined in discussion of all the separate units produced. The final result was four sets of student workbooks and teachers' guides, one for each environment.

The Trial of Materials

Schools to which workshop participants were attached were used for the trials. The major objective was to test the readability and comprehension of the written materials; a second objective was to test the suitability of the field work for Thai pupils. The teachers completed a questionnaire produced by the Pranakorn staff; these were collated and the revision of the materials carried out at Pranakorn.

WORKSHOP FOR SECONDARY/TERTIARY TEACHERS

Basically the programme was the same as for the primary teachers, but some of the methods were more sophisticated and the treatment was at greater depth, ecological principles receiving greater emphasis.

TEACHER TRAINING AT PRANAKORN

Due to input at Pranakorn Teachers' College from the environmental project, teacher training courses at that College have taken a new turn, and field trips, together with the production of written materials, have become more a part of the curriculum than before.

PROBLEMS TO BE FACED

It should not be assumed that the importation of Western methodologies in environmental education necessarily leads to ready assimilation. There are problems which need to be recognized and, if possible, dealt with. First, environmental education by its very nature is an inter-disciplinary study which requires an holistic approach. It must be realized that to attempt to deal with an environmental problem, such as excessive littering, or removal of forests, a community and its decision makers must face not only the ecological implications, but the social, cultural, economic, political and legal issues as well. Few, indeed, in any country of the world are those teachers who can with confidence embrace all the disciplines required for an adequate study of the environment, but the secondary and tertiary teachers of Thailand are strongly grounded in their special discipline and face the holistic approach with diffidence. A question to Joan Webb at the Banff Conference, 1984, led to a discussion of the continuing dependence of the Pranakorn team on the Australian "expert". The Pranakorn staff are convinced, enthusiastic, and dedicated to the environmental project, but their traditional disciplinary background leads to a lack of confidence when faced with a true inter-disciplinary study.

The teachers and training institutions of Thailand have responded with enthusiasm to Project Pranakorn; numerous invitations have been extended to Joan Webb to repeat the project at other Colleges. But the project needs to be expanded from within, as well as from without, and the Pranakorn team needs to form the nucleus of a nationwide project.

With the aim of helping to overcome this problem, the Australian team in 1985 is leading a training workshop for the Pranakorn staff. The plan is to expose the Thai lecturers to a number of environments not previously studied, having equipped them with a knowledge of basic ecological principles, basic social problems to be faced, and a number of specific objectives. The teaching strategies then proposed will be analysed and refined by group discussion. But Thai educators will fail to transmit the essentials of environmental education unless they change their thinking and orientation along one line of pursuit and take courage to explore in disciplines traditionally covered by their colleagues.

Allied to this problem of the inter-disciplinary approach, and the need to expand the project from within the local group, is the problem of the foreign "expert" who sees the need to take environmental education beyond the ecological level. As indicated above, environmental issues are closely linked with social and political aspects, and the foreigner who dares to venture into such fields, takes the risk of being accused of interference. Therefore, all the more urgent is the need for the local educators to grasp the importance of the broad view of environmental education and lift it beyond a purely ecological emphasis.

Second, there is a danger that the local educators will see the introduced methods as the only effective means of achieving the objectives. "Your methods are great", the Thai infants teachers said, "but how can we do that? Our school has no paper." Thailand has a national policy on environmental education for its schools, and not even Australia has that. The message for the Thai teacher should be that the policy must be implemented by as many methods as possible – if traditional methods work, use them, if the introduced methods work, and are possible, then use them. Thai teachers are dedicated, enthusiastic and intelligent; if they can be convinced that environmental education is critical for the nation's survival, then they themselves will develop creative and diverse strategies.

Further, if a country does have a national policy on any aspect of education, then government support should be available for its effective implementation. Environmental protection for Thailand, indeed for any country, is essential for survival into the 21st century, so education of the people needs government support.

Third, the average citizen is not aware of the critical nature of the environmental problems, and until he/she is convinced that environmental degradation is a bad thing, progress will be slow. Education needs to be supported by adequate legal protection, and laws that exist need to be enforced.

FUTURE PLANS FOR THE PROJECT

It is hoped to expand the project by giving in-service training to lecturers from teachers' colleges further afield. In addition, the number of workshops will increase to include metropolitan and district supervisors. This aspect of the project is crucial because the implementation of the national policy on environmental education depends not only on in-service work of classroom teachers, but on effective teacher training and on the policies and guidance given by district supervisors.

Support is also forthcoming in 1985 from Unesco to establish a field studies centre in a mangrove area at a secondary school in Petchaburi province. With help from the Australian team, Thai tertiary educators will study the area and develop student workbooks and a teacher's guide.

Thai initiatives taken in 1980 have developed into a worthwhile project because of the enthusiasm and encouragement from participating teachers at the workshops. Some teachers in Thailand have always taken their students for excursions, but this project is believed to be the first in Thailand to make field work more meaningful and more productive of the kind of attitudes needed in a developing country of the late 20th century.

Issue-based Learning at Primary School Level

A. J. YOUNG and J. E. MAGGS

If we are to incorporate *issue studies* into the primary schools, learning can no longer be based upon oral exposition by the teacher or upon printed texts whose contents are far removed from the environmental issues which confront the children. We are concerned with the development of children who will confront problem situations with a degree of confidence in their own ability to search for solutions. In attempting to achieve this through the formal educational sector, we must be aware of the necessary skills which need to be developed in young children, many of which are found in *knowledge studies*. However, they will not be directed to the same end, nor will they be best learned outside concrete experiences to be found in such issue studies. Active learning caters for the cognitive domain, whilst in the field of the affective domain, children must see the relevance of what they are doing. At primary level there needs to be an integration of issue-based studies with knowledge studies based on essential skills:

1. *Basic skills*
    (a) Collecting data; observing; interviewing; construction and use of questionnaires; use of archives and other historical sources, including industrial archaeology; experimentation.
    (b) Interpretation of data; classifying; evaluating; formulating hypotheses; formulating models; drawing logical inferences.
2. *Social skills*
    Participation in the organization of group activities, both in and out of the classroom.
3. *Basic skills*
    Mathematics; language and communication; creative activities; use of resource materials.
4. *Applied operational skills*
    (a) Agricultural/technical skills: care of plants and animals; soil studies, including the design and use of simple soil testing kits; making of

119

simple wind and water mills; techniques associated with the use of various tools; farms and their management.

(b) Art and craft skills; cultural craft techniques – old and new practices.

The introduction of issue-based learning, involving an analysis of the cognitive skills to be developed, would be a radical change in primary school methodology for many developing countries. The major problems would appear to be:

1. Selection procedures which endorse the existing curriculum.
2. Parental opposition to change and initiative which is obviously linked with 1, above.
3. The teacher's ability to cope with new methodologies, new content and to develop a more interactive relationship with the children.
4. The difficulty in evaluating children's progress in the affective domain.
5. A reluctance to change which is inherent in any well established system.

In spite of these difficulties, the authors' experiences in Indian primary schools indicate that it is possible to reorientate the educational approach to include activity methods based upon the environment and to extend this to issue studies. Once a teacher has the confidence to plan a study, many of the difficulties in implementation disappear. Teachers need practice in thinking through the implications of a particular study for the class. What is the nature of the problem? How can we begin the study? What means could be employed in the analysis of the information? How can the class be organized to carry out the enquiry? For example, using all the children to gather the same information might not be the best way to gain the breadth of information pertaining to the problem. In studies like these, the relationship of the teacher with the children will have to be somewhat different from that usually found in the authoritarian knowledge studies model. Children will not so much be talked to, but with. Discussion will be the norm and children will be required to think about a problem and suggest possible solutions. If they offer opinions, they may be challenged to produce evidence that will substantiate them. The children may have to decide, not only what information is necessary, but where such information may be obtained and thus they begin to assume a responsibility for their own development.

This kind of work could be attempted within the existing primary school system of many countries. For example, allowing children to participate more meaningfully in class lessons could be a major change in pedagogic practice, but one which would be reasonably easy to put into effect. Initially, the time devoted to an issue investigation could be as little as one afternoon per week, and the anxieties of parents could be more easily allayed if changes in existing practice were seen to be not only gradual, but relevant to future needs.

EXAMPLES OF PROJECTS UNDERTAKEN IN INDIAN PRIMARY SCHOOLS

From 1978, as a result of in-service courses in Environmental Studies, Mrs Mukerjea, of the Lajpat Nagar II School in Delhi, began to use the environment of the school and the wider community as a resource for the development of basic skills with her children of classes I and II. It became clear to Mrs Mukerjea that if children were to discuss, make decisions as a group and be generally more responsible for their own studies, such work must be prepared for from the beginning. She has thus analysed the local environment and seen its potential as the basis for a learning/teaching programme and has provided opportunities for out-of-class studies. The children were taken to a road near the school where the problem was one of traffic, and the safety of the children who needed to cross that road. A survey was made of the traffic passing along the road, especially at those times when the children came to school and left for home. The information was collected at the site using a tally method, and was illustrated using three-dimensional and pictorial representations. Stories of these illustrations were told by the children and the data were translated into numbers. This study concentrated the children's attention on the times when the road was most dangerous to cross and the solution to crossing the road practised. At this age the need was to introduce and develop early linguistic, number and measuring skills as the tools to be used in the solution of problems encountered.

In another exercise, leaves were collected from the trees and bushes in the school compound, and it was felt that this was not too early a stage to engage the children's thinking about the consequences of too enthusiastic a collection from trees and shrubs of either leaves or wood. This was to be viewed both from an aesthetic point of view (the beauty of the compound was stressed) and a utilitarian point of view (there would be no bushes to collect from next time). The leaves collected were sorted into sets with noticeable attributes and described: rough/smooth, long/short, wide/narrow, shiny/dull, colours and number properties. These sets were then compared quantitatively to develop number skills.

The children also observed the different birds visiting the school compound, and this led to classwork which varied from the writing of simple descriptive passages to a class discussion on the relationship between beak shape and the food eaten. (Some of the work may be seen on a slide–tape programme prepared by the British Council, India and lodged in their library.)

RAMJAS SCHOOL, R. K. PURAM, NEW DELHI

The Ramjas foundation is a private organization which sponsors a number of English-medium primary schools in New Delhi. Curricular initiatives are encouraged and project work is an established practice.

In 1982 Mrs Saroja Srinivasan and her class of 10-year-old children undertook one such project on the "Chipko" movement in India. The major aim of the project was to interpret the issues raised in the World Conservation Strategy handbook, with particular reference to Ramjas School and its pupils. The resulting children's work illustrated that they had been involved in a large number of learning situations and had sustained a high level of commitment throughout the project.

The children had used various mapping techniques to identify where extensive tree-felling was taking place and also to indicate where the most sensitive conservation areas were to be found in India. The biological implications of drastically altering established ecosystems appeared to be quite well understood by the children. The main emphasis of the project, however, was an examination of the sociological, economic and political implications of both tree-felling and using wood as a fuel. The children had obviously appreciated the dangers of indiscriminate and widespread wood-gathering and also realized the importance of reafforestation programmes.

The written work produced by the children was of a high standard, as was the associated art work; the latter, in particular, giving evidence of a highly motivated group of children, greatly concerned for their environment.

KOREGAON SCHOOL, PUNE DISTRICT

One of the best examples of the implementation of issue-based studies in a primary school took place in the Jeevan Shiksham Mandir at Koregaon in the district of Pune, Maharashtra State. The headmaster, Mr Judhao, had attended a number of in-service courses on environmental education given by the authors (under the aegis of the British Council) and had been convinced that a skill-based approach to the curriculum was particularly relevant for his rural school. He decided to examine, in a practical way, to what extent the study of local problems could provide the opportunity to develop a variety of cognitive skills in young children.

Initially the children were involved in monitoring wood-gathering activities around the village, and this led to a consideration of future needs and the pressure this would place on existing resources. Suggestions for solving the problem involved the children in finding out the growth rate of different trees and also discovering what were the most suitable species for planting in their environment. A piece of ground, close to the school, was cleared and prepared as a tree nursery. Seeds of local trees were gathered and the best conditions for their germination were discovered by trial-and-error experiments. Young seedlings were raised in simple containers and then grown outdoors under differing water and fertilizer regimes. The children and teacher also considered a simple strategy for managing the existing and future fuel resources of the area and this included such proposals as designating certain areas "conservation zones" in which no wood-gathering could take place for a period of years, extending the tree planting scheme and planning a timetable for the thinning out of young planted trees. This strategy was examined by village elders and the implications, for example, of making certain areas "goat-free" produced much agitated discussion. In the end, very little was attempted outside those activities which took place in the school. Nevertheless, the children had been involved in such activities as mapping, experimentation, information-gathering and analysis, and a wide variety of communication skills. Furthermore, all these important cognitive skills had been associated with a very relevant and immediate problem of the community.

The above examples illustrate what can be achieved by imaginative, resourceful and dedicated teachers. They all experienced problems such as parental misgivings, lack of resources and, occasionally, unhelpful and sceptical school inspectors who did not understand or appreciate what was being attempted, but, in the end, the teachers were sustained by the belief that what they were attempting was not only educationally sound, but also important to the children's future needs. Another common feature worthy of mention was that the studies elicited a high level of interaction between the teachers and the children. This was apparent in the quality of questions posed both by teachers and pupils, and also in the amount of genuine discussion which took place in the classroom.

Thus, in order to develop the flexibility and adaptability required in young children, a greater emphasis needs to be placed upon:

1.   Developing the Talents and Abilities of Each Individual Child

There will always be leaders and those who are led, but the successful leader will always be in need of effective contributions from others. Not even leaders have a priority on all talents, and the contributors themselves must realize that they have particular gifts and that they are able to use them. The task must not be as Ursula, in D. H. Lawrence's novel *The Rainbow* saw it, "to reduce sixty children to one state of mind, or being . . .", but to allow for sixty states of mind.

2.   Making Children More Responsible for their Own Studies

The authoritarian model of teaching would not be appropriate in the pursuit of the aims of issue-based learning. Such a model results in inhibition, rather than the desired flexibility of thought. Situations are to be explored, information is to be sought, classified, illustrated and interpreted. The teacher may provide the opportunity for doing this, assist the process and gently lead any discussions which may arise. The production of rote learning is inadequate for issue-based learning with its emphasis upon individual contributions to community evaluation of problems of immediate local concern.

3. Using the Local Environment More Extensively to Develop the Fundamental Skills of Language and Mathematics

Language does not grow in a vacuum, but in relationship to real materials and situations. There have to be opportunities for dialogue. Environmental issues are a fertile ground for the promotion of discussion, with the teacher as a participant, thus ensuring an exploration and enriching of the language in the process. The quality of the language used at this stage is crucial to the future intellectual development of the children. It should not be thought that the development of mathematics and language are mutually exclusive. The mathematically orientated parts of enquiries and associated discussions are often underused in the development of language. Issue-orientated material may be used as a basis for texts, whether nationally or locally produced, for use in the teaching of reading. Such material may also be useful in adult literacy programmes.

4. Utilizing the Existing Knowledge and Experience of the Children

Children are not passively waiting for an educational "topping up" process which may mean that they have an opinion in the end. In issue-based learning their "education" has been active. They have engaged in activities and experiences which allow for opinions, but the educational process must ensure that there is a reasonable foundation to this opinion. The authors were engaged with some primary school children on a road study and had posed the problem of allowing time intervals for the traffic signals. A discussion ensued in which the solution offered was found to be the very one (with modifications) which has been used by the local engineers responsible for traffic control.

5. Involving the Children in Making Simple Value-judgements

It must be realized that young children can be involved in the process of evaluating various features of their environment. Teachers must employ their professional skills to use suggested remedies/alternative practices in an appropriate teaching strategy.

The realization of the above objectives would inevitably mean a profound change in educational practice in many countries. There should be *less* emphasis on:

1. An Information-based Curriculum

Knowledge is largely wasted if the knowledge-holder cannot use it in the solution of local problems.

2. The Teacher Adopting the "Fountain of All Knowledge" Approach

Knowledge, to be useful in the solution of problems, has to be understood. Understanding, for the primary child, rarely comes about as the result of the verbal communication of some piece of information. We are interested in the pupil becoming self-reliant in the solution of problems not before encountered. Thus we are interested not just in instrumental learning, but in producing a learning situation in which relationships are sought.

3. The Class Lesson as the Main (and often only) Methodological Approach

The didactic approach is not ruled out entirely by issue-based education, but where it is used it will have to be in the context of the issue under investigation. It has a part to play, provided it is centred on things and events within the child's experience. Children often have useful experiences in their communities which are underused in their educational programmes.

4. Rote Learning and Class Chanting

This instrumental learning may have quick returns when remembered answers are trotted out to stock questions. Such learning is not easily retained, and as the scope of the educational experience widens, so the number of things to be remembered increases. This puts the relatively large number of low attainers with generally poor memories in a non-improving situation.

5. Competitive Examinations (almost entirely of a "recall" nature) as the Only Means of Evaluating Teaching Programmes

Such examinations are the servants of knowledge studies and have very little relevance to the communities we have in mind. The sole purpose of their use it to select those pupils who will proceed to further formal schooling. The labels attached to the unsuccessful as a result of these examinations are in no way helpful to them in facing the problems which beset them in the reality of their lives. In truth, nothing has been done to help them and a great deal has been taken away. It should be possible to educate positively and not negatively.

CONCLUSION

Environmental studies, whether issue-based or not, provide a basis on which to develop a progression of skills and concepts appropriate to the primary school child. In developing countries the environment can make up for a lack of those "in-school" resources which we take for granted in the West. Issue-based studies are more relevant to the lives of the children than most of the information contained within knowledge-based learning. A change to environmental education, issue-based, is not just desirable, but also eminently possible to achieve in the primary school.

Science Education for the Environment – an Indian Case Study

B. D. ATREYA

India has a long tradition of using the environment as a basis of learning. For example the movement of Badis Education launched by Mahatma Gandhi laid stress on correlation of the curriculum with productive activity and the physical and social environment. It is, however, only in the recent past that school curriculum designers have made a conscious effort to assimilate more and more environmental concepts and components.

The scope of this study is limited. Efforts at national level for the improvement of science education throughout the school, made during the past two decades, are considered with a view to identifying components that may be regarded as environmental. Also, an attempt is made to find out if there has been a trend over the years for making science curricula environment-related. The National Council of Educational Research and Training (NCERT) is an apex body which works at national level for the improvement of school education. So this study surveys the science curricula developed by NCERT for different stages of school education.

CURRICULUM DEVELOPMENT AT PRIMARY LEVEL

In 1963 the NCERT published an experimental edition of a general science syllabus, Classes I–VIII. The major criterion for content selection was to include those ideas and approaches of science which are essential for future citizens to live well-ordered lives in a rapidly developing technological society. The syllabus contents were organized into units, like "Air, Water and Weather", "Rocks, Soils and Minerals", which clearly had an environmental base. Some objectives of teaching general science stated by this syllabus had clearly an environmental relevance, e.g. to acquire knowledge of biological, physical and material environments including

127

forces of nature and simple natural phenomena, and to develop apprecia-tions such as impact of science on life. The syllabus stressed the need to encourage children to learn about things that are close to them around the home and school. Later on, their horizon may be widened to include their community, state, country or even the whole world. A holistic approach to teaching science was favoured, rather than teaching in separate disciplines. Based on this syllabus a teachers' handbook of activities for classes I & V was developed. This handbook laid stress on the product and process aspects of science, as well as on the nature of the learner, to determine how science should be taught. Some views expressed in the introduction to the handbook laid emphasis on the potential of the environment for teaching science even to rural children. The authors of the handbook felt that many science principles are illustrated on farms, in kitchens and in village bazaars. Children are affected as individuals by growing up in a modern world very different from what it was even one generation ago. A child growing up in this changing world of plastics, synthetic fibres, etc., must learn about the new features of his environment.

The emphasis on learning scientific concepts through the use of local environmental situations is obvious with even a cursory look at the activities suggested in the handbook. However, even good opportunities of conveying to the teacher that environmental resources should be con-served, or that they are being polluted by our careless use, are missed. For example, under the concept "Coal is formed from vegetable matter" efforts are made to teach children that it takes a long time for coal to form inside the earth. However, no mention is made of the need to conserve coal – a logical corollary to this understanding.

The development of textbooks, based on this syllabus and approach, took place during 1969 to 1973. Three textbooks were published, along with their teachers' guides. A major change from the handbook approach was that a primary science kit was also developed for use by the teacher in the classroom. All these curricular materials in science were implemented throughout the country during 1970 to 1975 under the Unicef-assisted Science Education Programme.

The use of primary science kits as a part of the teaching package created complications. Though many of the kit items were of everyday use, its presence with the teacher somehow led to the idea that science is linked with the kit, and not with the environment of the child. The emphasis on learning science concepts through environment advocated in the teachers' handbook was thus somewhat lost.

SCIENCE AS ENVIRONMENTAL STUDIES

In 1975, the NCERT, on the basis of the reports of the Indian Education

Commission, developed guidelines for the school curriculum published as "The Curriculum for the Ten Year School – A Framework".

The "Framework" identified environmental studies as an important area for accomplishing many objectives of the primary stage of schooling. It suggested that "since the environment and the experience of children outside the school vary from place to place, the activities provided in the school should also vary so that the edifice of knowledge be built not on the abstract concepts alone, but also on the solid foundations of the experience drawn from the environment of the child". In the new curriculum developed as a consequence, the physical and social environments are presented in an integrated manner in classes I and II. For classes III–V the curriculum of environmental studies has been prepared in two parts: environmental studies I covers the social environment and environmental studies II the biophysical environment.

The syllabus content for classes I and II has been organized into units such as: Our Family, Our Home, Our School and Our Neighbourhood. It is entirely new in comparison with the older primary science syllabus. The syllabus content for classes III to V is suggestive and flexible. For example, the unit "Living Things" for class III has only this to specify – Things Around Us, Plants Around Us and Animals Around Us, as science concepts. The three textbooks in environmental studies, however, are related to the older set of books though the use of the kit is obviated in the activities suggested. Instead, the local environment is used for organization of learning activities.

CURRICULUM DEVELOPMENT AT MIDDLE LEVEL

Major efforts in this area started in 1964 with the visit of the Unesco Planning Mission. The Mission gave in their report detailed recommendations for improving the teaching of science and mathematics. One important recommendation was that at the secondary stage (classes VI to VIII and IX, X, XI) science teaching should be arranged not as complex themes of general science but in three systematically taught sciences which are interconnected amongst themselves – namely, biology, physics and chemistry. The teaching of these subjects will ensure all-round ideas about the environment. According to the Mission a general science approach is permissible for teaching pupils in classes I to V but application of this approach to science syllabuses of classes VI to VIII would lead to inferior standards of science education.

Textbooks, teachers' guides and kits were developed under the Unesco project for teaching science in separate disciplines of physics, chemistry and biology during 1966 to 1969. Another set of curricular materials for teaching science as separate disciplines was developed under the guidance of study groups set up by NCERT. Both these types of curricular materials were adapted or adopted by the States and Union Territories to implement science teaching at middle stage initially under the Unicef project. While the Unesco project textbooks stressed the systematic development of the basic concepts and structure of the discipline concerned, the study group materials tried to relate the development of concepts and understandings of the discipline with the children's experiences in the environment. Thus study group materials in biology included elements of nature study, conservation, population and general ecological principles in a comprehensive approach to environmental awareness.

Another set of instructional materials was developed through an editorial board set up by NCERT in 1975 in pursuance of the recommendations of the "Framework". An integrated science curriculum was first drawn up, based on which the textbook *Learning Science*, in three volumes for classes VI to VIII, was developed. The presentation of content in the chapters of the textbook is generally divided into five sections, namely, (1) Observations, (2) Questions, (3) Let us find out, (4) Activities and (5) What have we learnt and how is it relevant? The first section includes a number of observations from the daily life experience of the child along with simple and obvious deductions. The questions of the second section follow logically and naturally from the observations. The activities suggested to find answers can at times be done by pupils in the school or their homes. Thus the entire approach lays great emphasis on the environment and first-hand experiences of the child. The level of integration attempted in these books is only preliminary.

CURRICULUM DEVELOPMENT FOR THE SECONDARY AND SENIOR SECONDARY STAGES

Three successive generations of instructional materials were developed by the NCERT for this stage. The first series comprised textbooks developed by textbook panels set up by NCERT for different subjects. The most popular in this series were the textbooks in biology published in 1967. These books stressed population explosion, food problems and conservation. Also discussed in detail were the topics of food chains and food webs and the biosphere as a whole.

The next generation of textbooks was developed by the study groups, in physics, chemistry, biology and mathematics. Here too the textbooks in biology followed a comprehensive approach to environmental awareness by presentation of such topics as conservation, population and general ecological principles.

The current generation of textbooks (1975–80) in biology has followed this trend of incorporating environmental concepts still further.

Human dependence on nature, adaptability of animals and man to their environments, population, ecological succession and eco-crisis, population and conservation, including community health, have featured in a well-thought-out and co-ordinated way.

It may be of interest here to mention briefly the difference in contents and approach of the two textbooks in chemistry for secondary classes. The first book, in the chapter on "Nuclear Chemistry", explains nuclear fission and mentions the destruction caused by the two fission bombs in 1945, but the environmental implications of the nuclear armaments build-up are not mentioned. Similarly, in the chapter on "Chemistry in Industry" no mention is made of the environmental implications of a reckless large-scale use of plastics, synthetic detergents, etc. The second textbook reveals a growing awareness of environmental problems. A full chapter in the textbook provides information about problems of environmental pollution (air, water and soil) and stresses the necessity of utmost care and intelligence on our part in the use of chemicals to maintain and promote the quality of our environment.

OTHER PROGRAMMES RELEVANT TO ENVIRONMENTAL EDUCATION

Non-formal Education (NFE)

The academic aspect of the NFE programme meant for children of the age group 9–14 consists of preparing prototype materials at NCERT, and specific materials at the State level. The dimensions of the NFE curriculum comprise, besides literacy and numeracy, such areas as health, environmental studies, social awareness and vocation. Since these areas are to be treated from the point of view of the needs and problems of the people, all of them have some relevance to environmental education.

Unicef-assisted Projects

The Science Education Programme (SEP) has already been mentioned in connection with the implementation of curricular materials in States at primary level, and for a few years also at the middle stage. Since 1975, two offshoot projects of SEP were implemented. One was for the development of a teacher's handbook on environment and local resources for use of science teachers at primary level. It ended as a Unicef project in 1980. The other one is Nutrition/Health Education and Environmental Sanitation at primary stage (NHEES). This project has attempted to develop a dynamic programme to carry relevant messages to school children as well as to the out-of-school population of the community, to help them adopt desirable nutrition, health and sanitation practices, so that they may participate intelligently in community health and environmental sanitation activities. Under this project a book, *The Curriculum Guide on Nutrition, Health Education and Environmental Sanitation in Primary Schools* was published. The curriculum content suggested in the Guide was fairly well linked with the primary science syllabus. Hence this project may be taken as a good sample of science education for the environment. It is more so because the project has a focus on desirable changes in practices and attitudes. Some messages extended from the school to the community through this project may be of interest in this context:

1. Use clean, safe water for drinking and cooking.
2. Keep your school, home and village surroundings clean.
3. Do not pollute sources of water.
4. Do not defaecate or urinate or spit anywhere but in the places provided.

There are many more messages of this type for implementation in the community through this project. In the first phase the project was implemented in five States. Subsequently it has been extended to 19 States/Union Territories.

Exhibitions

The National Science Exhibition for children organized by the Department of Education in Science and Mathematics (DESM), every year reflects the theme that environmental issues are one of our main concerns. Thus the themes of the 1975 and 1976 exhibitions were "eco-crises" and "human ecology" respectively. The national science exhibition is a big event for the school-going community since it is preceded by exhibitions (on the same theme) at various levels in the States. They wield an extensive and powerful influence on science education for the environment.

Teacher Preparation

No new trend in a curriculum can be effectively implemented without adequate preparation of teachers. During 1978–79 the DESM (NCERT) organized an in-service programme of training for teachers in environmental studies, with academic assistance from experts provided by the British Council. A very useful package of six tape–slide sequences on "Using the Environment to Develop Common Skills" was developed under this project. Six more workshops for orientation of resource persons in the States were organized during 1980–85. Still more needs to be done before one can expect desirable changes in attitudes and practices of the personnel involved.

Unesco Projects

NCERT undertook a number of projects that may be deemed to pertain to science education for the environment. For example, there was one title,

"Environmental Education Pilot Project in India – experimental implementation of environmentally based modules" (March 1979–July 1980). Twelve modules on science education developed in 1976 by the ACEID of the Unesco Regional Office for Education in Asia and Oceania, Bangkok, were tried out in four states of India. A few titles of modules are: Flood and you, The missing smile, Let us make our school clean and beautiful, Let us conserve nature and its resources.

There were good responses from teachers for many of the modules. But there was not a wide dissemination of new ideas under the project since the number of schools and personnel involved were quite limited.

CONCLUSION

Some textual materials and programmes developed and implemented by the National Council of Education Research and Training (NCERT), New Delhi, have been discussed to show how efforts to improve science education are also working for environmental education. A résumé of some of these efforts that the NCERT as a national body has made through its various departments and the Regional College of Education is given in a document *Environmental Education and NCERT*. At lower levels of school education there is greater emphasis on using the environment for science education, rather than the use of science for environmental education. Of course, there are some exceptions like the Nutrition, Health Education and Environmental Sanitation Project. At secondary and senior secondary stages there is a growing trend over the years to incorporate more and more of the environmental concepts in the syllabuses and textual materials. From the level of NCERT, there is dissemination of new ideas and approaches regarding environment throughout the country. However, dissemination of ideas about the need and contents of environmental education is one thing and the achievement of objectives of environmental education is quite another as envisaged in the Belgrade Charter in terms not only of awareness and knowledge but also of attitude, skills, evaluation ability and participation. Some beginnings have been made but we have still far to go to achieve the goal.

Syllabuses with an Environmental Emphasis in the Caribbean

J. GLASGOW

Injecting material into existing curricula/courses must follow one of two patterns. Either those teaching the material, out of commitment, interest and knowledge, must "push it in" from the "bottom up", or the educational system must be directed in such a way as to do this "from the top down".

In the Caribbean two factors contribute to the fact that the second method is the one more likely to succeed at present. Firstly, our teaching staff is neither large enough nor well enough trained throughout the entire region. Secondly, in the English-speaking Caribbean, 300 years of British rule have meant an educational system built up around the British model. This system, and the thinking of society as a whole, are very largely influenced by the philosophy of dependence on externally set public examinations. These decide what is taught in all educational institutions, with the probable exception of the University of the West Indies, which sets its own examinations.

Several organizations in the Caribbean have been involved at both the formal and non-formal levels in trying to work environmental content into schools. These include science teachers' associations, civic groups and various government departments such as health, environment, mining, natural resources and agriculture.

THE CARIBBEAN EXAMINATIONS COUNCIL

The single innovation, however, that is likely to be the most successful means of integrating environmental information and attitudes into secondary school curricula is the stance taken by the subject panels who have designed the science syllabuses for the Caribbean Examinations Council (CXC). All these panels – biology, chemistry, physics and integrated science – saw science as a route for making students intensely aware of the Caribbean environment and anxious to care for it. The new syllabuses that emerged from these panels in 1983 have made statements which declare their commitment to the task of educating, not just *about*, but *for* the environment.

As with any other innovation, it is necessary to put in the new without deviating too drastically from the old, if one wishes for a measure of success. Schools have been accustomed to a certain body of content, and style of requirements at this level. Although, for example, ecology had always been a part of the content of the biology syllabus for the Cambridge Examination Syndicate at this level, the topic was largely neglected. It was quite possible to attain success in these examinations without covering this content. Now there is the definite intent, built into the CXC system, that each student must be exposed to environmental experience within the syllabus if he is to succeed.

THE BIOLOGY SYLLABUS

The biology panel saw itself in a specially intimate position with regard to environmental education. The syllabus is divided into five sections, of which the first and last address environmental concerns most directly. They are named "Living Organisms in the Environment" and "The Environment and Man". In the other sections, which cover "Life Processes", "Continuity and Variation", and "Disease and Man", the emphasis, though more indirect, is still there. Although no prescriptions are laid down for a teaching order, teachers are advised to begin with the section on "Living Organisms in the Environment". The intent is, from the very introduction to the syllabus, to make the point that an environmental slant is being encouraged throughout.

THE CHEMISTRY SYLLABUS

As with the biology syllabus, environmental aims are concentrated in specific sections. Section C deals with "Chemistry in Industry", where students must select one local industry for in-depth study. The details expected include a consideration of the raw materials, principles underlying chosen processes, the economics of production, the generation of waste products, the possibilities for recycling and effects of the industry on the environment, including the social changes which may result because of the presence of the industry. Reference is also made to the environment in other sections such as energy, recycling of materials in nature and the consideration of the solvent properties of water including pollution. Throughout the entire material local examples are used to illustrate principles wherever possible.

THE INTEGRATED SCIENCE SYLLABUS

In pursuance of the establishment of links between the branches of science as expressed in the rationale, the syllabus lists several integrating threads which run throughout. Among these are that candidates should demonstrate:

1. An awareness that different forms of energy are interconvertible and that energy flows from the sun are needed for the formation of fuels and the photosynthetic process which is essential for life on this planet.
2. An awareness that the earth's resources are wasting assets and hence there is a need to: use wisely existing resources; in the case of energy resources, search for alternative sources of energy; actively strive for the maintenance and preservation of life.
3. An understanding that there is interdependence between the organism and its environment.

The arrangement of the syllabus is also in sections, with Section B "Our Environment and Its Resources" and Section D "Life and the Environment" exclusively devoted to environmental education.

EVALUATION STRATEGIES

This claim for the Caribbean Examinations Council is not that other examining bodies used in the region in these subject areas have not embodied environmental content in their syllabuses. Ecology is in the Cambridge syllabus. Similarly, their chemistry syllabus gives as one of its aims, "to show how the activities of chemists have social, industrial and economic consequences for the community". The claim for CXC, however, is that the evaluation strategies leave teachers no alternative but to include environmental aspects in a way that is very relevant to the student. This is the force which "gives" the desired direction or "push" from the "top down".

Two modalities, both reflecting the environmental emphasis, are used for evaluation in CXC: written and/or practical terminal examinations and a form of continuous assessment termed school-based assessment. The fact that all the syllabuses are divided into sections makes it easier to so control the design of the written papers that successfully performing students must cover the environmental sections. The attempt is made to spread questions evenly across all sections of the syllabus. There are the usual objective-type questions and compulsory structured questions. There is also an essay paper which, though not completely compulsory, does not carry an entirely open choice. Questions are arranged in pairs, which are chosen according to sections of the syllabus. Students are required to answer one from each pair, so that they cannot evade entirely the environmental concerns if they complete their papers.

Written questions may also be designed to tap not only factual knowledge, but attitudes as well. Although the biology and chemistry syllabuses will be examined for the first time in 1985, specimen questions which have been prepared for schools will serve to indicate the thinking on how these questions may be structured to evoke attitude responses.

School-based assessment has been designed to look, over a five-term period, at students' practical work. The assessment takes into consideration practical skills, some inquiry skills (usually interpretation), and an attitude component. In chemistry and integrated science social awareness is included in this component, and in biology not only environmental awareness but an additional sub-component under work habits, which looks for "a concern for the safety and care of living things and of property" is also included. In both integrated science and biology, care has been taken to reiterate that the ecological study is expected to be an integral part of this practical work.

CONCLUSION

In the Caribbean – where success in public examinations is, with some justification, regarded as the "open sesame" to the individual's progress – the Caribbean Examinations Council with its subject panels is a tool which can cogently be used to inject not only knowledge about the environment, but caring for the environment which has become so dangerously necessary in the world today. Civic-minded societies, government agencies and laws have done little to halt the march of often wanton destruction. The attitude of the upcoming generation must be changed, as of *now*.

Problems of Secondary Science Curriculum Innovation in Bangladesh

J. E. REEVES

Bangladesh is one of the poorest countries in the world. The average annual income per head of population is US$ 120. Barely 5 per cent consume an adequate quantity and quality of food. Almost 75 per cent are illiterate. The major priorities of the Government are to provide enough food and shelter for the teeming population.

The educational system has changed little since British colonial times, and remains highly centralized. Public examinations, conducted after class 10 and class 12, are administered by four semi-autonomous regional examination boards. Most secondary science teachers are graduates without any training beyond one or two 2-week in-service courses. About 1200 science teachers a year, after teaching for a few years, take a 1-year B.Ed. course at one of the ten teacher training colleges.

PRESENT CONSTRAINTS OF THE EDUCATIONAL SYSTEM

1. The rapid change-over of Ministers of Education and other senior personnel impedes change.
2. There is a grave shortage of senior administrative officers who have had professional experience in education.
3. Recruitment into the teaching profession is restricted by the rigidly defined promotion lanes, e.g. a headmaster will never move into the Ministry or even into teacher training.
4. There is no professional Inspectorate to help teachers or assist in curriculum development.
5. The science subjects are the traditional ones and science teachers are normally qualified in only one science subject.
6. Printed science materials are highly academic, and the poor quality of paper and binding allow a maximum life of 1 year.

7. The science and science methodology components of the B.Ed. course amount to only 8 per cent of the total time allocated, and what is included is taught formally in lectures.
8. In-service training courses accommodate approximately 150 science teachers per year out of a teaching force of 14,000 science teachers.
9. The teaching style in schools is formal and encourages rote learning.
10. Public examinations, essay-type recall questions normally set by university staff, determine entirely what shall be taught. Practical examinations in both physical and biological science do exist but are basically about routine laboratory operations.
11. Very little practical science work is done, as few teachers accept the value of doing practical work as a mode of learning.
12. There is a serious shortage of laboratories and scientific equipment.

Many of these constraints are common in developing countries, although it is perhaps unusual to find so many operating to the same degree, at the same time and in the same place. Senior government officials are aware of the need for change in the curriculum, and frequently say so in public. Resistance to change, however, comes from highly articulate university staff, teachers, parents and pupils whose objective is passing the examination by rote learning. A ladder of influence on the education system is given in Fig. 3.

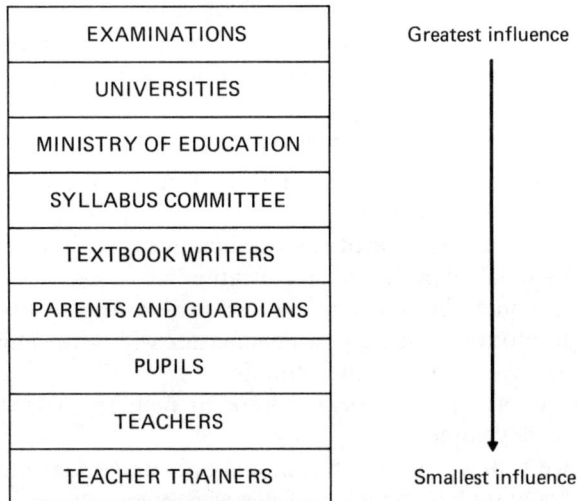

EXAMINATIONS	Greatest influence
UNIVERSITIES	
MINISTRY OF EDUCATION	
SYLLABUS COMMITTEE	
TEXTBOOK WRITERS	
PARENTS AND GUARDIANS	
PUPILS	
TEACHERS	
TEACHER TRAINERS	Smallest influence

FIG. 3 Ladder of influence in the education system.

THE INTRODUCTION OF NEW MATERIALS

Nevertheless progress towards changing the curriculum is happening. The essential elements in curriculum development – production and testing of materials for pupils and teachers, in-service training and relevant assessment procedures – are slowly being coordinated. To do it properly requires money and time. In 1976 a National Curriculum Committee was set up to prepare curricula in all subjects. Several relevant topics in the areas of health, agriculture and population were injected into science syllabuses. Unfortunately the opportunity was not taken to rid the syllabus of some of its dead wood, for example the conversion formula from Fahrenheit to Celsius remained, as did the anatomy of the frog. In 1983 a special committee reviewed the syllabus for classes 9 and 10 and modified it to emphasize man and his needs. Significantly secondary school teachers were included on this committee and were thus able to make a contribution for the first time. Now teachers' guides are being produced with detailed instructions for teachers. So far only two teachers' guides are available. Two copies of each are being distributed to every secondary school in Bangladesh, along with sets for use in teaching practice at teachers' colleges and at the in-service centre. An encouraging sign about the use of these guides is that new teachers are now enquiring about the availability of guides still being prepared.

New courses for teachers' college lecturers have begun, and a science teacher training manual has been produced. A major US$ 47 million project has just been launched with funds provided by the Asian Development Bank to equip the under-privileged secondary schools with laboratories and equipment. And science centres are being set up in each teachers' college to provide in-service training and resource materials.

CONCLUSION

It should be clear from this paper that curriculum development in Third World countries has its constraints. *But it can and does take place.* It is happening in Bangladesh, despite the enormous problems afflicting the country. The key to success lies in people. Teachers must receive adequate teacher training, both pre-service and in-service, in both quality and frequency. In addition to this, ways must be found of improving the motivation of the teacher by improving his terms of service, his working conditions, his opportunities for advancement into teacher training and educational administration work, and by increasing his involvement in development and decision-making about professional matters. It has to be realized that the public examination is merely an instrument of the educational process, and not its master, to be used for the benefit of those going through the system.

Towards a Relevant Scientific Curriculum for the Environment: a Case Study from Papua New Guinea

GRAHAM VULLIAMY

A recent survey of attempts to diversify secondary school curricula in developing countries, in order to make them more relevant to environmental and community concerns, has highlighted Papua New Guinea's Secondary Schools Community Extension Project (SSCEP) as one of the few models which can hold out some hope for the future (Lillis and Hogan, *Comparative Education* Vol. 9, 1983, p. 101). The project has attracted international attention as an ambitious, but carefully implemented, attempt to revise secondary school curricula so that they are more supportive of the government's strategy of rural development.

Following a discussion of the development of SSCEP, this paper will concentrate on the adaptation of scientific curricula to make them more relevant to environmental concerns and to rural development, with examples also from mathematics and agriculture. The literature on educational reforms in developing countries abounds with discussions of policies and plans. Where actual evaluation or research is entailed, it is usually of a type, such as questionnaires or short visits to schools, that results in the reproduction of the rhetoric of policies rather than an informed discussion of the constraints upon actually implementing the policies in practice. The latter requires the use of anthropological-style methods of participant observation and depth interviewing. Thus the author's research involved case studies of three of the five SSCEP schools (two of which were studied twice with an intervening period of over 2

143

years), when about 6 weeks was spent at each school on each occasion (an overview of the research findings is published elsewhere).

THE DEVELOPMENT OF SSCEP

SSCEP began as a pilot project in five secondary schools in 1978–83, and following encouraging evaluations has now entered a trial dissemination phase to further schools. Funded through the government's National Public Expenditure Plan, as the Ministry of Education's highest-priority project, it was designed to test the feasibility of providing a more relevant rural education, whilst avoiding the dangers of a dual curriculum split between academic and vocational streams.

The general aims of SSCEP are very broad. They include the production of school-leavers who are less alienated from village life and more capable of contributing to rural development through self-employment; the de-institutionalization of parts of secondary schooling both by creating outstations, where small groups of students go for a term, and by developing community extension activities and learning programmes in local areas; the redesigning of curricula in grades 9 and 10 (approximate ages 15 and 16) so as to relate academic and practical skills in a structured way; the improvement of teaching and curriculum development skills of teachers in SSCEP schools via an intensive in-service school-based training programme; and the maintenance of academic standards in the SSCEP schools in order that the opportunities for a small number of students to proceed to higher education are not hindered.

An important principle underlying the processes of curriculum development and community extension in SCCEP is that such developments should as far as possible be carried out within the schools themselves, albeit with the guidance of a four-person SSCEP headquarters team based in the country's capital, Port Moresby. There are two reasons for this. First, the programmes in the five different project schools are necessarily different in that they are related to very different community contexts. Second, it is felt that SSCEP is more likely to succeed if large numbers of staff in the school are involved in its planning and implementation from the outset. Experience from other countries supports this, in that centrally imposed curricular projects more often than not wither away in the school as soon as direct support from a central headquarters is terminated. Furthermore, if teachers are actively involved in planning new curricula, they are more likely to see the need to develop relevant new teaching techniques.

Each SSCEP school is allocated five extra staff – four project teachers and a SSCEP co-ordinator whose job it is to oversee the project within the school, whilst only teaching about half a timetable. This increase in school staff does not significantly affect SSCEP schools' staff–student ratios, because the project schools keep all their students on to grades 9 and 10, whereas conventional Papua New Guinean secondary schools until very recently required 40 per cent of their intake to leave at the end of grade 8.

Before proceeding to a discussion of the adaptation of scientific curricula, it is worth mentioning some positive aspects of SSCEP which differentiate it from similar attempts at relevance education that have failed in other countries. They include the following:

(a) An emphasis on *implementation*, where it is explicitly recognized that it is a change of teachers' *practices*, rather than simply a change of curriculum materials, that is required.

(b) The attempted maintenance of academic standards and consequent avoidance of a lower-status dualistic curriculum in SSCEP schools. This has been aided by the fact that the important national grade 10 examination in Papua New Guinea, in which SSCEP school students compete against those in the other conventional high schools, is a skill-based examination, rather than requiring the regurgitation of syllabus content. This fits well with the SSCEP aim of teaching both academic and practical skills.

(c) The secondary school system in Papua New Guinea is very recent and it is markedly less elitist and competitive than that in many other developing countries. There is little entrenched legacy of highly bookish academic learning. Instead, there is a pre-existing tradition of both self-reliance and agricultural/practical work in schools (most of which are boarding schools situated in rural areas).

(d) Papua New Guinea's general cultural and economic context is more conducive to such an innovation than elsewhere. For example, in many areas there are strong rural cultures, which facilitate the potential return of those secondary school leavers who do not get jobs in the formal sector.

THE ADAPTATION OF SCIENTIFIC CURRICULA

Core Projects

The core project was the main innovation around which SSCEP curriculum development was to be built. A core project is a practical project in which groups of students participate but, unlike the kinds of work parade (school maintenance) or self-reliance projects which operate in most Papua New Guinean high schools, it was to have aspects of an academic curriculum incorporated within it. Initially, the pilot schools were advised to select up to four core projects. Such projects were intended to develop students' practical skills in areas of relevance to the students' home communities, and they were to be as economically viable as possible. But the projects were also chosen so that they could develop certain academic skills from the four core subjects of English, mathematics, science and social science. Improved subsistence agriculture, poultry, trade-store maintenance, and furniture-making were examples of such projects. Within each school a project planning group, made up of the SSCEP teacher, who was to do most of the teaching for the project, together with other school staff, was responsible for planning the core projects in detail: their aims, objectives, sequencing, timetabling, etc. Such internal school planning for SSCEP took place during some of the timetabled sessions for in-service teaching, which characterize all Papua New Guinean high schools.

A second phase of the pilot schools' curricular development programmes concerned the analysis of skills in the core subject areas. A skill is defined by SSCEP as "a *process*, that is a skill is *doing* something, not merely knowing a fact". Examples of skills in this context would include evaluating information, observation, following instructions, drawing tables or diagrams, taking notes, or understanding cause and effect. Once the identification of core subject skills had taken place, the desired process of attempting to integrate the SSCEP core projects with the core subjects could follow. This was done in a variety of ways in the different SSCEP schools. For example, certain core subject skills could be taught directly in the core projects; alternatively, some core subject skills might simply be reinforced in the core project; and core subject teachers could also change the content of their syllabuses so that the skills were taught using a similar content to that in the core project. A cattle project, for instance, may require the teaching of certain mathematical skills, such as the calculation of the area of a piece of land suitable for grazing. If so, project teachers should liaise with students' mathematics teachers, who might try and base much of their teaching of the "areas" section of the mathematics syllabus on examples taken from the cattle project. Thus the aim is to redirect the schools' academic teaching away from traditional teaching styles, involving reproduction of abstract concepts and ideas, and towards a "learning by doing", which stresses the application of core subject skills to a practical situation.

A constraint on SSCEP from the outset was the decision that SSCEP students should participate in the same grade 10 selection process as students in conventional secondary schools, in order to avoid the emergence of a dualistic system. New assessment procedures were also to be encouraged in SSCEP schools so that practical project work did not come to be viewed as an inferior alternative to traditional academic schooling. The emphasis on skills in SSCEP has important implications for the schools' assessment policies. This issue of assessment is vital, because not only do examination criteria remain one of the most powerful influences on the practice of teaching, but also one of the assumptions behind SSCEP is that the "carrot" of entrance to higher education and salaried employment can be used to motivate all students in their SSCEP programme. It is then hoped that, having participated in SSCEP, students will develop a more intrinsic motivation to apply their skills to rural development projects. It is also hoped that, despite the insertion of more work into a student's timetable, academic standards will be maintained or even increased, so that SSCEP schools do not come to be seen by parents or the community as second rate.

Such an aim was aided considerably by the existing high-school assessment system. In July of their grade 10 year students took a Mid Year Ratings Examination (MYRE), which consisted of three multiple-choice papers (English language skills, Mathematical and logical thinking, Scientific thinking). Questions in this examination were skill-based rather than content-based (and therefore did not need memorization) and students' answers were dependent upon an understanding of such information or upon skills of manipulating or analysing it. The results of this examination were used to rate the different schools, determining the numbers of awards in each of the four core subjects to be given by each school. At the end of the year internal data, based upon continuous assessment throughout grades 9 and 10, were used to decide which students would be given which awards. Thus, whilst SSCEP students took the same MYRE as students in other provincial high schools, the selection of *which* students in SSCEP schools were to succeed was in the hands of that school's teachers and therefore was amenable to alterations in assessment procedures. Therefore, not only could individual students be rewarded for their performance in their core projects, but there could also be a realistic aim that the school's performance in the vital MYRE would not be impaired, given the skill-based nature of the questions and the fact that SSCEP students were reinforcing academic skills in a practical context. The initial evidence from the SSCEP schools was that their school examination results and consequent job record for school-leavers were better after the introduction of SSCEP than prior to it. However, later evidence may not be so encouraging, because changes to the national grade 10 selection process in 1982 had unfortunate, and largely unforeseen, consequences for SSCEP school students.

The above points will now be illustrated with reference to a specific core project being taught at one of the schools I researched. This "Experimental Agriculture" project was programmed to be taught intensively over a 5-week period at an outstation. Mornings were spent on project-related classroom work and afternoons on practical work based upon the morning programme. Excerpts from the project programme, most of which was written by the national teacher who was to teach it, indicate how it was designed to teach both practical project skills and core subject skills. Thus, in addition to project technical skills, such as crop selection and the application of insecticides, certain core subject skills were either taught or reinforced. In this case parts of students' preceding science syllabuses, such as principles of experimentation, the nitrogen cycle, and chemical elements, were revised, but in a specific practical context.

The kinds of scientific skills taught or reinforced in students' core projects included: performing simple experiments, observing accurately, tabulating data, measuring to scale, deductive reasoning, and interpreting graphs, diagrams, tables and maps. Students were tested on these skills (as well as on other core subject skills) and these marks were fed into students' core subject marks. These then had an important effect on students' life chances, given the continuous assessment system for ranking students within a school. However, such skills were also the type tested in the national MYRE, whose questions often involved situations of a practical nature. For example, the following question appeared in the 1981 paper on "Scientific thinking":

Work Schedule

	Peanuts	Beans	Cotton	Sorghum	Cassava	Maize
Planting begins	Feb.	Mar.	Jun.	July	Aug.	Mar.
Harvest	Aug.	Jul./Aug.	Feb.	Feb.	Dec.	Aug.

According to the work schedule, which crop has the longest growing period?
A. peanuts; B. cassava; C. maize; D. sorghum; E. cotton.

Many of the skills tested are those that SSCEP students had developed in a practical, as well as a classroom, context, unlike conventional high school students whose science lessons were in either classrooms or laboratories. Thus, for example, students in the experimental agriculture core project had conducted the exercise of plotting the height of a plant against its age as part of an experiment to determine the effects of fertilizers, and the interpretation of such graphs was required by another question in this paper.

While such skill-based questions are now widely used in many science examinations in the West, developing countries more usually have examinations which require some factual recall of information from the syllabus. Were that the case in Papua New Guinea, SSCEP students would undoubtedly be penalized in the MYRE, because they do not spend as much time on the national syllabus as conventional high school students.

Outstations

Outstations were an integral feature of the original conception of SSCEP, but the emphasis placed upon them by SSCEP headquarters lessened following the adoption of the school-based approach to curriculum development described above. However, during the pilot phase of SSCEP, two schools developed two outstations and another school one. These outstations were between about 3 and 40 kilometres from the main high schools and were normally located in a more village-like environment. Classes of students went there, together with a couple of teachers, usually for periods of a term at a time, participating in project work as well as continuing their general education programme. The major benefits of the outstations were seen to be: first, that they would be more suitable sites for the teaching of practical projects, and second, that they could incorporate more school–community interaction than would be possible at the main high school.

Where core subject teaching was carried out in outstations, attempts were made to adapt the syllabuses in order that full use could be made of special aspects of the outstation environment. This will now be illustrated with some examples of mathematics and science programmes being taught at outstations.

The "Hihila Mathematics Programme" was an adaptation, by a national mathematics teacher at the Hihila outstation, of the official Unit 2 "decimals and percentages" in the grade 9 mathematics syllabus. It was rewritten in such a way that all the examples used came from practical situations in which students found themselves during their stay at the outstation. These included operating the trade-store and keeping its daily accounts, which students took turns in doing, and the buying, weighing and selling of copra.

The science programme at the same outstation was based on the study of "Weather", and was originally devised by an expatriate volunteer teacher there. This programme included about half the material in the national grade 9 unit on "The Air Around Us", and made special use of the outstation environment and facilities. These included a small weather station, with recording instruments, located on the beach very near the outstation classroom. The year's first group of students had constructed this, according to guidelines laid down in the grade 9 unit.

At another outstation, two sections of the grade 10 Unit 1 on "Chemical Technology" were adapted. These were: first, the material on water and water treatment, where direct use could be made of a village water supply system which the outstation had installed with the co-operation of a neighbouring village. For part of their assessment, students were rated according to the cleanliness of the water emerging from small filtration drums they had constructed, using tin cans, coconut coverings, stones, gravel and sand. Second, the section on lime and lime-making was particularly suited to the outstation, which was situated on the sea. Students collected coral and produced lime by burning it on the beach.

CONCLUSION

Given the widespread opposition to most attempts in developing countries to make schooling more relevant to rural development and community needs, SSCEP has been fortunate in maintaining generally high levels of student, teacher and parental support. A principal reason for this has been a clear recognition of the dangers of a dualistic curriculum.

Moreover, unlike many such policies, SSCEP has promoted real changes in teachers' practices, including some good examples of relating academic science teaching to relevant community concerns in both core projects and outstations. The research indicated that there were important benefits for students both from core projects and from outstations. However, there were also many constraints on effective implementation, some of which had not been foreseen or identified by SSCEP headquarters. In addition, the evidence suggested that without the kind of implementation strategy adopted, especially the emphasis on school-based teacher in-service training within guidelines laid down by a central headquarters, many of the innovations developed by the schools would not have been sustained.

SSCEP adopted the kind of pilot school, gradualistic approach to reform advocated by Sinclair and Lillis, following their survey of relevance education innovations in the Third World (*School and Community in the Third World*, Croom Helm, 1980). Such a strategy is costly and also poses critical questions concerning its potential replicability on a wider scale. However, if innovations are to be any more than merely "on-paper" changes, then teachers require extensive support, especially in the early stages. The constraints on effective change, whether arising from the culture of the school, from conventions of the educational system, or from the sociological relationship between schooling and the wider society, are usually far greater than policy-makers recognize.

In such circumstances a pilot project strategy, deliberately embarking on an ambitious programme of reform in selected schools but within the general guidelines of the existing system of secondary schooling in Papua New Guinea, has been fruitful. It has indicated both what is possible in the way of innovation and the strength of the constraints which make other suggested changes impractical. An analysis of the transition of SSCEP in 1984 from its pilot phase to a trial dissemination phase suggests that important lessons have been learned to help sustain the innovations in new schools.

[In his original paper the author quotes many references relating to this Project – Eds.].

Sustainable Development: Agriculture and Environmental Education

A. BLUM

This paper is a description of a curriculum project which was one of the first to take up the challenge to teach students in a nationwide school system how agriculture can be further developed and, at the same time, how careful one should be in that endeavour. The curriculum is Agriculture as Environmental Science (AES) in Israeli Junior High Schools.

Since the foundation of the State of Israel, in 1948, non-vocational agriculture has been a regular part of the elementary school curriculum. Its aims were, above all, to educate towards the return to nature, to the soil and to productivity. At the same time the school garden was to serve nature studies. In practice, agriculture as a school subject in Israel faced problems similar to those of rural studies in many countries. Often routine work in the garden was not properly balanced by meaningful learning. In many cases the school garden was expected, above all, to provide produce and to occupy academically less able students.

During the 1950s and the early 1960s the socioeconomic situation in Israel underwent rapid changes towards intensive urbanization and industrialization. Agriculture continues to be the country's most sophisticated area of production. In each agricultural branch, fewer farmers, possessing a high professional standard, now produce higher yields. At the same time, a new wave of immigrants who did not always identify with the agrarian ideals of the early settlers contributed to a decline of the image agriculture had in the urban population. Even among educational decision makers many thought that agriculture might be a good topic for rural regions, but not in urban areas.

At the same time, traditional nature studies had come under attack as being too "woodsy-birdsy" and not scientific enough. As often in education, the remedial action tended to overshoot the target. When BSCS (yellow version), CHEMS and PSSC were introduced, their laboratory-centred approach was not balanced by outdoor investigations. The emphasis was on the structure of the disciplines. Applied and social issues to science were neglected.

In 1966 a national Curriculum Centre was established by the Israeli Ministry of Education and Culture. "Agriculture as Environmental Science (AES)" was one of the first six projects to start work.

A NEW APPROACH

When the AES curriculum was being planned, special attention was paid to the needs of the urban population. Rural children did not need to learn in school what modern agriculture is. They could see this at home. But youngsters in the concrete jungles of the cities needed a new approach to plants and animals which they could find in their vicinity. Therefore, flowers were to play an important role in the curriculum. At the same time flowers had become one of Israel's major export items and their production was based on an immediate translation of scientific research results into agrotechnical methods. So here was a topic which would show city students how modern and scientific agriculture works. It could also return to science teaching the applied aspects which had been neglected in the previous wave of curriculum change.

The AES project recognized that only a small percentage of the students will become agricultural producers, but all of them are already consumers of agricultural products. Therefore another criterion for choosing topics was set up: relevance to both producers and consumers. This became the basic philosophy, mainly in units on the DDT controversy, food spoilage, the world hunger problem and others.

Although in the past agriculture has been classified by the Ministry of Education as a "training subject", it was considered in the Curriculum Centre as part of the natural sciences. At that stage an amalgamation of agriculture and science was deemed desirable but not feasible, mainly because of the existence of two separate inspectorates in these two subjects. But planning the AES programmes was co-ordinated with that of the other science curricula. With the gradual and successful introduction of AES units into all schools in which agriculture is taught, the Ministry of Education and Culture decided to change the name of the school subject to *Environmental Studies and Agriculture*.

The AES project does not believe that environmental education and science teaching can or should be culture-free and uninvolved in social issues. Therefore from the beginning an effort was made not only to include in the texts contemporary and controversial social and environmental issues, but also to show how the cultural heritage contributed to developments in science and technology.

Many important discoveries, clever inventions and useful, environmentally sound, agricultural practices were developed 3000 years ago by our forefathers through observation and *experience*. The *experimental* approach is more fruitful and enables people also to answer why-questions, which experience cannot do. Scientific and technological progress, but also environmental mismanagement, grew at an exponential rate. But we look with respect and even admiration at some of the achievements of our ancestors. They used artificial pollination 2000 years ago and were familiar with the cycles of nature.

THE UNITS

The written materials are usually published in Hebrew and Arabic. Some units were partially or fully translated into English, but not published. All units are based on students' texts and teachers' guides. Where additional materials have been developed, these are mentioned in parentheses:

For Grade 6

Seeds Germinate; Be Host to Plants in Your Home; The Flowering Corner (also work-cards); "The Voice of the Turtledove is Heard in Our Land".

For Grade 7

Let's Grow Plants (also background materials for teachers, catalogue of materials and equipment, and blueprints for the planning of land laboratories).

For Grades 8–9: Let's Protect Plants

The Fruit Fly and the DDT Problem; Uncalled-for Guests (also a definer for weed seedlings and slides); On Moulds and Mildews and Other Fungi (also Life Cycle of Fungi learning game); catalogue of materials and equipment needed and background materials for teachers, for the whole Let's Protect Plants series.

For Grades 8–9 (other topics)

Fight against Hunger (also work cards, readers, End to Hunger – a simulation game); Let's Keep Bees (also worksheet for approximation of bee brood area and four filmloops); Let's Raise Chicks (also slides and a reader on the development of the human embryo).

The following is a synopsis of some of the units:

The Flowering Corner

The aim of this unit is to develop and foster pupils' awareness of the aesthetic value of plants on the school ground and in the neighbourhood. Students are involved in activities which contribute to the beautification of the school and its surroundings. This is done mainly by developing at least a corner in which plants flower during most of the school year. Students learn to choose a suitable spot, how to prepare the seedbed and the plants. Special attention is given to planning such a corner – first on the school ground and then at home.

Be Host to Plants in Your Home

This unit goes one step further. Pupils learn in an open-ended way how to grow and keep potted plants in their home. Special attention has been given to the illustration of the students' text in order to motivate students. Each of them receives two potted plants to keep at different places in their homes. Students observe the differences in the development of their plants and bring them back to school, once or twice during the school year, to compare them with those of their classmates and to discuss how to improve the results. The emphasis is on the development of a do-it-yourself approach.

The Fruit Fly and the DDT Problem

The pollution of food and the human body by pesticide residues is one of the ecological issues which should worry mankind. It is one of the problems arising from the human interference in nature which cannot be solved by an hysterical cry for an extreme measure – the banning of all insecticides, an action which would result in the death sentence for millions of people, by endangering them with insect-borne diseases and the shortage of food. Rather, an integrated plan of action should be adopted, based on a careful reappraisal of scientific research and technological progress, weighing the pros and cons of each possible action. To be able to do so, citizens need to be trained in the understanding of complex problems which can be solved only when civic action is taken on the basis of comprehending the underlying scientific issues.

The "Fruit Fly and the DDT Problem" unit was built around a case study starting with a major economic problem – the damage caused by the Mediterranean fruit fly. This problem was chosen because this fly is considered one of the most serious pests of citrus and other fruits in many warm climates.

After opening with a dramatic account of what insect pests can do (from the prophet Joel), the "Rise and Fall of DDT" is used as a case study.

Students experimentally explore the effects of DDT on various pests and their predators. In further experiments the potential of biological control is investigated. Students study the use of baits and other alternatives in selective control measures. Another chapter stresses the public controversy aspect of the pesticide problem. Students analyse controversial texts and are asked to differentiate between facts, comments and propaganda, as they are typically mixed in environmental controversies.

Fight against Hunger

The student text starts with a dramatic story of hungry Jasmin living in the shadow of a palace. Then different types of hunger, such as lack of calories and malnutrition due to an unbalanced diet, are discussed.

In the second chapter, the question "Is the danger of hunger imminent?" is asked. Conflicting opinions of different experts are cited and students try to understand the often unconscious motives that influence people when forming opinions.

In Chapter 3 students learn about the vicious circle: Hunger – Weakness – Illness – Ignorance – Apathy – Economic Backwardness – Poverty – Hunger, and are asked: "How can the vicious circle be broken?"

"What can be done to alleviate the problem of hunger?" is the question posed in Chapter 4. Students are referred to various resource materials, where they will find suggestions for unconventional ways to wage the war against hunger. Groups of students are then directed to the project cards and to the readers, which will help them to understand the complexity of each solution proposed, and the difficulties which arise when the ideas, so neat in theory, are actually implemented.

The last two chapters are on plant and animal breeding as one of the most promising ways to increase yields. Plant breeding was the starting point of the "Green Revolution". Basic concepts such as variety and breed, selection and hybridization are explained, and students engage in various field experiments.

The simulation game, "End to Hunger", serves as a culminating activity and summary for the topic "Economic Development and International Cooperation". Each student represents a wealthy or developing country. There are many factors, besides the efforts invested into work, that influence a country's chances to obtain food for an ever-expanding population. Among them are both natural and social elements. Students are led to discover that co-operation and education can benefit all of them and is essential for progress.

IMPLEMENTATION AND EVALUATION

According to the estimates of the Inspectorate on Agricultural and Environmental Studies, AES programmes are used:

1. in 6th grade by 14,500 students (420 schools);
2. in 7th grade by 18,000 students (510 schools);
3. in 8th–9th grade by 5000 students (150 schools).

No data are available on the dissemination of AES materials in secondary schools which use them in their biology courses. Some of the 8–9 grade materials are now also included in the new environmental studies course planned for senior high schools.

When a school decides to teach AES curricula and the teacher has attended the appropriate course, the Inspectorate on Agriculture and Environmental Studies supplies the necessary equipment. Living organisms are grown or collected and then distributed by a national supply centre at Kfar Hayarok Agricultural School. Teachers receive these materials either directly or through regional distribution centres and school farms.

Formative evaluation was based on teacher reports given at monthly meetings of trial teachers, analysis of teachers' written reports, and on students' work which was collected by the trial teachers who had received advice on how to choose the sample. Trial classes were also visited by members of the follow-up team.

Evaluation instruments included diagnostic multiple-choice achievement tests, questionnaires on interests and attitudes, students' preference scales for various activities (over a week and over a year) and teachers' attitudes towards various characteristics of the programme.

Special attention was given to pupils' reactions to drawings in their text and to the evaluation of a learning game.

When the "Let's Grow Plants" programme was adopted by about half the country's schools which offer environmental studies and agriculture, a comprehensive study on the effect of the programme on student achievement, mainly in applying the rules of experimental design to field experiments and on affective learning, was undertaken. When compared to pretests and to suitable control groups, AES students showed very significant improvements in drawing conclusions from experiments and in critically appraising experiment designs. They also found their students engaged in more leisure-time activities involving reading about, observing, experimenting with, and growing plants.

Issue-based Environmental Education in Developing Countries

G. W. KNAMILLER

It is convenient to look at issue-based environmental education in terms of learning modules. At the heart of a module is a field study that actively engages learners in systematically gathering, analysing, evaluating and expressing information for the purpose of identifying local development/ environmental problems and making decisions about relevant social action. This includes an examination of appropriate technological alternatives. Issue-based modules could be organized around such topics as:

malnutrition among under-5s in the community
local fuel resources and consumption patterns
time/energy costs for collecting water
production and marketing in local small-scale industries
controlling food crop pests
storing grain locally
the incidence of schistosomiasis and its relationship to local water
    resources
locally available family planning services
the siting of latrines and wells.

An issue-based curriculum development model might look as shown in Fig. 4. This is an action model for linking subject studies – science, geography, mathematics, social studies, technology – with the everyday experience of learners.

For Example

In September 1983 I had the good fortune to be able to teach for 2 weeks at the Gumbonzvanda rural day secondary school in Wedza District,

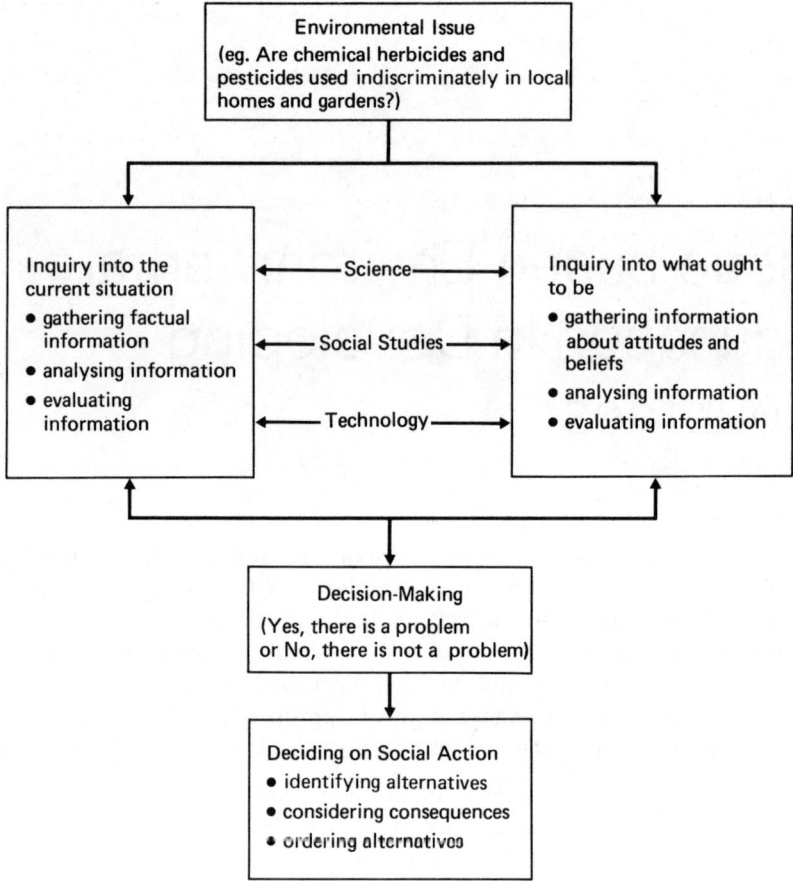

FIG. 4   Issue-based development model.*

Zimbabwe. The rural day secondary schools are community projects, arising after the civil war and independence in 1980. The purpose is to absorb into the school system the young freedom fighters and rural youth who had been denied access to formal post-primary education during the white regime.

In 1979 there were 177 secondary schools in Zimbabwe, enrolling some 66,000 students. Today, as a result of the rural day school programme, there are approximately 800 secondary schools with an enrolment of a quarter of a million. They are built by local communities with some financial help from the government which also provides teachers and materials. They follow the same syllabus, and aim toward the same external examination, as their established, traditional and better-endowed

*From G. W. Knamiller in *The Environmentalist*, 3, 1983.

sister schools. The curriculum is not locally based or immediately relevant to local, rural needs. (The agricultural science classes at Gumbonzvanda, for example, were doing a unit on pigs, which none of the 360 students have at home.)

I had three purposes in mind at Gumbonzvanda. The first was to see if issue-based studies could be natural out-growths of the on-going school syllabus. The second was to examine how well these rural students could gather and process information, particularly quantitative data, and make some sense of it in terms of describing and analysing a local community issue. Thirdly, I wanted to get a feeling for the response of students to doing issue-based learning modules related to local development/environmental problems.

One of the two science teachers, Joseph Maniyka, an 18-year-old secondary school graduate of 6 months (the other science teacher had also just completed secondary school), was just starting a unit on energy transfer with his first-form classes. He kindly, and most openly, let me share in the development and teaching of this unit. We decided to base the work around the theme of cooking food, and started with the energy cycle shown in Fig. 5. After quickly developing this diagram with students, the basic teaching/learning question put to them was – "How can we reduce the amount of energy we need to cook food?"

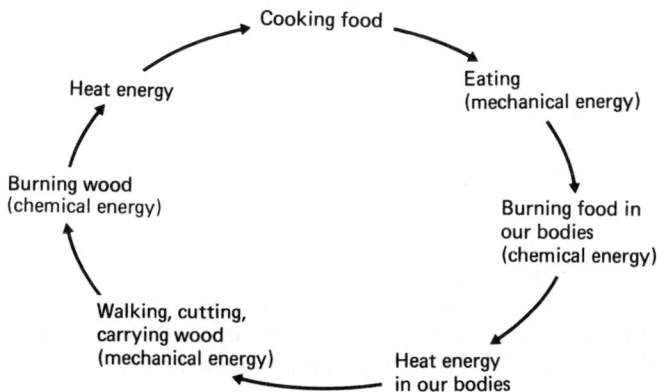

FIG. 5 The cooking food energy cycle.

What evolved over the 2 weeks was a focus on how we could reduce the mechanical energy required to collect firewood (as only two students in the four classes used fuel other than wood), and how to reduce the amount of chemical energy used, by improving the efficiency of the commonly used cook stove, the three-stone "maphifwa". Activities, then, revolved around:

1. producing a questionnaire and systematically gathering and analysing information about firewood types, consumption, collecting costs (distance, time, money) and local cook stove designs; and
2. designing and conducting experiments to see what kind of local woods are best for cooking and how the maphifwa might be made more efficient.

The information students collected from their own families was considered individually, and also combined for the class. The data on consumption and costs were extrapolated for the entire school population per year. Without going into the details of the local units of measure we used and our statistical manipulations, we came up with a figure of around 9000 trees, 3 metres high, consumed by the families of the total school population in 1 year.

This figure was questioned by the students. "Ah," said one, "but that's not enough, because we can use 10–20 'musinga' (bundle of wood) for a funeral (feast)." Another said, "We use trees to build houses and fences, and we did not get this information (in our survey)." When we considered the possibility of family and community wood lots and figured that each student in the school would have to plant around 25 trees per year just to keep pace with current demand one girl said, "But that's not so, some of these 'seedlings' will die." These and other similar comments left little doubt in our minds that these youths had a great deal of knowledge and feeling about their local firewood situation.

For the experiments, students brought different kinds of firewood from home. One experiment was to see which woods were most efficient for boiling water, using the traditional three-stone maphifwa. The second experiment required more invention. The school compound was littered with mud bricks used for constructing classrooms, and these were used to build various cook stoves. Attempts were made to design stoves (first through drawings and then the bricks) that would most efficiently boil water and also keep water at a certain temperature over a period of time. New "models" were compared with the traditional three-stone stove.

We could profitably have used more time on these experiments. Nevertheless, the students did seem to learn something about experimental methods, although these experiments were not as neatly packaged as typical experiments done in formal school laboratories, which at Gumbonzvanda did not exist anyway. Amazingly, most teams got clear, observable and positive results.

Maniyka and I felt that this experience into relevant science/environmental/technology education did help to raise the consciousness level of many of the students, not only to the local firewood situation, but more importantly to the idea that learning in school can be related to work at home and in the community.

CONCLUSION

In environmental education, as in all subject areas, we must keep asking ourselves the question that Gandhi was asking early in this century, a question which remains with us in the 1980s and will continue to occupy us in the 21st century: How is the current school curriculum in developing countries going to benefit those ever-increasing numbers of youths who will not achieve a school diploma (or its equivalent job-securing certification), who will not enter the formal economic sector, who will drift to the cities and, not finding a job, will either stay in the slums, searching, or return to the rural areas?

Issue-based studies in environmental education is one small attempt to address this question. It rests in the beliefs that rural youths' experience and knowledge of their environment is fertile ground upon which to base knowledge and skills; that a child's schooling should include field studies related to development/environmental issues experienced in their own lives; and that environmental education should be more technologically orientated than it is at present. The amount of knowledge content covered in schools is not nearly as important as students learning and practising the information-processing and decision-making skills. And even this has limited value if youths are not given opportunities to work with various technologies and technological methods in an attempt to do something productively about local problems. Implied in the environment and technology education link is the whole area of "appropriate technology". Perhaps standard environmental education equipment should be "appropriate" water pumps, latrines, cook stoves, biogas units, grain storage bins and so on, the type of equipment supplied by the Blair Research Laboratory in Zimbabwe and the Appropriate Technology Development Association here in India.

Teaching through the Environment in Elementary Schools in India

V. G. JADHAO, S. RAJPUT, S. MUKHOPADHYAY, A. B. SAXENA
and J. S. RAJPUT

In India attempts to relate the elementary curriculum to the environment have focused on teaching *through* the environment. The rationale for this approach is that the child's own environment should be the starting point for all teaching–learning processes. Also, using locally available resources reduces the financial demand for more expensive learning materials. At present precious financial resources are being used to achieve universal elementary education: to a degree the concern for qualitative improvement is secondary. Another possible advantage of teaching through the environment is that it decreases the drop-out rate of school-going children because it is interesting. Also it aims at developing a future generation more conscious of its environment in all its holistic aspects.

MATERIAL DEVELOPMENT

Several curricula have been prepared in India making use of the concept of "teaching through the environment". "Paryavarin Upagam", Environmental Approach, which offers detailed instructional material for teaching science and social studies for classes III to V, is one example. Many state education departments and other agencies have also developed similar teaching material based on their local environments. The State Institutes of Education of Madhya Pradesh, Jammu and Kashmir, Uttar Pradesh and many other states have conducted workshops for teachers and prepared such instructional material. Apart from these, the Educational Planning Group in New Delhi, Kishore Bharati and Hoshangabad have also been active in the propagation of this philosophy. Suggestions related to teaching through the environment can be found in the journals *Pathways,*

163

Primary Teacher, Education Quarterly, Shivira and the *Journal of Indian Education*.

RELATED RESEARCH

Several attempts have been made to test the efficacy of the "teaching through the environment" approach. Rao and Singh have prepared a test for the age group 14–16 which measures awareness and attitudes toward the environment. Deopuria has developed tests for finding out the attitudes of teachers and students towards environment and environmental education. Saxena and others have developed tests for measuring environmental awareness of children in classes III and IV. The results of all these investigations can be related to programmes where the approach is being applied.

Another dimension of research is to develop teaching–learning materials and methods, and to test them with respect to traditional classroom teaching. Jadhao and others found in a majority of schools that children in the new programme achieved higher scores on environmental awareness tests than those in "traditional" control groups. The extension of this study in terms of inclusion in the social studies curriculum, identification of teaching skills suitable for teaching through the environment and its implications for teacher training programmes is being carried out at the Regional College of Education (NCERT), Bhopal.

LIMITATIONS

A major limitation to getting the teaching through the environment approach operational in schools is the lack of an incentive system. Schools and teachers are not rewarded for being innovative. Also the centralized system of examination makes it difficult to selectively assess children in such a programme, which necessarily emphasizes local studies. Another constraint is that although elementary teachers have responsibility for the whole curriculum, instruction is subject-based. Many environmental problems that schools could tackle require an integrated, interdisciplinary approach. Teachers are not used to working in this way.

Perhaps all knowledge and skills required of children in elementary schools cannot and should not be taught through the environment. The point is not to stick to the environment at any cost, but to make the best and maximum use of the environment in order to make education meaningful to the learner. Efforts made by researchers in the area of environmental education often remain as theoretical exercises. The present need is to develop ways for getting positive results into practice in elementary schools. Materials and methods for teaching through the environment do exist. What must now be given serious consideration are innovative ways to deliver them.

[Editors' note: In its original version this paper gave references to much relevant research in India.]

Agriculture for Self-reliance

VINCENT MAPESI GONDWE

INTRODUCTION

This case study is based on personal attempts at developing a new approach to teaching and learning agriculture. A strategy is used which is relevant to a semi-subsistence economy and can be easily and cheaply implemented within the existing education system. It is set in Malawi, and if it is to be understood fully, an outline of the environment in which it originated becomes relevant.

Malawi is a small country, covering about 118,484 sq km, and lies along Lake Malawi (820 km long). High plateau and mountains line the Rift Valley which runs the length of the country. Although the lake and these highlands reduce arable land to approximately 68% of the total area, Malawi has great agricultural potential. The arable land is very fertile, and the climate, with rains falling from the end of October to early May, is suitable for the production of many tropical crops, most of which are grown during the rainy season.

Most of the 5.8 million people, over 85%, live by farming. Most of this farming is at a semi-subsistence level, and the policy of the Malawi government is to give priority to the development of small-holder farming. The policy has been so successful that small-holder farming in Malawi is considered among the best in Africa, accounting for 65% of agricultural exports.

The population currently grows at 3%, making children of school-going age a high proportion of the total population. All children above the age of 4 years can go to primary school, if their families can afford it. However, pupils have to compete for places on a 4-year secondary school course, and only 14% of the total number of primary school leavers get selected each year. To meet the aspirations of those denied places in secondary school, the Malawi Correspondence College with associated night schools has been established.

At the Correspondence College and at secondary schools the course is divided into junior and senior levels, each lasting two years. At the end of the junior course, examinations are given. Using the results, some are selected, including students from the College, to go on to the senior course in secondary schools. Those not selected can do the senior course at the College. A few go to teacher training colleges or for technical and vocational instruction. But many more go to urban areas without employment. At the end of the fourth year, candidates take the Malawi Certificate of Education examinations which are equivalent to G.C.E. ordinary level examinations. Less than 3% of these candidates, selected from the highest passers, enter the University of Malawi. Like junior certificate leavers, some compete for places in teacher training colleges and technical or vocational schools. Others prepare to retake the examinations. Those who fail, and the "unfortunate passers" as they are called, roam about in urban areas, hoping to get jobs.

At all levels of education sets of subjects are offered. In secondary schools, over ten subjects are offered, and agriculture is one of them. It was introduced into the school curriculum with the following aims:

1. To create an awareness of Malawi's dependence on agriculture.
2. To develop pupils' active interest in making the best use of the agricultural potential of the rural environment.
3. To teach and demonstrate basic agricultural principles and techniques through practical participation, and to show that good agricultural practices are profitable.
4. To show, through experiments, that agriculture is a changing science.

To achieve these aims, the agriculture syllabus covers the following:

(a) Detailed description and explanation of the Malawian climate, soils, water, population and the infra-structure as they influence crop and livestock production.
(b) Description, analysis and explanation of crop and animal growth.
(c) Management of crops and livestock.
(d) Some farm engineering, farm management and economic principles.

The Examination at the end of a 4-year course is set as follows:

1. Two papers on theory with a total loading of 140 marks (70% of total marks).
2. A practical paper with a loading of 25 marks (12½%).
3. A report on an agricultural project that a candidate did with a loading of 20 marks (10%).
4. Teacher's assessment of pupils' work in the field with a loading of 15 marks (7½%).

DEVELOPMENT OF MY IDEAS

Wanting to help increase the standard of living in rural areas, I took a degree in agriculture, and joined the Extension Services of the Ministry of Agriculture. My job was to advise farmers on modern methods of farming. Progress was slow, very slow, and I wondered whether I was as useful as I wanted to be. When I read the aims of the agriculture course in secondary schools, I began to believe that I could achieve more by teaching agriculture, and I became a teacher.

To my great surprise, few pupils wanted to take agriculture, and nearly all of them considered farming to be a lowly occupation which was good only for uneducated people. They hoped to get "decent" jobs in towns. I resolved to change this attitude, and I thought I could best do this by making everyone see agriculture as an easy subject to pass. I carefully studied past papers together with the syllabus, and discovered that there were specific areas of the syllabus which always appeared on the two theory papers. I called these the A, B and C of agriculture. They carried a total of about 90 marks out of the 140 marks possible on the theory paper. I then developed a teaching method that I was sure would help my pupils master A, B and C thoroughly. The method was simple: I made notes in point form in the simplest possible English, and then gave my students "guides" to study together with revision questions. Using these, my pupils never got lost when studying agriculture; they knew where to begin and what to do. They were always ahead of my teaching plan which made my teaching easier and more effective, allowing me to concentrate on "difficult" topics such as some principles of economics. The guides and revision questions also provoked discussions in class, and well discussed topics are not easily forgotten.

The method just outlined worked. My first candidates taking the Malawi Certificate of Education did very well, but it was the candidates of the following year that really "murdered" the examination. Out of 60 taking agriculture, 26 got distinctions of 1 and 2 grades and the rest got credits of 3 and 4, while the highest grade at a school that came close to us was a 4 grade. As desired, agriculture became *the* subject of the school, and the reputation that I was a "good" teacher spread far and wide.

With most pupils attracted to agriculture, my main concern became the relevance of the agriculture syllabus to life after school. I sincerely believed that whether one intended to become an engineer, a lawyer, a doctor or a pastor, there was something in agriculture that one would find useful throughout life. The syllabus ignored this fact. Also, by putting emphasis on the theoretical examination, the syllabus was ignoring school leavers who could neither go to college nor find jobs. Why impose a mainly academic posture in agriculture on a majority who would depend on growing their own food for survival? What was required, I thought, was a lot of practical teaching and a practical examination. Quite simply, the syllabus needed to be changed.

Knowing I would not succeed verbally in persuading the Syllabus Committee to change it, I thought that the best approach would be for me to influence other schools. Eventually the Committee itself, through observing good examples, might positively reconsider its traditional syllabus. All I needed was to find time for practical work, and ways of making pupils like this work. It then dawned on me that if I could expand my notes, guides and revision questions to cover the whole syllabus, I would not need to spend much time in the classroom. After all, most topics could best be taught through practical work, and notes, guides and revision questions would only help to organize the pupils' experience for the examination. Calculating the amount of work that needed explanation and discussion in the classroom, I found that I could comfortably spend 90% of the time allocated to agriculture in the field.

EDUCATION FOR LIFE

I made four specific objectives that our practical work had to achieve:

1. To develop a strong desire and determination in pupils, especially those who would not go to college, to become farmers.
2. To develop appreciation for the importance of nutrition and hygiene to health, and to show how lowly paid workers, who cannot afford sources of protein and vitamins, could easily and cheaply provide these in their free time.
3. To develop appreciation for the importance of the natural environment. With such an understanding and appreciation, ways and means of protecting and managing plant and animal species and their habitats can easily be found.
4. To make education for life more meaningful by developing the pupils' power of observation, enabling them not only to answer questions but also to formulate questions of their own.

Leaving aside the obvious need for highly educated farmers, one cannot help asking why at our level of development, with so much land which in most cases can be acquired free, lowly paid workers cannot raise five or six chickens or rabbits and grow a few vegetables to feed their large families? Just as surprising, the big, modern houses when occupied by Europeans had green lawns, flowers were blooming thoughout the year and shrubs were well-trimmed; but now, in our hands, lawns and flowers are gone, shrubs have grown formless and new yards have been left to God to beautify. Even more puzzling, in many villages where agriculture is taught in primary schools, devastating bushfires are still a common feature, pasture areas are still being overgrazed and steep hillsides are still being cultivated. Surely I could help to change all this.

My first method was to use a "hidden curriculum" – to influence through personal example without actually telling pupils to look at what I was doing. My house, like many big modern houses in Malawi, had a big yard, and it was very close to the school. In the backyard I grew all sorts of vegetables such as peas, carrots, tomatoes, beans, onions, rape and cucumbers. In front of the house I established a lawn and planted flowers. Every morning and every late afternoon – that is before and after school – I spent some time gardening, and pupils were seeing this. Close to my garden I raised rabbits, chickens and pigeons, just enough to feed my family and to give away as gifts. My wife made rations – livestock feed – from ground grains, beans and groundnuts. We both enjoyed looking after our livestock, and pupils were seeing all this.

Seeing a graduate freely applying "dirty" manure, working hard on vegetable beds and cleaning livestock houses, what pupil would think that manual work was degrading and fit only for the uneducated people? With flower and vegetable beds, the shrubs and the lawn forming a beautiful pattern, with rabbits of different colours jumping up and down in their paddocks, with pigeons fluttering from their house to the garden and then to the lawn, what pupil did not know that I had meat, eggs and vegetables whenever I wanted them? Who could not learn that gardening was a profitable form of physical exercise?

In my school, however, as in most schools, practical work was not taken seriously. Plots were not planned, maize and beans were the only crops grown, poorly for that matter, and livestock was not kept because "there would be no one to look after them during the school holidays". Whether it was weeding, applying fertilizer or harvesting, the class did the work as a group, with the teacher all the time present and shouting at the top of his voice. I had to change all this. Believing individual pupil involvement would be more effective than working as a class, I had to expand the school farm so that it could accommodate everyone, and also so that activities could be diversified. Fortunately when I explained my ideas to the headmaster he liked them, and he gave us three hectares of school land and bought us 64 hoes and other required tools.

Our land had fertile loamy soils with a gentle slope and a permanent stream passing through it. We opened 2.75 hectares for 8 classes of 40 pupils each. The only time we worked in groups was when we were marking out the area. Thereafter each pupil was given, and had to manage alone, a small section in each plot.

When choosing crops to grow and livestock to raise, we considered not only the environmental factors of the school but also their relevance to the lives of the pupils after school. Therefore, food crops that can be grown easily and cheaply in the villages or backyards were chosen. These were maize, groundnuts, beans, cassava and sweet potatoes as the main crops, and we settled for guava, oranges, bananas and paw-paw for fruits. We also grew 16 different kinds of vegetables and four types of trees. In all each pupil each year had to manage 69 sq m of main crops, 20 sq m of vegetables and a few trees or fruits.

Due to shortage of time, one pupil could not grow all the crops in one growing season. Groundnuts and sweet potatoes were grown by Forms I and III, beans and cassava by Forms II and IV, while maize, because it is our staple food, was grown by all classes. Vegetables were grown twice a year and in each growing season each pupil had to grow two different types of vegetables. Forms I and II grew trees, and each pupil planted two trees every January, and managed those that were planted earlier. Four-year-old trees were handed over to the headmaster to be cared for by school employees. Forms III and IV grew fruits and the management procedure was the same as for trees.

Pupils managed their crops during some of the agriculture class periods and whenever they found time. My presence in most cases was not necessary. I demonstrated each aspect of management in my sections and encouraged pupils to find more information from pamphlets published by the Extension Services of the Ministry of Agriculture. Pupils became so attached to their sections that they spent most of their free time on the farm.

Livestock was managed a little differently. The work we did in groups was assembling materials, building the houses, making food troughs and laying-boxes, but actual management was done by individuals. Forms I and III managed rabbits and pigeons, while Forms II and IV managed chickens and pigeons. Each pupil looked after the livestock for a day – that is, once in 40 days. During school holidays, school employees looked after them.

Apart from carrying on agricultural practices, each pupil kept field and financial records for his section. These were necessary for field management and, more especially, for calculating profits, for the headmaster gave a "loan" to each class in the form of inputs (seeds, fertilizers, insecticides, etc.). Working as a cooperative, the class shared the inputs, and each pupil was responsible for repaying his own share of the loan plus interest, which was set at 4%. After selling the produce (to teachers, the school or at the local market) the profits were spent on inputs such as improved seeds which each pupil took home for demonstration to farmers in his community.

To develop pupils' curiosity and power of observation, they were encouraged to note any disease, pest or other abnormalities seen in their sections. As guidelines, they would answer questions such as: Which part of the plant was attacked? What did the affected part look like? If it was a pest, what did it look like (drawing it if possible)? How old was the plant when the attack was first observed? How many plants were attacked? And so on! Reports on new observations were pinned on the school noticeboard under "Agricultural Discoveries of the Week". Very good reports were published in the school magazine.

Another important aspect of our practical agriculture was the projects the pupils had to do as part of their agriculture examination. Both junior and senior examinations allocated 10% of the total marks to a report on an agriculture project. Since we were doing quite a lot on crops and livestock, I encouraged my pupils to do their projects on conservation. Believing these projects could have some impact on the pupils' communities, I asked them to do their projects in their home areas during school holidays. I did not put any restrictions on the nature of the project to be undertaken, but I gave a few topics to serve as examples: reducing bush fires in my home area; attempts to set communal grazing areas as a way of reducing overgrazing in my home area; attempts at rational land use in my home area; making nature trails in my home area. (Additional information is given for each example, mainly in relation to monitoring relevant aspects.)

The syllabus requires that the projects be marked by subject teachers and moderated by a team of assessors chosen by the Syllabus Committee. I mark my pupils' projects as follows:

(a) Evidence of originality shown by reasons given for choosing the project, maps showing the physical features and the vegetation of the area where the project was done and the design of the project (10 marks).
(b) Presentation (logical sequence, correct grammar, etc.) (5 marks).
(c) Evaluation of the project (5 marks).

Although outside the syllabus, I included landscaping in our practical work. The headmaster gave me a free hand in landscaping the school grounds, and I used the "house system" in designing and implementing the programme. In Malawian secondary schools, unlike those in most developed countries, pupils stay in self-help boarding hostels. At our school two hostels, each with a capacity of 30 pupils, formed a house. Each house had equal number of pupils from each year. All "out-of-school" activities were organized in such a way that each house would do a given set of activities on a particular day. Thus, each house had a general work day during the week, and landscaping was the main part of this general work activity. Each house landscaped and maintained its yard and its section in the school grounds. I was available for advice, but I left it to house leaders to decide what to plant and where to plant it. Every week a different team of two teachers inspected the grounds, awarding marks from 10 down according to their impression. At the end of the term the "most beautiful" house of the term was given a garden party. The money for the party came from the interest pupils paid on their agricultural loan.

Taking profits home, publicity and parties were not the only incentives.

Best sections, and pupils who made the best suggestions on landscaping, won prizes, usually consumable items such as biscuits, soap, hardware, etc. I also found "field day" good reinforcement. Every second week of March (when the crops and the flowers are at their best) we invite guardians of the pupils, interested individuals and organizations, "good" farmers in the neighbouring villages and agricultural extension staff to come and see what we are doing. It is the most exciting moment of our practical work. Guests ask questions, praise us, take pictures, are given gifts from our farm, and at the end of the day we all have refreshments and are entertained by a comedy about a bad farmer.

EVALUATION

Although it is difficult to evaluate the success of my programme in concrete terms, it is evident that pupils enjoy their practical work. This is shown not only by the number of pupils taking agriculture but also by the enthusiasm they show in managing their crops and livestock, the observations they are making and the questions they are asking. I believe that learning which is enjoyable has a great impact on people's lives. That pupils do learn more is seen in the much improved examination results.

What is even more pleasing is that many of my ex-pupils, well-off or lowly paid, beautify their yards, grow vegetables and raise chickens. I have been flattered by the amount of correspondence I get from my ex-pupils inviting me to go and see what they have done around their houses. I have visited a few of them, and I have been impressed. From the many letters I get I have also learned that some of my ex-pupils have become successful farmers. How much impact these former pupils have on their local communities is difficult to evaluate, but considering the status that educated people, including secondary school leavers, are afforded in this country, their influence may be beyond our expectations.

Whether my programme can be introduced in other schools is another question. But one thing is certain: funds cannot be the limiting factor. The programme costs almost nothing. Instead, pupils can use loans to maximize their profits, learning good business procedure in the process. Some teachers can point to poor-quality land at their schools, but any resourceful, enthusiastic teacher can adjust the programme to the factors, resources and conditions of his school. Perhaps the real problem would be to find resourceful teachers.

I have seen the need for practical teaching earlier than most teachers, but as our population increases faster than our food production, and as more and more school leavers enter our pool of unemployed, more and more agriculture teachers will see that our hope lies *not* in advising old illiterate farmers (as the Ministry of Agriculture does) but in "cultivating" farmers from primary and secondary schools.

Teaching History and Environmental Protection

K. HORVATH

History, as part of environmental education, can teach children a kind of knowledge which is of primary importance for developing an environmental world concept. Dynamic, continuously deepening interactions between society and nature can be demonstrated. We can follow up antecedents of environmental problems and also their evolution. Concrete examples can proclaim how local problems have developed into regional, then global dangers. We can analyse roots of behaviours resulting in the ecological crisis of our time.

Our present environmental situation is determined by the complexity of previous economic and social development. People's influence on nature, its aim and mode, differs in different socioeconomic systems, depending on technical development and on the standpoint, interests and efforts of different social groups. These can deform the connection between society and nature, and can help or hamper the solution of environmental problems.

NATURE AND SOCIETY FORM AN ORGANIC UNIT

Society evolved from nature. Mankind developed in interaction with environmental evolution and the organization of society with it. A relatively separated system emerged, which was not identical with nature because of having its own rules of change but, at the same time, was not wholly separable.

Material exchange with nature is essential for the existence of society. Every living creature continuously exchanges materials and energy with its surroundings. Living creatures draw materials from nature, form them into their own substance and return their wastes to nature. The self-cleansing capability of natural systems makes them "disappear".

But men carry through a dual metabolism. On the one hand, they perform biological metabolism, while, on the other, they carry out a kind of material exchange during production processes. These two metabolisms are not independent of each other. Metabolism realized by production is only possible by the help of physical-intellectual forces produced by biological metabolism. Production consists of three phases: (1) Expropriation: people take certain things away from nature for given purposes and by given means. (2) Expropriated materials and energy are changed during production and become means of production and means of consumption. As a result, natural material significantly changes and becomes social, i.e. subordinated to social laws. For example, amortization of a machine is not only physical, but also moral. (3) Returning to nature: discharge of wastes, end-products and materials useful or neutral to nature. If people return too much waste nature becomes incapable of self-cleansing. This kind of metabolism as production not only fulfils existing demands but creates new ones, changing into the power for further development. Thus human beings transform nature according to their material needs and purposes.

As a result, people are decreasingly forced to accommodate to nature by changing their own metabolism. Unlike other living creatures, human beings do not change themselves but more and more consciously make tools and equipment. They become capable of creating their own living conditions anywhere in the world. That is how human beings became the dominant species of the biosphere.

People, therefore, do not now live under circumstances of virgin nature but in surroundings chosen by themselves. These bear the marks of activities of generations living under different socioeconomic systems.

Transformation of nature has become more and more significant during historical development. Humanized nature and society are the reflected images of each other, and each reflects the other's level of development. People's relation to nature also reflects their social relations. Finally, it is the development level of social relations which determines the relation to nature.

The lives of our predecessors took place in surroundings significantly different from ours, and they had more direct contact with nature. Understanding their everyday life is only possible by appreciating this.

Edward Brown made a journey to the Balkan Peninsula and Hungary. In his travel diary, published in London in 1674, he enumerated the different kinds of fish living in the Danube: trout, carp, perch, sterlet, salmon, mudfish, catfish, sturgeon. Miklós Oláh, Archbishop of Esztergom, reported catching sturgeon in his work *Hungaria*:

> Sturgeon migrate from the sea upriver late in the autumn and at the end of the winter. They find a hiding place on the bottom of the river. When the Danube is full of drift ice the fishers of Komárom enclose the river bed with posts but they leave a gap in the middle of it. In this

gap they drop a strong fishing net. From the bank they begin to cannon the water, upon which the sluggish animals get frightened and leave their hiding place. Sometimes one thousand sturgeons are caught this way. The sturgeon is 12 feet in length and sometimes one can be caught as big as a ton.

Upon analysing sources we realize how extraordinarily rich medieval Hungary was in fish, which can be understood only by considering the contemporary conditions of river regulation in the Carpathian basin. We get an idea of the importance of fishing, and this can be supported with other facts. In Hungary in the 11th–13th centuries 21 villages had names connected with fishing. We can come to know the contemporary methods of fishing. Sturgeon, which supplied 60 per cent of medieval fish consumption in this country became very rare in the 20th century. The last one was caught in March 1957. It was 280 cm in length and its weight was 134 kg.

Transformation of nature makes the development of an anthropogenic ecological crisis possible. While transforming nature, people themselves create conditions unbalancing nature and threatening their own basis of existence. Harmful effects of human activities could already be noticed in prehistoric times. Consequences of forest fires, for example, could worsen the living conditions of prehistoric people and result in local ecological crises. However, there were few people and a lot of space. Primitive people simply moved to another place after the development of a local ecological crisis.

According to many scientists the first regional anthropogenic ecological crisis took place during upper palaeolithic times following the death of big game. This crisis could have been the cause of the decay of upper palaeolithic culture. It is also probable that the population was decreasing significantly.

The problem was solved by primitive society itself as people changed over to farming and animal husbandry.

Environmental damage played an important role in slowing down technical development in Western Europe in the 14th century. Although it had very little importance compared to our problems nowadays, its effect could not be avoided at that technical–social level. The forests suffered large losses not only through building activity and agriculture, but through metallurgy as well. Four tons of ore had to be smelted to produce one ton of iron. This process needed 100 m^3 of wood. Coal was used not only for industrial purposes but for heating houses. London was the first town where inhabitants were protected against air pollution, between 1257 and 1288. A royal order in 1307 banned its use, because "unbearable smell has spread on the whole area to the highest discontent of dignitaries, citizens and other inhabitants".

Supply of growing cities could not be organized as well at the contemporary technical level. The 200,000 inhabitants of Paris ate up 188,500 sheep, 30,100 cattle, 19,600 calves, and 30,700 pigs in one single year (1293). The waste was thrown into the Seine. The slop water of tanners and dyers flowed there as well. The drainage system was not built everywhere, so litter and dirt flowed in the streets. In such circumstances cities were the hotbed of epidemics. From the beginning of the 14th century several epidemics of plague swept over Europe. The number of inhabitants decreased from 73 million in 1300 to 45 million in 1400.

We can read about the more and more frequently developing smog in Dickens's work *Bleak House*:

> London . . . Implacable November weather . . . Fog everywhere. Fog up the river . . . fog down the river, where it rolls defiled among the ties of shipping and the waterside pollutions of a great and dirty city.

Air pollution did not affect everybody in the same way. It did the most harm to those who had no power or influence to do anything against it. Those who usually made decisions were well protected.

While teaching history, we can explore the social roots and reasons of more and more striking environmental problems.

Industrial revolution and internationalization of technology facilitate two things. The first is that huge amounts of materials can be taken away from nature, which exceeds its regenerative capacity; the second is that wastes of such a quality and in such a quantity are given back to nature that natural processes cannot process them. These have both been facilitated by social circumstances. The aim of production is to gain profit, the most earnings on the least possible effort. Extravagant exploitation was the result of making profit the primary aim. Production has costs which are not covered by the manufacturer. These are called externalities, external costs. Free-competition capitalism endeavours to make most of the costs external and gain extra profit this way.

In this interpretation prime cost means production costs in the narrowest sense, the kind of costs which must be paid by the capitalist. Natural processes work free of charge; they make the harmful side-effects of industrial activities disappear without asking for wages.

Technology concentrates on raw materials, production, products and markets, and assumes plenitude both on the side of stocks and on the side of the waste-reception. It simply is not worth working hard on recycling waste.

Production is anarchical in character. There is a lack of scientific foresight. But, at the time of its development, a characteristic feature of morals was egoism. No attention was paid to long-term, common interests, but only to short-term, individual ones. Costs of preventing natural, environmental damages become production costs these days, enforced by imposing fines.

After the Second World War, mass consumption was increased by different means in developed capitalist countries. Mostly unnecessary needs were raised, partly by decreasing the lifetime of consumer goods and partly by means of advertising and mass communication. Individuals have to keep pace with changes in fashion and are frequently forced into status consumption. This kind of society, the so-called consumer society, wastes materials and energy, and, at the same time, pollutes natural systems by its immense waste. People are increasingly surrounded by objects, and they decreasingly feel or need nature.

Optimal relationships between human beings and nature can be revealed by analysing sensitivity to nature of different historical eras.

In ancient religions, every single natural phenomenon had its own god or goddess. The Romans personified even dirty water. Its goddess Dea Cloacina was figured even on coins in the times of Emperor Claudius. They identified the inexhaustible springs, the life-giving water, the aqueducts with the person of the god of rivers, or nymphs, and respected them very much. The area around the starting point of the water pipe was regarded as a holy grove. A well was built over every spring which was used as a chapel. On the festival of Floralia, after an offering at the forum, they went on a pilgrimage there and made a sacrifice to the gods personifying the waters which nourish the town.

Christianity deprived nature of its god-character and put an abstract god above nature and people. God created the world for the benefit of people. No things can have other purpose than to serve mankind. Christianity is the most anthropocentric religion, declaring that exploitation of nature is done by people for God's will.

In the philosophy of Augustine, nature, in itself, is guilty and damned and it is the glory of God which is realized in the power of man over nature. According to Lynn White, this is the explanation of the fact that European scientific thinking has always started from the necessity of conquering nature. European thinking can still be characterized by overstressing technical development and subordinating nature and mankind to this. Ideas of man conquering nature, and the naive belief that natural resources are inexhaustible and their use limited only by the profitability of commodity production, were still very popular in the 1950s.

People of our era can find positive examples of historical laws, aimed at defending natural resources and protecting nature. Ancient people endeavoured to make their surroundings healthier and more aesthetic. Julius Caesar, for example, prohibited coach traffic from dawn to sunset in order not to disturb pedestrian traffic. But, at the same time, rubbish carts could carry rubbish out of the towns even during the day. Streets and squares were not allowed to be barricaded by construction materials. House-owners were obliged to clean and repair the part of the street belonging to their house.

The first water pipe was built in Rome in the 4th century BC. Previously the inhabitants drank the water of the Tiber or other springs and wells. The demand grew parallel with the development of the town. In 33 BC an authority for water was set up, which became the best organized office at that time.

The drainage system was built up in Rome as well. Public lavatories were set up in the streets and squares. They were connected to the sewers which opened into the Tiber. The pavement before shops had to be watered every 2 or 3 hours. These strict measures served to prevent epidemics. The regulations of public sanitation often could not be carried out adequately, however, because of the lack of drainage.

Drainage, water systems and baths were built in the towns of the provinces too. The improvement of hygienic conditions contributed to growing life expectancy. For example, in Pannonia the average age rose from 27–30 to 38–42 in two centuries after the Roman conquest.

The consequences of inappropriate human interventions can teach people that intervening in the natural order must only be done cautiously, and by taking natural laws into account. The fates of cultures not capable of realizing the ecological consequences of their activities, can be warning examples.

Romans used a lot of wood for the construction of ships, towns and fortresses, for heating and for the production of potassium carbonate. Woods of the Apeninnes, Dinari Hills and Macedonia were destroyed at that time, devastating soil as well, and the territory became karstic. People still cannot restore these areas.

The Sahara turning into desert is a continuing process as well. Pictographs found in the South of Libya and the Tassili Mountains give evidence that today's deserts used to be savannah with a rich fauna of elephants, giraffes, ostriches and lions. Pictures of hippopotami and crocodiles show that these areas were rich in fresh water too. The age of these finds is estimated at 15,000–7000 years. The Tassili pictographs show grazing herds, relics of the shepherding age between 5000 and 2500 BC.

Desertification speeded up in the 7th century after cessation of Byzantine rule, and has not yet stopped.

Environmental pollution threatens our artistic values too. We can mention the accelerating damage to our cultural relics while showing them to our students. Acids in the polluted air blacken and eat away the marble and limestone of sculptures and old buildings.

We can analyse harmful effects of wars and the arms race when looking at the present period. Different from previous wars, modern wars not only harm the biosphere directly but also by their direct and indirect chemical and physical effects. Biological consequences of ionizing radiation are the most harmful and dangerous. Isotopes with long half-lives, developing during the explosion of atomic bombs, get into the atmosphere, then, after rain, into soil and water and, finally, into human beings through plants and animals.

Material and energy needs of the arms race cause ruthless exploitation, while at the same time drawing means and scientific capacity away from important tasks, e.g. from nature protection.

In our era we can consider the barriers to, and the chances of, unified action of humanity.

Spreading harmful materials on the earth is not limited either by geographical or by political borders. Their effects can be demonstrated far from the industrial areas. Their accumulated, long-term consequences threaten our whole globe. That is why the problem can be solved only by a global concentration of forces.

Short-range national aims must be harmonized with long-range global aims. A common policy and co-ordinated actions are necessary. Several levels of international co-operation have been developed, ranging from elementary co-operation between neighbouring countries through regional organizations to global co-operation through the specialized organizations of the United Nations. The co-operating partners, however, fix only the aims; putting them into practice remains the job of sovereign states. Their different modes of production, levels of technical development, special features of management systems and differences in level of infrastructure determine special conditions of environmental protection.

This short overview demonstrates that history, in its own way, can contribute to the development of environmental culture. Human beings have reached the level of consciousness which enables them to foresee the dangers threatening their future and to make efforts against them. History can contribute to these efforts by revealing the tendencies which prevent or help solutions, and by demonstrating the warnings of the distant and of the recent past.

In the course of its development, humanity got into other difficult situations and solutions were always found. These can also be drawn from history.

The Laws of Aesthetics are the Laws of Nature (Goethe)

ENIKO BADACSONYI

Though a study-cycle dealing with protection of the environment has been working in our school for only 2 years, we evolved the idea of environmental protection in our education a long time ago. Although our school specializes in music, we consider that children gain through learning different subjects and that developing the emotional basis of their responsibility for the environment is very important. Children cannot protect something they do not know, so we have to acquaint them with nature, and the emotional motivation for learning is very important, especially in childhood.

György Lukacs, the Hungarian philosopher, said that one can have personal experience of nature only if one gets into intimate contact with part of it, appreciating and comprehending its many aspects. Music and drawing lessons help to develop this emotional basis. The music which is part of the everyday life of the children influences the atmosphere of their environment. Each day begins with singing to dispel the sleepiness and chill of the morning. The motto of our school is a quotation from Kodály: "Singing beautifies our life, the singer beautifies the life of others." The music teaching is based on Hungarian folk music according to Kodály's method. Folk songs are the colourful mosaic picture of the complex, immemorial relation between Man and his Environment. These mosaics form the great *whole*.

Whenever children begin to learn a new song, the teacher discusses the text of it with the children. While they are talking about the meaning of the song, they enter into the spirit of it.

We find metaphors and images which use the pictures of nature in every folksong:

> Spring winds flood rivers,
> My darling, my darling.
> The birds choose their partners,
> My darling, my darling.

This Hungarian folk song expresses the wisdom of country folk. It describes the "natural history" of spring and also expresses personal feelings: "Who should I choose then?" Thus, through singing, I become a part of nature, I watch it and belong to it.

The following folksong is imbued with emotion:

> My flowers, my flowers
> Bend down with sorrow for me.
> My beautiful flowers
> Mourn for me, grieve for me.

Nature shares her joy and sorrow with Man!

Water is the life-giving substance in other songs, just as it is in one of the choral works of Kodály:

> Rain, rain, . . .
> We ask the rain to sweep through the grass, the trees and the bushes
> We ask water the symbol of life to keep plants alive.

A good example of this is in the symphonic poem of Smetana, the "Moldavia". In this, a small stream, flowing in a zig-zag path, joins many other brooks until it becomes a wide river, which on reaching the sea flows into the wide ocean.

The song of Schubert, "The Brook", is a picturesque description. We seem to see every tiny pebble through the translucent water, the muddy bends, the fast-moving current; we seem to hear the water and feel that this must be a crystal-clear mountain stream with its delightful touching music. Talking about this with children, questions surely occur: are our rivers and lakes as clear and beautiful today as was the brook in Schubert's song? If not, why not? The wish arises then to do something to make them clear again. Thus clear springs, green forests and singing birds become a part of our life. As the Hungarian writer, Aron Tamasi, said: "We are in the world to feel at home in it."

Children who have to spend their days in housing estates between high-rise buildings hear many kinds of noises, most of which are disturbing. The screech of brakes, the rumble of vehicles, the general clamour upsets hearing, so that willingly or unwillingly they speak louder and louder to out-shout the surrounding noise. The magic of silence disappears from their lives.

The whisper of leaves, the sound of birds are suppressed by loud noises. If then a child gets into an environment where loud noises are "natural", he cannot conform to new circumstances and he remains loud and noisy. In reality, children can be susceptible to the noises of nature and to the atmosphere of a new environment; they just have to be taught how to treat those sounds. Through drawing and through music lessons, they can learn how these sounds can be a source of beauty, full of delight.

Even the smallest children in our school know how to treat sounds. They learn that timbre and loudness may express feelings, and that noises may become components of music. Silence also is an element of music in the form of pauses.

They accompany the songs with clapping and knocking, and thus they compose music. Older children often make wonderful music instruments themselves, from nutshells, rubber bands or from the bricks of their younger brothers. These instruments also give noises which may express different atmospheres and feelings; this leads them to the ability to enter consciously into the spirit of the works of composers. The above-mentioned symphony of Smetana, or the songs of Schubert, show how music becomes the voice and harmony of nature through the ingenuity and brilliance of composers with the help of musical instruments! Though musical instruments made of wood or metal give sounds, we still seem to hear the voice of nature: the sounds of a babbling brook, a surging river, the roaring sea; and we let these sounds impress us.

Many people who visit our school envy us for our well-behaved children, who do not romp or run about in corridors, suggesting that we have an easy job on the grounds that we have selected children in our school. I do not believe in selection, but I believe in the educational effect and the magical power of music. Children may feel, perhaps not consciously, that what happens in music happens to them.

Most people do not accept the conditions and the environment in which they are born without reservations. We all try to find the best place to live where we feel well and can find beauty. We have to share the "space" in which we live with other people, so the space is common property. Its aesthetic questions are the questions of general culture. Thus the different branches of education, for example visual education, play an important part in making people realize the beauty of their environment, and this idea is also involved in the educational conception of our school. Visual education is not confined to teaching children how to use the power of sight. The aesthetic questions of forming our environment clearly show that the beauty of the home, the work place, the town and the land in which we live is closely connected to the morality of the society.

Our environment may praise us and justify our actions, but it may also blame us. There are troubles with discipline and morality in a country which has no beautiful gardens or parks, where the architecture and the handicrafts are not aesthetically satisfying. The air turning grey and the plants withering are unsightly not only because of being displeasing to the eye, but also because they reflect on our lives. Consequently, to create a culture and a philosophy of life of high quality must be the first step in beautifying our environment.

Art teaching in elementary schools may also serve this purpose. Our curriculum makes it possible to develop a visual culture which enables children to see things in motion, not only things at rest. They perceive forms to be the result of opposing forces that manifest themselves in the endless formation of surfaces.

It is characteristic of our art teaching to give up methods which substitute geometric structures for living forms. Why lock living and moving things in the "inanimate cage of geometry"?

The relationship between personality and the environment is different from the relationship between two objects. Personality grows into and irradiates the environment. The range of space around a person has a continuous consciousness-transforming role. Man "puts space on"; if he feels it tight he steps out of it; thus the surrounding space sometimes tightens and sometimes widens. This is why people are induced to explore, to fill and sometimes to monopolize their environment. The act of procuring and using the space we need belongs to the basic characteristics of our personality. In this way we can acquire from their buildings precise knowledge of the mentality of town-dwellers who lived in the past ages. Just as the shape of a shell characterizes the snail or the shell-fish which lives in it, buildings describe the people who live in them and who built them.

The purpose of art teaching must be not only to develop manual skills and the understanding of the arts, but to teach children to watch nature with an understanding eye and a feeling heart. We form our environment and its objects in our imagination, which is part of our intention to procure space. Hence our objects are usually anthropomorphic ones; they often strikingly imitate their creator, its shape and movements (just think about the manipulators of robots or about walking elevators) and they always reflect the relation between man and objects. Our machines become more and more clever; our objects (our artificial environment) become more and more practical. It depends on us whether they follow the wonderful laws of the material world and are beautifully shaped or not. The development of our personality in a certain sense means the cognition of the material world, and the objective world is the source of beauty.

Environment involves the inherence of many factors of nature and society – the connection of natural and social happenings, their realization in space and time. To make children recognize, understand and see the connection, the meaning and the purpose of these factors – this is the task of visual education. In our school we hope to bring children to internal human beauty. This would determine their relationship to the environment. They are led in their actions to do what is good and fitting without being constrained by rules and laws, only by an internal constraint to become creative doers, whatever profession they choose.

I hope you will agree that it is possible for school children to appreciate environmental protection with the help of music and art when you hear them singing, or enjoying the music they make, or creating their drawings.

The Resource Management Education Programme

GERALD A. LIEBERMAN

STATEMENT OF NEED

Public and private organizations have been working to develop conservation education programmes in the United States for the past two to three decades. Unfortunately, to date these programmes have not been adapted and disseminated to many of the developing countries where they are so vitally needed. The rapid growth of the populations and economies of these countries and the limited financial resources which are available for natural resource management programmes have worked synergistically to result in the rampant destruction of an irreplaceable base of natural resources.

RARE, Inc., a non-profit conservation organization based in Washington, DC, uses as its operating principle that conservation and wise use of natural resources are an investment in the future. Educating young people so that they understand the role of wise management of natural resources in the future health of the planet is the only means by which we can insure these investments.

After detailed evaluation RARE, in conjunction with several Latin American educators, determined that there was a need to develop an integrated system of basic resource management education. This system should provide the basis for understanding the importance of a country's natural resources, techniques for managing them, and the knowledge and experience necessary for the rational growth of society in conjunction with their prudent management. In addition, this system should provide the technical basis upon which sound management decisions can be made and which allows the possibility for an increased role of citizens in day-to-day as well as long-term planning for the wise use of their resources.

PROGRAMME

Goals and Objectives

The Resource Management Education Programme (RMEP), developed

189

by RARE for use in primary schools, represents a co-ordinated progression from basic awareness of resources – through the development of concepts, skills, values and attitudes – to problem-solving experiences and decision-making abilities. All of the studies are designed to augment the young citizens' abilities to make responsible decisions about their resources. In general terms, the goals of this programme are:

1. to develop an awareness of natural resources;
2. to provide the basic experiences and knowledge to develop the skills needed to identify and understand present and future resource management problems;
3. to tender the opportunities and encouragement which will allow students to become actively involved in the learning process and which will allow them to participate in basic resource management action and enhance their environment;
4. to cultivate a land ethic and resource conscience which will ensure the wise long-term management and use of the natural resources upon which we all depend for survival.

These goals are being reached through the development and dissemination of teacher and student training materials. These materials are designed for use by teachers in conjunction with teaching units in both the physical and life sciences.

To achieve the greatest possible degree of effectiveness, we believe that the participation of local professionals is critical to all stages of programme development. This methodology ensures that all materials developed recognize the socioeconomic and cultural context of the particular countries or regions where the projects are being implemented. Using this approach also allows RARE to have the greatest possible impact by helping to initiate conservation education activities in several countries simultaneously.

Programme Phases

Phase I – Develop In-country Contacts

The limited nature of RARE's involvement in the establishment and dissemination of the RMEP in each country necessitates the development of a strong local constituency. Establishing a network of contacts with local conservation organizations, university faculty and Ministries of Education is therefore of critical importance to the long-term success of the RMEP.

During this initial phase of the programme, contacts are made using all available means. As a preliminary step, with the aid of conservation professionals from within the participating country, RARE staff develop working lists of contacts in the particular country. First approaches are made via correspondence, with follow-up visits to the country to present the programme to the appropriate audiences.

The result of Phase I is the development of a team/network of professionals who work with RARE during all phases of the programme, to assure completion, success and continuation.

Phase II – Pre-pilot Review and Workshop

The pre-pilot review and workshop are used to adapt REMP materials to the needs of the specific country.

At this stage, modifications are made to the basic RMEP model materials so that they can best serve the participating country. Changes are recommended by the team of local professionals, with respect to the biological species and ecological conditions, teaching methods and curricula and special idiomatic needs. The extent of the necessary adaptations varies significantly from country to country and is determined by the team of local professionals in cooperation with RARE's staff.

Perhaps one of the more important aspects of this phase is that it provides for the active participation of the professionals within each country. This is vital to the continuing success of any such programme. The result of Phase II is the adaptation of the model RMEP materials to the participating country.

Phase III – Completion of Pilot Materials

After Phase II the RMEP materials are revised by the team of local professionals with the assistance of RARE staff. The package to be tested during Phase IV of the programme is then prepared and produced. Revisions generally include recommended biological, idiomatic and curricular adaptations of the texts and visual presentations.

Once these modifications have been made, the materials are available for testing and no further major changes are made until Phase V. The result of Phase III is the completed package of programme materials ready for pilot testing.

Phase IV – In-country Piloting of Materials

One of the main objectives of the in-country piloting of RMEP materials is to demonstrate the educational approach represented by this programme. Additionally, this test phase is used to ascertain the existence of any difficulties which might be discovered by the teachers.

The piloting is conducted with the co-operation and participation of the appropriate government agencies, generally the Ministry of Education, teachers and often local private conservation organizations. Representatives of these agencies and organizations (the local team of professionals) have the leading role in teacher training, implementation and evaluation of the results. The schools participating in the test are chosen to represent a cross-section of the cultural and socioeconomic structure within the country.

At the begining of this phase teachers from the pilot schools participate in a 2–3-day training workshop. During the workshop they are introduced to the educational methods used in the programme and have the opportunity to learn by sampling different activities. Generally, local conservationists participate in the workshop through presentations about important environmental issues of local concern. These presentations serve to motivate the teachers to action.

During this phase representatives of the Ministry of Education usually visit the schools where the programme is being tested. These visits allow the representatives to help the teachers resolve any problems which they may encounter with the materials and provide an important source of feedback for the future continuation of the programme.

The motivation and active participation of the teachers in this phase is critical because this provides them with the opportunity to make final adjustments to the materials during actual field testing.

The result of Phase IV is a review of teacher and student participation, effectiveness of the approach and materials and recommendations for final revisions.

Phase V – Final Revisions of Materials

At the end of Phase IV all the teachers who participated in the pilot testing of the programme are once again brought together. This time they are given the opportunity to discuss their experiences with the programme during testing and make specific recommendations on adaptation and further revision of the materials. The "final" revisions to the RMEP are made, based on the results of the in-country piloting, and are completed as a joint effort of the local professionals and RARE staff.

The result of Phase V is the completed package of programme materials ready for final implementation.

Phase VI – Disseminate Final Materials

The number of copies which is made available for use in each participating country is dependent upon available funding. Continued supervision and review of the programme is transferred to the Ministry of Education, which in our experience continues working in conjunction with the local teams of professionals. The in-country constituency for the programme, of teachers and students, has an important role in maintaining the government and

Ministry's interest in the long-term success of the programme and the training of future decision-makers.

The result of Phase VI is a fully operational Resource Management Education Programme supported by local people who will monitor and assure its continued success.

GENERAL SCHEDULE

The schedule for implementation of the RMEP follows one basic pattern in the different countries. Differences in the calendar year timing of the phases are of course dependent on the school schedules which are in use by the participating countries.

CONCLUSION

The Resource Management Education Programme (RMEP) has proved successful in Costa Rica, Colombia and Honduras. In Costa Rica, RMEP has completed 2 years of operation, training approximately 800 teachers and 28,000 children. In 1983 the Costa Rican Ministry of Education officially adopted RMEP as an integral part of its natural science curriculum. The Ministry of Education is extending RMEP to more public schools, while the Universidad Estatal a Distancia (UNED – State University at a Distance) is introducing RMEP into private schools. UNED is also using RMEP in its University environmental education programmes.

In 1982 the Secretary of Education and several environmental groups in Colombia began to develop a plan for environmental education programmes for Colombia's primary schools. In 1983 RARE was requested to assist in the development of a programme to train teachers already in the classroom and university students studying to be teachers. RARE staff worked with representatives of the Grupo Ecologico de la Universidad del Tolima (Ecology Group of the University of Tolima) and classroom teachers to adapt and revise RMEP to make it appropriate for use in various Departments (States) in Colombia.

In 1983, as part of the pilot phase, the Colombian RMEP programme trained 125 teachers from two Departments (Tolima and Quindio). Based on the success of this programme, the Ecology Group of Tolima received a grant from the World Wildlife Fund–US to expand the RMEP programme. In its second year RMEP, officially sanctioned by the Colombian government, trained a total of 464 teachers from 51 schools and approximately 25,000 students. As the programme expands over the next 5 years it is expected to affect more than 100,000 students in these two Colombian Departments.

In Honduras the Honduran Ecological Association solicited help from

RARE to develop an environmental education programme to train students who were studying to become teachers in normal schools. While the programme was successful, the Honduran Ecological Association and the Ministry of Education decided to modify the original plan and to concentrate on training teachers who were already in the classroom, because of their experience and the availability of students with whom to pilot the materials. The 1983 programme, which was funded through a USAID grant to the Honduran Ecological Association, will be expanded in 1985 concentrating on training primary school teachers.

A similar RMEP programme is being developed for Brazil. Presently Phases I and II are being initiated. It is hoped that RMEP will be operational by mid-1985.

As a result of RARE's Resource Management Education Programme more than 1500 teachers have been trained and more than 50,000 students involved. Through the use of RMEP, teachers and students have developed a strong understanding of their natural resources and a recognition of their responsibilities as future decision-makers who will impact the environmental quality of their country. It is anticipated that the teachers' and students' enthusiasm for proper resource use will spread up to the community through their families and friends.

TABLE 5

Phase		Number of months
I	Develop in-country contacts	3
II	Pre-pilot review and workshop	3
III	Completion of pilot materials	2
IV	In-country piloting of materials	5
V	Final revisions of materials	4
VI	Disseminate final materials	on-going

TABLE 6   Generalized Timetable

Phase	Month 1 2 3 4 5 6 7 8 9 10 11 12 13 14 . . . 24
I	<-------->
II	<------>
III	<---->
IV	<---------->
V	<-------->
VI	>>

Environmental Education Courses in Scotland: a Case Study of Theory Translated into Practice

FRANK CRAWFORD

INTRODUCTION: SETTING THE SCENE

This paper traces the theoretical development of a curricular model applicable to courses in environmental education and its influence on courses currently taught in Scottish schools. It will concentrate on the influences which the curriculum development process has on theory, the treatment of the final product by members of the teaching profession and the reaction of the end-users (school children).

The first of these, the curriculum development process in Scotland, is achieved by a careful balance between the influences of central institutions. Scottish education is, in the main, a highly centralized system due to the population size and the high regard which Scots have for centralized, external examination certificates. The main institutions involved in educational change are the Consultative Committee on the Curriculum (CCC), an autonomous body which has responsibility for overseeing the whole school curriculum, the Scottish Examination Board (SEB), which offers national certification of published curricula, and finally the Scottish Education Department (SED), which is the government body represented overtly by Her Majesty's Inspectorate. Major developments have been taking place in Scottish education over the last five to six years following the publication of the Munn and Dunning Reports, the former addressing itself to the structure of the curriculum of 14–16-year-olds, the latter to certification for the same age group and for all ability levels. This paper is chiefly concerned with a study of developments which come under the influence of the above two reports.

The Munn Report came down very heavily in favour of the existing and

195

entrenched system of a subject or discipline-based curriculum. The traditional fragmented structuring of secondary schools into subject compartments emerged virtually unscathed. The actual mechanism involved in bringing about curricular changes in Scotland can vary depending on whether the curriculum involved is to be certificated or not. If one wishes to make major changes, one has to set up a Joint Working Party consisting of representatives of the CCC, the SEB and the SED. This working party (JWP) then produces a public report which can be commented upon by a wide range of interested parties and is finally published as a national syllabus with national certification.

The second major aspect is the influence of the classroom teacher. It is of little value to publish pious hopes and rhetoric if this is to be distorted by inappropriate teaching methods. In the teaching of any aspect of environmental education, methodology is often as crucial if not more so than the actual content. Can one teach about an environmental ethic, for example, if one does not share this? Can it be taught didactically? Can one teach about personal involvement in local environmental management without oneself being involved?

The acid test of any theoretical curricular model is whether or not it works with the students. No claims will be made that rigorous pre-tests, post-tests or any other tests to measure the attainment of students have been carried out, but a detailed, descriptive evaluation of several environmental education courses has been completed, and personal reactions of students and staff are included in this evaluation.

DEVELOPMENT OF A MODEL

Environmental education in Scotland "entered the New Testament", in the words of the late S. T. S. Skillen, one of Her Majesty's Inspectors of Schools, in February 1977 when the Scottish Environmental Education Committee was formed at a conference organized by the Strathclyde Environmental Education Group (SEEG), an informal group of interested professionals, originally formed in 1975. At the above-mentioned conference there was a call for "a simpler, more clear-cut statement of basic definitions, aims and objectives".

The main aim has been defined as "enabling people to recognize the factors which determine the nature and quality of the human environment so that all may respect and appreciate it to the full and participate constructively, as individuals and as citizens, in its management and development".

The concept of a planned, coherent curriculum model was suggested by SEEG and one particular model was adopted, and is shown in Table 7. It is this model which formed the basis of some 8 years of development and testing in a wide variety of circumstances within Scottish education.

TABLE 7

Stage	Question	Activity
1. Observation	What does it look like?	Direct observation
2. Evolution	How did it get there?	Comparing/contrasting
3. Function Inter-relationships	How does it work? How do the bits fit together?	Analysing
4. Change	How does it change?	Investigating
5. Control of change	How is this change controlled?	Participating

Originally conceived as an holistic model giving a complete overview of environmental education it nevertheless is a valuable construct from which to plan a variety of courses, for example an essentially interdisciplinary course centring on "the home" theme to a Health Education course based on the main "environments" of man. The examples show what a versatile and rigorous tool such an overarching model can be.

Trials using the model concentrated on skills and attitudes. The ultimate goal is participation in matters relating to the environment. This can be seen as the full dissemination of democracy to the level of the individual, but to the individual as an active participant and not as mere voter in a ballot-box exercise. If pursued logically, in a world in which everyone cared for their immediate environment one would not even hesitate to question involvement in the international problems of conservation and pollution control; such problems would either cease to exist or be taken care of as a matter of fact, as a matter of faith, as a matter of conscience, as the *sine qua non* of progress of our human condition.

The Strathclyde Environmental Education Group provided back-up for the schools involved in the form of general aims, objectives and checklists for:

1. introductory components such as contextual statements;
2. curricular components such as suggestions for learning activities;
3. information such as resource lists;
4. assessment procedures such as student self-checks.

Not least important of all the considerations in the courses offered under the banner of environmental education is the methodology and teaching strategies adopted by staff. Many educationists now argue that the main difference between students in their ability to learn is one of pace, and that professional teachers are often unaware of the wide range of learning difficulties which are encountered *by students of all abilities*. That many students are also disadvantaged by social circumstances brings yet additional sets of learning difficulties which must be overcome.

Courses in environmental education offer opportunities to students to encounter a whole range of teaching strategies in what is usually a less formal teaching and learning situation. The classroom teacher, by careful choice of materials, approaches, media and pace, can help overcome many learning difficulties. From this point of view, multi-disciplinary approaches to the teaching of environmental education offer many advantages over the more traditional approach within the narrow subject-based curriculum.

The schools trying out the model produced a final report which was developed by SEEG and has now appeared in its final form. Bearing in mind that the curriculum in Scotland is particularly biased towards the subject-based approach, and that there is a distinct lack of political will to push for the cause of inter-disciplinary subjects like environmental education, the publication of this document, some 4 years after the school trials took place, is a milestone in Scottish environmental education.

Staff in the schools which tried out the model were certainly more than pleased with the structured approach to the development of courses in environmental education and with the methodologies suggested by SEEG.

> "The Environmental Topic is the best thing in our course. Children welcome the change in pace. The opportunities for learning in a less formal setting are huge."

> "There is no doubt that the SEEG model with its clearly defined stages is a very valuable aid both in the construction of an Environmental Studies course and also in the clear explanation to pupils of the logical progression of activity which seems to be apparent in most of what happens to and in our environment."

DEVELOPMENTS IN SCIENCE

One of the major recommendations of the Munn Report was that science should be a subject taught to all pupils up to the statutory leaving age of 16 years. Hitherto the only science available to pupils between the ages of 14 and 16 was either the specialist subjects of biology, chemistry and physics or courses in "science" which did not lead to external certification. A new subject called science was thus called for, though it was to be restricted to the lower 70 per cent of the student ability range, the top 30 per cent being catered for by the existing specialist sciences.

The new course in science was piloted (at the low ability ranges) in schools throughout Scotland. The original documents defining the course featured liberal references to the environment, and indeed the two main themes which encompassed the aims and objectives of the science course were:

1. Man's understanding of himself and his environment;
2. Man's inter-action with the environment.

These were expanded (originally) to identify five fields of study:

1. Healthy and Safe Living;
2. Man and Environment;
3. Man and Living Things;
4. Man and Materials;
5. Energy and its Uses.

It was detected quite quickly in the pilot schools that the fields of study relating to Man and Environment and Man and Living Things were proving to be problematic. As a consequence, these two were amalgamated, leaving four fields of study. There was then a further call for the complete removal of the environment issue from the new science course and, at a critical stage in the development, a small group of science teachers from Glasgow was asked to produce a paper outlining a complete and logical topic called "A Study of Environments".

This provided the opportunity for the influence of the SEEG philosophy and approach to be directed at the centre of the development of the science curriculum. The clear approach of developing from the small-scale, concrete, directly observable to the larger more abstract world via the five-stage model was outlined:

> "It is suggested that the environment be studied at three levels; firstly, a simplified mini-environment; secondly, a 'natural' environment readily accessible to the pupils; thirdly, a clearly man-influenced environment such as a town environment. The *five stages of study* should be covered at each of the three levels in order to take the pupils through the whole process with parallels being drawn between each level. The teacher should encourage the pupils to see the direct influence of science and technology as well as the usefulness of the scientific method in studying the environment."

The paper produced by the small group of science teachers was sent to the SED in a bid to influence the final structure of the environment topic. The paper suggested in more detail what could form the basis of study within the three main "environments" as follows:

Simplified mini-environment (e.g.) an aquarium, gerbil cage with burrows, locust colony. Identifying all its component parts, how these inter-relate, how it changes over time.

A "natural" environment (e.g.) woodland, freshwater stream, pond, seashore, moorland, meadow. Field work and appropriate experimental work. Identify common components – energy flow, material cycles, waste, pollution, population control, diversity, limiting factors, succession.

A man-influenced environment (e.g.) village, town, city. Observing use of space and materials. Visible impact of science and technology. Identify components – energy, waste, supply of materials, use, design of materials. Need for planning, compromise, conservation, participation.

The paper also suggested that to remove the environment topic would make a nonsense of the rationale of the whole science course. Edited, relevant statements for the draft science guidelines were submitted, a selection of which appear below. These are included as being highly relevant to any science course which purports to be concerned with environment and technology.

RELEVANT ISSUES

1. Science provides not only a way of approaching many of *the problems which people meet in everyday life* but also *helps them to make decisions on solutions*.

2. Knowledge encompassing man and his environment enables changes to be made in their inter-relationship.

3. A science course should aim to:
   (a) Develop in students a knowledge and understanding of themselves and man in general; of his environment; the effects of man upon his environment and the importance of science and technology and their relevance to work and leisure in a modern society.
   (b) Develop in students skills which will help them to acquire and communicate knowledge from first-hand experience; to use acquired knowledge to produce possible solutions to relevant problems; to make informed personal decisions.
   (c) Encourage in students the development of a willingness to participate, as an informed person, in democratic decision-making.
   (d) Develop in students an awareness of and an ability to cope with the changing world around them.
   (e) Develop the historical and social significance of science.
   (f) Help in the establishment of a public which is better informed on scientific and technological issues and the stewardship of resources.

4. Topics should be related to and then extend, pupils' own experience. Therefore, account should be taken of pupils' leisure interests, relevant socioeconomic issues and scientific and technological applications.

5. Attitudes should be inculcated and include the following:
   (a) An awareness of the value of co-operating with others.
   (b) An appreciation of the finite nature of the earth's resources, living and non-living, and a willingness to participate in the conservation of the natural environment.

(c) An interest and curiosity in themselves and their environment.
(d) An awareness of the contribution of science and technology to the economic, social and cultural life of the community.
(e) An awareness of the unique nature of living systems and the relationship between man and the environment.
(f) A willingness to search for patterns and relationships.
(g) An awareness of the responsibility of the individual to maintain his personal well-being and the well-being of the community.
(h) An appreciation of the advantages and disadvantages to society of the application of scientific development.

Happily, an environment-related topic eventually appeared entitled "A Study of Environments", but alas the basic five steps of the theoretical model had "disappeared", rejected as being "merely one way of looking at the world". The "mini-environment" too had disappeared in favour of studying only two environments – the school's environment and a "chosen" environment. The curriculum development process itself has severely distorted the theoretical model and produced the proverbial "horse designed by a committee" – the camel. It was noticeable that at the meeting to discuss the final structure of the environment topic, no-one who was involved with the model development was present!

All was not lost, however, since a few schools continued to develop their environment topic within science along the lines of the original model. The teachers concerned were convinced, despite what the official guidelines had to say, that they had a valid and useful model for an environment topic. It is fortunate that within Scottish education professional autonomy of the individual teacher still exists, and a variety of teaching styles and content structure is tolerable within general guidelines. One could argue that teaching could easily drift away from the norm towards poor educational practice, but again we are fortunate in Scotland to have a virtually all-graduate teaching force with a keen bias towards the encouragement of good educational practice.

The teachers who kept faith with the original model went on to develop their topic and were particularly inventive in field work. The pragmatic difficulties of taking some twenty students (many of whom would be poor academic performers) on a field trip has daunted the most enthusiastic staff. The key is advanced preparation and well-thought-out tasks. Student reaction can virtually cancel out the educational value of a course if it is not properly prepared and motivating.

Having carried out a pilot study in schools throughout Scotland to determine the feasibility of a nationally certificated science course for the lowest 30 per cent of the ability range, it was decided to extend the course to make it suitable for some 70 per cent of the ability range. Thus the official version of "A Study of Environments" was to be re-examined and could yet again be influenced by the five-stage model. Fortuitously, one of the science teachers involved in developing the model became partly responsible for the task of upgrading the official environment topic in the national science course.

A golden opportunity, one might think, to rationalize the topic away from its obviously fragmented and eclectic structure towards a more holistic and logical structure and to update the rather out-moded approach to certain environmental concepts and issues such as pollution. This might have been done along the lines suggested in Table 8, using the five-stage model; however, a full rewrite of the topic "A Study of Environments" was not possible. This was due to the constraints of the curriculum-development process. These were in some ways valid: the official version had been piloted, production of student materials was already under way, the environment topic had to be structured in a similar way to the other topics on energy, healthy bodies and materials, the topic had to be capable of being taught in 20 hours of class time and so the range of official constraints went on.

However, undaunted, the task was undertaken and the five-stage model was gently introduced in the preamble as "an approach" to the environment topic which appeared in the official national guidelines. The opportunity was also taken to rewrite some of the content, though wholesale changes were strictly forbidden at this stage!

TABLE 8   The Five-stage Model in Science: Environment Topic

	Ideas	Skills	Concepts
1.	Observe how resources are used	Observe, illustrate, record, estimate, measure, discover, generalize	Environment, resource use, use of space structure/function relationship
2.	Historical context, development of environment	Compare, contrast, construct/use questionnaires	Patterns in time, effects of technology over a period
3.	Environmental components, inter-dependence of components	Identify, analyse, interpret, classify, discriminate, define operationally	Whole made of components, inter-dependence, eco-system, community, food chains
4.	Effect of humans, population, pollution, succession	Identify changes, identify constraints, predict, experiment, field work skills	Resource limitation, waste, pollution, energy flow, diversity/stability, relationship
5.	Control in nature, conflict, compromise, planning, waste management, participation	Infer, predict, plan, assume, manipulate variables	Recycling in nature, limiting factors, conservation, planning, recycling waste

Thus the questions associated with the theoretical model now appear in the national guidelines for science. The model also appears in the guidelines for another new subject in the curriculum of 14–16-year-olds – Contemporary Social Studies. These guidelines appeared a year after science but the questions are the same: What does it (the environment) look like? How do the parts fit together? How does it change? How is this change controlled?

DISCUSSION

There are three main contentions in this paper:

1. The curriculum development process can distort theoretical approaches in the search for compromise and in the avoidance of changes in curricular provision which appear too radical.

   There is a theory in Scottish education about the existence of an establishment conspiracy to maintain the status quo: a naturally conservative establishment will not allow shifts from accepted norms. The conspiracy theory is, of course, a mirage and simply a paradigm of what is merely system bias, that is, the propensity of any complex system to remain stable.

   This phenomenon, nevertheless, when encountered can be extremely frustrating. The paper has demonstrated by example how a particular approach can be vastly altered in the process of development by those within the development process. If there is to be anything learned from this it is that any theoretical approach should be tried in as "pure" a form as possible, and then documented to be considered by those whose task it is to develop the curriculum. Another and perhaps less controllable factor is the presence or absence within the curriculum development process of advocates of a particular approach. Although there are many real constraints, at least the true nature of a suggested approach can be argued at first-hand. It is perhaps more by accident than design that certain good practices are adopted in the curriculum.

2. The teaching profession itself can distort the suggested curricular diet of students. This was demonstrated in the case of the science teachers who, on hearing that their own suggested approach had been officially rejected, continued to operate with their original structure, despite the official guidelines. This is defensible in that good practice was adopted, but there are inherent dangers in a system which allows for total freedom of approach without some sort of accountability, for example the adoption of poor teaching techniques which are not consistent with official guidelines.

3. The students themselves can reject even the most enlightened of ideas if these are not properly presented. The schools which tried the theoretical model in an inter-disciplinary setting constructed their

courses as close to the original model as possible and used a wide variety of teaching approaches. The pupil reaction in these cases was very favourable.

On the other hand, the teachers who developed the field-trip tasks did so as much to preserve their sanity as for any other reason and the result was good quality learning materials. Originally the students worked in groups on rather loosely-defined tasks. Problems arose, however, in the form of lack of direction, boredom and self-destruction. The sight of fifteen to twenty young students cavorting through a woodland with trees being subjected to all sorts of indignities via various pieces of scientific equipment is less than joyful to the thinking teacher. Sanity can prevail and the careful redesign of the materials eventually produced a hugely successful student response.

Thus, if one has a sensible and logical construct for a particular curricular development, one should take cognizance of the changes which might take place when the construct is adapted by the curriculum developers, the teachers who will implement the course and the students at the receiving end. Above all, one needs patience, stamina and a modicum of contrived interference.

III Community-based Environmental Education and Links with Other Conference Themes

S. JAKOWSKA

The structure of this part is different from that of the preceding ones in that it places most emphasis on what happened during the workshops focused on community-based and informal approaches to environmental education, and also on those shared with other conference themes. Some of the papers relating to this part are reviewed in the account which follows; others appear elsewhere in the book.

1

Highlights of the Prevailing Trends and Recommendations

The workshops dealing with informal community-based education took a very important direction which emerged from discussions summarized by John Smyth, through increasing the emphasis on "action-orientated" school-based education. Effective approaches have involved a combination of formal and non-formal education, using a multiplicity of aids and methods, including actual work on individual or community projects, use of national heritage and history, and use of ecologically positive beliefs and customs. Games, audiovisuals, music, dance and drama have also been most effectively integrated for environmental education within the school.

The group identified teachers and teacher training as key catalytic factors essential for the long-term success of environmental education in conserving the environment. The emphasis must be to integrate environmental awareness into all disciplines and faculties, and to integrate action-based approaches into teacher training programmes rather than to make environmental education a theoretical concept outside the other school subjects.

Equally important is the fact that environmental education is moving into the community at large and demonstrating the interdependence of conservation and development. This can be effectively done through providing positive and feasible alternatives to environmental problems and encouraging a holistic approach to development issues.

A combination of strong grass-roots movements along with influencing key decision-makers and creating public opinion was found to be the most effective approach.

For school-based, university-based and community-based education, partners can and must be found within the community. Government and non-government agencies, industry and workers' unions, religious, social, scientific and cultural groups can all become important advocates of the environmental conservation ethic.

Some important elements which emerged as guidelines for future action were: (1) the need to make environmental education in schools *issue-related* through case studies, *"do-how"-related* through practical projects, and *community-related* through the use of the child's immediate environment, rural or urban; (2) the need for environmentalists to *reach out* to colleagues in other disciplines, professions, and groups, both for understanding environmental issues in their totality, and for working together as partners for change; (3) the need to *reach into* the resources available within the participants and within the traditions of the community, e.g. art, music, dance; (4) the need to make the environmental education message a tool for sustainable development; (5) the need to disseminate information about the large bank of innovative educational tools and techniques which are now available.

With this summary in mind, we can now examine in greater detail some of the most significant contributions and interventions which took place at the conference, around this theme. Their value lies in showing the diversification of present-day environmental education which, rather than being just another curricular item with a rigid syllabus, spills out of school into the life of the children and their community to become a basis for a life-long conservation habit.

The cases presented show how people other than science teachers traditionally involved in environmental education can stimulate positive action and contribute through the arts and the mass media to spreading a conservation philosophy. These cases also show how teachers who claim closer affinity with physics and mathematics than with the life sciences become convincingly and effectively engaged as "doers" and leaders in culturally integrated environmentally positive community action.

2

The Place of Ethics, Humanities and the Arts in the Environmental Education of Children

To date, most of the efforts in environmental education as a whole have been directed along the guidelines of science and technology. Obviously, all of us felt the need to use the arguments and the knowledge derived from up-to-date information on natural resources and the ways in which science and technology contribute to preserve them. It was felt that much environmental damage was due precisely to ignorance of the complexities and inter-relationships in the web of life, not to speak of the economic and social realities involved.

Thus, in the more affluent societies, children are being raised today with considerable faith in science and technology, and some live with the illusion that these alone will resolve all problems, including those that they themselves are creating with increasing consumer demands on raw materials and energy resources. For each of the forms of ecological aggression there seems to exist some form of scientific response and technological solution that will at least neutralize it. This, however, is the great hoax of our times which environmental educators are unwittingly keeping alive simply by not insisting more that there is a limit to what we can do with our space and our natural resources, no matter how effective our scientific evaluation and our technological remedies may be.

Under the guise of science and technology, some of the mass communication media, through the audacious and entertaining genre of science fiction in comic strips and films, lead some children to believe, for example, that the animals that become extinct may be easily replaced by robots and gadgets with comparable utilitarian qualities, that the world devoid of trees and other living things will be just right for superior human beings, without emotions and clad in some sort of spacesuits, and that they

209

or their children will become that way in order to rule over the world.

While this false image of what is called a desirable future is being offered to our children as entertainment and even as education, let us rejoice that in some of the most developed parts of the world people are already experiencing, individually and collectively, a "nature hunger" or a subtle yearning for an affinity with something more than the present or the future, which they find both rather dismal and insecure.

This "nature hunger" cannot be appeased with the promise of a sterile antiseptic world. It needs the sound of rushing waters, the sparkling light filtering through the foliage, the companionship of other living beings, seen and unseen, and a feeling of unity and harmony with the rest of the world. This hunger can be appeased only in human beings that are sensitive to nature and capable of appreciating and protecting it.

The survival of today's people does not depend exclusively on contributions from science and technology. Human survival requires more than the protection of the material world in which we live. It depends on more than the casual recognition of our responsibilities for the physical world. Collective guilt feelings, if any exist anywhere, must give way to positive expressions replacing fruitless efforts to assign responsibility for the ecological crisis to this or that religion, philosophy or system. It is time to seek out and to make known the ecologically positive components of each way of thinking and of each way of life, so that they may contribute, individually and collectively, to our global strategy for survival.

We should not be reluctant to speak of patterns of human conduct in terms of ecological virtues and of a value system derived from the depth of human experiences, carried through as oral and written tradition from generation to generation. We have now reached the point where traditional environmental education, based chiefly on science and technology, must expand to the dimension of environmental culture. The term was coined in 1978 in an effort to recruit into the field of environmental education and the defence of the natural heritage all kinds of professionals, especially those from disciplines other than science and technology. At that time there appeared to exist a strong "non-scientific" and "non-technological" concern for the environment, but it seemed to be more of a desire for an encounter with what we were then led to believe were two cultures, separate and different.

No doubt the level of technology available determines in some way the speed, the scope, and the intensity of the interactions of people with their environment, but human attitudes that result in human actions do not depend on material factors alone. If we consider that human actions defy our biological nature and transcend any biological discipline, we must identify those factors that mould culture and society and blend them effectively into our efforts for conservation.

In terms of ethics, humanities, and the arts we should consider children a very high priority. Children of today, no matter where they live, should not grow up thinking that they are merely products or producers of modern science and technology. Science and technology are undeniably a birthright of any child of this century, but we should never offer a child science and technology as solutions to all problems, except in the sense that they permit us to extend human capabilities, just as the instruments we use are the extensions of our senses. Human nature is more than the sum of the biological components of the body. This is something we must be sure that children understand, within the context of their specific culture.

We share the assumption of the philosopher Matthew Lipman, Director of the Institute for the Advancement of Philosophy for Children, that children are by nature interested in philosophical issues such as truth, fairness and personal identity, and that they should learn to think for themselves, to explore alternatives to their own points of view, to consider evidence, to make careful distinctions, and to become aware of the objectives of the educational process. Traditional philosophy may be stripped of its formidable terminology and rephrased in children's own words. Children need not know that they engage in discussion that adults might term "metaphysical", "aesthetic", "ethical" or "logical", but they do need the many specific thinking skills that produce reasoning.

The early childhood curriculum employed by Lipman at grades 2–3 includes an introduction to environmental education; it considers animals, space and time, and many other aspects of nature. At grade levels 5–6 children are shown what it might be like to live and participate in a small community where children have their own interests, yet respect each other as people and are capable of engaging in co-operative inquiry for the satisfaction of doing so. An ethical inquiry programme for grades 7–8 is meant to sensitize children to the moral aspects of everyday life, heighten their consciousness with regard to the problematic and contestable (and in certain cases soluble) aspects of these moral issues, and introduce them to the procedures which make ethical inquiry feasible.

Both the opportunity to learn thinking skills and the time to think represent an important background for an effective environmental education, one that will permit them to make value-judgements and responsible decisions. Meditation may also be a means of achieving inner involvement with nature, adapting reflection-generating words and statements, or visual stimuli, to the specific age group and the cultural and temperamental characteristics of the children involved.

When we think about how much has been entrusted to us, and how much depends on how we use our talents, the task before us appears immense. But we must simply gather the courage to liberate the potential within us that was timidly hidden away when we feared to express opinions in other than scientific terms. As we liberate and recruit talents for the cause of conservation, we are able to give an ecological slant to practically every discipline, even to those that once seemed incompatible with science and technology.

As conservationists, anxious to get support from everyone and from everywhere, we should ask ourselves now if we have been neglected by those who could see conservation with a wider perspective than those of science and technology alone; or have we been so concerned with the material aspects of preserving and protecting the earth that we have failed to identify and to hear the voices trying to come to our aid?

Perhaps the answer is "yes" to both questions; and perhaps the problem is due to our own educational deficiencies or to the fallacy of two separate cultures that some of us have been taking it for granted.

The Bangalore Conference gave us the opportuity to see the environment and its resources as a cultural heritage bound to national or ethnic, as well as to individual identity, to judge human actions in terms of ecological virtues such as moderation in the use of natural resources, or of ecological vices such as consumerism and waste. We also started raising our voices, as some on the outside have already tried to do, insisting that nature be preserved to achieve a better quality of life with an added spiritual dimension, and in terms of values such as beauty capable of inspiring human creativity and inner growth, and leading us, eventually, toward a reconciliation with nature.

3

The Use of Art, Music, History and Other Topics in Environmental Education

A trend to integrate environmental education with the humanities and the arts, or to make these meaningful in an environmentally positive way, already seems to exist. Enikö Szalay-Marzsó of Hungary collected, analysed and summarized a number of case studies dealing with the social sciences and the arts and their relation to environmental education.

The cases included the contributions of E. Badacsonyi (see p. 183), H. Hass, K. Horvath (see p. 175), K. Schilke, and G. Trommer. In all cases there is an important point of agreement concerning the natural order which shows inherent stability against a tendency to disorder, and which becomes irreversibly affected by any intervention. This awareness prompts a strong desire to maintain the original natural order, of which man is part, and within which man seeks the "quality of life" that satisfies his material and non-material needs.

The first objective in this direction should be to mobilize a worldwide action of experts to provide environmental education programmes that develop knowledge, skills, and attitudes leading to a new system of order, values and conservation ethics for a wiser management of nature. In this integral form, environmental education must be taught from kindergarten through to postgraduate level by teachers who share these ideals.

But the teaching must be spread to the whole community, because people must learn to relate cause and effect in general terms and not think in terms of subject matter such as history or geography.

Environmental studies can become the unifying factor in effective teaching of the natural and social sciences and the arts, for future human needs. Every form of teaching aid and communication medium, as well as every form of artistic expression available, may be employed to enhance and to advance environmental education in order to stimulate ecologically positive attitudes, creativity and practical applications for action.

In workshop 4 Enikö Badacsonyi (3), who teaches biology and

environmental protection in the Zoltán Kodály Music School in Budapest, showed, with an audiovisual aid, how music and drawing lessons help children to develop an emotional basis for a responsible attitude towards the environment, and how social sciences and biology are incorporated into a music and art curriculum (see p. 183).

This mutual interest of music and environmental educators offers an opportunity for further collaboration. The human voice, everyone's musical instrument, is not only capable of producing sounds with different tone, vibration and texture: it can produce speech that conveys meaning. This meaning, combined with a melody, is an effective educational tool and should be used more extensively in environmental education.

Advertising jingles with catchy slogans produce the desired effect of increasing the sales of advertised goods. What we need now is more impressive and meaningful environmental lyrics for familiar tunes that everyone can hum, that can be used for dancing and for marching, as well as for working. Some may help people dream and hope for a better, greener world. Why not environmental ballads, operettas, or even operas with environmental plots that people can understand?

In this fast-moving world, where many good songs fall into oblivion, it would be good to prepare a list of the existing environmentally positive songs, and to record some folk songs, such as the Punjabi song about the cranes, before they get forgotten.

But let us not forget that children and school teachers are quite capable of producing locally relevant as well as universally appealing songs and other forms of ecologically positive artistic expression. Specific situations are the best stimulus for creativity.

Appropriate musical background helps sensitize people to the message of an audiovisual programme. Dilnavaz Variava of Bombay produced one, aimed at the rural population, which emphasizes non-resource species. It shows how our "gift of a sense of wonder" permits us to observe and to appreciate "the gift of colour", which provides protective colouration and mimicry in the living world. The message based on aesthetics is easily understood: "There is so little we can leave our children except the wonders of nature."

Children ought to have more opportunities to sing about things that they must learn to appreciate and to love. This reminds me of a song made popular by Polish scout cubs, with lyrics by Wanda Chotomska (*Panorama Polska*, Feb. 1978, No. 2259) which develops from a simple encounter with a roadside wildflower: "Don't step on the daisies by the roadside, because though a daisy may be small, each one contains the sound of music, each one is like a drop of poetry. People become enriched by these tiny flowers, and that is why we cry out today: do not trample daisies nor feelings!" There is a poetic as well as an ethical dimension to this joyous marching song which conveys concern for nature, with aesthetic rather than utilitarian aspects.

Something similar was pointed out in a Spanish children's book (*Amigos del Cocodrilo*, Jakowska, 1979) about a non-resource species: "Crocodiles are important, not because they are eaten, not because they are used, not because they are sold. They are a form of life that's different yet similar to us. They enrich the earth with their presence."

Fortunately there is a trend among educators which stresses the need to develop an aesthetic capacity in humankind to enjoy and to use the intangible values provided by the natural environment. Perhaps people, as children, can still learn not to destroy a blade of grass, or not to step on a roadside daisy. But both opulent and poverty-stricken societies are guilty of waste: we must help children to develop an urge to plant and to grow living things, not only for food but to draw upon their intangible values.

Childhood in highly industrialized societies, with computer games and entertaining electronic gadgets, does not offer so many opportunities for aesthetics. We have pointed out on many occasions that the natural heritage contributes to the national heritage on equal terms with the cultural component, and that it must be loved and protected. Thus, if respect is due to the flag or to sites of historical importance so it is also due to ancient trees and forests that witnessed a people's past, caves, mountains, shores, and all of the flora and fauna with species that are unique. It is here that the affective aspect may be nurtured in terms of patriotism and national identity.

History as a social science is also a valid vehicle for the environmental message. K. Horvath (see p. 175) firmly believes that history offers concrete lessons in environmental education. The ecological conditions and the level of exploitation of natural resources during different epochs may be reconstructed from the existing documents, and ancillary sciences help complete the picture, even for pre-historic periods. Thus, a historian who is environmentally orientated can provide a more realistic interpretation of the past and better delve into the "ecological errors" as well as into their roots.

Fortunately environmental history has already gained its place among other scholarly approaches to the past, and it is hoped that educators in social and environmental sciences on every level will draw upon it as a source of information, and of inspiration.

Writers, poets, and illustrators ought to be encouraged to collaborate in the production of children's books relevant to conservation. However, since in the Third World most children lack elementary texts and other school supplies, it would be unrealistic to think that some of the books on nature-related topics which we have seen would be available to such under-privileged children. Nevertheless, a way must be found so that, in the words of Huang Min-Yung (27a) "easy and interesting textbooks for children's environmental education should be published to supply the teachers with teaching material". And we may add: inexpensive, illustrated, preferably in full colour, and in very large editions.

Conservation and survival can be achieved only through the educational development of people by taking into consideration human nature, social implications and cultural background of each population. Non-formal community-orientated education must take up this challenge because there is no formal education programme in existence that can accomplish this. Unless, of course, all our education were revamped and given an environmental orientation.

Children, as a group, must grow with the feeling that the world was meant to be better than it is, and that they, as individuals and as members of a society, are able to do something about it.

4
Children as Partners in Conservation

Sophie Jakowska (29a) offered creative educators a great number of possibilities for designing displays, exhibits, performances, work-like activities, games, etc., for a sort of children's environmental fair or festival, to be held preferably in connection with some conservationist event, permitting mutual interaction and shared experience of children and adults.

Conceived as modular units, to be used independently or together, the plan resembles in some ways traditional audiovisual environmental exhibits, arranged by themes such as "the world to care for", "the world of animals", "the world of plants" and "the world of water". But the distinguishing feature of this programme lies in the four creativity modules or areas dedicated to Meditation, to Plastic Arts and Graphic Expression, to Music, Dance, and the Performing Arts, and to Verbal Expression and Communication, the latter with a model Press Room. The description of these areas provided in the publication is but a suggestion for more extensive children's activities.

The minds of today's young may hold the solution to many of the world's problems. We must make ourselves receptive to their creativity and listen to what they may have to say. We must inform them well, we must instruct them and aid them in every way, as they are willing to accept our help, individually and collectively, to be responsible for a better world of tomorrow, as sincere and incorrupt partners for conservation.

A child may be led to learn to consider the natural heritage of the homeland as something to be loved, preserved, protected, developed through work and planning, and shared by all while used by all with moderation. Without abandoning the fruitful paths of science and technology in environmental education we must seek elsewhere for the source of inner strength that will help us guide the young and provide them with the hope and the faith which, if not one that moves mountains, will at least fill them again with the vision of green forests and sparkling streams they were meant to hold.

In today's world the children of the poor and of the rich are bound for slavery, physical and spiritual, unless we open them to influences that will help them face the world of tomorrow. Those who work with children are right in seeing them as the most endangered representatives of our species. They are right when they point out that children as a group and as individuals are actually powerless before the laws and other man-made institutions.

Yet children are an arsenal of "the Divine Grace", if we may use this expression, of innocence, and "a form of matter as close to the angels" as one may imagine. Their intrinsic spiritual power is what makes them grow, develop, and survive even when chances are very slim. This power may be directed in our effort to save our world. But we must sensitize children to urgent ecological and human needs by offering them opportunities to share in productive work as partners for conservation, and to feel the joys that generosity of sacrifice and effort of daily work can bring.

Two samples from this modular plan have been developed in detail, in the form of teacher's packs for the Bangalore Conference, and they were presented for study and discussion in the workshop under the over-all theme of Children as Partners for Conservation.

One of these, an easy-to-imitate work–activity programme, stems from a case report on a small organization in the Dominican Republic, which sets a pattern for community action spanning two nations on the island of Hispaniola, with children as principal agents in a reforestation effort in both urban and rural areas. The programme promotes the principles that small is beautiful, that no-one is so poor as to be unable to give, and that those who are the least powerful can accomplish a great deal in the struggle to stave off forest depletion, becoming true partners for conservation. This activity does not require great knowledge of trees, silviculture or great understanding of specific deforestation problems or reforestation practices. More than anything it needs a sincere feeling for trees and an understanding of their role on earth, resulting in a personal and permanent commitment to reforestation.

It is important to make children understand that trees and other green plants contribute in the primary and most significant way to life on earth and show them that "trees solve people's problems if people only let them live and grow and produce long enough to make it worthwhile to use them". Children deserve to know the facts about the danger of world-wide tree depletion. We must support with data, appropriate for each age, how ignorance and greed cause the destruction of trees, how urgent the need is to replace trees that are being lost, and how moderation in the use of these resources and work directed at planting trees may help counterbalance forest disappearance.

On the other hand, we might consider simply telling them something like this:

"Children can do something very important by learning how to grow and to plant trees. Each of us, in our lifetime, ought to plant a tree. Those who have not planted a tree have not lived. There are many old people who have not lived yet. We must help them to plant trees and to live.

When a child is born we must celebrate and plant a little tree for the occasion. The community must protect the children and the trees, so that they may grow strong. The children and the trees enrich the community. A child that plants a tree prepares a better future for all of us and builds a better world. We must protect the trees that the children plant so that some of them may become the natural monuments, landmarks of the community, and a true national heritage.

Those who destroy trees usually do it through ignorance, but at times from a necessity for which we must find alternatives. We must prevent tree vandalism, teaching everyone what trees really mean to all of us: trees are people's best friends. We are important when we plant trees: we become symbols of our homeland, lastingly evergreen."

Or perhaps we should just tell the children to love trees as much as do the villagers of the "Chipko" movement of India, who embrace trees to save them from being cut down.

The case report describes how small centres can operate in the heart of a needy community, where children and youth are taught the basic civic concepts of conservation and reforestation, tree identification, seed collecting and growing seeds in mini-nurseries. A child is considered old enough to become a member of the group when he/she understands the responsibility for care of the trees. Each child takes home 25 small plastic bags with soil and seeds and cares for the seedlings, watering them each day for 3–4 months, an optimum period for most of the trees produced in this programme, and an achievable accomplishment for most children.

Trees produced in these mini-nurseries are selected for their special qualities and value. *Moringa oleifera* (horse-radish tree) and *Sesbania grandiflora* (flamingo-bill tree), both originally from Asia, are known to produce edible grain and pods of high protein content, about 38 and 46 per cent respectively. Trees such as *Leucaena glauca* and *Cassia siamea* are fast-growing and good for fuel. Leaves of *Leucaena* are suitable as food for tilapia, rabbits, and even as human food, but acceptance must be developed gradually. *Prosopis juliflora* (mesquite), *Samaneus saman* (raintree), and *Catalpa longissima* (West Indian "oak") are also produced for fuel and as replacement for the dry forest.

At community gatherings, when certificates are awarded to members with 100 trees to be given away, the youngsters and the adults enjoy singing and hand-clapping to simple tunes, naming all kinds of trees they grow and plant, and singing the praises of trees. Colouring contests are held, in which the children produce mini-posters with conservation and tree-orientated slogans, which later adorn their homes. Rice with moringa or sesbania pod usually follows.

The charisma of this movement resides in its appeal to the under-privileged children and youth, who become instruments of environmental education and reforestation. The members of this organization, known as Operación Convite, may be correctly described as the richest children on earth for, no matter how poor they may be, they enrich the world through the gift of life they produce with their work.

The teacher's pack describing this activity included some facts about forests and deforestation, information on the Dominican Republic pertinent to the case, an illustrated story about the children of this organization titled "A tree that sleeps by night", and samples of tree-orientated colouring sheets for mini-posters. The latter, designed by Sophie Jakowska, carry simple slogans such as "The forest loves us", "The gift of life – plant a tree today" and "Trees solve people's problems", or more detailed information for older youth and adults on "Tree that feeds us" and its high protein content.

As a comment on this case study Bernt Hauge (Norway) stated that an International Youth Reforestation Programme will be developed for 1992 as one of many projects under the umbrella of the International Forest Decade. We should aim, he stated, to hold a "work jamboree" on the island of Hispaniola, lasting 2–4 weeks, and with the participation of young people from different countries. Schools, clubs, and other organizations should send delegates for tree planting and other reforestation activities, as well as for seminars, discussions, excursions to places of historical and ecological interest, singing, dancing and drama for greater cultural enrichment (see p. 252).

There is a need for a study to make decisions as to the selection of reforestation sites, and species to be planted, as well as other tasks such as irrigation systems, cleaning up the shores, building something (e.g. club houses) that will remain as a lasting memory of this jamboree.

La Isabela, on the Atlantic shore of the Dominican Republic, where in 1992 the replicas of Columbus' ships will arrive, ought to be the principal site of interest. Since it is in dire need of reforestation it is already the concern of the new Conservation for Development Clubs forming in the area of Luperon. These clubs, inspired by the call from the new president of the International Union for the Conservation of Nature, Dr Swami-nathan, are known in the Dominican Republic as "Laureles de Quis-queya", and were started in July 1985. Together with the "barefoot children" of various grass-roots organizations already involved in reforestation action, these clubs will take an important part in the preparations for 1992.

The second sample of children-orientated activities taken from the modular plan was also presented in the form of a teacher's pack consisting of all the necessary information, instructions and text for the production of an ecological play entitled "The Flight of the Flamingo", inspired by the wildland fire on one of the islands of the Archipelago of Galapagos in 1985, which forced a colony of these birds to flee from danger across the sea. The plot of the play involves a group of young adult flamingoes, with one old lame bird among them, that carry on the activities of daily life on a muddy bank at the water's edge. It is time for courtship, pairing, building the nests, and eventually laying eggs and raising chicks. But nesting is not possible because of a nearby wildland fire, which forces the young flamingoes to fly away across the sea to another island. The old flamingo cannot fly and perishes in the fire. Mother Earth acts both as narrator and as collective conscience, thus adding the dimension of community involvement to group and individual performance. The script is based on nature studies provided in the pack, and combines humanistic and scientific disciplines with artistic expression.

The script was written especially for the children of India, a country which is the home of large colonies of the Greater and the Lesser Flamingoes, but is meant to be "open" for change and adaptation. The participants and the educators must decide on the depth at which each of the issues of the play should be explored. Such an adaptation was presented to the workshop by a group from Aditi School in Bangalore.

The activity is meant as a game, a performance, a form of entertainment for parents, students, and the community at large, as well as a teaching instrument. It is intended to develop a greater sensitivity towards the living world for which we must learn to care, and to teach how to assign values, other than utilitarian, to the environment and to natural resources.

The teaching staff and children of Aditi School presented *their* version of the play, just as any teacher can do to suit particular needs. At this workshop they performed in a limited space, hence they had to modify the scenery, but they used somewhat more elaborate costumes and appropriate musical selections on tapes to accompany dance sequences.

The Aditi School version combined the sequences on awaking and feeding into one unit. The script modification produced a statement in which Mother Earth addresses the plants: "Breathe, breathe, so the air is clean and fresh", shifting the emphasis from photosynthesis as a food-producing phenomenon to oxygen production, which is correct, but should not be referred to as "breathing", which could be confused with respiration. The dialogue of the feeding flamingoes omitted "funny" remarks about flamingo chicks being fat (which is true), but this version introduced another interesting detail. Since all the children, small and older, were to participate, the modified script introduced both the greater and the lesser flamingoes, both species living in harmony in large colonies in North-Western India. This introduced another dimension, the concept of food-sharing, and a message about moderation in the use of natural resources. The Aditi script included a decision on the part of the flamingoes as to where to feed in view of man-caused damage to the environment. The relation of carotenoids in the diet to the bright pink colour of the flamingo feathers was handled in a way that appealed to the young girls in the group, as was the "flirting" in the "more than two" sequence of the play.

There is some obvious anthropomorphism in the original script and in the Aditi version, meant to help people identify with the plight of the flamingoes. But the allusions to the horror of extinction, or destruction by fire were somewhat mitigated. The message of Chief Seattle, an American Indian, was omitted, appropriately for this age group. The last two sequences, Smoke and Flight, were combined in strikingly beautiful choreography, and there were interestingly attractive costumes for the children representing fire. The acceptance of death by the old bird, the need for survival of the species, and the comments of Mother Earth on death as a return to nature seemed compatible with the local way of thinking. The last word of the original script "You must help as you have pledged", were substituted with a more direct "You must have the will to do this", directed at the audience. The child carrying the sign "Is this the end?" produced the impression that the play is open for discussion.

The script, and the accompanying instructions, were meant to be used in the workshop and modified by the participants for children of different ages and cultural background. In the Bangalore Conference we had a sample of what teachers and children can do within a relatively short time allotted for rehearsals. We are grateful to all the teachers, the children, and especially to Mrs Anne Warrior, Principal, for making this performance a memorable experience for all the participants.

Perhaps we might add the statement of David Hancock from his book *Animals and Architecture* (1971): "Man is the only animal who both laughs and weeps, for he alone sees things not only as they are, but as they could be." Most of us felt deeply moved as we saw the children perform.

V. Gangadharan of Homi Bhabha Memorial Science Teacher's Library of Senior Cathedral School in Bombay described how song and dramatization are used to bring knowledge about medicine to the people, and the message about the importance of trees for water supplies, for villagers in their different languages and in the official language of India.

Dilnavaz Variava, representing the Save Silent Valley Committee of Bombay, described how traditional "Katakali" dance and song performing style is used in the State of Kerala to transmit environmental, health and science information to the villagers during the annual caravan for Science and Technology as Instruments of Social Progress. Dance, drama, poetry and music are used to convey environmental messages in a 37-day marathon march from one end of the State of Kerala to the other, crossing 300–400 villages on a 6000 km route. This caravan is an outgrowth of the people's movement that was instrumental in preserving the integrity of a very important wildlife area through raising consciousness.

Puppetry, traditional in some parts of the world, is another form of performing art that may be used to enhance the environmental message. In India it is taught in puppetry workshops for teachers at the Vikram A. Sarabhai Community Science Centre in Ahmedabad, where, as Jayshree Mehta reported, children also perform plays on water, rain, trees, and other environmental topics. Puppets are also used in conjunction with camel cart shows, which serve as village communicators during 2–3 days in each place. Recently, in the Dominican Republic, a 16-year-old boy organized a puppet theatre and adapted the text of a children's book *Amigos del Cocodrilo* (Friends of the Crocodile), which he presents at different conservationist events.

5

Special Approaches to Non-formal Environmental Education of Children: Integrating the School and the Community

Workshops emphasized the direct contact and interaction between educators and children, and stressed the need to recognize certain approaches that extend the action of the school into the community.

Environmental science, as it is frequently taught, is replete with examples of the consequences of our "ecological crimes" and presents the future in apocalyptic terms. While this may have a salutary effect with the adult public the approach is not advisable with children.

Elstgeest (17), Hauge (25), Hass (24), and Jakowska who chaired the workshop, all favour non-formal education. Instead of confronting children with global environmental issues which they are incapable of resolving, this approach stresses issue-related, community-rooted, action- and service-orientated programmes that integrate the sciences and the humanities with aesthetic experiences, and permit the children to participate in community projects, rather then being told about them or performing "environmental exercises".

Thus, Elstgeest speaks in a special way about this:

> Environmental education is not a matter of telling the children *about* it. It is necessary to use the unique environment of every child as a source of information, as a ground for learning, a mine of wisdom. Only then can we expect our younger children to accept the responsibility for the earth they share with others. When this feeling of responsibility becomes ingrained in their personality, they shall be able to carry it into their adult life, when our problems become theirs.

225

Huang Min-Yung (27) from Beijing, China, where love of nature is considered a virtue, stressed the aesthetic and social values in the special approaches to environmental education of children. Chinese children are guided through positively orientated personal experiences into the appreciation of the relationships of water, air, sounds, and people. They are given information about the beneficial birds and insects that protect the crops, about the negative and positive environmental factors that affect human health, and they are told about the vibrations that are both the source of musical sounds that make people happy, and a source of noise that makes them irritable.

Environmental education of children, besides using the scientific experimental approach and the traditional audiovisual methods, must include more subtle ways to influence their character and their thinking through activities such as planting trees and flowers, and beautifying the school yard and the classrooms. Attractive study and teaching aids are an essential element for the aesthetic ingredient of environmental education. Bernt Hauge (25) was very explicit in his insistence on preparing children for adulthood and parenthood as an essential feature of a responsible environmental education. Educators must recognize that they are dealing with people who hopefully will learn to live and to love, to carry on a culture, to find their role in society, to achieve self-respect, to take on responsibilities, and eventually become the parents of a new generation.

Understanding depends on real experience, be it learning how to read and write, to master a foreign language, to swim, or to use an axe. The same applies to social experiences that teach one how to live in a society, in harmony with others, to understand one's own value, one's place and role in the community. Children must be given every opportunity to interact in a natural way in society, outside the school, in order to gain this kind of understanding.

Unfortunately, as Hauge pointed out, school in the Western world continues to keep children segregated by age and subject to a rigid curriculum. School keeps the children away from productive work and from direct contacts with nature. School, as it is now, seems to imply that all this is not important and that children are nonentities, who are not needed and whose background is of no interest to anyone.

Under these circumstances, should the child's environment outside the school fail to compensate for these curricular deficiencies, it would be a very serious matter. Life in and out of school must be seen as complementary, and there has to be a way for co-operation. Both are environments for growth.

Care must be taken to make children feel needed and loved, in an age-integrated setting, where they have tasks and responsibilities. In such a setting children should be guided towards an understanding of their parents' role in society, and of the functions of the family and of society.

They must come to grasp their own identity and beliefs through contacts with people of other cultures, and through the exploration of beauty, diversity and plurality on every level.

An environment for growth must give the children an opportunity for fantasy and curiosity; for play, exploration and discovery; for hiding away, meditating, and dreaming; for inventing and for building. And, as for understanding nature, nothing is more important than experiencing the ways of primary and secondary production, the steps from nature to product, and back to nature again. The direct experience with nature that shows children their role and permits them to interact with nature is better than any formal lesson on ecology for developing a feeling of responsibility for the environment. It is for these reasons that natural sciences and social sciences ought to be taught together.

The school has much to learn: not only to respect and to value life and learning outside the classroom, but to care and be responsible for this form of education. The school must learn that both environments are the most important textbooks, and it is only fair to expect that the school should want these to be as good as possible, and want to become an integrated and an integrating part of society.

Environmental problems require more than knowledge, or even an understanding that permits people to argue and to discuss them. They require preparedness for the challenges and tasks of a responsible group of adults who will be the parents of a new generation. Thus we should carefully examine ourselves as an interesting part of the environment, as representatives of science, technology, politics and education, that children view as part of their very own environment. Are we good enough to be interesting textbooks from which they can learn?

Bernt Hauge insists that as environmentalists we must do more than teach and be accessible to children. We must make an effort to learn more about them and their situations, to make their interests and rights our own interests and the dominant part of our studies, with the highest priority in our work. We must also see our responsibility for the knowledge we produce and for the way that it is used. We must work against what is bad and in favour of what is good for children, world-wide.

A number of participants described their experiences and interactions with the boys and girls from the high-school division of the Poornaprajna Educational Centre in Bangalore, with whom they established person-to-person contacts during the days preceding this workshop at the suggestion of Bernt Hauge. Some adults from Western countries were surprised at the relative maturity and discipline of these youngsters, and at their candid form of expression on matters of mutual interest. The children answered various questions posed by the participants and listened carefully during meetings, but were a little reserved in expressing their opinions, as would be expected under these circumstances. There was a cordial feeling between the adults of different nationalities and these English-speaking children of India.

The participants cited some school and out-of-school activities that involve the children in their countries in real environmental projects. As anticipated, some of the more interesting ones came not from the "curriculum powers", notably the USA and the UK, but from less developed countries such as Mexico, Ghana and the Philippines. In Norway intermediate school students carry out projects on the use of water, garbage disposal, etc., with the co-operation of their families and of the community including various of its institutions, municipal and central governments, private enterprises, and civic groups.

But Hauge also feels that young people have to be exposed to experiencing in some way the needs of countries other than their own, especially of those that are geographically and culturally removed. North–South and East–West linkages are opportunities for much-needed positive action. He cited specifically the case of famine and civil rights struggles in Africa, and reforestation of the island of Hispaniola (see p. 220).

The European Community Environmental Education Network Project, reported by Frits L. Gravenberch and Jacques van Trommel (see also p. 60), also encourages teachers to help students carry out community-based studies such as the assessment of the quality of air or water, and other pressing community issues.

In the same vein, Gary W. Knamiller (see p. 157) insisted that in the developing countries all environmental education must be issue-based and must focus upon the principal human needs such as nutritious food, fuel, clean water and sanitation, health care, adequate housing and demographic pressures.

Another case history, in which school can generate activities in the service of the community was presented by Helmut Hass (24a). He stressed that the young need more than objective knowledge to be motivated towards a commitment with nature. In his own words: "The search for self-realization in individual freedom may easily come into conflict with the demand of the natural and social environment. This conflict, however, disappears as soon as the individual perceives himself as a *part* of this environment: the 'object' environment is taken over as a personal responsibility, a prerequisite for self-determination."

In present-day society children are faced with controversies about environmental aims, and situations arise where rationalists are as dangerous as highly emotional persons or those who, as doers, demand action at all costs. An imbalance of thought, feeling and action may lead to catastrophic environmental results. But with children one may exploit positive values in the structural framework of environmental education because of their innate awareness of the principles of order.

One must logically aim at action starting in the pupil's personal sphere, with change of habits, e.g. saving energy in one's home, rejection of a throw-away mentality, etc. The action may extend to improving or repairing the local environment, at school or in the community, and spreading eventually to the public at large. Such environmentally positive ideas and actions must be given public exposure with the hope that others will adopt them as their own.

This "output phase", or conscious action on the part of the students, becomes an experience with lasting educational value, preceded as it must be by a "process phase" in which knowledge initially acquired in the "context phase" is fortified with research and discovery, carried out in small groups to encourage teamwork as well as independence.

Pupils pick out an environmental problem, analyse all the relevant newspaper reports from the local press, follow up with questionnaires at community level, question themselves in brain-storming sessions as to their own understanding of the situation, make their own on-site observations, seek out the opinions of the experts and of the representatives of the public, and become familiar with all the related government agencies and non-government organizations. They also become involved in public discussions where they share the results of their findings with others, and take conscious action in decision-making processes and in the execution of the projects.

It is not possible to include all the short comments made during the workshop, some describing very interesting experiments in education. But the workshop results may be summed up in the statement of Joyce Glasgow of Jamaica, West Indies, who, speaking of syllabuses, states that a non-formal education system is indispensable.

M. A. Partha Sarathy (41) summed up the ideas with a reasonable degree of optimism (see p. 351).

6

Environmental Education and Coexistence with Protected Wildlife

Special approaches to environmental education are required when there are conflicts between community interests and conservation needs. Such are the problems of populations which must establish new criteria for coexistence with natural resources that were traditionally theirs to use but are now declared under protection.

People who live on the edge of national parks, reserves or wildlife sanctuaries, or who are used to hunting species now on the endangered list, suffer considerable hardships in the absence of appropriate alternatives for subsistence, and may face a cultural crisis when their way of life becomes interrupted.

In other instances the traditional way of life is threatened by progress, e.g. the construction of a dam with all its consequences. Often the people concerned are the last to realize that their way of life is doomed, with the rest of the web of life being sacrificed for development or profit.

Cecil J. Saldanha, conservationist of Karnataka State in India, points out that environmental management is for the people and has to be achieved with the people. The community becomes the measure of success of environmental programmes as it tries to establish the basis for coexistence and respect for protected wildlife. It is strengthened when the community can contribute in some way to the change in attitudes towards wildlife, rather than just complying with wildlife protection laws imposed by the government.

Two cases illustrate these situations; one from Canada and one from India. Kathleen Blanchard (8) described a recent educational programme on the remote North Shore of the Gulf of St Lawrence in Canada, an economically depressed area with a high level of unemployment, where food and other supplies must be brought in by ship and aircraft. This paper has already been referred to on p. 67, and appears on p. 369.

The Bandipur National Park is another example showing how coexistence with protected wildlife may be achieved.

The Bandipur National Park, located in Karnataka State on the Mysore plateau, comprises a wilderness zone of 523 sq km, a buffer zone of 260 sq km, a tourism zone of 82 sq km, and an administration zone of 1 sq km. It is managed by a staff of 6 Park Wardens, 20 Foresters, 103 Park Guards and 8 Park Watchers. Each Park Guard is provided with an assistant known as a Tracker, who accompanies him and helps in apprehending smugglers and poachers, and fights fires during the summer.

M. A. Partha Sarathy made some pertinent comments that served as an introduction to our field visit there. He pointed out that India has a large inheritance of nature awareness, with worshippers of trees, tigers, and elephants, and many social and/or religious observances with an ecological meaning. There are also familiar sayings such as the one (Dasaputra) likening a tree to 10 good sons, since a tree provides 10 important needs of people: food, fodder, fertilizer, fibre, fuel, air, water, soil, shade and beauty.

In India it seems easier to get people back to nature, and the trip from the city to the countryside is never too long. All species in India are in crisis, if not endangered, and the younger generation realizes that their own life is threatened. And India has the added problem: it needs to communicate in so many languages.

In the media there is now less interest in "sensational wildlife" and listeners ask for more nature programmes on radio and television. This may explain why people come to science centres, nature camps or to the National Parks, which in India, unlike those of Africa which are geared towards the foreign tourists, are orientated to serve the local public.

Naturally, the measure of success of nature camps and similar non-formal education is determined by the subsequent contribution or participation in environmental activities. The Nature Clubs and camps have been organized by WWF-India, first for the English-speaking pupils, but since June 1984 tribal children from rural schools at Bandipur have been enrolled. A 3-day Nature Orientation Workshop was given ahead of that for rural teachers. The significance of this cannot be overestimated.

These tribal children live with their families on the outskirts of the National Park, where the largest predator, the tiger, has been saved from extinction through the energetic co-operation of India and international conservation organizations starting in 1973–74. The presence of this predator is an occasional threat to human life and wandering cattle from the neighbouring villages. Other carnivores include leopards, wild dogs, jungle cats, small Indian civets, and mongooses.

The park also harbours herbivores that were in the past available for hunting to the tribesmen, including elephant, chital, muntjac, sambar, gaur, wild boar and others. The bird and reptile fauna is also varied and rich. The reserve consists of Southern tropical moist mixed-deciduous and Southern tropical dry deciduous forest types, with teak dominant among rosewood, sandalwood, laurel, bamboos and others.

The establishment of this National Park required the relocation of forest villages of Gundre and Banur, which were inside the Reserve. During 1978–79, 41 families with 120 head of cattle were relocated at Hosalli and Gendathur. Each family was given 4 acres of land in a cleared part of the District Jungle and a just compensation. Six cattle camps existing in the Park were uprooted in 1976, and the vacated fields and gardens now serve as meadows and provide good grazing grounds for wildlife. The cattle from the nearby villages are barred from entering the reserve for grazing. In spite of this the carnivores occasionally prey on stray cattle belonging to the villagers, and in such cases the owners receive compensation. Cattle destined for the slaughterhouses in Kerala are forbidden to cross the Park on foot to prevent the spread of foot-and-mouth disease and other ungulate diseases to wild herbivores.

Experience has shown that where human needs are given attention, conservation efforts can be successful. Elsewhere in India attempts to conserve habitat without considering the needs of the people who live nearby often failed. Wildlife managers have realized that National Parks and Reserves have no future unless the people who live around such areas are reasonably well off, i.e. they must have home, enough food, decent clothing, and education for their families.

In other words, the objectives of conservation and social reform are two sides of the same coin. Keeping these points in mind, efforts are being made to foster an awareness of the importance and benefits of wildlife reserves among the surrounding communities, through a non-formal nature education programme.

Rural school children living at the fringes of the reserve are brought to Bandipur by park vehicles and taken around the reserve to show them trees, wildlife and birds. They are also told about the importance of flora and fauna and their role in the maintenance of nature's balance, and how that is responsible for human survival. They are shown films on nature and wildlife before returning to their home village. So far 1380 children have participated in this programme. It is hoped that it will indirectly influence the parents not to be antagonistic toward the forests and wildlife.

Rural youths and members of village communities who undergo training in nature education workshops are appointed by the park authorities as "Honorary Park Wardens" to enlist their co-operation. Nature education to members of the tribal community may mean a change in attitude that will help nature serve them better. The park also provides the local villagers with work such as deepening and desilting water holes, weeding and maintenance of roads and fire control. Some tribesmen are employed as fire watchers and for anti-poaching squads. Villagers are taught to adopt certain devices to scare away wild animals rather than to use guns and explosives. The park is building an elephant-proof trench along the periphery abutting the cultivated fields, which also prevents the cattle from entering the reserve.

These and similar practices that make the villagers feel the concern of the park authorities for their welfare and development are very important in the process of achieving environmental awareness.

Our own visit to the Bandipur Park left an overall impression of excellent organization and planning. Our hosts were most solicitous for our personal comfort. In the tourism zone, before departing, we could see families coming and leaving the education centre, all with the same look of people who feel they are doing something important. We came back enriched.

7

Public Awareness Activities in India

Sálvano Briceño served as rapporteur for a workshop dedicated to case studies on public environmental awareness activities from the host country. These were presented by T. N. Khoshoo, Jayshree Mehta, and Dilnavaz Variava. For some details we drew upon the written materials submitted by the speakers.

T. N. Khoshoo (32) (in a paper which is also cited on pp. 25 and 401), stressed that education is an investment of the highest order, and that environmental education in particular must be promoted because our whole life-support system and survival depend on the way we manage our natural resources.

Environmental education must be extended to those who are most needy and to those living in remote rural areas. For them the problems that plague Western societies, such as acid rain, are not a major issue because the monsoon rains seem to wash it out, but clean drinking water, latrines, garbage disposal, fuel for cooking, food, fodder and shelter are some of the urgent necessities.

Most educated people in India recognize the need for environmental education, but few have had actual experience of working in remote rural areas, with tribal people and with slum-dwellers, where they also encounter additional language barriers. In schools, environmental education cannot be a separate subject matter in the highly overloaded formal curriculum, but should rather permeate all subjects. The central Department of Education and the school authorities in each State have to make their own decisions. However, primary school headmasters must be first sensitized to environmental needs because they have the power of the spoken word and authority in the community. Their help must be enlisted before we talk of any conservation practices and sustainable development: it is necessary to create awareness through real-life education aiming at all, including the lowest level of the illiterate.

It is important to understand that in India being illiterate is not synonymous with being uneducated. Illiterate people often participate very effectively in community affairs and communicate through traditional dance and song forms, puppetry, etc., during festivals and other community celebrations. They are able to establish personal contacts, which are essential for creating environmental awareness. It is necessary to recognize the value of the various traditional forms of transmission of culture which may prove fruitful in environmental education. But emphasis has to be given to the individual (person), to children, youth, and women.

Tribal people also deserve special attention in the environmental effort. They do not denude the forest because the forest to them is what water is to fish. They produce low-yield but resistant low-demand crops. Their traditional existence is closely bound to natural areas that also deserve protection.

Handicapped children and youth in general must receive practical environmental education and become involved in an appropriate form of conservation and development efforts. Youth in India has literally "embraced" the Chipko movement, meant as a protest against felling trees. In the State of Karnataka, where the conference was held, the movement is called Appiko, which in the local Kannada language means the same, i.e. "hug" or "embrace". The movement has contributed to a greater emphasis on reforestation by people at large.

By educating the children we educate a new generation, but we must also bring the environmental message through techniques that permit "learning by doing". We must provide public opinion with proper data on conflicting environmental issues, use the mass media, train administrators, make lawyers understand science and technology, and seek international co-operation. Most of all we must motivate the highest levels of leadership. The late Prime Minister Indira Gandhi was very sensitive to conservation needs and reaching her on any specific environmental issue was an assurance of success.

Jayshree Mehta (39), joint director of the Vikram A. Sarabhai Community Science Centre in Ahmedabad (see p. 397), described their approach, which follows the philosophy of its late founder whose name the Centre bears:

> The development of a nation is intimately linked with the understanding and application of science and technology by its people. An ability to question basic assumptions in any situation is fostered by probing the frontiers of science. It is this ability rather than an empirical hit-and-miss approach which proves most effective in tackling the day-to-day problems of the world.

The core of scientists and professionals who formed this highly motivated group felt that new ideas in science and mathematics education should be tried out, and they set out to develop new teaching–learning aids for formal and non-formal programmes, for students and teachers. But for more than a decade the Centre has been involved in programmes of environmental education and awareness for pupils and for the community at large, in an effort to make science a living meaningful experience, developed against the backdrop of the local scene and patterns.

Ahmedabad is often called the Manchester of India, with half of the country's textile mills located there. People pose questions such as: Can we avoid pollution without stopping our textile mills? Why is our river dry during the major part of the year? Why is our river dirty? Why do we have desert plants around us? What sort of insects eat away cotton flowers? What can be done to improve the shanty dwellings? People who pose such questions, children and youth, families and teachers, from rural and urban areas, visit the Centre daily. They are exposed to a variety of educational approaches, and seem to develop interest, ability, and motivation to appreciate, understand, and conserve nature.

The experience of the past 15 years suggests that combining formal and non-formal educational activities is useful, but it is necessary to develop a prolonged individual interaction. It is important not to expect that all programmes will be successful, but basically, in order to produce any observable change in society, programmes must be done in depth and for a long period of time. Village communities require different approaches, such as the use of puppeteers rather than audiovisuals, or the camel cart instead of a bus for a mobile resource centre. A live snake show proved quite successful, proving to people that most snakes are not harmful: those who saw the show no longer tried to kill them.

An interesting case of misunderstanding due to lack of communication was reported by Mehta. At a rural school, after a flood, one of the boys said that "we must cut all the trees because trees bring rain". Ensuring that the message comes through correctly requires a lot of planning, the right type of communication skill and a follow-up.

As to experiences with real environmental problems, Mehta cited the instance when Lake Kankaria in Ahmedabad became polluted by toxic wastes. Although all life was wiped out in the lake, no action was taken against the offenders owing to insufficient public support. The vegetarians did not feel affected by the fish kill and the newspapers did not continue with the story since "they were not paid to print it".

While this happened two years ago, recently in Ahmedabad the government rescinded on building a five-star hotel in an area with more than 300 trees. This was possible by building up public opinion through various media and is a successful example of public awareness. The hotel will be built in another place without destroying a wooded area.

The Centre co-ordinates a project to evaluate the pollution of the River Sabarmati, which happens to be one of the most polluted rivers in India, with the hope that the sampling will lead to a possible action plan.

A tremendous educational effort is required to make people understand the inter-relationships between them and their natural environment. Such programmes are effective for those who visit science centres or national parks and sanctuaries, for they are already motivated and become more sensitive to environmental problems with proper educational input. Local action groups are also very important because they are economically, socially and emotionally attached to local issues and problems.

The Saving of the Silent Valley (p. 355) presented by Dilnavaz S. Variava of Bombay Natural History Society, is a classical case of environmental education in action.

This was one of the most important and motivating workshops of the Conference. People from other countries were encouraged to find out more about the Indian experience which was considered a very important one for environmental education. It was pointed out during the discussion that the United States, with King Valley experience, has similar problems in facing construction of such major dimensions. It is crucial to know how to say "no" to such big projects but with a positive approach, helping to look for other solutions and other alternatives, instead of just opposing the project.

It has been pointed out that religion and tradition may be used to motivate people for ecologically positive action, as was done by the Forest Protection Society in West Bengal, where the "Deva" concept was invoked to protect individual trees by declaring them sacred.

The Bandipur National Park, already described, also offers a rich programme of environmental education and training for environmental awareness. A comprehensive non-formal nature education programme was drawn up especially for the benefit of the rural communities living around the reserve. It correlates its activities with international events, such as Year of Forests, IUCN's Man and Biosphere Reserves, World Environment Day, World Forestry Day, Kenya Wildlife Tourism Week, International Year of Youth, and Republic Day.

As to Nature Camps, these are aimed at rural and urban audiences consisting of environmental science students, photographers of wildlife and birds, naturalists, wildlife lovers and environmentalists, tourist guides, travel agents from tourist organizations and travel agencies, representatives of hotels involved in tourism recognized by Karnataka State, planners, decision-makers and executives, rural women, the general public, and those who can trek in the forest.

Such well-programmed encounters with nature not only provide personal experience and knowledge, but also help to nurture love and concern for wildlife among people in all walks of life, and in particular among the young.

8
Ethics and Environment

John Smyth served as rapporteur for this session, one of several in which members of the environment group joined with those of another group. The workshop aimed to identify ethical issues which people need to be made aware of in order to develop a teaching approach.

A leading speaker took the issue of chemicals in the environment as a means of exploring social responsibility, the equation of industrialization with pollution, the reaching of decisions without sound knowledge, the global effects of chemicals and the need to pay heed to popular wisdom.

Dr Thilla Chelliah, of the University of Malaya, defined the aims of economic growth in terms of quality of life which must include a healthy environment. Participatory attitudes were required among all citizens. She distinguished between ethics (relating to how people treat the environment) and social responsibility (the accountability of managers).

Fr C. J. Saldanha of the Indian Institute of Science in Bangalore described a case study of a mining operation in Goa. Ethical decisions might seem obvious, but could be argued either way.

Participants were then divided into groups and asked to discuss examples of environmental issues in terms of their ethical dimensions, considering how they might be packaged for teachers in secondary schools, the methods that might be employed and the sort of encouragement that might be given to use them. Examples included a dam, the nitrification of lake water, a power station, a mining operation and deforestation.

We report here on the work of one group as an example of the procedure followed. This group decided upon a 1956 dam project that posed, after the event, certain questions of ethics and social responsibility. The case involved a dam built to produce electricity to be sold to a neighbouring country. Although scientists were included in the decision-making process, the project was decided at national level and without any involvement of the population affected by the project.

For teaching material the group decided to produce a fact sheet with as much information as possible, and with as much accuracy as possible, assuming limited access to some official data. Some of the facts were to include:

1. the location and physical characteristics of the project (size of the dam, volume of water, electric power generated, etc.), with maps and plans;
2. former characteristics of the land (geology, soil quality, previous uses in agriculture, etc.) and of the water systems that were affected by the project;
3. background information on the negotiation methods employed and the involvement of national and foreign interests;
4. economic benefits to the country where the dam was built, to the foreign country and/or foreign companies, as well as to the population displaced by the project;
5. social costs of the project in terms of health problems, including "river blindness" and emotional and mental illness resulting from displacement of the population;
6. cultural costs of the project in terms of alienation produced by unfamiliar housing conditions, in a strange environment provided by the government, and the loss of community identity, customs, traditions and way of life;
7. value of this case as a lesson in retrospect in terms of the need for community involvement, people–government relations and communication, the role of compromise and settlement, and the existing means to correct the environmental and social damage caused by the project.

This group proposed to leave the fact sheet "open-ended" to encourage investigation and further fact-finding (e.g. oral history) on the part of the students, and to leave the methodology to the initiative and creativity of the teacher.

A site visit, if possible, and/or a slide show would help familiarize all the persons concerned with the area under study.

The following points arose from this and other groups in this workshop:

1. the need to expand into every possible discipline;
2. the need to give teaching freedom;
3. the question whether the teacher should be neutral or devil's advocate;
4. the need to generate activity;
5. the possibility of role-playing;
6. the need to generate alternative solutions to provide democratic decisions;
7. the need to provide both qualitative and quantitative data (considering the status of this as science);
8. the obligation to avoid driving solutions in one predetermined direction;
9. the importance of starting off questions of ethics from issues in which children are themselves engaged.

We are gradually coming to realize that human awareness of natural beauty stimulates the formation of environmental ethics. As Richard Cartwright Austin points out (*Environmental Ethics*, **7**(3) 197–208; 1985):

> We experience beauty intuitively: it is an affecting experience which motivates thought and action. The experience of beauty gives us a stake in the existence of the beautiful. Ecology can explore the relationships of natural beauty scientifically: it may be a science of the beauty of the Earth. The beauty of the world is necessary for its survival. Beauty is manifest in the interplay of interdependence with individuality, yielding diversity. The most beautiful relationships are those which recognize diversity, support individuality, and empathetically span the distinctions between beings. The sense of beauty is not a luxury, but a distinctive human vocation.

Psychologists have identified Man's basic animal and social needs, but there are also human needs, of a higher order. The best society aims at fulfilling these needs.

9
Health and Environment

Health is usually defined in negative terms as the absence of disease, but it can also be viewed in positive terms as a full development and achievement of life. Since the options and the limitations for this are determined by the environment, there is a need to consider jointly health and environmental education, as was done in the workshop devoted to this topic.

Gerhard Schaefer from West Germany introduced the "Total Human Health System" as a concept showing that human health depends on the interaction of five factors: the body, the natural environment, the social environment, the personal mind (including the conscious and the subconscious), and the transpersonal transcendent "self" (the religious dimension).

He presented the results of an analysis of the leading biology textbooks for health and environment-related contents, showing that body health is the principal concern in most Western societies, except in Canada where major coverage is given to the natural environment. In Japan, on the other hand, the social environment receives major attention. He also showed how the most frequent associations given to the key-word "health" differ in countries such as West Germany (where it has a strong "disease-orientated" connotation) or the Philippines and Japan (where it is more "ease-orientated").

The question of how health is defined, as a "state of . . ." or as a "process of . . .", and other similar questions, were explored through the "burr-model" with a tripartite structure consisting of the name, the logic core, and the associative framework. Although educators lack the basic understanding of what is biological equilibrium and health, they recognize that both are dynamic processes of continuous equilibration, which compensate for the disturbances of life. An associative framework permits us to explore attitudes and often reveals the effects of a negative education in respect to health and environment in Western countries, which produces a kind of "pollution of the mind" caused by mass media and advertising.

Gerhard Schaefer feels that there is a great need for positive health education and for positive environmental education, both starting from the notion of life developing at its best. Only at a secondary stage should there

S. JAKOWSKA

be reference to the negative aspects. Through this kind of education the students might develop and maintain a positive picture of their world which would give them imagination and motivation to find solutions for their health and environment problems. At this time, in West Germany, the study of association profiles indicates that there were practically no associations of health and environment, either in the physical (natural) or the social part. A corresponding investigation on the key-word "environment" also revealed a negative associative framework, i.e. destruction- and threat-orientated. There were also no noticeable associative bridges with "health", suggesting that in West Germany at this time Environment and Health are apparently not connected with each other on the level of spontaneous reactions.

Helmut Hass, also from West Germany, reported that associations gained from little children about the environment of a *specific* living being (e.g. dog, bird or man) were more positive than negative, judging from drawings made by the children. Apparently for small children at the primary level there is a certain *order* in the environment of a living being which they regard as positive. The awareness and the understanding of the complementarity of an organism and its environment, which represents a "system of higher order", is the main objective of environmental education.

Hass carried out a psychological study with the semantic differential (polarity profile), a special bond-association test where students must make choices between pairs of strongly emotive words, e.g. beautiful/ugly. When "man" was given as a key-word, there was a strong positive correlation between "order" on one side and "healthy, safe, valuable, good, friendly, happy, beautiful" on the other. This correlation continued through all the age groups, although the absolute values decreased during puberty (15–16 years old), and increased again afterwards.

A teaching model was designed to show how the concept of "order" (or "disorder") may serve to connect or to "translate" the general principles from the abstract quantitative thinking of the scientific world to concrete, qualitative daily-life thinking in more colloquial terms.

Both speakers pointed out that in many curricula the motivation lies in problems with strong negative tones and dealing with disorder in nature and in society, which may lead to avoidance and fearful expectations in children that need a basic trust in the world. The pre-scientific feeling of order shown by children must be developed in a positive way. We need a basic trust in the creative power of man and in the capacity to preserve and to develop the world, by seeking to discover and to understand the *natural order*.

Questioned during the discussion as to whether the concept of "order" is appropriate for the development of positive attitudes towards health and environment, since order to one person may mean disorder to another,

Gerhard Schaefer pointed out that this relativity is only superficial, and that there are specific orders with a higher priority to survival and life, such as those listed as his 12 principles of life on which to base positive health education. Denying this would mean denying the fundamental difference between the living and the non-living world.

He defended his "Total Human Health System" as a holistic rather than a reductionist approach to health and life, since the sub-systems proposed are open systems, and infinite as a causal network, and 11 of his 12 principles are formulated on a high level of generality, i.e. in terms of systems theory.

As to the reliability of the word-association test which he used, it was admitted that experts in linguistics may be needed to interpret fine connotations and to solve semantic problems.

The attention of the workshop participants was again drawn to the children's health and environment magazine called *Pied Crow* (see p. 59). Also of interest is the fact that in some African countries primary school children learn to prepare a life-saving physiological solution, using water, salt and sugar in correct proportions by making paper measuring-cups of specified dimensions. Science, mathematics, and health studies are integrated into a concern for one's own brothers and neighbours sick with diarrhoea.

10

The Presence of Children at the Bangalore Conference

Many years of experience went into the preparation of some of the workshop materials. It is significant, inspiring, and perhaps even auspicious, that a number of people from different national and professional backgrounds coincided in their views about what the main object of their attention as environmental educators should be. They presented cases, dissimilar, and yet so very much alike.

The children stood at the forefront of strong position papers. Their presence at the conference, which was not anticipated by the organizers, became so urgent, so important, that some of the participants became obsessed with the need to include them in all the major activities.

The arrangements were made by M. A. Partha Sarathy and put into practice a week before the conference by Bernt Hauge and Sophie Jakowska, who made several visits to two teaching centres in Bangalore and established close relations with teachers and students during their normal daily school activities. Thanks to the co-operation of the principals, Mrs Anne Warrior of Aditi and Mr L. V. R. Iyengar of Poornaprajna, it was possible to plan the participation of the children and select those who would make special contributions.

Nine-year-old Rohini Sachithanand of Aditi School addressed the conference plenary session dedicated to the environment theme with the words of Bernt Hauge, harvested from the depth of his own experience as teacher at Ugla School in Trondheim, Norway. The day was close to the 40th anniversary of Hiroshima:

Good morning　　　　　　　*I'm a child.*
Good morning　　　　　　　*I represent the children,*
Good morning　　　　　　　*children of all colours,*
　　　　　　　　　　　　　　all over the world.
Didn't you expect me to come?
It's me this conference is about!　*Look at me.*

Do you think I'm beautiful?
All children are beautiful!

Do you think I'm unique?
Do you?
All children are unique.
We are not a category.
Every one is unique.

Didn't you expect me to come?
I am the future!
It's me this conference is about!

Look at me.
Do you see me?
I'm a girl.
Girls are as important as boys.

Are you innocent?
I'm innocent.
Can you say the same?
Are you innocent?

Do you remember what happened
40 years ago?
40 years ago in Hiroshima.

I am afraid.

Can I trust you?
Can I trust you?

Who contacted me
before this conference?
Me or another child?
Tell me.
Which of you contacted a child
before this conference?

Are you afraid of children?
Your homework for this conference
is:
to find a child to talk with,
and to follow into her world in
Bangalore.

What does she do?
What does she feel?
What does she think?

Your homework is to learn to know
me.

Let this be your homework,
always before making a decision
to learn to know me.

These words set the mood for all the child-orientated workshops. Children, whom the conference organizers did not expect to come, became true participants, the most important delegates.

Another girl, of the Poornaprajna Educational Centre, read some reflections of Bernt Hauge in which he urges a dialogue between the educator and the pupil as essential to the learning process, with an insistent refrain: "Who ought to learn?"

It was at this workshop that the participants reported their impressions on the interactions they had with the high school students who chose to be their companions during the conference, and to exchange views on life in and out of school, their interests, concerns, and hopes for the future.

The children of Aditi School, with the help of their teachers, prepared with great care a performance of an ecological drama "The Flight of the Flamingoes" written by Sophie Jakowska, through which they became both the subjects and the agents of environmental education (see p. 221).

The pupils of both these schools represented urban well-to-do Bangalore families. However, during the visit to the Bandipur National Park the delegates had an opportunity to come in contact with some children of rural India. These were the tribal children, whose parents live and work in the perimeter of the Park. Unlike those in Bangalore, these children could not speak English or Hindi and not even the language spoken by most people in the State of Karnataka, but they had no trouble communicating with their eyes, smiles, and gestures the trust and the friendship they felt towards this group of strangers.

These children are not "environmental illiterates". India has a large inheritance of nature awareness, and trees, tigers, and elephants are worshipped. But in today's India all species are in crisis, if not endangered, and the younger generation realizes that their own lives are actually threatened. Thus a great part of educational emphasis of the national park programme is on the people who live near such nature sanctuaries.

In spite of the fact that the structure of the Conference had already been decided at the time that children's participation was proposed as an integral and indispensable feature of certain workshops, "this conference was blessed with the presence of children", as Sophie Jakowska stated at the closing plenary session. And she went on to say:

> Has it ever occurred to you as educators that children are becoming an important yet powerless majority?
>
> In many countries children are *used* as instruments for environmental destruction, forced by their elders into preparing their own doom. Shouldn't these children rather be equal *partners* for conservation, working towards a greener and healthier world, so that *their* children may live in it some day?
>
> Last, but not least, let the children lend us their hidden spiritual power, nurtured in some parts of the world by age-long beliefs and traditions of life in harmony with nature. Let the children lead us in a moment of prayer for *our* reconciliation with nature, a prayer for peace, at the same moment, all over our plundered planet. And may hope rise that through our efforts as educators, and by working together as *partners for conservation*, we may leave a better world to those who look up to us for guidance.

In community-based environmentally positive action, the youngest teach while being taught, and the adults learn while teaching. The process becomes a source of constant individual and collective interaction that releases all kinds of hidden creativity, stimulates performance, and makes life more meaningful for all as the community draws closer, within its own contexts, towards environmental culture, our last hope for survival.

11

Conclusions and a Guide For Action

The following statements express conclusions and guidance for action as drafted in Bangalore.

THE PLACE OF ETHICS, HUMANITIES AND THE ARTS IN ENVIRONMENTAL EDUCATION OF CHILDREN

Ethics is now an inseparable element of environmental education, meant to prepare people from an early age to make appropriate value-judgements. Combined with religious and tribal traditions, such education must draw upon the cultural heritage, seeking out beliefs and practices that have an ecologically positive meaning.

To reinforce and sustain the positive attitudes, typical of young children, we must avoid starting environmental science with a list of ecological disasters, pollution problems, radiation dangers and such, but rather nurture an interest in nature and love for the living world. This was very aptly reiterated by many delegates.

Developing the affective part of a positive attitude may benefit from:

1. The input of ecological history and the treatment of natural resources as part of the national heritage.
2. The exploitation of the best elements from the humanities and the arts in environmental education (literature, plastic arts, music, dance, folklore).
3. The encouragement to writers, painters, sculptors, composers, and performers to learn about environmental problems and to place themselves and their talents at the service of conservation.

NEW TRENDS IN ENVIRONMENTAL EDUCATION

The most profound new trend we can read from the contributions is *action-orientated* school education. A corollary of this is an emphasis on *co-operation with others*. This can give new learning possibilities, more effective action, better motivation, and transform this form of teaching into a lasting part of the school's programme.

Usually the partners in this co-operation will be found within the community, e.g. municipal and national government, non-government organizations, commerce, industry, workers' unions, the religious groups, cultural organizations, social clubs, etc.

In some cases school may become a major resource for short-term actions, as in drought catastrophe in Africa, or in long-term international projects, such as the International Forest Decade.

CONSERVATION FOR DEVELOPMENT THROUGH ISSUE-RELATED EDUCATION

There is a general agreement as to the educational value of grass-roots movements, both urban and rural, that generate ecologically positive action and an improvement in the quality of life in response to some acute or chronic problem.

When such a problem is solved through an enlightened intervention of those involved, the effect may be both lasting and multiplicative, since it increases overall awareness.

The delegates felt a commitment to encourage in their home countries ecologically positive civic action and to provide professional assistance, and when necessary, to address the relevant international organizations for information, consultation, and support.

EDUCATION FOR SHARING AND MODERATION IN THE USE OF THE NATURAL RESOURCES

The finite nature of world resources and the limitations of science and technology should be presented in a realistic way to people in both the developed and the developing countries. The need for sharing and moderation in the use of the resources should be encouraged as a condition for achieving sustainable development.

OPERATION NEW WORLD 1992

The following very specific proposal was made by Sophie Jakowska.

In recognition of the historical and cultural significance of the 5th centenary of Columbus' discovery of America, to be celebrated in 1992, and the serious deforestation problem faced by the countries of the New World, the delegates propose to:

1. Encourage all government and non-government organizations to counteract deforestation by joining in their respective nations the International Forest Decade 1990–2000, and working in anticipation of this memorable occasion.

2. Start a reforestation campaign on the island of Hispaniola, shared by the Dominican Republic and the Republic of Haiti, as soon as possible, and continue this process through the rest of the continent, country by country, in the order of their discovery after 1492.
3. Plan a conference in Santo Domingo, Dominican Republic, with a theme relating environmental issues to the historical, social, and cultural background of the various nations of Latin America.

MULTIPLYING THE EFFECTS OF THE CONFERENCE

In the hope that this conference will lead to action as well as to a publication, the participants proposed the following suggestions for multiplying its effects:

1. Home-directed feedback, i.e. information on activities to be made known through the mass media of the home country.
2. Action programmes entrusted to delegates for further elaboration and execution in their home countries: projects, teaching aids, and publicizing the conference spin-off.
3. Regional and North–South, East–West conferences for further discussion and application of the new trends in environmental education.

IV Tertiary, Professional and Vocational Environmental Education

In this Part the first three papers introduce the ideas underlying the papers and workshops. There follow country-based papers and one issue-based paper, and finally some of the main conclusions and recommendations that arose from the workshops.

1

Introduction
Environment in Technology
and Engineering Education

CONRADO BAUER

THE CHALLENGE OF THE ENVIRONMENT

By dominating his natural environment, man has, since the dawn of time, attempted to create healthy surroundings in which human skills, intellect and spirit can be developed to their highest potential. This has propelled growth and consumption of goods and energy on an exponential curve, and threatens to destroy the equilibrium of nature, and to jeopardize the destiny of mankind.

Some visualize, as a result, a tragedy of collective and total destruction, brought about by a nuclear conflagration or by excessive genetic manipulation. Others imagine the less rapid but increasingly worrisome advance of environmental deterioration with its attendant destruction of our planet's capacity for endurance which could bring us to the point of no return.

Man's ability to understand and dominate has developed simultaneously with the power to debase and destroy. On the one hand there has been considerable progress in understanding the processes of nature: the macro- and micro-cosmos, the earth's homeostasis, the life and energy cycles and behaviour of ecosystems. On the other hand, demographic and techno-logical explosions and the depredation and pollution of natural resources have dangerously weakened or eliminated many of the factors that make human life pleasant, or even possible, on earth.

The process by which man has tried to survive by protecting himself from nature's threats has brought him to a crossroads at which he is the dominator as well as the destroyer. He must now consider whether he can survive physically and spiritually in a ravaged natural environment or even without nature at all. The moment has arrived when Man's behaviour must be modified to defend nature. Man must search for a dynamic and creative balance in which the interaction between man and nature will favour the life-giving exaltation of both.

If we take into account that this is happening at a time when there is an almost opulent minority and a destitute majority, where a large part of the world population is plunged in underdevelopment and where hunger and misery cause havoc, we must admit that finding a safe path to a positive future will be very difficult. The magnitude and the ever-increasing speed of the processes involved make it imperative not to err along the way.

THE OBJECTIVES OF THIS PAPER

The above scenario makes it necessary to revise all aspects of the present human condition. We must seek constructive criticism from all sectors of the world and inquire what each region, each country and each individual can do to correct the dangerous course we are on and avoid the destruction which lies ahead; a danger which defies us with its ethical, philosophical and political implications. How can we motivate the people of the world to take concrete steps toward strengthening solidarity and love among men, to promote harmonic integration with the environment, and simultaneously to preserve our own free will which is the essence of human dignity? How shall we advance and improve, within the bounds of justice and security and without threatening our future with irrevocable destruction?

These dilemmas preoccupy a growing number of people and have inspired important movements and actions of preservation, particularly during the last two decades. Well-known thinkers, scientists and politicians, acting individually or through civic and other organizations, have made recommendations on the subject and have promoted specific programmes. Nevertheless, the persistence and seriousness of the existing problems demand a redoubling of concerted efforts. On the one hand we must arrive at a correct diagnosis of the evils – their importance, their causes and their possible evolution. On the other hand, courses of action must be found and executed to overcome these evils.

A major premise of the Bangalore Conference was that improved education in science and technology provides the soundest base for decisions toward a better future and the satisfaction of human needs.

SCIENCE, TECHNOLOGY AND ENGINEERING

Although science does, in a sense, embrace all systematic knowledge, we consider it important to note certain differences between "science", "applied science", "technology" and "engineering".

Although all four are closely related and interact reciprocally, we can categorize them according to the pre-eminence of certain objectives and motivations, whose extremes – often superimposed – are truth and usefulness. Thus we recognize that science starts with the search for truth: it discovers, investigates and critically and rationally organizes data. Applied science in turn projects the scientific methodology and discoveries of science in search of their practical uses. On the other hand, technology using scientific or traditional knowledge, invents objects and procedures which modify the environment and human habits. It recognizes a practical but generalized aim. Its characteristic "products" are prototypes. Finally, engineering responds to the demand of socioeconomic activity in the physical environment; the engineer selects the scientific discoveries and the technological inventions, adapting and transforming them with genius and creativity, to solve practical problems. Sometimes, while creating, he may make scientific discoveries and invent new technologies, but his prevailing mission, when practising engineering, is to apply technology to concrete matters, to give effective and acceptable answers to his "client" (a superior, an organizational entity, or an independent person).

The predominant activities engaged in professionally by an engineer are: to plan or design systems or objects, to produce processes, working methodologies; to direct and administer their physical fulfilment; to put them into operation; to correct and perform maintenance; to transfer knowledge; to train and lead people; to measure and control; to rate goods. The engineer is the great selector, fulfiller and evaluator of the technology associated with the physical world; he gives advice and projects and directs its utilization to respond to human needs.

Summarizing, we may state that science investigates and discovers, technology invents, and engineering fulfils.

The attempt to respond to real or perceived needs directly related to the environment often identifies and brings together significant sectors of the technology and engineering communities. This suggests the possibility of developing parallel methodologies for the academic education of those who, aiming to obtain results which have a physical expression, will devote themselves to both engineering and technology.

But education for science is different in rigour and style, putting emphasis on investigation and it differs even more from engineering and technology education when it deals with the social sciences rather than the basic sciences.

Science moves from the local to the universal, while engineering, due to its eminently practical and fulfilling characteristic, interacts directly with the possibilities that uphold it, and the needs it must serve, and, consequently, with the cultural, socioeconomic and geographic circumstances which lead to its implementation. This determines a close relationship between engineering, environmental transformations, and the development of nations. The fulfilments or omissions of engineering are the main causes of the modification (improvement or deterioration) of human surroundings. It is therefore necessary to appraise the function and the social and environmental responsibilities of engineering, as well as the ethical considerations of its professional exercise from this point of view.

Finally, quoting A. V. Baez (*Innovation in Science Education Worldwide*, Unesco, 1976) we can complete the comments on the engineer's role in this way:

> [I]t is the engineer who applies existing knowledge to the solution of problems. He . . . has to exercise creativity and to make recommendations based on value judgements. He has to generate a product for a client who has the power to make the final decisions on whether to accept his recommendations, but he can nevertheless exercise some social responsibility because he should base his recommendations not only on technical factors of engineering . . . but on other and equally important grounds, including economic, safety, aesthetic, legal, diplomatic, psychological and cultural factors.

ENGINEERING, ENVIRONMENT AND DEVELOPMENT

Engineering and the technology which upholds it, interact with the entire physical surrounding. Based on a scale of increasing intensity of human intervention, we can distinguish: (1) nature, or the natural environment; (2) the environment modified by man (regions affected by primary exploitation, the construction of infrastructures, artificial forestry, etc.); (3) the environment urbanized or constructed by man (cities, industrial concentrations, etc.). In each case ecological science analyses the respective ecosystems composed of matter, both that which is inert and that consisting of living matter and beings: plants, animals and man himself, and the bearing resources (earth, water and air), which are driven by flows of energy and information, and by life itself, fulfilling the great cycles of production, consumption and decomposition.

These analyses show a fundamental difference: the natural ecosystems maintain their own dynamic equilibrium consuming energy from the sun and regulating their production and decomposition cycles; the more diversified their structures the more stable their behaviour and the better their resistance to exterior aggressions which gradually transform them. On the other hand, as the intervention of man grows, specialization increases their vulnerability; the input of additional, artificially supplied energy needed to uphold the dynamic of the ecosystems increases; the amount of goods which must be incorporated (food, fuel, agricultural or industrial substances) increases; residues and pollutants causing deterioration of the environment unless treated or eliminated (also artificially, with additional consumption of energy) are also greater. These processes, especially in urban concentrations, demand massive extraction, production or transfer of substances and energy which deteriorate the natural environment over vast regions, altering its balanced performance, as well as progressively damaging some aspects of the quality of life in cities themselves, all the more when badly managed.

These considerations lead to a conservationist strategy for development: obtain a maximum profit from the natural processes, protect their variety, respect and imitate nature. This is not only for ethical reasons, because nature is our "road companion" and, if we are believers, God's creation, but also for practical and even selfish reasons: the more we let nature work, the less men and women will have to work and the more stable will be the consequences.

From this we draw our first synthesis of recommendable action for all men, and particularly for engineers: reduce harm to nature to a minimum and increase the yield of the production processes to a maximum so that the consumption of energy and inputs, as well as the generation of polluting residues may be reduced to a minimum. Any optimization strategy must, of course, incorporate requirements basic to human nature: health, welfare, social solidarity, beauty, etc.

This challenge is so complex that it greatly outweighs the objective of searching for procedures that may temper the cascade of energy degradation, and lead to a variety of sometimes confusing interpretations.

Ever since Carnot, entropic fatalism has announced with scientific rigour the destruction of life as we know it. Now there are other "fatalisms", without rational justification, whose limitations unsettle the conscience. Some people maintain that any technological activity is contaminating. These people abhor all technology and push the responsibility for all ills upon it. Others trust that technological creations will solve all problems. They face the squandering of resources and pollution with indifference.

We believe that an engineer's education should thoroughly analyse these two extreme opinions and warn against their ambiguous and paralysing consequences, striving for constructive and prudent action, which may make the need for a just development compatible with the preservation of the positive aspects of nature and the rational administration of goods.

The above challenge demands, and will demand much more in the future, for engineers enough knowledge and capacity for analysis and observation to enable them to distinguish true from false, fundamental from accessory and beneficial from harmful. It should also enable them to organize information and experiences to make possible a correct understanding of causality which will permit them to anticipate and control consequences. We seek, therefore, an education that pushes engineers to search for the most adequate solution for each problem, considering economic, social and environmental aspects, circumstances of time and place, and technological and human possibilities. These considerations should relate not only to the finished and operating object (building, machine, process, consumer goods, etc.), but also to all the activities inherent in the period of its execution until it is used or sold, as well as during its performance, operation and maintenance throughout its useful life.

The "environmental" viewpoint requires that each creation of the engineer, besides solving a specific problem, favours, or at least does not damage, the life scope in which it is set or for which it is destined. This must be foreseen, and any possible damage or "contamination" controlled during the aforementioned stages.

With these aims we can name as "polluters", in a broad sense, all kinds of substances (solid, liquid or gaseous), living beings (humans included), energy (in all its forms) or information, which damage health or man's well-being or unsettle ecosystems in a way that, in the short or long term, could produce negative effects on mankind. According to the analysis suggested above, we can distinguish three stages in the contaminating effects of each human achievement: (1) Those which take place during the application of the system or method of manufacture of the "object" (first generation pollution); (2) those taking place while using the product (second generation); (3) those occurring when the "object" ends its useful life and turns into a residue (third generation pollution): for example, the production of a car, its performance and its final destiny when obsolete, or the manufacture of an agrochemical product, its use and its residual effects, or agricultural tasks, sowing and production, and the harvest and its destiny.

Those concerned with improving man's living conditions (quality of life) expect the engineer and producers of technological accomplishments and all physical modifications to take into account and reduce contamination risks to a minimum. They should thoroughly study the environmental impact of their projects, examining all their consequences, at the same time carrying out cost effectiveness and cost benefit analyses, to choose the best alternative, rejecting all those incompatible with existing regulations.

We also expect these analyses (and the engineer's attitude) to ensure that the projects are useful to man and his environment, and that the contamination generated is related adequately to the self-purifying capacity of nature. In addition, we contemplate among other equally significant factors: (1) not to unsettle the landscape's beauty and, wherever possible, improve the natural or artificial surroundings (urban), preserving at the same time the historic and cultural heritage; (2) rationally use natural resources, substances as well as energy, not squandering the non-renewable ones; (3) consequently, to take into caring consideration animal and plant life, nature conservation, genetic diversity, the complexity that protects and enriches life; (4) conveniently control processing or elimination of residues produced by the metabolism and the usual activities of man and other living beings; (5) adequate use of information and feedback in a fertile dialogue. Technological decisions must not be authoritarian; options must be explained and evaluated, consulting the groups and people who will be affected by them, respecting their opinions and free will, within the established legal frame.

We must not forget that engineers and technologists, as members of a complex society, may give their opinions and advice, but society as a whole must decide on the extent and limitations of technical action, through the organization and legal rules it may have adopted.

In other words, engineering and technology must serve men, the men of today and the men of the future, in all geographical areas, always subject to their regulatory limits. To respect this they must not do what is prohibited, but must apply their ethics and responsibility to recommend and do what is best.

THE ENVIRONMENTAL EDUCATION OF ENGINEERS

For general reference we note the following points:

1. Within current institutions, habits and legal norms of his working scope, the engineer must establish himself as an agent conscious of healthy and sustainable socioeconomic development, co-operating toward a wise management of nature and the improvement of the human environment. This should be borne in mind when including environmental subjects in an engineer's education, carefully weighing all the aspects of his own geographic and human scope.
2. As a creative professional within an expanding discipline, the engineer must possess scientific quality and methodological strength, always being open to learn what is new.
3. An engineer should never abandon specialization: he should be thoroughly familiar with at least a portion of the professional spectrum which will allow him to apply correctly the updated and selected know-how to solve concrete problems with the greatest efficiency, within tight security margins, capable of adapting and innovating in order to face real situations that may arise. Once he is conscious of his mission to generate sound development, this specialization will allow him to accomplish satisfactorily certain aspects of his environmental responsibility: economize in the use of raw materials and energy, use available resources best, reduce the generation of pollution to values compatible with established rules and propose modifications and controls, when noticing anything that could disturb the objectives of nature conservation and improvement of the human surroundings and of the quality of life.

We hope to obtain the following from the environmental education of all engineers in the "graduate" stage regardless of their specialization: (1) a basic knowledge of and a special sensitivity and responsibility toward environmental problems: (2) a capacity to understand reality from systematic viewpoints and to integrate it with criteria of synthesis, complementing the classic analytical methods of the exact sciences; (3) a predisposition to discuss and work in a team with other professionals such as physicians, ecologists, chemists, geographers, biologists, anthropologists, psychologists, sociologists, architects, lawyers.

This implies that engineering studies should include topics like ecology, natural resources, ecosystem dynamics, contamination, which could be taught during the first cycle (their intensity would vary according to the knowledge gained during previous studies, e.g. preparatory and high school). On the other hand, the "professional cycle" should include, within each subject and activity, concepts referred to their respective relations with: use of resources, the working environment, appropriate technology (for the regional circumstances of the students), clean technology (with minimum consumption and residues), activities requiring interdisciplinary treatment and methodologies of approach, evaluation of environmental impact, cost–benefit analysis, cost effectiveness, risk assessment, etc.

Finally, in the postgraduate cycles, these subjects should be complemented or intensified according to the characteristics of each speciality. In all cases the teaching methodology must stimulate the creation of a real community-orientated mentality for the professional, beyond the search for "technical prowess" which is often absurd. This requires close contact with the socioeconomic environment and the local community, development of ethical conduct, social communication capacitation, teamwork on matters relevant to the regional medium, etc.

We think it possible that a branch of "environmental engineering" could adopt some working methodologies similar to those of other specialities, as was suggested by M. Hubert Curoen, Minister of Research and Technology of France, in his statement addressed to the World Industry Conference on Environmental Management (Wicem, Versailles, November 1984). As an example: engineering design of resistant structures with synergistic and probabilistic considerations that guarantee their stability, within tolerable deformation limits and minimum utilization of materials, made compatible with the required durability and with a security margin in accordance with the type of possible failure evaluated and with the damage that this failure could produce.

With this kind of methodology in mind, conveniently adapted to the extreme complexity of the problem, it would be possible to train engineers as coordinators or members of interdisciplinary working teams to manage the environment. They could analyse the characteristics of ecosystems, and design their utilization and conservation limits.

The discussion about employers or clients who hire engineers to be "docile and apolitical" is beyond the scope of this paper. However, we are convinced that environmental education should provide engineers with sufficient expertise and opinions about problems to enable them to reject any complacency with projects or actions which may conspire against the health, security and well-being of the population, or against the preservation of nature, even though the country's laws may not condemn them as crimes. To that effect, a "code of ethics", establishing what should not be done where environment is concerned, should be set by their professional organizations and respected by engineers. This conduct will be one of the main signs of success for the environmental education of engineers.

Finally, in spite of recognizing that the hierarchy of values is mainly transmitted by exemplary behaviours (beginning with those of teachers and professors) environmental science could offer assistance in distinguishing and stimulating discussion of central questions in the area of values. Axiological education would benefit from and reinforce the attitudes of respect for life and nature developed by environmental education.

FINAL CONSIDERATIONS

In this paper, following the definitions of the United Nations' Conference (Stockholm, 1972), we have analysed the education of engineers, considering the surroundings as "human environment", and consequently we sponsor the pursuit of a better quality of life for man on Earth, his planet. The concept of "quality of life" includes health, housing, nourishment, work, education, culture, recreation, use of free time, the appropriate surroundings (healthy and pleasant), and diversity, open options and the dynamic balance of man and environment.

However, in order to avoid misunderstandings, we must point out that this anthropocentric viewpoint aims at improving the quality of life of all mankind and not only privileged countries or groups. Therefore, we can under no circumstances permit the claim to protect, preserve or improve the environment to be considered a luxury, an extravagance or the whim of an élite or a hedonist dream. We must encourage the prudent administration of reserves which allow us to uphold development and life and the preservation of the variety and beauty of nature. We must insure that the urban habitat protects human physical and mental health and stimulates creativity, work and recreation. We are sure that all of this constitutes a programme for the benefit of all men, and for the continuity of the human race on Earth. When we say "the benefit of all men" we are thinking not only of the poorest among them, whose living conditions must, of course, be substantially improved, but of "all people", as a guarantee and support of social harmony and peace. It is a proposal, with a profound social content of international solidarity, which summons us to fight and to put under control or eliminate the main causes of environmental deterioration: war, misery, ignorance and natural disasters. At the same time, further threats consist of human neglectful activities, like the excessive and ravaging exploitation of natural resources and the contamination of water, air and soil, aggravated by the dizzying growth of population during the last century.

The advance of science and technology, and the marvellous capacity of the human race to adapt itself to changing situations have allowed us to overcome and/or overlook many of those problems. Besides, the material conditions of well-being and comfort, intellectual stimulation, and the duration of life itself have increased over the last centuries together with people's progress, particularly in the more developed countries. Even so, it is undeniable that this has been carried out at the cost of suppressing or excessively limiting the traditional possibilities of enjoyment and spiritual expansion of mankind.

But another limitation has emerged: the occupancy of the earth space has reached such a degree that the marginal advances of a policy of expansion of economic frontiers are extremely expensive. Perspectives for an extension to outer space which might solve these limitations are not for the foreseeable future. Even leaving aside relevant ethical matters, these sole, almost elementary circumstances of space availability make us realize that population and consumption growth, which doubles the global demand for energy, food and other goods every 15 or 20 years, cannot be upheld indefinitely by the earthly resources within the thin layer of the biosphere, further attacked in its support capacity by this "ravaging" style of "progress".

Only a sound environmental development, which delays the pace of increasingly jeopardizing events, can offer the possibility of re-establishing the natural dynamic equilibrium of the biosphere, and the possibility of a sustainable future for all of humanity. It could be accomplished if we find educational methods and living experiences to change human goals and behaviour, affirming such values as fairness and harmony.

We must not curse science and technology, or reject them due to a mistaken management of values. This misunderstanding could aggravate the misery of poor countries and reduce the opportunities for development. On the contrary, we must direct and apply them correctly with a criterion of social and environmental justice, coupled with common sense. I think we can put our trust in them without falling victims to the cult of the rational, which could lead us to scepticism lacking a superior goal. We are convinced that science and technology can solve many or perhaps all the material problems we face, particularly those of production of food and energy. We are further convinced that human intelligence is an inexhaustible resource. But even so, the question is: will their findings be made and implemented in time?

Since we believe in our cleverness, conservation instinct, intelligence and transcendent destiny, we trust that mankind will overcome those crises without incurring a tremendous cost. We cannot accept that the human race should repeat the destiny of some species which have disappeared from earth, or that humanity should forget the lessons of history and the fate of outstanding civilizations that faded out as a result of their mismanagement of the natural resources which sustained them.

The task and responsibility of finding new formulae for development and living together with nature falls on all men. But they are even greater for those people, like engineers and technicians, who perform particular decisive functions in the transformation of the physical world. The evolution and utilization of technology will play a role of increasing importance in determining the future of mankind.

University-level Environmental Education

GEORGE R. FRANCIS

ESSENTIAL FEATURES

Four main questions must be addressed in planning for any university-level environmental education programme. The essential characteristics of any one programme can be summarized by the way in which these questions have been handled. Case study examples should address these explicitly.

1. The Educational Objectives

Educational objectives can be defined in terms of awareness, knowledge, skills, attitudes and commitment, all of which are necessary to deal effectively with environmental issues. Each programme will have its own balance and emphases in terms of which objectives it is striving most to achieve; if skills are uppermost it will likely be viewed as a training programme rather than an educational one. The appropriate balance and emphases also depend on the assumptions made about (a) what the students already know and know how to do, i.e. which objectives they have already achieved to some extent, and (b) what kinds of employment or other social roles the students are expecting (or expected) to take up after they graduate.

There are five distinct approaches for achieving these educational objectives evident in ongoing environmental programmes in universities. Much depends on how the higher education system itself is organized.

(a) A general introduction to themes, perspectives and basic knowledge about environment is given in secondary schools and/or undergraduate (first cycle) courses at university. Students then specialize in concurrent/sequential study in related disciplines and professions, or in some environmental speciality.

(b) Environmental topics are introduced as an integral part of professional and technical training at the undergraduate (first, second cycle) levels.

269

Some students specialize in the environmental aspects of a particular profession.

(c) Postgraduate courses for a mix of people with different prior education in one of the various disciplines or professions. Emphasis is often given to learning about the environmental implications related to each person's main field of study, and to developing the skills needed to co-operate effectively in problem-solving teams.

(d) Focus is on graduate level research. Students apply their particular disciplinary or professional training to some environmental research topic as part of the work required for an advanced degree.

(e) There is a deliberate attempt to create a new discipline or profession to deal with environmental concerns. Tbilisi* advised against this, but pressures to specialize in universities encourage trends in this direction.

2. Knowledge Used as a Basis for Instruction

Environmental issues require knowledge from a number of different subjects (disciplines) if they are to be properly understood, and skills from a variety of technical and professional fields if they are to be effectively resolved. There is no single discipline or technical profession which is sufficient in itself. It is also impossible to teach everything, hence some balance among all the main areas of knowledge and expertise has to be drawn upon to give the appropriate instruction.

The selection and balance of subject matter is reflected by the curriculum for the programme. University programmes commonly rely on one of three general approaches for selecting and organizing the "content" of their programmes, although there can be a number of variations and combinations among them.

(a) By "clustering" traditional subjects
   - environmental sciences, with the emphasis almost exclusively on biophysical sciences and scientific research methods;
   - environmental studies, tending to give more emphasis to human and institutional factors;
   - environmental ethics, which stress important philosophical questions of quality of life, development and environment, etc.
(b) By grouping topics under broad themes
   - environmental design, combining aspects of architecture, physical planning, landscape architecture, industrial design, etc.;
   - environmental health, combining aspects of the biomedical sciences, public health and hygiene, occupational health and safety, sanitary/chemical engineering, etc.;

*The Unesco–UNEP Intergovernmental Conference on Environmental Education, Tbilisi, USSR, October 1977.

- environmental protection or management, combining aspects of forestry, water resource management, agricultural land use, pollution control, energy conservation, protection of nature, etc.
(c) By particular emphasis given to man–environment interrelationships
  - man's impact on environment (hence "ecosystem management" emphasis);
  - impact of environment on man (hence "human ecology" emphasis).

3. Integrating Knowledge, Teaching and Learning

Environmental education because of its inherent scope (in drawing upon the natural sciences, social sciences, humanities, and applied professional specialities) has to provide some degree of interdisciplinary integration in order for effective teaching and learning to occur. This raises the questions of what kind of "integration" is being sought through the programme and what means are used to achieve it.

Three kinds of "integration" are commonly sought as follows:

(a) unity of practice, integrating knowledge and skills from various sources to solve problems;
(b) unity of the person, each individual "integrates" own knowledge and experience and develops more of his human potential;
(c) unity of knowledge, integration of concepts/theories into some larger or more "powerful" intellectual construct.

The first of these, "unity of practice", is the most common interpretation found in environmental courses. The second, "unity of the person", may be just another way of defining what education itself should do. The third, "unity of knowledge", leads into some difficult philosophical questions about concepts and theory.

In practice, environmental courses have used various means to help integrate teaching and learning, as noted below. It is important to be certain that some kind of integrating device is incorporated into *both* the instruction and the learning experiences. Interdisciplinarity can be sought through:

(a) Organizing subject matter by:
adapting existing theory, e.g. systems,
use of a central concept, e.g. "energy",
use of a core subject, e.g. ecology,
use of techniques, e.g. computer simulation;
(b) Organizing learning process by:
teamwork around some real problem situation,
in-service training, on-the-job experience,
"experiential learning", participant–observer, field studies.

4. Application to Development Issues

University-level environmental education has to deal with questions of how whatever is taught about environment should apply in the context of development. This is often done by addressing the theme "environmental management" which in turn raises the question of what specifically is to be managed through environmental management. Among an array of existing programmes, different approaches are used which focus primarily upon:

(a) Organizations whose activities impact on the environment
  - Focus is on the role of planners and managers.
  - Challenge is to identify the particular environmental components they need to know and act upon.
  - Examples: Centre d'Etudes Industrielles (Geneva), Asian Planning and Development Institute (Bangkok).
(b) Protection of the environment from impacts associated with economic production/consumption
  - Focus is on project or site specific development and how impacts can be minimized by technological innovation or remedial activities.
  - Challenge is to go beyond limitations of reacting only to each situation as it comes along.
  - Examples: Most courses in industrialized countries.
(c) Maintaining ecosystems to help assure sustainable development
  - Focus is on ecosystem structure and functioning, and on management either to prevent degradation or bring about rehabilitation of major ecosystems.
  - Challenge is to develop an effective "ecosystem approach" to management, including the "behaviour of institutions".
  - Examples: Emerging perspective in a number of countries; urged by the IUCN World Conservation Strategy.
(d) Management of socioeconomic development itself so that it is ecologically sound, hence sustainable
  - Focus is on the technological/economic processes which undermine the ecological basis for their own continuance.
  - Challenge is to "re-think development" in part to avoid this.
  - Examples: ENDA (Environment and Development in Action, a non-governmental organization in Dakar, Senegal) and other courses based on "ecodevelopment" urged by UNEP as the proper role for environmental management.

Environmental Science Education and Future Human Needs

M. K. WALI and R. L. BURGESS

In many parts of the developing world, the critical application of science and technology to pressing problems of human society is severely constrained by a lack of adequately trained scientific manpower, and the requisite educational structures to produce this necessary resource. This has been the case, particularly with respect to environmental problems, be they related to forest ecosystems, water resources, agriculture, or energy development. Consequently, a survey of educational systems, concepts, and techniques around the world can serve to identify common threads of success that can then be implemented by developing nations to build the scientific, technological, and educational cadre that will contribute to problem solution at local, regional, and even global scales.

Few events in recent history have elicited such emotional and enthusiastic response as the concern for environmental quality. These articulations have been long overdue. Burgeoning human population, overexploitation of natural resources, degradation of air, land and water quality, input of teratogenic organic compounds, unprecedented amounts of hazardous waste products – all brought a clamour for quick remedial measures.

In the developed nations, landmark legislation, intended to guard against irrevocable decisions and irreversible damage to biological resources including man, was led by the United States. However, the fulfilment of each legislative mandate posed questions never before asked, and demanded new information never before collected.

While ecosystem structure and function remain at their very core, environmental science education and research must encompass much more. The understanding of and solutions to contemporary environmental problems transcend disciplinary boundaries. They must integrate the classical and traditional scientific disciplines with the problems of technological development, of generated residuals and associated risk, of economic and social choices. Response from educational institutions to these new needs has been slow, and in some cases, not forthcoming at all.

We discuss two case studies here that we consider reasonably successful and with which we have first-hand experience. The first of these is a vibrant and dynamic graduate programme at our present institution, part of the State University of New York (SUNY) system, the largest public university in the world. The second case study comes from experiences at Oak Ridge National Laboratory (ORNL) in conjunction with Oak Ridge Associated Universities (ORAU). Together, these prime examples illustrate both concepts and methods of education and training designed to prepare students for functional roles in society that involve social and economic issues, technology development, and the preservation of environmental quality.

Formally approved master's and doctoral programmes in Environmental Science began in 1975 at the State University of New York College of Environmental Science and Forestry. The College, chartered in 1911, had been granting advanced degrees in traditional scientific disciplines for many decades, but the interdisciplinary Graduate Program in Environmental Science was an innovative thrust in response to recognized societal needs. For purposes of the programme environmental science "is the field of enquiry in which the knowledge and principles of physical, biological, and social sciences flow as systems processes within the contextual framework of unifying public policies. These policies, in turn, determine the design, the plan, and regulation, seeking mitigation of environmental problems."

The centrality of the programme mission, constituted on a campus-wide basis, lies in the "transdisciplinary education and research to foster the effective use of natural resources while protecting the environmental base from which all sources flow". The programme prepares students to deal scientifically with environmental problems and to perform as environmental professionals by stressing: (a) a multi-disciplinary approach – recognition that environmental problems require input from several disciplines; (b) a holistic philosophy – awareness and deference to the interdependence of ecosystem elements; (c) a sound grounding in at least one concentration – competency to understand and apply the principles of an environmental discipline, and with that strength interact with other disciplines; (d) a realistic experience – through internships or focused projects which provide direct interaction in economic, political, and social institutions which underlie decision-making; and (e) problem-solving tools to permit students to go beyond traditional paths.

Within the framework of environmental policy, the programme offers training in six areas of concentration: (1) Land Use, (2) Water Resources, (3) Energy, (4) Urban Ecosystems, (5) Waste Management, and (6)

Environmental Communication. These concentrations are in line with the strengths and expertise of the resident college faculty and the larger scientific and educational community of central New York. The programme has a faculty of 54 and, for the past 5 years, has averaged 70–80 graduate students per year. A total of 129 have thus far received graduate degrees from the programme, and a recent college survey revealed all to be either gainfully employed, or in the process of further specialization.

The programme fosters internships and working experience with both private and public agencies, at state, regional, and national levels. Students routinely take courses and participate in research with faculty members at Syracuse University's Maxwell School of Citizenship and Public Affairs, the S. I. Newhouse School of Public Communications, School of Management, and the College of Law. Graduate exchange programmes permit students to study at the State University of New York Centers at Albany, Binghamton, Buffalo, and Stony Brook; City University of New York; or New York State College of Agriculture and Life Science at Cornell University. A perusal of the 1984 Petersen's Guides to Graduate Study shows that there are few such programmes in North America.

The second case study, from Oak Ridge National Laboratory (ORNL) and Oak Ridge Associated Universities (ORAU), began in 1971 when the Environmental Sciences Division at ORNL mounted a vigorous educational programme at both graduate and undergraduate levels. ORNL staff members were appointed adjunct faculty at the nearby University of Tennessee, and many graduate students from the university were afforded the opportunity to undertake thesis and dissertation research at the National Laboratory. ORNL researchers regularly offered courses at the university, served on committees, and greatly broadened the range of environmental sciences available to university students. In addition, contracts with several other colleges and universities provided for paid student internships. These brought qualified master's and doctoral candidates to ORNL for periods ranging from 6–12 months, to actively engage in major projects in environmental assessment, ecosystem research, simulation modelling, risk analysis, and policy formulation.

The Environmental Sciences Division recognized its capability to contribute regionally and nationally to the education of environmental scientists. However, this was not the only goal of the internship and other undergraduate and graduate programmes. As a matter of policy, management recognized the healthy influence upon established staff members of working with and guiding bright young minds. In a word, this activity "keeps our staff young and alert". While progress toward such a goal is difficult to gauge, it is important to recognize the benefits of this interpersonal interaction. Realistic acknowledgment of this goal places students with many staff rather than overloading a few staff members with a majority of students.

A number of programmes for undergraduate student participation in research and assessment projects provide a continuing opportunity for interaction between students and staff. Over a period of several years, 30–35 undergraduate students regularly participated in environmental science programmes. Students came from established programmes of various consortia (e.g. ORAU, the Southern College University Union, the Great Lakes Colleges Association, Carnegie Corporation) or from contractual arrangements with individual institutions (e.g. Emory University, Jackson State University, University of Wisconsin–Stevens Point).

Students are assigned to individual advisors who guide them through an experiment or project associated with one of the Division's programmes. The student is required to document results in a report and to present a seminar to the other students and laboratory staff. This research participation experience is designed to expose the student to the research process; and the greatest benefit to students is frequently an improved outlook on career opportunities in research and an understanding of practical approaches to environmental and technological problems.

The Environmental Sciences Division provides an opportunity for graduate and postdoctoral research consistent with the mission of the National Laboratory. Normally between 12 and 18 graduate students were supported through contract with the University of Tennessee Graduate Program in Ecology. Students receive stipends administered by the university and are guided in their research endeavours by selected staff members, one of which serves on the student's academic guidance committee at the university. In addition, research conducted by students not requiring Division support is accommodated on a more limited basis. Several students, supported by Oak Ridge Associated Universities, University of Tennessee, and Vanderbilt University, have conducted research and assessment projects over a span of several years.

As the number of graduate students participating in research has increased over the years, so has the need for formalized guidelines to ensure the timing and quality of the research. Graduate student guidelines reflect current Laboratory and Division policy consistent with the academic goals of participating institutions. A number of graduate students were also supported through research subcontracts to various universities.

The Environmental Sciences Division is also involved in continuing education, both through ORNL "in-house" staff improvement programmes and at the University of Tennessee. The laboratory encourages continuing education by rescheduling work hours and tuition reimbursement, and provides an incentive for staff improvement through course-work.

ORAU is a consortium of over 50 colleges and universities, primarily in the southeastern United States. Originally incorporated to deal with educational needs for the peaceful uses of nuclear energy, it is expanded to encompass programmes in radiation research, medicine, environment, biotechnology, socio/economic analysis, and alternative energy systems.

In addition to organizing and implementing full-time university and continuing education courses, ORAU maintains research and educational programmes for undergraduates, graduate students, and faculty at the National Laboratory. These programmes bring participants together with staff for periods of a summer, a semester, or a full year. A major theme is the application of science and technology to societal needs, and participant selection and tutorial involvement is most often predicated on this premise.

In addition, ORAU, drawing heavily on ORNL research staff, provides a Travelling Lectureship programme. This activity makes a variety of excellent teachers and seminar speakers available to small colleges that otherwise would not be possible.

In summary, this array of innovative mechanisms has accomplished a great deal in the training of new scientists, the spread of knowledge, and the application of recent advances in science and technology to the pressing problems of human society. In developing nations, similar programmes based at existing institutions can stress the interdisciplinary nature of national problems. They can utilize the consultative expertise available through United Nations programmes and the array of non-governmental scientific institutions, and effectively break the educational and technological barriers to the continued enhancement of the quality of life for all of their citizens.

2

Country-based Studies
The Teaching of Sanitary Engineering and Environmental Sciences in Venezuela

GUSTAVO RIVAS MIJARES

The teaching of sciences related to the protection of the environment in Venezuela was, in the past, done through the presentation, in some of our universities, of the so-called traditional sanitary engineering subjects. This situation was radically changed when the many new environmental problems that appeared during the past two decades forced those universities and some other centres of higher education in the country to establish new and more comprehensive courses that could prepare professional personnel to find better and more rational solutions to the complicated and sophisticated environmental problems which had arisen. The number of such courses has increased considerably to attack the causes that are producing an increased deterioration of our environment.

A study made by the author has shown that there are seven universities in Caracas that have been offering programmes closely related to environmental sciences and that there are six other programmes functioning in other cities of the country.

Of the undergraduate and graduate programmes now being offered in Venezuelan universities, nineteen can be classified as directly related to sanitary engineering and environmental sciences, twelve as undergraduate programmes, four as "options" within traditional undergraduate curricula, and some twelve others leading to Master's and Doctor's degrees.

The teaching of traditional Sanitary Engineering Sciences in Venezuela was established in the Universidad Central de Venezuela (UCV), located in Caracas, in 1956. Before that date in this university and in the

Universidad de Los Andes (ULA), located in the southwest of Venezuela, only a few subjects within the Civil Engineering curricula were offered in that area of knowledge. These included courses such as "Water Supply and Sewerage" and "Municipal and Rural Sanitation".

Later, starting at the UCV, some additional subjects were offered toward the fulfilment of the so-called Sanitary Engineering Option, a kind of pseudo-speciality taught during the last 5 years of undergraduate studies in Civil Engineering.

In the 1960s the Pan American Health Organization (PAHO) – the regional office for the Americas of the World Health Organization – in conjunction with the government of Venezuela, established an Education Programme called "Enseñanza de la Ingenieria Sanitaria en Venezuela" (Teaching of Sanitary Engineering in Venezuela), to establish sanitary engineering teaching in the UCV and ULA Universities already mentioned and in two other Venezuelan universities: La Universidad del Zulia (LUZ), in the northwest of the country, and the Universidad Catolica Andres Bello (UCAB) in Caracas.

The optional programme in Sanitary Engineering at the UCV was included within the ninth and tenth semesters of the civil engineering course, including the following subjects: sanitary biology, sanitary chemistry, water supply and sewerage, water and wastewater treatment plants, biostatistics and epidemiology, solid waste disposal, and municipal and rural sanitation. At the other three universities the following subjects were established: basic environmental sanitation, water supply and sewerage, and a brief course related to the corresponding water and sewage treatment installations.

Lately, those initial programmes have been developed and extended to other higher educational centres in the "Environmental Sciences Programmes" that will be described in the following sections of this paper.

There are today thirteen university level institutional centres with nineteen programmes directly devoted to the teaching of environmental science in Venezuela. Four of them are graduate programmes, specifically directed toward Master's and Ph.D. degrees in Environmental Sciences and as mentioned previously, four of them in the civil engineering schools to prepare engineers in the sanitary and environmental engineering sciences.

At UCV a Department of Sanitary Engineering has been functioning in the College (Faculty) of Engineering, within the Civil Engineering School. Under the "Sanitary and Environmental" option, subjects having some relation with environmental sciences have been offered to engineering students of the ninth and tenth semesters of the course. Subjects common for civil engineering students are hydrology, applied geology, fluid mechanics, environmental sanitation, water supply and sewerage. Subjects properly belonging to the option include sanitary chemistry, sanitary biology, water treatment, laboratory for water and waste-water analysis, sanitary microbiology, epidemiology and biostatistics, plumbing, and special graduate work (a kind of preliminary research in areas already mentioned).

Under the Master of Science programme including "Water Quality" and "Environmental Engineering" a wider range of subjects is offered.

The *Centro de Estudios Integrales del Ambiente (CENAMB)* is a branch of the UCV where an interdisciplinary university centre was created to co-ordinate environmental programmes offered by the university, to investigate special environmental problems existing in Venezuela, and to offer postgraduate programmes integrally presented in the area of environmental sciences. Since its inception the centre has been working in the following programmes:

1. Environmental model to design an environmental ideogram (already accomplished). A descriptive model is under study.
2. Five critical units for the study of five existing environmental degradation problems of the country.
3. Research projects related to alternative sources of energy (other than petroleum).
4. Research projects related to the integral effect and system synthesis of the environment synergism in the Guayana Region of Venezuela.

The *School of Biology, Faculty of Science of UCV*, offers a range of undergraduate, Master's and Ph.D. programmes in general ecology.

Universidad Simon Bolivar (USB) created a Department of Environmental Studies directed toward study and research in subjects directly related to environmental sciences, particularly in the areas of biology and ecology, including introductory courses, formative courses (2nd cycle of general studies) and professional courses including two courses in general ecology and their corresponding laboratory programmes, four courses in evaluation of biology problems, and elective subjects depending on the particular interest of the students taking the graduate programme.

Universidad Catolica Andres Bello (UCAB) has a Department of Sanitary Engineering and offers some undergraduate subjects directly related to the principles of environmental protection sciences.

Metropolitan University (UM), a private university, offers courses within the Civil Engineering School and operates an air sampling station for air quality control with the Ministry of Health (MSAS) of Venezuela. This station is collaborating with the Pan-American Net for the quality of air.

The *Venezuelan Institute of Scientific Research*, a high-level educational and research national centre, has been offering a Master's Degree programme in environmental engineering. The specific areas of research are aquatic chemistry, water quality, ecosystems pollution, water treatment and atmospheric chemistry.

Instituto Universitario de las Fuerzas Armadas (IUFAN), which is at the university academic level, offers a Master's Degree programme in environmental administration which prepares graduates to study, to diagnose, to control and to evaluate environmental situations, and to look for practical solutions to the problems found in the system under study.

Universidad de Los Andes (ULA) in the city of Merida, has undergraduate programmes in sanitary engineering, ecology, forestry and environmental law. Graduate programmes are in public health, forestry sciences, tropical ecology and chemical engineering including geology and emulsions transport, animal and vegetable waste utilization, fruit and vegetable conservation and lactic products conservation.

Centro Interamericano de Desarrollo Integral de Aguas (CIDIAT) operates in connection with the Faculty of Engineering of the Universidad de Los Andes (ULA) and presents a variety of national and international courses, among them graduate courses in hydrology, hydraulic works, irrigation and drainage and soils under irrigation. Some short courses also have been offered.

Universidad de Carabobo (UC), located in Valencia in north central Venezuela, has been offering an option in sanitary engineering within the civil engineering programme (in the ninth and tenth semesters of the undergraduate programmes).

La Universidad del Zulia (LUZ) is located in the city of Maracaibo in northwest Venezuela and has been offering programmes at both the undergraduate and the graduate levels in the Civil Engineering School and the Chemical Engineering School and postgraduate programmes in environmental engineering.

Escuela Internacional de Malaria is located in the city of Maracay in the north central region of Venezuela and has been offering graduate courses in malaria and environmental health. These courses have been directed toward graduate students from engineering and medical schools and are mainly devoted to their preparation in the area of malaria control and the control of other transmissible diseases.

Universidad Experimental de Los Llanos Occidentales Ezequiel Zamora (UNELLEZ) has recently established an undergraduate course called "Conservative Engineering", requiring ten semesters of studies. These new *conceptual engineers* have been prepared to work toward a rational handling, planning, utilization and administration of natural renewable resources.

Environmental Sciences in Engineering Curricula: Reflections on the Growing Interaction between the Engineer and Society in a Developing Country

RUY CARLOS DE CAMARGO

INTRODUCTION

The aim of this paper is to illustrate the manner in which scientific and technological knowledge related to environmental problems can be integrated into formal engineering programmes in order to improve the training of engineers, preparing them not only to meet the development challenges of the society within which they live, but also to be sensitive to the environmental dangers that can result from the very process of development.

THE BRAZILIAN EDUCATIONAL SYSTEM

The formal Brazilian educational system consists of federal and private universities and colleges, federal technical schools, and the state educational system which includes state and city primary schools in addition to state universities and colleges.

The Minister of Education has responsibility for the co-ordination of the federal educational system while the various state Secretaries of Education co-ordinate the state systems. The government agency responsible for setting standards for higher education at both the federal and state levels is the Federal Council of Education. At the primary level the state Councils of Education have a similar responsibility.

Legislation establishes "minimum standards" in terms of programme content and duration at the higher education level. These requirements, established in 1961, constitute a structure "sui generis" characteristic of the Brazilian educational system and are perhaps justified not only by the country's stage of development, but also by the wide regional diversity that exists in a country of continental extension.

Graduate programmes, on the other hand, are not subject to these specific "minimum standards". Structurally they are more flexible in spite of the fact that both master's and doctoral programmes must be accredited by the Federal Council of Education.

Although the first undergraduate engineering programmes in the country were initiated in 1810, more than a century ago, formal graduate programmes in their present form, which are similar to the North American model, were started only 15 years ago.

Today in Brazil 321 engineering programmes are offered by 126 public (federal, state and municipal) and private universities and colleges. Twenty-five of these institutions also offer 90 graduate engineering programmes at the master's degree level and 35 at the doctoral level. Twenty-five thousand new professionals graduate annually, joining the almost 250,000 engineers already at work in the country.

ENVIRONMENTAL SCIENCES IN ENGINEERING PROGRAMMES

The present minimum standards for graduate engineering programmes were established in 1977 and it was then that coursework in environmental sciences was made mandatory. This core curriculum includes study in basic sciences (mathematics, physics, chemistry, etc.), general coursework (including environmental sciences) and advanced coursework in the six areas of civil, electrical, mechanical, metallurgical, mining and chemical engineering. The basic and general coursework is required for all students while the advanced class requirements depend on the student's area of specialization.

Since 1977 the study of environmental sciences has been a requirement for all engineering students in the country. Those engineers graduating within the last three years (1981, 1982, 1983), representing a total of approximately 70,000 professionals, have already received training in this area.

The area of environmental sciences as it is defined by the Federal Council of Education covers the following topics: the biosphere and its equilibrium, the effects of technology on ecological equilibrium, and the preservation of natural resources. Each educational institution has the liberty to expand this list in order to establish one or more courses that specifically cover these areas. At the same time presentation of these topics can be integrated into other courses within the engineering programmes when considered convenient.

Soon after the establishment of the minimum standards requirement that made the presentation of material on environmental sciences mandatory, the Minister of Education, on the basis of a study made by a Commission of Specialists, publicly stressed that the environmental sciences requirement constituted an important innovation in engineering programmes. Recommendations were made to help engineering schools adapt their programmes to include this type of material:

> Having in mind the aims and objectives earlier expressed it is recommended that the material covering environmental sciences should be taught in a one-semester course with a minimum of 30 hours' duration in which the following topics will be presented:

1. Introduction to biogeochemical cycles with examples of applications of environmental sciences to engineering. Environmental consequences of technological development, demographic growth and the distribution of resources. Interferences in biogeochemical cycles.
2. Major elements of ecology with special attention to the interdependence of human beings, the concept of ecosystems and application of ecology to engineering and to public health. Special ecological problems of Brazil.
3. Considerations with respect to the natural environment, highlighting the physical environment, the ecological niche, man and his place in nature, man in society, pollution and contamination, planning and protection of the natural environment.
4. The terrestrial environment with respect to the air and soil, their properties and quality requirements, the role of vegetation in the production of oxygen and atmospheric humidity, the role of vegetation and micro-organisms in the quality of the soil. Air pollution; heat and thermic comfort. Soil pollution, degradation, erosion and wastes.
5. The aquatic environment, the importance of water in the ecological environment as a heat regulator and as a source of nutrients and energy. Properties of water and quality requirements. Water pollution and methods of protection.
6. Energy and mineral resources, sources of consumption, exploitation, depletion of reserves and methods of protection.
7. Considerations concerning radiation, highlighting the various types and their effects on the environment: destruction of human beings, genetic and ecological imbalance. Levels of radiation, radioactive contamination, radioactive wastes: danger, disposal.

In the development of the outline for this course educational institutions are expected to give special attention to topics that relate to local and regional characteristics always stressing the need to protect the environment when planning and executing engineering projects.

It is always worth keeping in mind the important connection between topics relating to environmental sciences and other topics that are covered in coursework relating to the humanities and social sciences and to studies of Brazilian problems, as well as in more advanced coursework such as that relating specifically to basic sanitation in the area of civil engineering. It is the responsibility of each educational institute to take advantage of the flexibility permitted in the composition of courses of study to integrate this new material in an harmonious manner avoiding unnecessary redundancy.

Recently at a congress sponsored by the Brazilian Association of Engineering Education recommendations on material related to environmental sciences and a bibliography were discussed. Consequently, a discussion forum was opened in the *Review of Engineering Education* based on the position that "the teaching of environmental sciences should awaken within the future professional an awareness that:

1. the quality of life can be harmed by the activities of man;
2. nature is balanced within certain limits;
3. man has sufficient knowledge (and if he doesn't he should look for it) to guarantee that projects presently under way preserve life and respect the limits of nature;
4. considerations with regard to possible consequences of man's activities; the future should be based on the experience of the past."

In view of these priorities and in the context of the above-mentioned forum a new programme for the establishment of relevant coursework was proposed, consisting of the following five units.

Unit 1: Availability and Distribution of Natural Resources

With the objective of making the future engineer aware of the need for rational utilization of natural resources, recycling, and the utilization of alternative energy sources within the context of population growth this unit includes the following topics:

1. The current availability and distribution of mineral resources and of food.
2. The prospects for the future with respect to the needs of a growing population and terrestrial limits.
3. The capacity of the earth to absorb wastes produced by man.

Unit 2: Elements of Basic Ecology

The objective of this unit is to make the future engineer understand how nature is structured, how it functions, and how the activities of man affect its stability. This unit should cover these topics:

1. The biotic community; ecosystems; ecological niche.
2. Food chains and networks; interferences.
3. Biogeochemical cycles: the carbon cycle (photosynthesis and respiration), the nitrogren cycle, the phosphorus cycle; interferences caused by human activity in the balance of these cycles.
4. Energy flows in the biosphere.

Unit 3: The Aquatic Environment and its Degradation

The objective of this unit is to make the future engineer aware that the disposal of waste products into the aquatic environment not only endangers the population who must use contaminated water, but also disrupts the aquatic balance thereby destroying the biotic community. It is also an aim of this unit to alert the future engineer to the existence of techniques for the treatment of effluents and to the legal requirements with respect to the characteristics of effluents and of the aquatic environment. The topics recommended for this unit are:

1. The hydrological cycle and the properties of water.
2. Water contamination by toxic substances and by pathogenic organisms.
3. Water pollution and the process of natural repurification.
4. Legislation; patterns of quality of water and effluents; basic principles and techniques for the control of water pollution.

Unit 4: Soil and its Degradation

The aims of this unit are more limited, dealing with preservation of the soil and disposal of solid wastes. Only two topics are recommended:

1. The importance of vegetation cover in the maintenance of soil fertility; erosion.
2. Solid wastes and their disposal.

Unit 5: Atmospheric Pollution

The objective of this unit is to make the future engineer understand that the emission of certain substances into the atmosphere can significantly alter its properties. When these substances are toxic they can also endanger the health of populations that live and breathe in the affected region. Like Unit 3 this unit also is intended to make the engineer aware of the existence of techniques for the control of waste emissions and of the legal requirements for air quality. This unit should cover these topics:

1. The evolution of the atmosphere and its present composition.
2. Global effects of air pollution; stratospheric ozone; the hot-house effect; particles and atmospheric dust.
3. The effects of specific pollutants; toxicology.
4. Legislation; patterns of air quality.
5. Processes of formation, sources of air pollutants.
6. Basic principles and techniques for the control of air pollution.

It is hoped that experience acquired since 1977 can contribute to the refinement of the teaching of environmental sciences in engineering programmes. In the next few years the impact of the introduction of this new material will be monitored to learn what effect it is having on the performance of engineers.

The Brazilian Association of Engineering Education has just finished an important study on professional profiles of engineers in which an evaluation was made of the contribution that knowledge of environmental sciences is making toward the improvement of engineering activities. Preliminary results indicate significant concern with the interrelationship between engineering and the environment among civil, mining and metallurgical engineers. However, in the areas of electrical and mechanical engineering, and surprisingly in the field of chemical engineering, this concern was significantly less important. Relatively frequently engineers in these fields justified their lack of direct concern with the environment by the fact that their companies had departments specifically responsible for dealing with environmental matters. Unfortunately, this seems to a certain point to indicate a lack of professional awareness and concern about the environment.

Since more than half of the professionals interviewed in this study, however, graduated more than ten years ago, the above results are relatively promising, especially if the country's stage of development is considered. A particularly positive sign is the preoccupation with the environment demonstrated by professionals whose activities involve hydroelectric projects, mineral processing plants, quarries and foundries, in addition to those working specifically in the areas of sanitation and pollution control.

ENVIRONMENTAL ENGINEERING IN ENGINEERING SCHOOLS

Present engineering programmes in Brazil offer students six areas of specialization: civil, electrical, mechanical, metallurgical, mining and chemical engineering. Each educational institution has the flexibility to develop its own curricula based on the material specific to each of these six areas, building and expanding the required minimum coursework curriculum in order to meet the particular priorities of the school, regional characteristics, and interests of the students.

Specialized courses which do not reflect a direct expansion of the minimum core of required coursework can be inserted in engineering programmes (thereby making up the so-called "full curriculum") depending on the priorities of each institution. Those advanced courses which are characterized by an expansion of material related to the six areas in general are labelled "eclectic courses". Those which deal more specifically with material of one particular area are called "courses with specific emphasis". Finally, a third group is represented by those courses specific to a particular engineering specialization without being directly related to any of the core material presented in the minimum coursework curriculum. These are referred to as "specialized courses".

Examples of courses with "specific emphasis" related to the environment offered by six educational institutions include Basic Sanitation. An example of a "specialized course" related to the environment would be Sanitation Engineering. This course within the area of civil engineering is characterized by the presentation of the following material:

(a)   Water, Air and Soil Quality

Sanitation chemistry; sanitation biology; microbiology and sanitation parasitology.

(b)   Treatment of Water Supply and of Waste Water

Water treatment; treatment of domestic and industrial waste water.

(c)   Hydrological Resources

Integrated planning for the utilization and conservation of hydrological resources: domestic and industrial water supply, generation of energy, irrigation, water transport, fishing, flood control, recreation.

(d)   Environmental Sanitation and Applied Ecology

Water, air and soil pollution, public health problems, ecology applied to environmental and natural resource protection.

Programmes in Sanitation Engineering are relatively new, dating only from 1978, and they are only offered by six engineering schools around the country. As seen in the above outline for sanitation engineering courses environmental sanitation is stressed as much as basic sanitation.

It is worth noting that graduate programmes in sanitation engineering were established in Brazil even before undergraduate programmes. In fact in the 1940s the then São Paulo Institute of Hygiene (today the University of São Paulo's College of Public Health) initiated a graduate programme with coursework in the area of sanitation. This was followed by the creation of a similar programme by the National School of Public Health in Rio de Janeiro, today the Castelo Branco Institute of the Minister of Health's Oswaldo Cruz Foundation.

Today, in addition to the two institutions just mentioned there are five formal graduate programmes offered by universities in areas of concentration related to the environment. These programmes originate from civil engineering programmes that are dedicated to research in the field of water supply and waste water. There are also groups working within universities that dedicate themselves to the study of environmental problems in a more general way, such as the Centre for Hydrological Resources and Applied Ecology created over ten years ago within the University of São Paulo's São Carlos School of Engineering.

Recent findings of the National Council of Scientific and Technological Development resultant from a study entitled "Evaluation and Perspectives 1982" highlighted the evolution of research activities in the area of sanitation engineering in connection with the preparation of professionals. This study evaluated the perspectives for the further development of research activities in a comprehensive way, looking at many related areas of research including that of environmental engineering.

The development of research in the area of water supply and sewage systems was particularly stimulated in 1968 by the establishment of the National Plan of Basic Sanitation, whose objective is to make drinkable water available by the end of the 1980s to 100 per cent of the Brazilian population and to provide sewage systems to serve at least 70 per cent of the population. A natural evolution of research activities in this area is apparent. Initial research focused on systems of water supply and sewage collection, but with time emphasis has shifted to the control of water pollution, with specific attention given to the planning and utilization of natural resources, the fight against pollution, and the development of new techniques for the treatment of wastes.

It is worth noting the awareness demonstrated by researchers with respect to the peculiarities of environmental problems in Brazil and the need to make use of techniques which are appropriate considering national conditions. Special conditions include a vast territorial extension with low population density, abundant energy whether in the form of solar radiation or hydroelectric power potential and the availability of relatively abundant unskilled labour.

The establishment of programmes in sanitation engineering since 1978 has made possible the training of approximately 200 sanitation engineers

(1982 and 1983 graduates). Graduate programmes existing since 1971 have led to the awarding of more than 100 masters' degrees and about 30 doctorate degrees.

Although higher education programmes in sanitation engineering, and by extension environmental engineering, are relatively new in Brazil it is already possible to witness their impact not only in the activities of researchers working to treat environmental problems that result from national development, but also in the manner in which new engineers creatively design and implement projects, mindful of their environmental ramifications.

This is further reflected by the fact that numerous agencies at the state level are being established to develop research activities and standards designed to preserve environmental quality.

THE CONTRIBUTION OF SCIENTIFIC AND TECHNOLOGICAL KNOWLEDGE BEING TAUGHT TO THE ENGINEER IN ORDER TO MEET THE DEVELOPMENT NEEDS OF THE COUNTRY AT ITS PRESENT SOCIOECONOMIC STAGE OF DEVELOPMENT

Scientific and technological training related to the environment for engineers in the country has been most concerned in recent decades with those aspects that deal with basic sanitation. These concerns include appropriate techniques for water supply systems from the source to the treatment and distribution of potable water, as well as sewage systems involving techniques of collection, treatment and disposal. The collection, transport and disposal of urban trash has also been a concern.

The development of intensive agricultural activities, accelerated industrialization and uncontrolled population growth in the country's major urban centres (in particular in the metropolitan regions of São Paulo, Rio de Janeiro, Belo Horizonte, Porto Alegre and Recife) are main causes of recent environmental problems not traditionally considered a concern of basic sanitation. To deal with these problems it has become necessary in engineering education to give a greater emphasis to the area of environmental sanitation. This discipline covers topics such as methods for the management of hydrological resources (and by extension natural resources) considering not only development of their full economic potential, but also the maintenance of balanced ecosystems.

The establishment of a National Policy for the Environment by federal legislation in the past 3 years has played an important role in consolidating the research and teaching activities orientated to the solution of environmental problems, including those which affect large portions of the population, those which present high immediate risk to health and well-being, those which cause damage that is difficult to correct, and those which permit a better knowledge of the country's natural resources.

The establishment of this national policy reflected the recognition of the need in the planning of scientific and technological development for prioritizing a national policy for the area, quantifying and qualifying hydrological resources and agents of pollution, elaborating new norms and standards, and developing production processes and specific technologies to deal with environmental problems.

Several cases can be mentioned which illustrate the importance of scientific and technological knowledge transmitted to the engineer with the aim of preparing him to deal with actual and future human necessities in the country.

Initially, with respect to the relatively recent development of intensive agriculture for the production of fuel alcohol, the development of mechanized agriculture in all areas of production and the development of an industry for the processing of vegetable raw materials both stand out. Although these developments help solve the national energy problem related to liquid fuels, they also are responsible for potential threats to the health and well-being of both rural and urban populations due to the enormous volume of residues which result from these production and transformation processes. The problem resulting from the need for treating these residues has been the focus of numerous research studies and today it is possible to project viable solutions for the recycling of these wastes or for treatment adequate to preserve the equilibrium of ecosystems affected by the return of these wastes to the environment.

With respect to accelerated industrialization the implantation of the Industrial Pole of Cubatão provides an illustrative example. This pole serves as a base for heavy industry such as the steel and petrochemical industries and although it contributes significantly toward the economic development of the country's principal state, it also causes serious ecological damage to surrounding areas. In addition, the health of the local community is severely affected by consequent heavy air pollution. These problems have been the object of exhaustive research studies which have served to alert the authorities and the local community to the serious need for action to protect the environment. They have also provided ideas and techniques potentially useful for the solution of these problems.

Finally, in relation to uncontrolled urban growth, although it seems to represent a conquest for the rural population that has moved to cities in search of a better standard of living and although this influx has led to a concentration of labour that has facilitated industrial development, in reality this phenomenon will have future consequences that are difficult to predict in terms of water supply, flooding and air pollution in other areas. Again these problems have stimulated a series of research activities designed to find an economical solution while guaranteeing the necessary preservation of environmental quality. The monitoring of watersheds for the control of water quality, the substitution of aerobic processes (with the necessary reversal of energy flows), the development of models for the prediction of flooding using meteorological radar, and the monitoring of air quality and the establishment of norms and standards together with the development of antipollution techniques have all become concerns of environmental engineering.

In this way one can see the important role played by science and technology incorporated specifically into engineering training in order to provide the knowledge necessary to solve environmental problems resulting from economic development in the country. It is worth noting that the "corrective" mentality which has been generally reflected by the performance of engineers has gradually given way to a "prevention" mentality, due to the efforts made to emphasize environmental education in the training of engineers.

CONCLUSION

This summary of the evolution of the Brazilian educational system with respect to engineering education and concerns for the environment attempts to illustrate the importance given to the incorporation of specific scientific and technological knowledge into engineering programmes in the country.

Unfortunately the simple integration of new coursework itself does not insure that professionals incorporate concerns with preservation of the environment into the planning and execution of engineering projects. In spite of the positive evolution observed in engineering education in Brazil in connection with the environment, it is apparent at the country's present stage of development that there is a lack of a deep-rooted conservationist mentality diffused through the various segments of society. One of the causes for this is probably the lack of emphasis given to science and technology in the country's educational system.

Accelerated economic development in a country such as Brazil, together with the preservation of natural resources in order to guarantee an acceptable quality of life to the population, can only be accomplished together through the wise application of scientific and technological knowledge, not only to solve existing problems but to prevent future ones.

An evaluation of the effects of the new orientation being given to engineering programmes with respect to the interrelationship between engineering and the environment will be completed by the end of the decade. It will permit a complete appraisal of this new orientation and should provide an excellent case-study for countries with characteristics similar to those of Brazil.

The Teaching of Ecology to Students of Engineering at the National University of Lujan (Argentina)

LEONARDO MALACALZA

In this paper the consequence of including "general ecology" as a subject in the study plans of all UNLU courses is analysed and commented upon. Ever since 1973 there has been a common core of general studies in our university which is in the first year of study for every course. It consists of three subjects: general ecology, socioeconomic analysis, and elements of logic and systems.

The courses offered by this university are: food engineering, agricultural engineering, business administration, educational science and social development. Approximately half of our students belong to the first two categories listed. There are no significant differences in the performance of the students from different careers; those majoring in engineering show great motivation and a high level of achievement in cnvironmental topics.

The results of 2500 objective multiple-choice tests given to 1250 students over a period of 6 years were considered, all necessary information being duly recorded. Those tests were given together with the examinations required to pass the course. One was administered in the middle and the other at the end of the corresponding examinations. The required passing grades were maintained unchanged during the period under control.

The marks presented range in the scale 0–10. Successes as well as failures were included.

The subject programme includes the following topics: Part One: (I) Life and energy; (II) The biosphere and its evolution. Part Two: (III) The ecosystem; (IV) Populations; (V) Dynamics of the ecosystem. Part Three: (VI) Human environment; (VII) Human populations; (VIII) Environment pollution; (IX) Preservation and administration of natural resources; (X) Brief history of ecology.

In Part One basic elementary biology concepts are given in order to prepare the students for Part Two; the latter deals with the theory of ecology which is, in turn, necessary to interpret Part Three, related to "Man in the biosphere".

The three parts take up 15, 35 and 50 per cent respectively of the 108-hour course, which is developed in 4 months. Field and laboratory work represent 30 per cent of that time.

The grade averages obtained in each field were as follows:

Food engineering	:	5.60 (n = 242)
Agronomical engineering	:	5.32 (n = 405)
Business administration	:	5.03 (n = 401)
Educational science	:	5.20 (n = 95)
Social development	:	4.83 (n = 93)

The passing grade is over 4. Consequently, it can be inferred that the majority of the students achieved the goals of the programme; in particular those in food engineering and agronomical engineering.

The common core of general studies supplies information about the general fields of knowledge and current problems. We believe it is convenient, and have demonstrated that it is possible, for all university students to study the same topics, because this facilitates the dialogue among professionals, allowing them to understand the problems associated with those topics. Each profession should then deal with them from its own point of view, assuming that, in general, solutions are possible through interdisciplinary work groups. At the present time the environment is one such problem.

Doing general ecology before biology has proved successful in our case for both food and agricultural engineering. The idea is to place biology in a broader context, within which other specific disciplines of those fields are included.

Environmental Teaching in the School of Engineering of Buenos Aires University

JULIO C. DURAN

Courses in civil engineering at Buenos Aires University were created in 1881, and since then have expanded continuously to meet the growth needs of the country. It is at present the largest in Argentina and one of the most important throughout the world in terms of enrolment. The total number of students enlisted is approximately 10,000.

The teaching of environmental subjects was introduced in the School of Engineering due to the interest shown by sanitary engineers who extended their traditional operating field – water supply and sewage disposal – to include a wider range of environmental health topics.

A new graduate School of Sanitary Engineering developed a postgraduate course in the area of interest of the National Enterprise of Sanitary Works (OSN). By this contract, OSN was held responsible for the financial support of the school and agreed to grant scholarships to participating students. At the beginning the applicants had to be civil engineers of the hydraulic branch, but later admission was extended to engineers of other kinds.

The postgraduate programme includes academic courses in sanitary chemistry and microbiology, water supply, municipal sewage, industrial water wastes, water pollution, sanitary policies and legislation, and economy and finance of public sanitary works.

Support given by the Ministry of Public Health permitted the establishment of public health engineering postgraduate courses during a period of 7 years from 1967. Special attention was given to city and rural sanitation, sanitary education, sanitary planning, food sanitation and public health administration. The courses were discontinued when the Ministry of Public Health withdrew its support.

In the meantime an Environmental Engineering Research Centre

298 JULIO C. DURAN

(CIIA) was created, in close connection with the Graduate School of Sanitary Engineering. The objective of CIIA was the training of a team of engineers to develop technologies applicable to environmental problems caused by industries. Their scope included industrial air pollution abatement, industrial waste water treatment and the evaluation and control of the labour environment. Recently it was extended to low-contamination industrial technologies.

The activity of CIIA gave way to an integration of teaching with technological research and field work. This is of mutual interest for engineers and for the industry involved.

In the meantime, the Graduate School of Sanitary Engineering was being transformed into an Institute for Sanitary Engineering, under the supervision of the Dean of the School of Engineering.

The introduction of environmental courses into engineering started in 1974 when the Department of Environmental and Labour Engineering was created. Two new courses – industrial health and safety, and natural resources – were added to the curriculum. Experience in this case proved to be negative due to the relative lack of interest of the students, who were mainly concerned at this first stage in acquiring a more ample knowledge of basic scientific disciplines and did not yet have a wide knowledge of the specific work of an engineer.

A further reform led to replacing the course on natural resources by an introduction to environmental engineering, which offers students a wider panorama of environmental issues and is directed towards specific engineering activities.

The evolution of environmental teaching at the Buenos Aires University School of Engineering has not been the consequence of orderly planning but the result of favourable or adverse circumstantial factors. In all cases it has been promoted through the personal efforts of a few pioneers who foresaw the constant and increasing impact of technology in engineering activity on the balance of nature.

The evaluation of past experience permits correction of distortions or requirements of the teaching programmes. It can also be taken as a useful guide to planning for other institutions or schools.

Engineering "is a profession which has a mission to transform the power and resources of Nature, producing goods and services with maximum yield and minimum cost".

But in this traditional definition the sense of "cost" must be interpreted, nowadays, to take into account the different economic, social, cultural and even aesthetic values determining the quality of life.

That is why, in the environmental training of engineers, the following two different objectives must be distinguished:

1. To make engineers aware of the existence of the environmental impact

of their specific work, which can appear directly and immediately, or as a consequence of complex and subtle disturbances of ecological balance.

2. To train specialists in environmental engineering to evaluate, prevent and correct the undesirable effects of environmental impact.

Attainment of the first goal requires the introduction into all engineering careers of a course relative to the value of environmental quality and providing information regarding the negative and detrimental aspects of human activities.

In accordance with our experience, the above-mentioned course will become more effective and have a better reception when it is included in the last undergraduate year.

The training of specialists must be effected by post-graduate courses which must include a solid basis of ecology, and as a minimum the study of the consequences of abuse of natural resources, the environmental impact of development works and the evaluation and prevention of man-made pollution.

In every case engineers should be prepared to work in multidisciplinary teams. It is recommended to complement academic teaching with actual case studies.

Environmental Protection in Engineering Education

H. P. JOHANN

The protection of the environment, and of man himself, against detrimental effects of technical activities, which are ultimately of anthropogenic origin, confront the engineer with new responsibilities which he must fulfil.

New demands are likewise being imposed on technology, which has hitherto been concerned primarily with the most efficient means of producing and processing goods within the framework of industrial manufacturing operations.

A prerequisite for the fulfilment of the demand and responsibilities thus imposed is the contribution by educational institutions through appropriate instruction and research.

On the one hand, basic knowledge and understanding of environmental problems in our industrial society must be provided in order to impart a proper understanding of, and objective approach to, questions of environmental protection. This is especially vital for promoting environmentally compatible behaviour and co-operation in efforts to achieve suitable solutions to environmental problems in various private, professional, or social situations. On the other hand, new approaches must be sought for realizing operations in industry, and especially for applied technology, in order to decrease the strain on the environment and ensure the preservation of wholesome living conditions.

The engineer must be properly prepared to meet this challenge.

At present the responsibilities and activities of engineers in practice are already being affected to an increasing extent by problems whose origin is associated with environmental protection in the broadest sense. One approach for counteracting the educational deficit thereby evident is the inclusion of environmental aspects in the general framework of practice-orientated instruction in all applied engineering fields. This implies that education in the field of environmental protection should no longer be conducted unsystematically, incompletely, and randomly, but rather must be subject to the same principles as the traditional courses of study.

301

The general requirement for practice-orientated instruction implies that curricula be designed to reflect the demand imposed on future engineers in practice. A correspondingly orientated system of didactics at educational institutions must ensure optimal matching of practical requirements, on the one hand, with the objectives and contents of courses of study, on the other.

Basically, the criteria for selection and justification (validation) of learning objectives (study objectives), and for the associated course contents, are derived from the following conditions:

1. demands and requirements imposed by society;
2. needs and motivations of the students;
3. demands, responsibilities, and problems encountered in practice;
4. requirements imposed by the institution of learning, the respective subject, and the respective science.

For the field of environmental protection, many companies are currently being compelled to prepare young university graduates for operational practice by means of company-internal training and continuing education programmes, in order to decrease the educational deficit which is becoming evident in this field.

For this purpose, the previous selection of course material for engineering education must be critically examined and supplemented to conform to the altered requirements encountered in practice.

ENVIRONMENTAL RESPONSIBILITIES IN THE ENGINEERING PROFESSIONS

Through the media of the press, radio, and television, the citizen is almost continually confronted with measures and problems which are directly or indirectly associated with environmental protection. This confrontation is increasingly evident in both daily business and plant operations. Its influence on the activities of engineers working for the companies involved is especially pronounced, as has been revealed by an investigation conducted by the Verein Deutscher Eisenhüttenleute, from which it emerges that secondary activities associated with environmental protection take up to 10 per cent of company time in operational practice as related to primary activities in engineering fields, such as production, plant construction, and maintenance.

However, the investigation described does not provide detailed information on the distribution of environmental activities among individual environmental fields, such as filter technology airborne pollutants, sewage treatment, methods of processing solid wastes, etc. For mixed smelters, an approximately uniform weight distribution can be assumed for these fields of activity. In the densely populated Ruhr district noise emission has about the same importance as air and water pollution or waste disposal problems. In the case of rolling mills, in contrast, the noise and vibration emitted by the plants and products are the predominant source of emission.

From this survey of conditions actually prevailing, it can be deduced that operational problems have arisen in the environmental field, and that the engineers involved will have to cope with the situation. Operating experience shows that an adequate means of decreasing the qualification deficit has not yet been provided for solving these problems.

In nearly all companies, departments responsible for environmental protection have been established, partially because such measures are explicitly demanded by legal regulations, and partially because the companies themselves have implemented the measures on the basis of their own experience.

Nevertheless, difficulties encountered in coping with environmental problems are often still due to insufficient familiarity with pertinent technology for environmental protection, as well as the related possibilities and limitations for application.

The number of laws and legal specifications relating to environmental protection is steadily increasing and placing progressively more stringent demands on the companies, and above all on the managers, who are viewed as the responsible operators in the legal sense. For satisfying these demands, the requirements imposed on the available knowledge and ability are becoming ever more rigorous, too, and the discrepancy is still very large in practice.

In order to help close this gap, about 1000 predominantly technical managers at the domestic and foreign plants of the Mannesmann Combine alone are receiving instruction at internal seminars on current environmental problems, orientated to practical operational problems and case studies. Other companies have adopted similar measures. External possibilities for extending education are also being utilized, for example at the Haus der Technik in Essen or at the Federal State Institution for Emission Control. The problems faced by the industry have been recognized throughout the Federal Republic of Germany during the interim. In April 1978 the Technical University of Berlin, the Technische Überwachungs-Verein, the Chamber of Commerce, and the VDI have established a Centre for Continuing Education for the Protection of Health and Environment as a joint venture in Berlin. As a supplement to specialized courses of study, the purpose is to provide company engineers occupied in environmental protection with an educational possibility beyond that usually offered. An examination of the courses offered shows that these features are not available, or not sufficiently comprehensive, at most institutions of learning.

The enthusiasm demonstrated by the attendance at the relevant seminars is evidence of the prevailing insufficiency, and of the efforts on the part of practising engineers to cope with the demands and responsibilities imposed.

The position can be summarized as follows:

1. As a rule the technical managers are not sufficiently well informed about environmental problems, and not adequately prepared to assume such responsibilities in the course of their education.
2. The response to training and continuing education courses in the field of environmental protection indicates that knowledge of this kind is very much in demand for the fulfilment of operational responsibilities.
3. The emphasis placed on environmental protection by industry can be deduced from the fact that companies are prepared to spend money and time for educational programmes for the period necessary.
4. In the long term, the discrepancy between requirements and abilities can be eliminated neither by the companies nor by external instruction through the organization of seminars. This responsibility and challenge must be assumed by the universities.

The education of engineers is generally regarded as a preparation for assuming operational responsibilities. During the past 10 years these responsibilities have changed – especially because of the increasing importance of environmental protection. They must be reflected in curricula and course material.

THE COMPANY ENVIRONMENTAL SPECIALIST

What does industry expect from an environmental specialist? This question cannot be isolated from the attitude of the legislator toward this matter. The object of the following discussion, however, is to comment on the various educational concepts from the standpoint of operational practice.

In a study relevant to the question whether or not engineers can be trained for the entire field of environmental protection, the VDI has urged that the education of engineers should be governed by the requirements imposed on graduates in operational practice as early as 1973. The literal statement is as follows: "A well founded, specialized course of study must continue to constitute the core of training." The fundamentals of environmental technology, which are required by the engineer for fulfilling the responsibilities conferred on him in practice, are to be imparted by means of parallel or supplementary courses of study.

For the safety engineer employed at a plant, whose duties encompass responsibilities for environmental protection, the field of activity is frequently quite compatible with the requirements of the company. This is evident from the immediate professional relationship for a course of study in safety engineering. In many cases the safety engineer will in practice also have to assume the responsibilities for environmental protection at the plant, particularly in small and medium-sized businesses. This combination results from the high degree of coincidence between the duties involved, the systematics, and the methods of solving problems, as already explained, and this is, of course, desirable. As responsibilities of safety engineers, noise abatement measures implemented at work stations, for example, in compliance with the UVV Noise or Ordinance for Work Stations, simultaneously serve the purpose of environmental protection through the observance of noise emission limits in the vicinity. The same considerations apply to dust, noxious gases and vapours.

A comparison of the various responsibilities and requirements for occupational safety with those for environmental protection illustrates the mutual conformity of their objectives and confirms the possibility of fulfilling both, through the same engineer in certain plant departments and fields of operation. The purpose of occupational safety measures is to avoid hazards to personnel resulting from the operations, as well as from the overall department. Environmental protection measures are likewise intended to prevent hazards to human health. These hazards are, of course, anthropogenic from the very start, since they result from man's own technical activities. They pollute or otherwise impair his environment and living conditions. Thus, a kind of feed-back results between human activity and human health.

The broadening of experience of environmental protection extends the educational basis for the safety engineer, and simultaneously improves the opportunities for later professional advancement. Such a broadening of operational experience can provide a welcome enhancement of career opportunities and professional qualifications – precisely in view of the present employment and environmental situation. The simultaneous responsibility for both safety engineering and emission control at a plant can thus prove quite beneficial.

However, the extent to which the approach just discussed can be applied to various fields is questionable. An equally attractive solution is a postgraduate or supplementary programme of study with a duration of 2 to 4 semesters in the field of environmental engineering, as a follow-up to a course of professional study in some field of engineering. In this manner, it would be possible to complement specialized engineering training with the aspects specific to environmental protection. A further advantage of this approach is its interdisciplinary nature.

Besides these possibilities, the establishment of an independent, professional course of study in environmental protection engineering as such is also conceivable. In this case the object would be the establishment of a "pure" environmental specialist.

The thought of training two different kinds of engineers, that is one who pollutes the environment as a result of production, and one who eliminates the damage thus caused, must be approached with caution. Otherwise there is a risk of totally by-passing the objective of environmental protection, and also of missing the significance of the preventive measures adopted by the legislator, as well as the introduction of environmentally compatible manufacturing processes which do not pollute the environment in the first place.

In most cases these demands can be met in conjunction with specific engineering considerations on production, and from the processes employed. A professional course of study in engineering, as well as relevant experience, are, of course, prerequisites. Application-orientated, environmentally compatible technology can be designed only on the basis of a well-founded, specific education in the corresponding field of engineering. A specialized, purely environmental engineer without a basic course of study in some specific engineering field can provide such a contribution only within the framework of interdisciplinary teamwork – in this case, as the synthesizing team leader for a project.

CONSEQUENCES FOR INSTRUCTION IN THE FIELD OF ENVIRONMENTAL PROTECTION FOR EXISTING COURSES OF STUDY

For the engineer, responsibility for environmental protection can arise in two concrete cases:

1. The environmental specialist with a full professional degree in environmental protection, as just described, is employed as team leader with a synthesizing function. In this case the demand is certainly not as great as might generally be assumed.
2. The plant engineer must be thoroughly familiar with environmental protection simply because his duties in numerous areas involve topics in this field. He should be qualified as environmental specialist in his field. This means that he must be fully aware of the possible effects of his production on the environment, be familiar with the pertinent legal specifications, regulations, and requirements for approval, and have at his disposal the knowledge and experience necessary for counteracting these effects on man and his environment, and for proposing appropriate solutions.

In conclusion, the following assertions can be made on the basis of many years of operational experience in this field:

Every engineer – regardless of his field of specialization – should have at his disposal basic knowledge of environmental protection upon his arrival in practice. Moreover, he must possess general knowledge of the mutual interaction between technology and environment, and especially for his own special field, in order to be able to recognize operational environmental problems, solve simpler problems himself, or avoid them if feasible.

This goal is to be achieved through integration of environmental protection into the educational programme, with the following alternatives:

1. lecture series in conjunction with professional courses of study;
2. postgraduate or continuing education;

or, where feasible or advisable,

3. the integration of environmental protection into the required course programme in subjects and fields environmentally relevant to operational practice, such as steel production.

The steadily increasing importance of environmental protection for the future of mankind and of his natural environment requires a large measure of familiarity with effects specific to production and the resulting interactions between man and his living environment. This imposes special demands on engineers in operational practice, since they are directly responsible for manufacturing plants relevant to the environment.

Everyone is responsible for the protection of our precious environment, now and in the future: society, the economy, and the individual. However, universities and other institutions of learning bear a special responsibility, since they are educating precisely those people who will share in the shaping of our environment tomorrow – the technicians and engineers. Thus, environmental protection constitutes an increasingly vital task of social policy and engineering education, whose content and objectives must be orientated towards the desired quality of life.

Environmental Education for Engineering and Technology – An Analysis of Experience in India

R. D. DESHPANDE

Environmental problems vary widely in nature, magnitude and complexity in the countries of the Asia–Pacific Region. It is increasingly being realized that, if truly harmonious relations have to be developed between people and their environment, certain economic and technological orientations which would have an adverse effect on the quality of the environment and the conservation of its productive potential, must be reviewed. This has led to the adoption of legislation concerning the environment, setting up apex decision-making bodies in environment at the national level and incorporation of an environmental dimension into the education process.

While planning environmental education for engineers and technologists two fundamental ideas have to be borne in mind. The first is that environmental education is not to be regarded as a new discipline representing simply an addition to already existing subjects. It should comprise contributions from all disciplines concerned with knowledge and understanding of the environment and the solution of its problems and its management. The underlying principle has to be that environmental education is not meant to bring about minor changes in the pattern of learning but to promote new basic knowledge and new approaches within the framework of an overall educational policy. The existence of so many environmental problems today is partly due to the limited number of people who have been trained accurately to identify and effectively to solve complex problems. Traditional engineering and technical education have been unsuccessful in preparing individuals to face the changing complexity of environmental problems. Progress towards sound environmental management has been rather slow due to the fact that although the problems cross the boundaries of many "disciplines" these have been looked into by "specialists". Only recently has there been an effort towards an integrated approach to environmental management and consequently towards interdisciplinary education of environmental engineers. The interdisciplinary approach has been introduced in varying degrees. It has ranged from the mere introduction of an environmental component into the different traditional subjects to an approach combining several disciplines with some affinity in their ideas and methods. According to information contained in the Unesco *Directory of Engineering Education Institutions* (2nd edition) there are 119 engineering education institutions in India. Of these, twenty institutions offer postgraduate courses in environmental engineering. A number of institutions plan to start courses in different fields of environmental engineering in the coming 2–3-year period. In 1974 a review committee appointed by the Ministry of Works and Housing of the Government of India examined the existing curricula in all Indian institutions, and made important recommendations for establishing a standard curriculum to meet the objectives of postgraduate training in environmental engineering.

To improve the academic competence of faculty members in engineering institutions the Ministry of Education of the Government of India initiated a Quality Improvement Programme (QIP) in 1970, which enabled the teachers to study for masters' and doctoral degrees at carefully selected institutions. In addition, short-term courses and curriculum development programmes were also sponsored under the QIP scheme. In-service education is also imparted to practising engineers at selected institutions under a scheme financed by the Central Public Health and Environmental Engineering Organization (CPHEEO), Ministry of Works and Housing. This has been in operation since 1956, having been started by the Ministry of Health in that year.

During the past few years the National Environmental Engineering Research Institute, Nagpur, has been organizing several refresher-type continuing education programmes of 1–3 weeks' duration for the benefit of engineers employed in government engineering departments, water and air pollution control boards and industries both in the private and public sectors. Some professional societies, e.g. The Institution of Engineers (India), also organize 1–4-week duration programmes for the benefit of members on topics of national priority. Some municipal bodies, with the help of academic institutions, organize training programmes to update the technical knowledge of their engineering staff. Training is thus considered an essential element in all undertakings dealing with environmental engineering in India.

On 5 June 1985 (World Environment Day) the Indian Institute of Technology, Bombay, set up the Centre on Environmental Science and Engineering. The Centre offers an interdisciplinary postgraduate programme with a balanced training in scientific, engineering and social aspects of environmental management. The curriculum has been designed to meet the requirements of industry, and planning, design and research organizations. The programme provides for a set of compulsory core courses along with an ample choice of electives to facilitate an in-depth study of various environmental problems. Candidates with bachelor's degree in any branch of engineering or master's degree in physical/ chemical/biological sciences are admitted to the postgraduate programme, consisting of study courses in the first year followed by a research project in the second year.

The concern for integration of environmental components in the process of planning for economic development has prompted some engineering institutions to introduce elective courses dealing with life sciences, environmental impact assessment and environmental control for all undergraduate students in engineering. There has been considerable debate as to whether specialization for environmental engineers should take place at the postgraduate or undergraduate level, or both. It is recognized that some environmental input into professional engineering programmes would be desirable at undergraduate level, with courses geared to the respective branches of engineering, e.g. water pollution to civil and chemical engineering students, air pollution to chemical and mechanical engineering students and noise and vibration to mechanical and electrical engineering students. This is particularly to be expected when it is realized that the majority of students seek employment after the first degree. It is, however, realized that the multidisciplinary nature of environmental specializations can only be fully appreciated and handled by those who already have a level of expertise in one or two of the contributing disciplines. In response to the possible increase in demand for environmental engineers, the Environmental Science and Engineering group of the Indian Institute of Technology, Bombay, has examined the possibility of introducing an undergraduate programme. For this purpose a survey was conducted to estimate the present and future demand for environmental engineers. The study brought out some interesting results. The general consensus was that there were only limited employment opportunities for first-degree graduates while the job potential for postgraduate degree holders was rated as excellent. It also brought out that in spite of given conditions in industries, governmental agencies and consultancy firms, most of the postgraduates seem to be appropriately employed in terms of their training. They also seem to have excellent avenues for mobility comparable to those obtained in other newly emerging areas in engineering. Some employers indicated their preference for graduates with specialization in environmental engineering, maximum job opportunities available being in air pollution, water pollution, industrial effluent treatment and land use. Some experts in engineering education strongly argue for postgraduate rather than undergraduate programmes, because the undergraduate training severely reduces employment options by reducing the amount of traditional "hard-core" engineering content in the course – without removing the need to specialize at the postgraduate level in order to be qualified as an environmental engineer. They feel that it is easier at the postgraduate level to inculcate in the students the ability to acquire, analyse, synthesize and evaluate existing knowledge, an ability that will enable them to play an active part in devising environmentally appropriate solutions. All of the institutions offering postgraduate specialization in environmental engineering, apart from some formal teaching, insist on students undertaking projects especially in the engineering context and allocate to this an appropriate number of credits.

One of the significant developments in environmental education at the tertiary level in India has been the appointment of a Committee on Environmental Sciences by the University Grants Commission. The Committee in its report has stressed that environmental education has to be seen as a process during which the students are made aware of the environment and of the interaction of its biological, physical and sociocultural components. The Committee has recommended a postgraduate master's course for degree-holders in physical sciences and engineering. This recommendation would be examined by engineering and other institutions directly receiving support from the UGC.

Decision-makers and educational planners have become aware of the increased manpower needs for well-trained environmental engineers and the inadequate output of the engineering institutions. It is fully realized that such a comprehensive training can be provided at only a few institutions having highly qualified faculty and physical facilities, and which are also fully involved in solving the environmental problems faced by industry and government. Trained environmental engineers are expected to face the challenge of a broad variety of environmental problems which have social and political implications. They therefore have to be exposed to social science disciplines during their academic training. Most institutions providing training for environmental engineering agree that the focus of training should not be confined to traditional public health administrative activities such as the supply of municipal water, treatment and disposal of industrial and municipal waste water and of municipal solid wastes. Environmental engineers must now be trained to deal with a broad spectrum of environmental problems arising from rapid and poorly planned industrialization. They need to have innovative minds to tackle problems in an environmentally appropriate manner involving minimal social costs. A survey of environmental engineers already employed has indicated that they would like the existing curriculum strengthened by the addition of more electives, e.g. project management, communication techniques, financial planning, environmental law, environmetrics, and simulation and modelling.

Education in environmental engineering is being given increased recognition because of the role that the environmental engineers are playing in identifying environmental problems and suggesting sound solutions. The nature and content of interdisciplinary training received by them needs to be constantly reviewed so that they understand the complexity of the environment and are better prepared to improve or maintain its quality. Knowledge, attitudes and skills acquired should enable environmental engineers to take a more active part in social decisions which have important environmental consequences.

Science and Technology Education in Darjeeling– Sikkim Himalayas

G. S. YONZONE

INTRODUCTION

The mountainous region of Darjeeling–Sikkim Himalayas with an area of 10,284.5 sq km is part of the great Himalayan range of India. There are more than 14 snowy peaks, of which Mount Kangchenjungha at 8585 m is the third highest mountain in the world. These peaks are the source of a number of perennial rivers and streams which divide the region into several valleys and spurs.

Despite the region's vast natural wealth of physical and biological resources it is staggeringly backward in the field of science and technology education.

We must think of science and technology education in relation to a holistic concept of the region's environmental characteristics and of its natural resources.

Existing environmental problems include:

1. *Overpopulation*. The total population in the region has reached a figure of 1,339,268 from only 324,794 in 1901.
2. *Depletion of forests*. The main reasons include wanton clearance of forests for short-term commercial gain, major dependence on forests for fodder and fuel, uncontrolled grazing and theft and pilferage of trees, and extension of cultivation into forest areas due to population pressure.
3. *Soil erosion*. Although a perennial feature of the hilly terrain, soil erosion has been accelerated by a faulty traditional agricultural system, random construction of roads and houses without examining scientifically the stability of the soil, and indiscriminate tree-felling without considering the concomitant environmental hazards.

4. *Overstocking of cattle.* Overstocking of cattle by almost every rural family, without adequate fodder resources. This compels people to plunder the reserved and sanctuary forests.
5. *Destruction of scientifically unstudied flora and fauna.* Lack of responsibility, and of the knowledge that survival of man depends on the survival of plants and animals.
6. *Lack of post-harvest technology.* This is still an alien subject in the region.
7. *Poverty.* Offspring of the above problems.

These problems are swelling in dimension as they threaten conservation and sustained development. We should remember that conservation and development are mirror-images of each other and this deserves widest possible propaganda. What is called development has resulted in ecological backlashes. It is a double tragedy, since not only is the money spent on some development works lost through bad investment, but additional money has to be spent to correct the new problems created. Only careful study, research and prior planning can ensure a net benefit to the people. Otherwise it will only be a temporary economic benefit for a vested interest. One could visualize a great deal of science and technology education within the body of the environmental problems enumerated above.

NATURAL RESOURCES

The region is very rich in the following resources:

1. Humid climate favouring the cultivation of a large number of agro-horticultural plants. The region is especially famous for tea, cardamon, orange, ginger, guava and plum.
2. Forest vegetation, although it has now declined to less than 30 per cent against a minimum requirement of 60 per cent of the total geographical area in the hills.
3. Wildlife. Diversity of flora and fauna is a valuable genetic asset.
4. Perennial rivers.
5. Tropical, temperate and alpine climatic zones.
6. A beautiful natural landscape.

NEED FOR CHANGES IN THE EXISTING CURRICULA

The existing curricula of graduate and post-graduate courses of teaching under the University of North Bengal falling within the region offer only fragments of the physical and biological aspects of science specific to the region, while technology education with the aim of developing the learners themselves has been totally omitted. Certain science courses lack qualified teachers to teach them. There also appears to be very limited scope for teachers to receive adequate training in the subject. As the curricula are not issue-based, the students become helpless onlookers on the growing socioeconomic problems that have almost engulfed their society.

I suggest the development of technology education in the following subject areas keeping in view the present and future needs of the people of the region:

1. As tea is the main industry of the area employing the largest number of people, and as Darjeeling tea is famous for its flavour, there is tremendous scope in the field of tea science and technology for further improvement of tea qualitatively and quantitatively from the time of plucking to the stage of made tea.
2. Floriculture is one of the most prosperous industries of the region. There are thousands of different kinds of Himalayan flowers peculiar to this region, which is regarded as a botanical paradise of India. One or two private flower nurseries have been doing very well, but the field has remained wholly unidentified from educational and economic points of view.
3. Mushroom cultivation and cultivation of fruits, medicinal, aromatic and spice plants, plant tissue and cell culture, plant breeding and hybridization, horticultural economics and marketing.
4. Forestry – social forestry, farm forestry, silviculture.
5. Non-conventional energy sources as an alternative fuel to wood.
6. Food and post-harvest technology.
7. Meat and vegetable processing technology.
8. Dairy and animal husbandry technology.
9. Computer technology.
10. Art and craft industry.
11. Hill fishery.
12. Sericulture.

CONSERVATION AND ENVIRONMENTAL PROTECTION

There is vast scope for economic development in the region through the cultivation of economically important plants. Phytochemical investigation of some wild plants has shown promising results. The following areas of research deserve consideration in the postgraduate science curricula:

1. A systematic survey of the ethnobotany of the region.
2. A systematic survey of the chemistry of all the plants which are reported to be medicinal, aromatic or poisonous.
3. An ecological study of all economically important plants.
4. Studies of the physiology, cytogenetics, breeding behaviour and other aspects relating to the synthesis of active principles.

5. Studies of cultural methods and propagation of high-yielding clones.
6. Studies of phytopathology, pharmacology and pollination biology.
7. Studies of environmental interaction.

Of the various economic plants, medicinal plants form one of the chief natural resources of the region. A policy can be evolved to encourage the farmers to cultivate these in place of economically less viable agricultural crops whose yield is comparatively lower. Many other important medicinal plants grow at higher elevations in the temperate and alpine zones. Cultivation of these plants can also be envisaged with profit.

FOUNDATION FOR SCIENCE AND TECHNOLOGY EDUCATION

No education can be possible without proper institutions and teachers. While our horizon of knowledge has greatly expanded, and many new subject areas have come up, we are lagging very much behind in evolving an effective strategy to cope with ever diversifying research in science and technology. There is therefore a widening gap between what we are and what we ought to be. It is sad to notice an unhappy contrast between existing poverty and the very rich natural resources which, if handled well, could assure economic prosperity for all, good food for all, good health and education for all with the other benefits of modern life. We have overlooked the fact that past, present and future are intimately connected. The past is the foundation for the present, as the present is for the future. Science and technology education, the emancipator of mankind, should have a foundation which is presently lacking. The establishment of the following institutions is necessary for all sections of the people:

1. A multidisciplinary environmental research institute for all kinds of environmental planning, education, research and training.
2. Departments of Environment at District and Sub-Divisional levels, with the avowed objective of bringing about mass awareness and involvement in monitoring, safeguarding and enhancing the environment.
3. Botanical and zoological gardens, parks and sanctuaries at District and Sub-Divisional levels, which will not only help in conserving the vanishing flora and fauna but also serve as centres of environmental education for all. They can also act as gene pools.
4. A natural history museum with full provision of educative materials on environment for teachers, students and the public.
5. An economic botany museum at each Sub-Division.
6. Science and technology museums at each Sub-Division.
7. A post-harvest technology centre for preservation and storage of foods and grains.

8. A bio-fuel or non-conventional energy centre for training the people.
9. An electronics centre.

It seems we have now got to fight a double war: one against the grave omissions of the past, and the other for meeting the needs and aspirations of the present and the future.

Environmental Education
in China

HUANG MIN-YUNG

With the development of modern reconstruction of China the importance and urgency of environmental protection are becoming more and more outstanding. The development of the cause of environmental protection in China is mainly restrained by two factors. One is insufficiency of economic power; it is unable to commit much to the treatment of environmental pollution. The second is the underdevelopment of science and education and the lack of scientific and technical personnel, including people whose speciality is environmental management. With the development of the country's economic reconstruction, funding is expected to be increased gradually. The problems of personnel depend on popularization and improvement of education in China for their solution.

China has made great efforts to train specialized personnel and to improve qualifications of in-service engineers and technicians in the field of environmental protection. From 1974 up to now special facilities, departments and institutes have been established to meet the needs of environmental protection in 64 colleges and universities. Eighteen secondary specialized schools in this field have also been set up in the country. Now eight universities are preparing to offer courses on environmental protection. They will cover the following subjects: environmental engineering, environmental chemistry, environmental biology, environmental earth science, environmental protection for agriculture and environmental medicine. Towards the end of 1983, 1724 students and 114 postgraduates will have completed their studies in the departments of environmental protection. Now there are 3950 students and 226 postgraduates studying environmental sciences at the universities. Two thousand six hundred students have gone through the secondary specialized schools on environmental protection.

For want of specialized personnel most of the in-service people were transferred from other units. Since working objectives and fields of science had changed, they had to learn new subjects. Towards the end of 1983

321

Ministries of the State Council and bureaus of all the provinces and municipalities involved in environmental protection operated 193 courses for training managers and technicians in the field. The number of trained people reached 25,400. All the managers received training, in rotation.

Environmental sciences are frontier sciences, resulting from overlapping of many sciences, including not only natural sciences but also social sciences. In order to equip cadres with new knowledge to satisfy the needs of development in environmental protection the Ministry of Urban and Rural Construction and Environmental Protection has established a base for training technical cadres at Tongji University, Shanghai, where in-service personnel are trained half a year. There has also been established a secondary specialized school only for training managers in environmental protection at Qinghuangdao in Hobei Province. The length of study is 2 months. Nine seminars have been organized and the number of trained people has reached 836. Apart from this, several classes for further studies have also been provided in Beijing University, Tsinghua University and Beijing Normal University. There the participants systematically learn technology and theories on environmental sciences.

According to the directive of the Ministry of Education many institutions of higher learning have opened a course entitled "Introduction to Environmental Sciences", as an optional subject so that graduates, working in different fields, may take notice of environmental protection and may work to lessen environmental pollution.

The central and local authorities also launched work to spread environmental education in society. For example, in March 1980 and from March to April 1981 – propaganda month – active propaganda for environmental protection was carried out all over the country. Through the press, radio, television, films, lectures and photo exhibitions, knowledge of environmental protection was spread among the people.

China will strengthen co-operation and exchange experience with foreign countries to improve the work of environmental protection. At the same time it will contribute its share to the cause of world environmental protection.

[Editors' note: the author in collaboration with Jing Wen-Yung also presented information concerning a competition in Beijing on special approaches to the education of children and other environmental education activities in Tsinghua University of Beijing.]

Ecological Education of Engineers in the USSR

E. ZNAMENSKY

Optimization of relations between society and nature and minimalization of man's influences on the latter is an important ecological problem, comparable with the prevention of nuclear war. Its solution has as its aim to preserve life on earth and to contribute to the advance of civilization. The measures to ensure an effective solution of that problem include the education and, above all, the ecological training of engineers.

In accordance with the Constitution of the USSR and education laws, this country has, and is unceasingly improving, a single system of public education. The system provides both a general education and professional training, and guarantees extensive development of higher education founded on a close connection between human life and production. An integral part of the system is a programme of ecological education of engineers to form in all engineers a conscious perception of nature, a conviction of the need for thrifty and rational use of natural resources, and an understanding of how important it is to increase the sustainable natural resources of the biosphere.

Government solutions of ecological problems are most effective when involving direct participation of broad sections of the public. This country has scientific and technical societies, nature protection societies and societies for the dissemination of scientific knowledge. Engineers are enabled to solve problems competently on a social basis both through their high level of education and professional training and their direct participation in the work of such societies. A contribution to the same end is also made by the press, radio, television, cinema and other mass media.

Ecological training of engineers is at present done in more than 250 higher schools in 21 specialities. In the past 5 years over 200,000 specialists have received a higher and ecological education. Besides specialization at the higher schools, use is also made of even more specific preparation for particular engineering lines, which makes it possible to use time for

323

providing additional ecological information. Moreover, the extension of such information is achieved by the choice of ecological subjects for the higher-school students' yearly and diploma designs, and by various forms of practical training.

Essential in the scheme of ecological education of engineers are three successive directions consisting of separate stages. The first one shapes an ecological outlook; the second is training in a particular branch of engineering ecology; and the third is training in nature management economics. The first direction comprises the ecological principles of nature protection, philosophical questions of interaction between society and nature, and practical nature protection activities. The second investigates the factors and sources of damage to the environment, no-waste technologies, a system of environmental protection measures, and rational use of natural resources. The third involves calculation and economic estimation of natural resources, bioeconomic evaluation of engineering schemes and of the techniques of organization of nature management and no-waste technologies on the scale of a region.

At these stages students are given a special course, including environment protection subjects, as an independent branch of social and specialized disciplines. Practical nature protection work is done by the students at the humanities department and when undergoing practical training in their special field. The total time assigned for the entire course of ecological education at the institute is 120–140 hours including 30 hours for the special course.

Ecological education at the Byelorussian Technological Institute is conducted consistently, without interruption from the first to the ninth or tenth semester. In the first and second years of study an ecological outlook is formed and during the remaining years engineering ecology and economics of nature management are taught.

Environmental protection retraining of engineers is done at special departments of a number of higher schools. Thus retraining in the speciality "Ecology and More Effective Uses of Natural Resources" is annually provided as day-time instruction at six higher schools to about 200 specialists with higher education. Such retraining is offered to engineers with a length of service not less than 3 years. They discontinue their work during the 6 months' term of instruction.

Important positive experience has been gained by the higher schools for advanced training of managers and specialists at a number of ministries, such as the Ministry of the Chemical Industry, Ministry of the Oil-extracting Industry, Ministry of Electrical Engineering, Ministry of Non-ferrous Metallurgy and others. As an example, a brief analysis might be made of the practice of advanced training of engineers at the Ministry of the Chemical Industry. The high rate of development of chemical industry necessitates special environmental protection measures at its enterprises. Hence the great responsibility for the instruction of leading managers, engineers and designers in scientifically substantiated designing and functioning of no-effluent and no-waste flow-lines, the development of new methods and improvement of existing methods of purifying and sterilizing industrial waste, its utilization, and reliable operation of purification works. The ministry has adopted a long-term complex plan for advanced training of all managers and specialists in environmental protection and rational use of natural resources, which includes a wide range of subjects: legal, economic, sanitary and hygienic, and technical. At the present time the ministry accentuates instruction in the theory and practical applications of low-waste technologies, no-waste processes, including the creation and introduction of closed-circuit water systems, of reuse of water, contributing to the main trends of scientific and technological progress in the solution of ecological problems.

In the past decade over 10,000 persons in the Ministry of Chemical Industry alone have received full-time advanced training.

A number of aspects of ecological instruction of engineers, as a specific, relatively new sphere of education are yet to be carefully investigated, reinforced and improved. All useful initiatives to improve ecological education of engineers, both on the national and international level, must be supported and encouraged, to provide ecologically competent, cultured engineers capable of tackling problems of nature management, with the least economic expenditure and, at the same time, with the greatest socioeconomic and ecological effect.

Better preparation of engineers in environmental matters requires raising the effectiveness of national and international nature protection measures, extending the knowledge of nature through the exchange of information on organization, programmes and methods of training and advanced training of engineers, co-ordinating concepts and adopting generally accepted terms.

No less important in engineers' ecological education appears to be its orientation to the future. In the near and more remote future, the main ecological problems, despite the measures taken and even the satisfactory solution of some of them, will require more attention. Considerable effort will probably be needed to make technical means and methods of nature management not only ecologically compatible but also safe.

A great deal is being done in the USSR to create, improve and materialize the potentialities of new machinery, technology and methods of economic activities harmless for the environment. Such is the purpose of scientific research, and technological, experimental, engineering and other development activities. It is therefore very important that ecological education of the engineer should without delay absorb the latest ideas, the achievements of scientific and technological progress, the tendencies of interaction of technology with the biosphere, and possible consequences of economic activities, and thereby provide the trainees with the knowledge not only of the past and the present but also of the future.

3

An Issue-Based Approach
Education and Research Options for Addressing Social and Environmental Issues in Water Resources Planning and Management

WARREN VIESSMAN, JR

INTRODUCTION

Social and environmental goals and objectives are continually changing, and often difficult to quantify. Consequently, water resources professionals may find it difficult to maintain currency with them and to see that they are appropriately reflected in their professional endeavours. Yet these social goals and objectives are the keystones of decision-making actions; plans and proposals prepared in ignorance of them have little chance of being accepted by the public and implemented. Water resources professionals face a challenge of great proportions, one of exerting their technical expertise in a manner compatible with, and constrained by, the broad and ever-changing inclinations of society. Education is a key factor in this process.

THE DYNAMICS OF GOALS AND OBJECTIVES

The attitudes of people toward how the nation's water resources should be developed and managed have shifted markedly in recent years. The only constant has been the resource itself. Floods, droughts, and pollution remain serious problems, even though they have been mitigated to some extent. What has changed significantly has been society's focus. It has shifted from technical issues of hydrologic systems – physical, biological, and chemical features of water bodies – to the social and environmental aspects of how water is used and misused.

DEALING WITH SOCIAL AND ENVIRONMENTAL GOALS AND OBJECTIVES

Given the changing and often intangible nature of social goals and objectives, the question is, how can they be accommodated as plans are developed and management decisions are made? Several paths have been followed, all with shortcomings, and there is wide recognition that new ideas and approaches are needed. Professionals must fully understand and be aware of pertinent regulations, societal attitudes, and political practicalities. And here the importance of education and research should be recognized. Although most professionals do not make the political decisions that dictate broad water resources policies, they have an obligation to use their expertise to provide hard data to clarify the implications of trade-offs that must be made in the political arena. Unfortunately, decisions regarding attainment of social and environmental goals are often made on the basis of pressures from uninformed popular opinion, and emotions may tend to get in the way of rational and factual thinking. Educators, engineers, planners, and scientists should see that those making decisions fully understand the consequences of their actions. If they do not do this, they cannot avoid bearing some of the responsibility for actions that are not economically, technically, or environmentally sound.

All water resources professionals should be concerned with the identification and understanding of environmental goals and objectives; and the meaningful incorporation of them in planning and managing processes. It seems appropriate that: (1) the process of identifying goals and objectives should be emphasized and given increased attention; (2) the scientific community should be encouraged to participate actively in social and political processes; and (3) that university researchers should actively pursue development of more contemporary measures of project and programme efficacy. Revised planning standards, if developed co-operatively with environmentalists and other professionals who understand prevailing ecological, social and economic systems, could lead to more efficient and equitable solutions to water and water-related problems.

Ways in which professionals concerned about water (educators, planners, managers, engineers, and scientists) can play a more active role in relation to understanding social and environmental goals and objectives and incorporating them in their activities include: lobbying; participating in local, state, and national government; education and research; publishing; interacting with the public; and analysing existing systems. Creating an awareness of the opportunities presented for professionals to become effective participants in government, for example, should be actively pursued by those educating the water resource planners and managers of the future.

If one accepts the notion that the real purpose of water resources management, planning, and policy is to enhance the well-being of people, then the social dimension must be considered an integral component of water resources education. In particular, there is a need to understand how social well-being can be achieved by fair and equitable processes.

Education ignoring the benefit of the social, behavioural, and political sciences will not adequately prepare engineers to perform credible jobs as water resources professionals. Because political decisions involving engineering works are usually reached through compromise, engineering designs cannot be viable unless they are responsive to the inclinations of decision-makers and the interested constituencies representing different sectors, regions, civic groups, and stakeholders. An understanding by engineers of how decisions are made and implemented is just as important as an understanding of physical laws governing their designs.

The multidisciplinary nature of water-related problems strongly suggests that engineering departments must effectively include in their curricula courses that address political, legal, and social dimensions if they are to meet today's educational requirements. Furthermore, those who are assigned the role of advising water resources engineering students must realize that the social sciences are disciplines of equal importance to engineering when trade-offs are to be made in the design of programmes of study. The need to add a political–legal–social dimension to the education of water resources engineers has long been recognized but, except for lip-service, has mostly been ignored.

An added problem is that the system of rewards, including promotion and tenure, used by many universities actually discourages the engineering faculty from collaborating with their colleagues from the arts and humanities in what could be most valuable and rewarding research or educational programmes. As noted by Haimes (at an "Urban Water 84" Conference in Baltimore), "The term 'soft' sciences – referring to the social, behavioral, and political sciences – carries a connotation that discourages the junior faculty from collaboration. As a result, capabilities for teaching the necessary material are never developed." Specific training in the social, behavioural, and political sciences must be integrated in water resources curricula. While some universities already do this, they represent a minority.

There are some indications that engineering education is changing and that the political and social dimensions of society are beginning to be recognized more as integral parts of technical studies. For example, a 1985 textbook on water management by Viessman and Welty (*Water Management: Technology and Institutions*, Harper & Row Inc., New York) contains the following statements in its preface:

The engineers and scientists of tomorrow will require ethics of practice that permit them to range beyond the technicalities of design and into the realm of shaping policy that ultimately specifies what those designs should be. Imaginative and creative individuals are needed who can perceive and respect technical, nontechnical, and combination solutions to society's problems; who can set forth and assess viable alternatives; and who can understand environmental issues and design workable systems accordingly. Engineers and scientists, in particular, should be prepared to take leadership roles in guiding those in decision-making capacities to create the best possible programs and regulations for the management of water and other resources. The challenge is to produce technically qualified individuals who can relate their knowledge to the realities of the political, economic, and social settings in which all water problems must be solved.

The avenues for fostering and encouraging education and research designed to prepare students to influence the goals and objectives of society and to reflect these appropriately in their applications of technology include:

1. Promoting and supporting undergraduate and graduate programmes at colleges and universities which include instruction in the procedures for, and the importance of, incorporating social and environmental considerations in planning and management processes.
2. Sponsoring continuing education programmes to acquaint practitioners with state-of-the-art technology and the roles of various disciplines in addressing social and environmental issues.
3. Conducting sessions at professional meetings or holding special seminars to address issues related to dealing with social and environmental goals and objectives and with determining how the water resources community can be influential in affecting laws, regulations, establishment of planning criteria, etc.
4. Encouraging research directed toward linking the technical dimensions of mathematical modelling of water resources systems with interactive computerized systems which decision-makers can use to evaluate the consequences of their decisions in terms they can understand.
5. Designing approaches which effectively translate research findings into formats suitable for use by decision-making bodies.
6. Encouraging public discussion and participation by pursuing media outlets and speaking at social functions about current environmental issues. The focus should be to outline steps the public can take to rectify detrimental behaviour as well as ways to influence legislators to make constructive policies.

Water resources professionals should be encouraged to participate more directly in citizens' groups and meetings. This could involve active participation in special interest group meetings and other forums. Furthermore, active membership in special interest groups having a stake in water resources development or management could aid significantly in the process of conflict identification and resolution at an early stage.

CONCLUSION

Social and environmental goals and objectives shape water programmes. They must be clearly understood by all concerned with water resources so that as proposals are generated to address various issues, they will be developed in the context of prevailing social moods. This is not an easy task, particularly since society's attitudes are continually shifting. An added difficulty is that historic goals, translated into statutory form, are frequently left in place long after they have outlived their usefulness. Thus it seems that the professional has a role, not only in helping to see that society's interests are identified and included in new designs, but also in aiding decision-makers to shape new policies, seek ways to implement them, and to bring about statutory and regulatory reform.

The key to much of this appears to be education. On the one hand it will be necessary to instruct students, lay-persons and professionals in the importance of their involvement in the areas of goal-setting and policy-structuring, and on how to function effectively in a political–social–natural environment. On the other hand, the issue is how to get information on viable alternatives to decision-making bodies relative to the issues they are concerned with. The objective is to present well-informed choices, ones that are socially acceptable, technically sound, and economically efficient.

Students must be taught the art of problem-solving in the context of constraining influences, natural and social. They must learn to assess options objectively and to present their findings so that those without technical expertise can understand and use them. A possibility for creating this setting lies in stronger interaction between practising professionals and university faculties. Perceptions, by professionals, of the world outside their areas, must be broad and tempered by the realities of what should and should not be manipulated.

The time is now for increasing the scope of educational influence so that the achievements of tomorrow will be innovative and efficient, rather than reactions to misinformed or poorly-made decisions.

4

Implementation Strategies

Implementation Strategies
at the Tertiary Level – an
Example and a Proposal

G. R. FRANCIS and G. RIVAS MIJARES

The example is from Canada and the proposal from Venezuela.

EXAMPLE OF AN UNDERGRADUATE PROGRAMME AT THE TERTIARY LEVEL

A 4-year Bachelor of Environmental Studies (B.E.S.) degree at the Department of Man–Environment Studies, University of Waterloo, Canada, was started in 1970. It enrolls about 60 students in year 1 each year, most coming directly from secondary school.

About one-half of the course credits required for a degree are taken from the home department and the remainder are electives which students take elsewhere in the university. Arrangements with other departments in the university allow students to combine environmental studies with study in a related discipline (such as biology, chemistry, geography, economics, sociology, mathematics, etc.) or theme (a set of related courses orientated to such fields as natural resource management, energy studies, peace and conflict resolution, or urban studies).

The environmental studies "core" has three distinct components:

(a) Introductory overview of environmental issues and approaches to analysing and resolving them, followed by required courses in ecology and the social sciences.
(b) Introduction to systems analyses and the use of computers followed by required courses on research methods and data analyses.
(c) Individual or small group projects, often related to community organizations, which each student undertakes in years 2, 3 and 4.

333

The teaching faculty is a multidisciplinary team with backgrounds and experience from the natural sciences, social sciences, systems engineering, law and communications science.

Graduates holding the B.E.S. degree have entered a wide array of employment in government, business and industry, community organizations and teaching, as well as a wide array of postgraduate studies. Generally employment depends on what else besides the environmental studies core the students studied during their undergraduate years and/or for a postgraduate degree. Those who go on to postgraduate work tend to select professional programmes such as environmental design, planning, law, administrative studies, health sciences, or natural resources management.

A PROPOSAL

Engineering studies focus mainly on science and technology applications whose objective is to conceive, to design, to construct, to operate and to maintain engineering works. Knowledge of the basic sciences, physics, mathematics, chemistry and biology, are also taught to supply the minimum background engineering students will need to understand the subjects of academic curricula.

We present here in a practical way a programme that could be approved by universities all over the world, with a minimum of the resistance often found in educational establishments.

What is most important for engineers to understand and to apply in the daily exercise of their profession is how to adjust traditional practice to conform with the most elementary principles for protection of the environment, taking into account the fragility of the surrounding space and the inability of the environment to reverse resultant degradations. To build under no restrictive rules and regulations is today recognized as detrimental to living creatures. A well-balanced, synoptic and detailed environmental course at undergraduate level in engineering schools should be devised and evaluated by those who have been working in this area.

For this purpose an international working group should be convened to outline such a course. After this a competent group should take responsibility for writing such a book, basing chapters on the crucial problems that arise in the areas of the course under consideration.

A mechanism could then be established to print the book at a reasonable cost, affordable by engineering staff and students at both undergraduate and graduate levels.

Parallel with the publication of such a textbook, whose title might be *Environmental Engineering*, additional guidelines should be prepared concerning specific topics related to the main engineering areas: civil engineering (hydraulic, structures, highways and sanitary engineering), mechanical engineering (petrology, energy, thermodynamics, thermo-electronics, nuclear generators, etc); electrical engineering (electronic computation and control); system analysis and communications; geology and metallurgy (physical and chemical metallurgy, geophysics), chemical engineering (process design, transport phenomena, thermodynamic and kinematic) and petroleum engineering (transport, distribution and refining).

In each of the formal engineering departments, seminars should be convened to emphasize, for each discipline, the problems met most frequently relating to the protection of the environment, especially when designing and building engineering works.

The seminars should consider this question: At what time during undergraduate studies should the specific subject "Environmental Engineering" be presented? It could be at the end of the basic cycle of undergraduate studies or within the last four semesters of the so-called professional subjects studies cycle.

What seems to be very important is the need to offer specific subjects within the undergraduate engineering course and the guidelines within the junior and senior students' cycle differentiated to be specific for each engineering department, and also for graduate students working for higher engineering degrees.

Eventually some other complementary actions could be taken to carry on the programme under consideration: seminars, conferences, short courses and any other activity that could reinforce this important subject of environmental education for engineers.

For the high school level some successful programmes have been reported. For example, in Venezuela a pilot project was established by Unesco entitled "Environmental Education for Engineers".

It would be advisable to review the multidisciplinary book on this subject published in 1982 by Unesco, written by a multidisciplinary international team.

Finally, it would be very helpful to invent a mechanism whereby all engineering projects take into account the environmental implications of their work.

Conclusions and Recommendations

G. R. FRANCIS

The following statements summarize the conclusions and recommend-ations arrived at in the workshops dealing with tertiary, professional and vocational environmental education.

1. Environmental education has been incorporated into a number of tertiary institutions in all regions of the world at both the undergraduate and postgraduate levels. There are five distinct approaches to doing this:
   (a) A general introduction to the requisite awareness, knowledge, skills, attitudes and commitments is provided at the pre-university and/or undergraduate (first cycle) course at university. Students then specialize through concurrent and/or sequential study in a related discipline or profession.
   (b) The environmental dimensions are introduced as an integral component of professional and disciplinary education at the undergraduate level. Some students specialize in the environmental aspects of their chosen profession or discipline.
   (c) Postgraduate courses enroll persons with quite different prior education in the various disciplines or professions. Emphasis is then placed on having students understand the environmental implica-tions of their individual discipline/profession and learn to work together effectively in problem-solving teams.
   (d) Graduate-level research provides the focus for learning. Students apply their special disciplinary or professional training to particular environmental research topics as part of their thesis requirements.
   (e) A deliberate attempt may be made to create a new discipline of "environmental science", or a new profession as an "environmental-ist" which would be analogous to existing professions in terms of accreditation procedures, codes of ethics, and so on.
2. There is a general consensus that environmental education at the tertiary level should, as a minimum, emphasize

ESTE-L

(a) A multidisciplinary approach which recognizes that the understanding and solution of environmental problems requires inputs from several disciplines and professions.

(b) A holistic philosophy, utilizing a systems perspective, and acknowledging the goal of striving for ecologically sustainable development.

(c) A sound grounding in at least one area of concentrated study, such as a profession, discipline, or some other relevant skills and abilities.

(d) A realistic understanding of the social, economic, political and institutional contexts within which environmental problems arise, decisions must be made and solutions have to be implemented.

(e) Problem-solving tools and abilities which permit students to transcend conventional disciplinary approaches. (For details, see Wali and Burgess, p. 273.)

3. There are two options for developing such programmes. The first is to establish completely new programmes at undergraduate and postgraduate levels which have these characteristics. The second is to introduce environmental education components progressively into the curricula for existing science and technology education. In each case the education and training for environmental scientists and professionals at the tertiary level must be seen as continuous and interdependent with the learning attained at primary and secondary school levels. Each level contributes to the requisite awareness, knowledge, skills, attitudes and commitment needed to help resolve environmental problems. Tertiary-level programmes must adopt the appropriate balance and emphasis in their approach to take account of the prior education students attained at pre-university levels as well as the particular kinds of employment and other social roles students are expected to take up after graduating from university.

4. Examples of the first option are programmes developed by the Department of Man–Environment Studies, University of Waterloo, Canada, the School of Environmental Studies, Jawaharlal Nehru University, New Delhi, India, and the Programme in Environmental Science, College of Environmental Science and Forestry, State University of New York, Syracuse. There are many examples of the second option (for example in the background papers from Brazil, USSR, etc.).

5. The future goal should be to have environmental components incorporated and/or strengthened in all courses for scientists, engineers and other professions having considerable influence over environmental design and management, e.g. architects, foresters, agronomists. The challenge is to decide what additional awareness, understanding and skills each professional or scientific specialist should have over and

above that provided by standard training. The goal is to have practitioners become more sensitive to and responsible for the environmental consequences of their practices. This may be a matter of beliefs, values and attitudes rather than additional knowledge and skills. Some persons may specialize in the environmental protection tasks associated with their particular profession.

It must be recognized that most environmental problems and issues require knowledge and skills from a number of specialists if they are to be understood properly and acted upon effectively. No one discipline or profession is sufficient to achieve this.

The challenge is to have diverse specialists able to work together effectively in teams. Each participant must master some "group process" skills, learn to communicate with other specialists (hence must know the basic concepts, language, and paradigms of other disciplines and professions) and be able to relate their own knowledge and skills to the larger societal context (e.g. to the concerns of the public, decision-makers, etc.). The appropriate pedagogy differs from that used to train scientists and most professionals and hence becomes very demanding of both instructors and participants.

6. With particular reference to the training of engineers, it was agreed that:
   (a) It is desirable that all engineering students obtain an awareness and some understanding (to the level of basic concepts, "language", and limitations) of ecology, socioeconomics, and systems analysis as these relate to the role and responsibilities of engineers.
   (b) Engineering students must also understand the principles of urban, rural and regional planning which guide development and the importance of local involvement in planning and decision-making.
   (c) Case studies of various kinds should be used to demonstrate the relevance of these wider considerations to the practising engineer.

A number of institutional constraints must be overcome to introduce these modifications into professional training for engineers (and others). They include: the attitude of professors and senior administrators of universities, the conservative traditions of professional associations, and the already large amount of content in the curricula which it is deemed necessary to maintain.

7. Nevertheless, strategies to introduce these modifications into the curriculum should consider the following:
   (a) Compilation of case studies of various development schemes which failed because those larger considerations were ignored.
   (b) Introducing modifications first into those fields of engineering which are potentially the most socially, economically and ecologically "damaging" when they are practised too narrowly.

(c) Developing an elective course first in order to "experiment" on how best to organize and teach the substance of it.

(d) Assigning senior, experienced professors to the course in order to emphasize the importance and seriousness of the matters discussed.

(e) Use of thesis topics at graduate level which must incorporate engineering, ecological, planning and socioeconomic considerations into their conception and elaboration.

8. Taking account of the general educational specifications and different possible approaches to developing programmes within tertiary institutions, working committees should be convened to develop curriculum guidelines adapted to particular needs of different professions and disciplines so that some practitioners from each field can also become environmental scientists or professionals. Guidelines for developing these curricula should cover:

(a) Supplementary educational and training objectives (to those objectives already attained by the discipline or profession being considered).

(b) The scope and organization of the additional subject matter (academic content) to be covered and its relation to the discipline or profession being addressed.

(c) The methods to be used to integrate the subject matter in both teaching and learning processes, i.e. to attain the requisite inter-disciplinary core for the programme.

(d) Application of the particular kind of environmental knowledge and skills to issues of ecologically sustainable development (e.g. the objectives of the World Conservation Strategy).

9. The World Federation of Engineering Organizations is committed to promoting the incorporation of environmental components into engineering curricula. The Committee on Engineering and the Environment of WFEO has already taken some initial steps towards this. ICSU/CST should promote the same goal with reference to training scientists and other professional groups.

V Non-Formal, Public Environmental Education

1

Introduction

LAURIE WAYBURN

Environmental education is increasingly recognized to extend well beyond the academic and formal teaching fields into the public forum of everyday life. It involves a variety of practical local level issues as well as regional, national and international concerns ranging from natural resource management to law, social aspects and religion. One of the best ways to better inform and educate the public on the consequences of their daily decisions affecting the environment – and on possible alternative courses of action – is to use public and non-academic media such as film, slide shows and popular media such as comic books and posters. Efforts involving community talks, newspapers, radio and films are increasingly effective in heightening grassroots public understanding of environmental issues and creating new alternative practices in sustainable use of resources.

Environmental education concerns not only school children or those in academic research fields, but also the general public whose daily decisions affect resource use and determine our everyday environmental quality. Perhaps the most useful, easily acessible and practical means of teaching this public about their environment is through the popular media using non-academic audiovisual techniques. Non-formal, issue and practically orientated teaching methods are also perhaps the most appropriate means by which to increase public environmental awareness as these already form a familiar part of people's daily lives. In these circumstances, environmental education becomes a very practical and open concept combining immediate concerns (such as how to improve water quality) with longer-range, more theoretical concerns (such as understanding the role of water cycles in maintaining a balanced healthy ecosystem). Many innovative local-level efforts – as well as regional and global ones – have recently been made in this field, ranging from travelling poster shows carried on camels to environmental radio and TV campaigns, to multi-purpose slide–tape shows and simulation games for planners and administrators. The recognition that effective means of public communication are a very powerful tool for increasing overall environmental education – especially at the grass-roots level – was a major theme in the presentations made and discussions held during the Environment theme of the Bangalore Conference.

The Environment group held one session specifically devoted to the use of non-formal means – primarily audiovisual – of improving environmental education, and two sessions relating to this theme on community action and on the use of simulation games. It was also evident throughout the meeting that audiovisual techniques are increasingly used throughout the entire spectrum of activities related to furthering public awareness about the environment and to their role in improving and maintaining environmental quality. Among the examples of such activities described were various slide–tape shows on wildlife and general environmental conservation, local and national media campaigns in India on environmental protection and a poster-based information effort on natural resource management alternatives carried out world-wide by the Man and the Biosphere (MAB) Programme of Unesco.

DESIGN OF PUBLIC ENVIRONMENTAL EDUCATION MATERIALS

Some important common design features in these public-oriented environmental education efforts are that they should:

1. be multipurpose, adaptable and flexible for use on many levels and occasions;
2. use a common and accepted medium;
3. be economical, durable and utilize simple, easily maintained materials;
4. use relevant local themes to demonstrate broad issues (which may go well beyond local perceptions, such as the need to preserve genetic diversity);
5. use both practical experiences and scientific knowledge as the basis for proposing alternatives to current environmental practices.

ADAPTABILITY AND FLEXIBILITY: MULTIPURPOSE MEDIA MATERIALS

An important consideration in designing materials for public information and education is ensuring that they be multipurpose. Poster exhibits, slide shows and photographic displays are relatively inexpensive, and can be built up or down to serve as the core or the whole of an information/ education session. By having a "skeleton" narrative, script or scenario which can be adapted to many situations along with such core material, a variety of "lesson plans" can be developed from limited means.

The utility and desirability of such a communications programme was well demonstrated by Mark Boulton of the International Centre for Conservation Education (ICCE). ICCE has concentrated on producing multipurpose slide and slide–tape shows. These can additionally be used as the source for still photography illustration or for photo sheets, with or without full text, with fact sheets, etc. This ensures that their material, with relatively low production costs, is equally suited to rural field use, conferences or school rooms.

USE OF COMMON POPULAR MEDIA

By using locally available media, such as newspapers, radio, television or theatre, and also local facilities such as schools, museums, agricultural or health extension services, one can greatly increase the extent of acceptance and distribution of public environmental education. Examples of this kind of project include running environmental comic strips and books in local papers (East Africa, Asia), designing calendars with monthly illustrations demonstrating agricultural techniques (Nepal), using a puppet show to illustrate various land use problems and solutions, and a travelling show on water conservation using camels to carry information posters (India).

ECONOMICAL, SIMPLE, DURABLE MATERIALS

Particularly in developing countries, low-cost, long-lasting and easily maintained educational materials are essential. Equipment-intensive pro-grammes such as interactive video may be useful and appropriate in some situations, but they also require that supplies or repairs be easily available. For primarily rural efforts addressed to illiterate – although not necessarily uneducated – audiences in areas with variable supply facilities, low-cost, low-maintenance materials make more sense and are often better suited to local educational levels. In these cases, posters, radio and slide shows or films accompanied by talks and discussions are perhaps the most appropriate means to use.

LOCAL ISSUES AND CONCERNS

To be effective on the local level, environmental education must address tangible aspects of people's daily lives. While many environmental issues such as pollution or wildlife conservation raise considerable global interest, educational efforts to change local resource management practices in order to eliminate pollution or save animals will only be effective when the issues concerned are shown to make a difference in people's daily lives. Feasible, practical alternatives must be offered.

It is also useful to incorporate local community organizations, and to take advantage of local knowledge and practices in developing educational materials. By getting the support and participation of key local leaders in religious, business and community welfare groups one can facilitate the introduction of often-misunderstood concepts and practices. Building local institutional co-operation is an important part of long-term environmental education.

PRACTICAL AND SCIENTIFIC BASES

Environmental education may have different emphases in different situations. In industrialized countries, for example, environmental education often concentrates on building an understanding of the natural world. In parts of the Third World, however, it may concentrate on introducing environmentally sustainable agricultural techniques. However, the overall aim is the same: to improve the understanding and management of our environment. This objective often requires change in common resource uses and that alternatives be introduced. Such changes will come about only when feasible proven means are shown to implement these alternatives. The experiences of the Unesco Man and the Biosphere's "Ecology in Action" exhibit (see the paper by Damlamian and Hadley, p. 385) show that there is a high success rate in having alternative concepts and practices in natural resource management understood and accepted when these are based on sound research and are well demonstrated. The exhibit, which consists of 36 colour posters and is produced in English, French and Spanish, is based upon the results of some 10 years of field research in countries all over the world, and has been used as the core of thousands of local exhibits and educational efforts on environmental management as well as in academic forums. By using a multidisciplinary and multilevel approach, it is equally effective with many audiences, engineers, range managers, teachers and members of the public, in building an understanding of sound ecological alternatives in resource management.

WHEN TO USE WHAT TECHNIQUE

Discussion during the Environment theme also highlighted the question of how to choose the most appropriate medium to achieve a specific objective. The example given by Dilnavaz Variava of the campaign to save the Silent Valley (see p. 355) from an unwarranted hydroelectric project provided an excellent illustration of how a variety of public media – newspapers, radio, television and film – were (or were not) used in a public environmental education campaign to save the Silent Valley. These efforts were designed to heighten public awareness of, and participation in, a decision affecting the natural environment. Many stories were run in local and national papers to reach the broadest public audience, as well as policy-makers. Door-to-door efforts were made by local people. In contrast, a film developed for national and international audiences on the subject was made but never released: this allowed for calm negotiations rather than the raising of an emotional and political confrontation between the different interest groups involved.

This campaign also illustrated the potentials of different techniques. Pamphlets and newspaper articles were produced for local use, radio programmes for regional use and film materials for national and international use. Local talks were given to build community understanding of the issues involved. Large-scale international efforts were avoided as being counterproductive and alienating for the local public and decision-makers involved. Thus, consideration must be given to establishing which priorities are to be achieved and when, and then matching the communications tool to suit them. A final point raised in this campaign was the need to reach all levels of the public, regardless of their education, profession or institutional connection. A broad-based public environmental awareness is vital in improving environmental quality.

2

An Overview of Selected Papers

The following selection of papers gives an overview of the range and diversity of experiences in non-formal education presented at the Bangalore Conference. Some of these case studies were also presented to other workshops – edited versions of them are presented here as they highlight certain aspects of non-formal environmental education.

Environmental education is a continuous process, often part of a wider social campaign. D. Variava's work (51) shows this very clearly, demonstrating the need for an integrated, co-ordinated effort across the entire spectrum of society – from politicians to academics to local farmers – and at all levels, local, regional, national, and at times, international. She also highlights the need to demonstrate tangible benefits of environmental campaigns on the local level if long-range changes are to be achieved.

K. Blanchard's work (8) on increasing community environmental awareness and involvement in Canada parallels and complements that described by Variava.

M. Boulton's work (10) on audio-visual communications techniques provides a useful guide to assessing one's needs for these in environmental education and also gives several options in designing such a programme.

J. Damlamian and M. Hadley's case study (14) describes one international programme designed to heighten public awareness and understanding of the practical applications in ecological theory and research resources management.

A. Blum (96) and P. Fensham (18) take another popular tool – simulation games – to show how these can help demonstrate the practical applications of environmental education.

M. A. Partha Sarathy's work (41) in community and regional conservation in India shows clearly the importance of respecting and incorporating local cultures and customs – with all their diversity – in environmental education for the public.

J. Mehta's work (39) at an Indian community education centre shows both how necessary and how welcome such work is as a way of linking an

349

individual's curiosity for the natural environment to a greater environmental awareness and involvement.

T. Khoshoo's essay (32) on the India experience emphasizes the crucial role of public environmental education in recognizing that the environment is our common heritage, and we must all understand our role in protecting and maintaining it.

Finally, in addition to the published papers, mention should be made of a presentation given to the workshop by Dr James Connor (12) on the use of popular media in environmental education.

A highly successful experimental programme, run by Dr Connor, has been using comic books as the medium for its message. *Rainbow*, a comic book originally launched in Nairobi, Kenya, has addressed a wide range of environmental issues, from air and water pollution to tree planting and energy. It is geared not only for traditional school-age audiences, but also for use in adult literacy and university extension programmes.

The project has now spread to Uganda, Indonesia and Thailand, with plans to start similar projects in Nepal, Bangladesh and India. While all current material is in English, translation into Spanish (for a Honduran project) and French (for several West African countries) is foreseen in 1986.

Rainbow has been sponsored by a number of international and bilateral aid donors as a supplement to formal environmental education programmes in schools. These include CARE, UNEP, UNICEF, NORAD and DANIDA. Subjects covered in comic book form include: beekeeping, wetlands development, soil conservation, air and water pollution, family health, population issues, energy and tree-planting.

Dr Connor's experiment in raising public awareness and understanding of environmental issues through this medium has found a wide response. It has proved an effective complement to more formal academic approaches to the subject and has broadened the general public audience for environmental information.

Range, Opportunities and Applicability of Non-formal Environmental Education

M. A. PARTHA SARATHY

Available options in non-formal environmental education are much wider than one usually thinks. The importance of exploring every avenue of non-formal education available for introducing the environmental message does not appear to have been recognized to its full extent.

In a broad definition, any system of education that is outside a school can be called non-formal. However, even among school-going pupils there is room and need for non-formal opportunities. Non-formal systems also encompass a very large number of adult populations outside educational institutions, literate as well as illiterate, urban as well as rural, in positions of power as well as in positions that are not only devoid of power, but also susceptible to the effects of a variety of powers – economic, political or developmental.

Added to this is the fact that two-thirds of the world's population is in developing areas, where the level of literacy and access to schooling are limited. From this point of view further importance is added to non-formal systems, and their value should be explored to the fullest extent.

One more aspect of non-formal educational systems is worthy of special recognition, and that is that the village communities of the world have evolved information systems of their own, of communication, entertainment and education, which have stood the test of time and are therefore effective tools with which the environmental message can be conveyed. Some examples are folk art, folk music and community singing. Often the environmental message can well be an integral part of another message, that is either being conveyed from time to time to an audience which has already been conditioned to listening to this message, or to an audience which has made it a cultural habit to receive this message. All these are valuable tools which are not only cost-effective but also psychologically effective. There are also, of course, limitations to the applicability and effectiveness of these forms of communication which are often restricted to a particular culture or nation.

I will now discuss the broad areas of non-formal environmental education commonly available world-wide. First, let me divide the receiving audience into two categories – urban and rural. Let me again sub-divide these two into two sub-categories, adult and non-adult. Let us once again sub-divide these into available-for-school-opportunity and not-available-for-school-opportunity categories. Let us further divide these into decision-making and non-decision-making. We seem now to have 16 different categories. While the temptation to describe a system of education relevant to each of these categories is great, I will not yield to it. Instead, having described the multiplicity of *types* of target audience for non-formal education, let me mention some *means* of non-formal education.

For literate audiences the primary media are newspapers, periodicals and books. Some of these have incorporated an increasing quantity of information on the environment. My submission is that the teachers of science and technology have yet not fully developed these means of communication.

Radio is still a powerful and prevalent tool for conveying the environmental message. An example is the success story of agricultural self-sufficiency in India which is largely attributed to a very effective agricultural information programme on All-India Radio. Environmental education can be readily added to this, not only in India, but in most Third World countries.

Practical demonstration of aspects of the environment and description and methods by which environmental management can be improved are effective in non-formal education.

Audiovisual media such as film, radio, television, slides, photographs and photography exhibitions are certainly worth a lot of consideration. However, developing countries are restricted in this field by the need for equipment and energy. Many villagers in developing countries wake up at sunrise and go to sleep at sunset, either by choice or of necessity. Audiovisual techniques must be adapted to this kind of constraint.

Training in the technology and psychology of audiovisual messages is growing in importance. The creation of public awareness through attractive, factually correct, easily understandable environmental messages, along with demonstrations and exhibitions wherever possible, is indeed very effective. The scientific community, and those involved in the teaching of science, could help to increase the quality of such messages by providing information and techniques, and by participation in such events.

One last word about an area of education in environment, which should be applicable to all areas of the teaching of science and technology. I refer particularly to vocationally orientated teaching. In today's world, where unemployment is growing, admission to schools is becoming more difficult, and the number of people who cannot afford to go to college is increasing. We must evolve an educational system in the environmental field in which the out-of-school as well as the in-school content prepares a person at an early stage to take up environmental protection as a professional occupation.

How do we do this? One method is by the creation of more Nature Camps. These camps introduce nature and environmental education to groups of participants, often school-going children but frequently non-school-going people also. This concept deserves to be widened. The syllabus and the tools with which such education is supplied needs to be examined so that these camps can become effective as vocational guides. Here the teaching community can play a vital role.

The Saving of the Silent Valley: a Case Study of Environmental Education in Action

D. S. VARIAVA

In 1929, when an enterprising British engineer sat down and identified the Silent Valley as one of the best potential sites in Kerala for a hydroelectric project, he could not have imagined that 50 years later this tranquil valley would be the centre of a raging controversy.

Protected over millennia by its virtual inaccessibility, this 8950 ha valley of tropical wet evergreen forests forms part of a magnificent block of almost 40,000 ha of contiguous forest. The Silent Valley itself is one of the few areas in India to have been almost free of human habitation and intervention (not more than three or four trees per acre were felled for railway sleepers; a coffee plantation in the 19th century was started, and almost immediately abandoned).

Here wildlife, which has been almost eliminated from other parts of the country, still survives – the tiger, the nilgiri langur, the giant squirrel and, most valuable, one of the only two viable populations of the lion-tailed macaque – one of the world's most endangered primates. More exciting is the fact that in the dense vegetation are found wild relatives of pepper, cardamom, tobacco, black gram and other commercially valuable species – a genetic resource essential for the survival and development of their cultivated counterparts – and many medicinal plants which could provide the basis for modern life-saving drugs.

Unfortunately, as so often happens, environmentalists woke up to the existence of this area, and to the devastating effects of the proposed hydroelectric project, at a stage when the project had already been cleared by the Planning Commission of India for implementation. In fact, preliminary work had already started in 1973. The first I heard of it was in

1974 when, as the then chief executive of WWF–India, an article arrived from Romulus Whittaker for the WWF–I Newsletter. In 1976–77 a Government-sponsored Task Force for the Protection of the Western Ghats recommended that the project be dropped, but, anticipating that the odds against this happening were too great, added a series of safeguards if the project were to be implemented.

HUMANS VERSUS MONKEYS: THE ELECTRICITY BOARD'S CASE

Ironically, it was the over-anxious Kerala State Electricity Board which contributed to saving this valley by rushing to the press with its condemnation of the report, and thus drawing the attention of environmentalists to an area which might otherwise, like so many others, have been quietly destroyed. The subsequent ding-dong battle, which lasted over 6 years, saw the deployment of all types of arguments on both sides.

The protagonists for the project triumphantly paraded the following facts:

1. That the project, situated in one of Kerala's poorest regions, was an economic necessity for Kerala, generating 500 million units of energy, irrigating 10,000 ha of land and providing employment for 3000 people during its construction phase.
2. That the Silent Valley dam site provided an ideal – almost a textbook – location for a hydroelectric project, in a state which would have a power deficit by 1985 without it.
3. That every single political party in Kerala had joined forces to demand from the then Prime Minister, Shri Morarji Desai, the implementation of the project. (The only other occasion when such unanimity was achieved was when the Kerala legislators voted an enhancement of their own emoluments!) In fact, no political party in Kerala which valued its votes, dared ask for the abandonment of a project so avidly sought by the people of the economically backward Palghat district of Kerala, where it was to be located. The project was cleared by the Prime Minister, on the State Government undertaking to enact legislation ensuring the "safeguards" listed in the Task Force Report.
4. That the Kerala High Court had cleared the project for implementation.

With the promotions of 22 engineers at stake, as well as many lucrative contracts for timber felling and construction, the Kerala State Electricity Board (KSEB), and its unions, mounted an "environmental education" campaign of its own.

Unknown college professors were projected overnight as "eminent scientists" and directly or indirectly funded to produce no less than six books denigrating the importance of the Silent Valley, and scores of such articles for the local press. The objective was to project to the public, and to key decision-makers, that "scientific opinion was divided " on the value of this forest.

Words like "unique" and "virgin", which had been loosely applied by environmentalists to this valley in early stages of the campaign, were pounced upon and torn to shreds. Busloads of legislators and journalists were taken to the dam site, already denuded of trees, to show them how ecologically poor the Silent Valley was, and that the campaign was motivated by smugglers and antisocial elements who did not welcome the healthy intrusion of the Electricity Board personnel.

Eminent scientists and environmentalists who called for the dropping of the project were dubbed imperialist stooges, or cranks who were more concerned about the welfare of monkeys than of people. Officials, especially Keralites, who occupied key positions in the Central Government (including the Chairman of the Central Water Commission, an authority concerned with implementation of such projects throughout the country) were assiduously lobbied and provided with distorted information about the biological wealth of the area and the ecological impact of the dam.

The sentiments of the local population were whipped up, on the grounds of economic deprivation, so that environmentalists who went there ran the risk of physical assault if they advocated dropping the project.

MAN AND MONKEY: THE ENVIRONMENTALISTS' CASE

Environmentalists, on their part, mounted an unprecedented national campaign to create public pressure for stopping the project. Starting in 1977, when a few naturalists in Kerala visited the area after reading the KSEB-sponsored barrage in the newspaper, the campaign gained national momentum by 1979 with "Save Silent Valley" groups springing up in different parts of the country. The key elements of this campaign were the following:

1. A group of intellectuals in Kerala, who became concerned with the implications of the Silent Valley hydroelectric project, began expressing this through newspaper articles and speeches. Among these were scientists, poets, economists and political activists. The seeds of public debate on the wisdom of the project were planted.

2. The Executive Committee of the Kerala Shastra Sahitya Parishad (KSSP) was inspired, primarily through the persuasions of one of its members, Prof. M. K. Prasad, to undertake a "techno-economic, socio-political" assessment of the implications of the Silent Valley project. The report produced by its multidisciplinary Task Force, consisting of a biologist, an electrical engineer, a nuclear engineer, an

economist and an agricultural scientist-cum-economist, provided a turning point in the Silent Valley campaign. It exposed the undesirability of the project, not only on ecological grounds, but on technical, economic, and social grounds. While the little grey booklet would have found few customers from the general public, its cogent analysis provided environmental activists with important data; namely: that the energy contribution of the SV project was really marginal in the context of Kerala's power requirements, that alternative sources for augmenting power existed, that ground water provided an effective and economic source for irrigation, and that far more employment could be generated in this economically backward region through medium- and small-scale industries than through this one major project. More important, it convinced the 60-member Executive Committee of the KSSP to take up the fight to save the Silent Valley.

The KSSP's 7000 members – consisting of teachers, doctors, engineers, lawyers, scientists, agriculturists, trade union workers and others, all of whom were committed to taking science to the people as a tool for social uplift – were an invaluable weapon in the battle to save the Silent Valley. These members, and especially some of the leading intellectuals of the KSSP's Executive Committee, encouraged and participated in public debates in different parts of Kerala. The youth, especially the college-going youth, were convinced.

Through its unique annual Jatha – a 37-day marathon march from one end of Kerala to the other – KSSP members focused on the effects of deforestation through traditional cultural media like dance, drama, poetry, music, etc. The Jatha covers 300 to 400 villages along its 6000 km route.

3. Eminent scientists, and nationally or internationally renowned environmentalists, were persuaded to make public statements regarding the importance of preserving an area like the Silent Valley in a country which had already lost most of the genetic wealth that such areas represent. Members of the Government-sponsored Task Force on the Western Ghats were persuaded to state that they had been mistaken in recommending the so-called "safeguards", which had been misused to negate their substantive recommendation that the project should be dropped and the area preserved. They also stated that the safeguards could not really prevent major ecological devastation of the area, but were only an attempt to save what remained on the assumption that the project could not be dropped. The national press was constantly fed with such information by the Save Silent Valley Committees in Bombay and Madras.

4. International and national organizations like the IUCN, WWF, Bombay Natural History Society and natural history societies in other parts of the country, Friends of Trees and other organizations adopted

resolutions, lobbied through members' letters and made representations to the Central and State Governments.

5. A Court case, though eventually lost, brought an invaluable stay on
   KSEB operations, thereby providing time for the education campaign
   to have full effect.

6. Key decision-makers in Government were convinced of the importance
   of saving Silent Valley – or, at least, of keeping the options open till a
   future date, when all other power-generating options in Kerala had
   been exhausted. They became the most valuable forces in stopping the
   Silent Valley project.

Dr M. S. Swaminathan, who was then Secretary for Agriculture, India,
prepared a report highlighting the genetic wealth of the area and the
desirability of postponing the project until this resource could be studied
and tapped. Mr E. M. S. Namboodripad, Secretary of the powerful (in
Kerala) Communist Party of India (Marxist) left the matter open for
debate within the Party, having been convinced that the proposed project
was not an unmitigated blessing for the people of the area.

Above all, Mrs Indira Gandhi, who became Prime Minister in 1980,
played a critical role in asking the State Government to halt further work
until the Central and State Governments could explore the implications of
the proposed project and the alternatives that were available. A
Committee with representatives of the Central and State Governments was
set up by her, under the Chairmanship of Prof. M. G. K. Menon (then
Secretary, Department of Science and Technology) to look into the
ecological implications of the project.

THE OUTCOME

In November 1983 the Silent Valley hydroelectric project was officially
declared to have been shelved. Steps have been initiated to create the
Silent Valley National Park. In the context of an environmental education
campaign which covered all segments of society, from three successive
Prime Ministers to the peasants affected by the project, what insights can
be shared?

THE MESSAGE

A major requirement of such a campaign is a constant sensitivity to what is
the most appropriate message, to whom it should be addressed, and by
whom. Lion-tailed macaques were useful in obtaining support from
international and national conservation bodies, but counterproductive at
the local level. The "genetic treasure house" concept was effective both for
decision-makers and the general public. The Silent Valley name was

deeply evocative, and if such an advantage does not exist in other cases, it would be useful to search for some element that could create it.

Above all, however, the environmental education effort must start with an effort to understand the needs of the local people and project how the proposed conservation movement is directly beneficial to them.

THE MEDIUM

Since dropping the project involved convincing many different levels in the decision-making process, different media had to be used.

At the Prime Ministerial level, letters from such an eminent naturalist as Dr Salim Ali, the report prepared by Dr M. S. Swaminathan and representations from reputable international conservation bodies, carried weight.

At the popular level, the use of the press created national interest in the fate of the Silent Valley. In Kerala itself it was a combination of press reports and public debate that had the maximum impact. The KSSP's annual Jatha took the issue of deforestation to the countryside. An unprecedented drought in 1983 made the effects of deforestation a living reality for the people of Kerala. A special 12-day Jatha was organized during April/May 1983, covering all districts in Kerala which still had forests. Signatures were collected from 200,000 people asking the Government of Kerala to declare a moratorium on all development projects in forested areas and to stop all clear felling, especially on steep slopes.

The decision *not* to use a particular medium is often as important as a decision to use it. At the State level, representations from international conservation bodies, with their headquarters in Western countries, would have been counterproductive because of the prevailing communist ethos in this State, and were not used. Similarly an excellent little pamphlet produced in English and in the local language, Malayalam, for the legislators of Kerala, was never used for this purpose since an over-obliging printer had done the job, free of cost, on such exquisite art paper that it would only have helped confirm the allegations of those who contended that the campaign was a capitalist plot!

A 35 mm film on which one of our Committee members had laboured for days and nights was never released for screening to millions of people through the Films Division because, by the time it was ready, the campaign had moved into a phase of behind-the-scenes diplomacy rather than public outcry.

In the final stages of the campaign, key officials in the Central Government were looking into alternatives, and trying to find a possible solution. In a 4-hour discussion with the initially hostile Chairman of the Central Water Commission, it was decided that the best strategy would be to call a halt to the public controversy so that positions would not harden further, and the Central and State Governments could work on resolving the problem in the right atmosphere. There was accordingly an immediate de-escalation in the press campaign on the part of the environmental groups, and a corresponding de-escalation on the part of the supporters of the Electricity Board.

At all times, if the medium is treated only as a tool in achieving the larger aims of the campaign, and if the cause takes precedence over individual ego-needs, the choice of the appropriate medium becomes an easier one.

METHODS AND STRATEGIES

Some of the following strategies paid dividends and may be useful elsewhere.

1. Having a multidisciplinary report, so that the benefits of the project itself can be questioned. Economic considerations generally take precedence over ecological ones, always putting the "burden of proof" on conservationists. If environmentalists can convince a few of their colleagues from other disciplines to help them assess the true costs and benefits from proposed "development" projects, they could shift the ball to the other court.
2. Leading the supposed beneficiaries of development projects to look at and question the benefits which the project promises to bestow. Without this it is difficult for economically deprived people to sympathize with environmental positions which require them to sacrifice even small short-term gains in the interest of sustainable development.
3. Asking for a "postponement" of the project until other alternatives have been exploited, rather than demanding a dropping of the project, can bring public support and provide a "face-saving" escape from the project.
4. Time and energy expended in convincing key decision-makers, either directly or by using the good offices of those in whom they have confidence, is invaluable. Government officials who do not have a vested interest in a project, either in terms of potential income or prestige, can be most helpful. Those who have an open mind should not be blamed if the pro-project lobby does a better job of communicating with them than environmentalists do.
5. Good rhetoric is not a substitute for hard work and good data in convincing such decision-makers. In fact, the Chairman of the Central Water Commission strongly resented the last-minute delay in the implementation of the project on vague environmental grounds, and

not until he had received satisfactory answers to the many distorted facts fed to him by the KSEB did he suggest joint de-escalation of the confrontation through the press.

6. Though the Prime Minister's personal interest was invaluable, it does not provide for a simplistic solution to such a politically sensitive problem. There is a need for public education to make the decision a politically acceptable one.

7. The press can play a crucial role where literacy is high. In other situations the people have to be approached through more direct contact. Where a science-for-the-people movement as effective as the KSSP does not exist, environmentalists must take the trouble to convince other organizations working in the field of rural uplift to take up their cause.

8. Co-ordination in strategy formulation, and decentralization in action, proved necessary for powerful campaigning. Although Silent Valley groups had sprung up spontaneously and independently in different parts of the country, a division of functions emerged. Groups in Kerala created public awareness in their respective areas, the Friends of Trees unit in Kerala pursued the court case, the Society for Environmental Education in Kerala (SEEK) worked largely with children's groups. The Save Silent Valley Committee in Trivandrum, capital city of Kerala, provided a meeting point for important activists from different walks of life and from different political parties.

   The Save Silent Valley Committee in Bombay, the most active group outside Kerala, provided support to the efforts in Kerala. This consisted primarily in providing access to the national press, particularly important when the local press stopped giving exposure to the environmental point of view. It also played an important role in approaching eminent scientists and decision-makers in the Central Government and in keeping communications flowing between different groups for effective strategy formulation and implementation.

9. The ability to respond with speed and flexibility to rapidly changing situations was very important in contending with the strong, and financially powerful, vested interests involved in such a major project. A number of private contractors had a great deal to lose, as did some KSEB officials, if the project was dropped.

The established conservation bodies, with their multi-tiered organization structures, were less effective in responding to the demands of a rapidly evolving situation. An ad-hoc group, like the Save Silent Valley Committee, Bombay, strongly focused on a single environmental issue, with no hierarchical structure and no requirement to perpetuate itself once the campaign was over, could draw together interested members from various organizations and pool their valuable contacts and expertise.

CONCLUSION

It is difficult, even at this stage, to pinpoint precisely all the factors that contributed to the shelving of the Silent Valley hydroelectric project at the eleventh hour and in the face of formidable odds. Many aspects, especially in the realm of human motivation, will always remain as "grey areas" and conjectures. But if an objective criterion is required that the environmental education campaign worked, it is to be found in the fact that there was no outcry in Kerala when the project was eventually dropped. In the Palghat district of Kerala where the project was to have been located, and where those who called for the dropping of the project had to face the possibility of physical assault, the people suggested to the KSSP activists that a felicitation be held for the Prime Minister for dropping the project!

In the conservation field no battle is ever final. The Silent Valley campaign, where environmentalists intervened at a very late stage in the life of the project, and with a very inadequate data base to begin with, made the task more difficult, more bitter and more costly than it need have been. Now that a respite has been won, the search should be for ways in which such movements for ecologically sound development are based on planned and timely interactions between governmental and non-governmental agencies, with an objective assessment of costs and benefits. An approach of this type would be an appropriate expression of the holistic approach, which is part of the conservationists' own philosophy.

AVEHI: Audiovisual Educational Resources Centre

D. S. VARIAVA

OBJECTIVES AND FUNCTIONS

This Centre, the only one of its kind in India, is a non-profit organization which makes audiovisual material available on loan to those individuals and organizations in Bombay who wish to use this tool for imparting education and creating social change.

The Centre obtains material such as films, video-films, slide shows, flash cards, charts/posters, exhibitions and flannelograms, and makes these available on loan to those groups which are actually engaged in the work of social or economic uplift, but who do not have knowledge of, or access to, material which has been produced. With the permission of producers, AVEHI does an excellent job of modifying available material to Indian conditions, and of making them appropriate for the target audiences. The audiovisual material is translated from English into suitable Indian languages by AVEHI.

For a nominal membership fee, and screening charges which can be as low as Rs. 5 for a 2-hour screening of slide shows, members have the facility of pre-viewing material, borrowing an advance copy of the script for preparing their session, and having a projectionist arrive with equipment and slide shows on a prearranged date. An evaluation and feedback form is required to be filled in by the user, and is available for review by agencies who have donated the material.

A PROFILE OF USERS

During 1984, 57 schools and colleges, 38 organizations working in slums, 25 professional groups, 10 women's organizations, 10 hospitals and dispensaries, 6 rural organizations and 6 industrial organizations made use of the audiovisual materials available from AVEHI.

An analysis of the audiences attending the programmes at which audiovisual material borrowed from AVEHI was screened, yielded the data shown in Table 9. From the feedback and evaluation forms an analysis was made of the user's response to the question of level of satisfaction with the material and services provided. It should be noted that this analysis is an assessment of the reactions of social workers and others who had borrowed the material, and not of the audiences. In other words, it assesses the effectiveness of the tool provided to the change-agent.

Satisfied   87.6%
Not satisfied   6.7%
Not known   5.7%

TABLE 9

Socioeconomic background (%)		Educational level (%)	
Low income	42.9	Illiterate	21.5
Middle income	25.4	Semi-literate	28.4
High income	5.7	Literate	30.5
Not known	26.0	Not known	19.6

SUBJECTS COVERED

The Centre seeks and stores material on all subjects which could be useful in inculcating scientific perceptions or in bringing about socioeconomic uplift. Since many of the users are working with low-income and low-literacy groups, the initial demands are for material most directly related to the lives of these people, namely material on subjects relating to health, nutrition, etc. At later stages the demand moves to materials pertaining to more distant long-range concerns, namely environmental issues, social topics, etc. Since AVEHI works on a shoe-string budget, mainly relying on donated audiovisual material, the following data on subject break-up of material screened also partially reflects the availability of material.

Health   31.7%
Peace   22.5% (due to excellent films on Hiroshima)
Stories for children 11.2%
Social issues   8.6%
Women's issues   8.1%
Ecology   5.8%
General education   5.2%
Other   6.9%

[Editors' Note: The AVEHI has proved a successful information centre and catalyst for educational efforts in poor urban communities. It may serve as a useful model for similar efforts, particularly in developing countries of the Third World. It is highly unfortunate that AVEHI's entire stock of materials was destroyed in the 1984 Bombay floods. Despite many efforts to rebuild this stock, their work has been considerably hampered since that time. AVEHI would welcome any contributions of audiovisual materials adaptable to Indian conditions. For further information on any aspect of the Centre, contact AVEHI, c/o Indian Education Society, Napoo Road, Hindu Colony, Dadar, Bombay 400014. Tel. 451317.]

Developing Wildlife Education Programmes in a Remote Section of Canada

KATHLEEN BLANCHARD

INTRODUCTION

Natural resource managers have long known that most wildlife problems stem from people and their interactions with wildlife. It follows, then, that successful management of wildlife populations and habitats must involve conservation education both at the onset and later on as an important means of environmental conflict resolution. Combined with research, law enforcement, and habitat protection, it is a vital component of a well-balanced management plan.

Science educators today face a special challenge with respect to wildlife management. The challenge stems from the widening interface between traditional wildlife management and education. Today wildlife managers are confronted with public dissatisfaction over such issues as recovery of endangered species or effective and ethical ways to manage those that are overabundant. Often managers find themselves ill-equipped to research the socio-economic and cultural factors that motivate the public and to communicate their message effectively. Here science educators can assist the overall conservation plan by researching root elements of the problem such as people's knowledge, attitudes, and interactions with wildlife, and implementing education programmes that target those elements in ways that benefit conservation.

This paper examines a wildlife problem on the remote North Shore of the Gulf of St Lawrence and a regional education programme that was developed to address it.

THE PROBLEM AND ITS CONTEXT

Marine bird populations on the North Shore of the Gulf of St Lawrence have experienced several fluctuations since the time of European

369

exploration as a direct or indirect result of human interaction. Nesting populations declined dramatically during the 1800s, when exploitation for seabird eggs, meat, and feathers was rampant. Numbers increased during the 1920s–1950s, following the establishment of sanctuaries and the implementation of rigorous protection measures. However, recent decades have witnessed serious declines among species such as Common Eider (*Somateria mollissima*), Razorbill (*Alca torda*), and Atlantic Puffin (*Fratercula arctica*).

Causes for the declines may be varied, but numerous authors have pointed to colony disturbance and the illegal harvest of birds and eggs by local residents as important factors influencing the declines.

Pertinent to the problem were the findings of a research project, which unveiled the magnitude of the harvest and identified relevant concepts and attitudes held by residents. For instance, residents claimed that an average of 75 per cent of families in their particular village harvest seabirds and eggs. All bird species considered, with the exception of the Common Eider, are legally protected under the International Migratory Bird Treaty, yet 94 per cent of the people interviewed believed they were justified in hunting them for food. Public opinion differed considerably from the law; for instance, 81 per cent favoured an open season on the Common Murre (*Uria aalge*) and the Thick-billed Murre (*Uria lomvia*).

Residents, both adults and youths, displayed little knowledge of concepts pertaining to seabird biology and the law. For instance, 65 per cent of the adults surveyed did not know that murres were protected. In a related study of children, 85 per cent did not know that the harvest of seabirds in general was illegal, though 94 per cent of all children sampled had previously eaten seabirds or their eggs. Furthermore, results of an historical analysis showed that no formal conservation education programme had ever been attempted by wildlife agents charged with protecting and monitoring marine bird populations of the coast.

The Biophysical Environment

The North Shore of the Gulf of St Lawrence forms the southern coast of the Quebec–Labrador peninsula in the northeast part of mainland Canada. The biophysical environment is largely influenced by climate and ice conditions and the mixing of waters from the Gulf of St Lawrence with that of the cold Labrador Current. Winters are cold, summers cool, with snow and ice persisting over seabird islands even after the birds have returned. Fog is abundant and the growing season too short to sustain most crops under normal circumstances.

Tundra and shrubby thickets characterize the offshore islands; coniferous forests and muskeg occupy the interior. Seabirds are the most conspicuous wildlife of the coastal region. Less than 100,000 occur along the Gulf of the St Lawrence North Shore, with 15 species occurring as breeders.

The Sociocultural Environment

The population of the Quebec Lower North Shore subregion is approximately 5900 residents, including some 720 Amerindians. Francophones reside in three of the 15 villages and comprise approximately 21 per cent of the white population.

Immigration to the coast is low; 84.3 per cent of current heads-of-households have lived there nearly all their lives. The most important economic activity is the fishing industry, with 53.7 per cent of heads-of-households employed as fishermen and a large proportion of non-fishermen employed at fish plants. Most fishing is for Atlantic Cod (*Gadus morrhua*) but the season lasts for only 3 months. Most residents receive unemployment insurance and depend upon temporary work projects.

Transportation along the coast is limited to passenger ferry during ice-free months or by aircraft.

The average number of years of formal education among heads-of-households is 7.4. Educational services are limited, with secondary schools only beginning to develop. During the years of this study, the maximum grade level offered was Secondary III (grade 9), offered in only a few villages. Students wanting to attend school beyond the grade levels offered in their own village travelled to another village or to a school outside the Lower North Shore. Most school teachers are not from the coast, and the turnover rate from year to year is high.

Modern changes in the economy and lifestyle of the North Shore have influenced the nature of the harvesting activities and brought new pressures on the seabird populations of the coast. The rapid development of improved services, greater varieties of imported foods, increased leisure time, and enhanced purchasing power has meant that subsistence activities and family-run enterprises, once necessary for survival, now serve a variety of cultural and psychological needs, such as tradition, recreation, and social esteem. The harvest of seabirds and eggs requires an expenditure of cash; it is a function of a changing economy and of the needs and preferences of the people performing the activity.

While motivating influences are strong, barriers that would prevent the harvest from occurring are weak or nonexistent. For the past decade the bird sanctuaries have been without caretakers, and there have been only two migratory bird officers stationed full-time on the Lower North Shore. Violators of wildlife laws are seldom caught, and peer pressure among males favours the harvest. The introduction of outboard motors and semi-automatic guns facilitates access to seabird colonies and a harvest that exceeds sustainable levels.

THE MARINE BIRD CONSERVATION PROJECT

The Marine Bird Conservation Project (MBCP) began in 1978 on the Quebec Lower North Shore as a partial solution to the problem of illegal harvest of marine birds. It developed from the principle that good wildlife management involves educating people. Its premise was that education, sanctuary protection, law enforcement, and research were all vital ingredients of a comprehensive management programme for seabirds of the coast. Its purpose was to fill the gap in seabird management by providing an education programme that would address the illegal harvest, teach people about seabirds and the law, and inspire in them conservation attitudes and behaviours. The MBCP was designed to encourage learning that would lead to conservation practices by enlarging people's conceptual realm about seabirds and laws and providing them with opportunities and guidance for the expression of attitudes and behaviours about wildlife. Objectives of the project were:

1. to teach seabird biology and conservation to youths and adults;
2. to promote conservation attitudes and lawful, sportsmanlike behaviours; and
3. to establish a locally run support base for conservation.

Given a low public image of wildlife law and conservation agents, it was necessary that conservation education programmes be dissociated from the government in a formal sense. As it was, the MBCP was conceived, sponsored, and implemented by a private, non-profit organization called the Quebec–Labrador Foundation (QLF), through its environmental division, the Atlantic Centre for the Environment. Programmes depend on foundations and other supporters and are led by trained staff who work for little or no pay.

Project implementation occurred in three phases, each emphasizing important strategies that were tailored to the biophysical and sociocultural environment and aimed at producing long-term solutions to the illegal harvest problem.

Phase I involved strategies that would introduce the project in a low-key manner and would reach out to as many residents as possible. Youths and teenagers seized upon the MBCP with great enthusiasm, for it offered them an inexpensive and enjoyable week of learning about seabirds at a residential programme based at a light station and seabird sanctuary, approximately 11 km from the mainland. There they gained first-hand knowledge of ornithology, confronted daily the issue of poaching, and learned the skills and etiquettes of working with birds. Children and young teenagers from seven of the 15 villages attended the programme. They returned to their families with eager enthusiasm and infectious conversation about birds.

In a follow-up study of teenagers who had attended the programme 4 or 5 years earlier, it was found that their perspectives on wildlife had broadened from merely utilitarian to include aesthetic, scientific, and ecological perspectives, and that the vast majority of past participants were concerned about conserving seabirds.

Fostering interactions that would encourage learning among past participants and their families was an important strategy of Phase I. Numerous interactions were documented, as in the following account where the names of individuals have been changed.

> Fred (age 21) spoke up at the dinner table about going gunning for birds. Both Laurie (age 10) and Jim (age 12) blurted to their brother that if he brought birds home to the table they wouldn't eat them. (Both Laurie and Jim had participated in the MBCP.) Following their remark, their father admonished Fred's intentions and began to expound on the life history features of puffins.
>
> At dinner the next day, the family ate razorbill and murre that Fred had shot. Sally (age 16) and Jim explained, "Well, if you had only seen the birds out on St. Mary's – seen them up close and the way they live – well, you wouldn't be able to kill them for sure!"

Phase II more directly confronted the issue of seabird conservation and the long-term effectiveness of the project by engaging the active participation of leading adult members of the communities and training them to assume much of the teaching responsibilities. School teachers did not receive the training, as their turnover rates from year to year were too high.

Workshops, films, and evening lectures were offered free of charge and on a regular basis in the communities, and carefully scheduled so as not to conflict with social and religious events. Adults who showed interest were taken on one-day field trips to the St Mary's Seabird Sanctuary. Meetings were held weekly with the Parents' Committee (a powerful committee of parents whose children attend the local school) to discuss ways of incorporating conservation education into the school system and creating a wildlife society for the coast. From the workshops and meetings there emerged a body of adults who possessed the interest, motivation, and local authority to begin to assume positions in conservation education. Under the guidance of the MBCP staff, the group incorporated itself as a conservation society under the following purpose:

> In these changing times, this society will provide an opportunity for adults and children to learn about their past and the natural environment of the Lower North Shore. It will seek to preserve the cultural and environmental heritage of this area for future generations. An important goal of the club will be to promote the wise use

of native plant, fish, and wildlife populations through education and through acting as a collective voice to insure conservation.

Officers were selected, funds raised, and memberships solicited for this first locally run wildlife society on the coast. By 1983 the society had raised enough funds to purchase the oldest building in one of the villages as site for a meeting place and heritage museum.

During a 3-year period, MBCP staff worked diligently to train a local resident to conduct the conservation programme for youths, known as the "Hawkeyes", specifically tailored to the North Shore environment. Regional and provincial government agents took notice of the local initiative, along with news articles and radio, and encouraged the group for its important work.

With the training of local leaders teaching materials were developed and a school programme initiated. A poster was created that portrayed the important seabirds of the coast. It was distributed free of charge among families, schools, and community centres, and hung conspicuously on ships, wharves, and in general stores. It was carefully designed to portray only those concepts that were considered essential and yet lacking in people's knowledge of seabirds and the law. Such concepts as delayed maturity and low reproductive output are important contributing factors in causing seabirds and their populations to be vulnerable to disturbance. The poster was aesthetic, highly relevant to the North Shore, and nonaggressive in its pitch, "Help conserve our precious wildlife."

Also created was a slide-tape programme that utilized photographs of local children and familiar scenes. It was used in schools in conjunction with a lesson and discussion about seabirds.

Phase III of the Marine Bird Conservation Project was targeted at broadening support for seabird conservation and facilitating the gradual take-over of conservation education activities by local people. Strategies included a study tour of the coast for representatives of appropriate conservation organizations. It succeeded, and several organizations are now actively involved in helping the cause.

In 1984 a major breakthrough occurred when the Government of Canada awarded the project a major grant which allowed the hiring of twelve residents during a 20-week period. Employed as teachers, boatmen, carpenters, and assistants, the local people were supervised and trained by the MBCP staff. Thanks to employment opportunities provided by the government, the MBCP took a giant leap in popularity and effectiveness on the coast.

Other strategies important to the success of the MBCP include:

1. local leaders giving public testimony to the need for conservation;
2. popular and well-known figures from outside coming to the coast to speak in support of conservation;

3. local teachers trained in conservation continuing the work in schools as volunteers;
4. frequent meetings with federal wildlife agencies to ensure that the educational programme fits suitably with overall management goals.

Long-term effects of the project were revealed in a follow-up study which showed that children who had previously participated in the MBCP were more knowledgeable about seabird biology and ecology than those who had not. In addition, the attitudes of those who had participated were more diverse, developed, and positive. Short-term effects of the school programme were that knowledge of seabird ecology increased and attitudes broadened from primarily utilitarian views to ecological and aesthetic ones.

CONCLUSION

The biophysical and sociocultural environment of the North Shore of the Gulf of St Lawrence plays a vital role in the problem of illegal harvest of seabirds; recognition of such should be an important element in the design of an educational programme. Opportunities for expanding knowledge, attitudes, and experiences contributed to effective learning about conservation. Programmes aimed at changing people's knowledge, attitudes, and behaviour about a controversial subject in conservation should involve those people early in the planning and operational phases and train them to assume leadership roles in the project.

[The author provides numerous references to research work associated with this project – Eds.]

Audiovisual Techniques for Conservation

MARK N. BOULTON

It has become increasingly evident in recent years that progress in the field of conservation and development is, to a large degree, dependent on an informed and sympathetic public. Whilst modern science continues to develop a bewildering variety of new technology for the would-be communicator, the purpose of this paper is to underline the important role that even the more modest audiovisual techniques can play in conservation education.

Although, strictly speaking, any presentation which links images with the spoken word can be termed "audiovisual" – from the live use of a blackboard or flip chart to the present-day video disc and three-dimensional holography, this paper will confine itself to the relevance of filmstrips and slide presentations to the field of conservation.

WHY AUDIOVISUAL?

If, as the Chinese proverb suggests, "a picture is worth a thousand words", then a series of dramatic visuals accompanied by a carefully narrated text should prove to be an extremely effective way of spreading the conservation message. Research on the efficiency of information transfer suggests that the average student remembers less than 10 per cent of what he reads, about 20 per cent of what he hears, and about 30 per cent of what he sees. However the combination of sight and sound together increases retention to more than 50 per cent, and subsequent discussion can raise this above 70 per cent. Since audiovisual by definition utilizes both sound and sight – usually simultaneously – then its potential as a tool for communicating conservation is clearly evident. Having made the decision to use AV techniques, however, the potential user is left with a mass of unanswered questions on the different methods of presentation, the nature and cost of the equipment, whether to "buy-in" prepared programmes or prepare programmes oneself, and where to obtain further advice and information.

WHY FILMSTRIPS AND SLIDE PROGRAMMES?

Why use filmstrips and slide programmes in preference to films and video? Whilst all these media have their own contribution to make in the conservation field, filmstrips and slides do offer several distinct and in some cases, unique advantages.

Economy   Both are relatively cheap to purchase and to produce. It is generally reckoned that the production of a slide–tape programme costs less than 5 per cent of a comparable 16 mm film, and copies of a pack of 60 slides may cost less than UK£10 each compared with the average 16 mm film at UK£300 or more.

Flexibility   A programme purchased as a 60-frame filmstrip for around UK£5 can be used unaltered with the script provided, or may be cut into separate frames and mounted to make slides. These in turn may be rearranged to suit the "live" message of the presenter, or mixed with other resource materials as required. Programmes are also readily updated by substitution or addition of new material.

Quality   There is a widely held view that filmstrips and slide duplicates are necessarily "inferior" to the more sophisticated film and video materials. In fact the reverse should be the case! Original slides (and good-quality copies too) may be enlarged using a good projector to 4 metres or more across, and the sound quality from a well-prepared cassette far exceeds that of a 16 mm film optical sound track. Mix slide and tape well with a good twin projector "cross-fade" system and the audience is never quite sure whether it has been watching a film or a slide show – but is usually very impressed with the presentation.

Speed   The production time for filmstrip and slide presentations is much shorter than for 16 mm films (which are rarely completed within a year). Trainees at the International Centre for Conservation Education (ICCE) have completed slide–tape programmes within a fortnight!

FILMSTRIPS OR SLIDE PROGRAMMES?

Although it is possible to originate AV programmes so that they can be distributed as both filmstrips *and* slide-packs it is appropriate to consider the relative advantages of each.

Most of the early AV materials – certainly those used in schools – were supplied as *filmstrips*: continuous lengths of 35 mm film comprising a series of images or frames. Some of these were "full-frame" (image size 36 × 24 mm) others were "half-frame" (image size 24 × 18 mm). Such filmstrips were cheap to produce, light to distribute (especially overseas) and also eliminated the risk of losing individual frames – always a danger with slide-packs. Once the user established how to thread the filmstrip correctly into the projector (some readers will know from bitter experience that even the humble filmstrip can be loaded in four different ways, only one of which projects a picture the correct way up and the right way round!) the sequence of appearance of the pictures is fixed and the frames cannot be projected in the wrong order. However early filmstrips were often very poor quality and it was sometimes difficult to tell whether they were colour or black and white!

Fortunately there have been substantial improvements in quality in recent years. Some found the inability to change the sequence of pictures a serious disadvantage, and unless fairly sophisticated production facilities are to hand, updating of filmstrips is impossible. In general, filmstrips are also unsuitable for use with pre-recorded tape/cassette commentaries although there are a few manufacturers who market filmstrip projectors which incorporate a cassette recorder. Such units automatically advance the filmstrip one frame at a time in response to signals received from the "synch" track of the cassette. Perhaps the greatest advantage of filmstrips is their low cost – about half that of a comparable slide-pack. Those on economy budgets may consider it worth purchasing AV programmes in filmstrip form and then cutting and mounting the individual frames into standard slide mounts. Before doing so it is wise to check that a "full-frame" filmstrip is being purchased and not a "half-frame" version.

Slide packs would now appear to be the more popular way of presenting AV programmes. Most colour slide films are returned from the processing laboratories in "ready-to-project" card or plastic mounts, and a wide variety of 35 mm slide projectors are now available to suit most pockets. Relatively basic projectors utilizing straight trays or magazines into which 36 or more slides are pre-loaded can be purchased for around UK£40, and some of them include remote-control facilities. Rotary magazine projectors such as the well-known Kodak Carousel, which carry 80 (occasionally 140) slides have become the accepted standard for "professional" presentations, though at the top of their range these will cost UK£500. Such projectors have many additional facilities including built-in spare bulbs, exchangeable lenses, thermal cut-outs to prevent damage by overheating, and remote sockets allowing sophisticated electronic control and coupling with other projectors and even computers for multi-image/multi-screen presentations. Fortunately even some of the cheaper projectors now carry the "DIN" socket, which is necessary if the projector is to be coupled with a tape/cassette recorder for automatic presentations.

A universal requirement for both filmstrip and slide projectors is of course a source of electricity. Some projectors can be adapted to operate from 12-volt car batteries, though they draw heavily on the current and the batteries must be recharged very frequently. Where mains electricity is not available all will operate perfectly well from even the smallest petrol generators (the World Wildlife Fund is using dozens of these for rural conservation education programmes in developing countries).

THE "LIVE" PRESENTATION

The potential of the "live" presentation should never be underestimated – though its final impact will depend to a great extent on the skill and knowledge of the presenter. Thorough preparation is essential and slides should be chosen not merely for their technical and aesthetic value (though both are important), but so that they form a logical series of visual images which help to guide the theme of the talk. Time spent preparing title slides, occasional graphics and end credits make for a more professional approach. Whenever possible the projector should be situated at the rear of the projection room (rather than in the middle of the audience) and it may often be necessary to use a long-focus lens (180 or 250 mm). The projector should ideally be controlled by the presenter, and this is usually accomplished using a remote hand control on a long extension lead (although infra-red cordless controls are becoming more readily available). Care should be taken to avoid talking too directly about the projected slides (the "this as you will see is a tiger in long grass" approach!) since this undervalues the intelligence of the audience. The most effective presentations are often those where the visuals form a "structured background" to a talk which would be interesting in its own right – even without the pictures.

SLIDE–TAPE PRESENTATIONS

There will always be those who, for reasons of time, or lack of specialized knowledge or confidence, prefer to utilize pre-recorded narrations. Although these are less personal and direct than a live presenter, they have the advantages of a professional voice, music and/or sound effects, and of being predictable in length (unlike some "live" presenters!). Whilst it is possible to use such slide–tape packages by playing the cassette on a domestic cassette recorder (assuming the sound output is adequate) and advancing the slides manually, this requires very thorough preparation and complete concentration during the performance. Those considering the regular use of such presentations would be well advised to consider purchasing special slide–tape equipment.

Although a number of "magic boxes" are advertised which can, in theory, link any slide projector to any cassette/tape recorder, the serious user will need access to a cassette recorder having an "AV head". Although such units still use the standard international compact cassette, they are specially constructed to respond to control pulses (or "cue-tones") carried on track 4 of the cassette tape, whilst the audio (narration/music/ sounds effects) is carried on tracks 1 and 2. Track 3 is usually left blank to avoid any possible interference between the "inaudible" control pulses and the commentary (though on some recent formats tracks 3 and 4 are used to increase the reliability of detection of the pulses). It follows of course that AV cassettes can only be used "one way" – they cannot be turned over and used on the other side like domestic cassettes. It also follows that if one is confronted with a troublesome cassette which does not appear to operate correctly with a slide–tape unit, it can be turned over and played "upside down" to find out if the control pulses are present. A number of manufacturers make basic units which, apart from their AV head, differ little from ordinary domestic recorders. Examples are the Philips AV cassette, and the Hanimex synchrocorder. Much better, however, are units made especially with slide–tape in mind – such as the Coomber 353 AV machine (around UK£225 in UK) which combines a high-quality amplifier and public address system (with large built-in speaker) with the AV cassette unit. ICCE has designed a special "Pandamatic" system for use under tropical field conditions where the electronics are protected against dust and adverse climate by enclosure in an extremely durable rigidized aluminium case. With such equipment, all that is necessary to present a pre-recorded slide–tape show is to load the slide magazine onto an appropriate projector, link it to the "Pandamatic" with a single lead, place the cassette in the AV cassette deck, and press the play button. The pre-recorded (1 kHz) pulses automatically change the slides at the correct places in the narration.

More sophisticated units can control two or more projectors – not merely advancing the slides automatically, but fading or dissolving from one image to the next – thus avoiding the blank/black screen interval which occurs in most single-projector presentations. Is such an expensive technique justified? (This system costs at least double that of an ordinary single slide–tape unit.) The answer depends very much on the intended use, the level of sophistication of the audience, the budget available, and the experience of the operator. Such units are ideal for permanent installations in visitor centres, for major lecture tours, and other special presentations – but in a "Third-World" situation it would almost certainly be preferable (budget permitting) to purchase two single AV units, and to use them in different locations. There is little doubt, however, that the two-projector system is an extremely effective medium, whether used "live" or with pre-recorded cassettes. It allows for very professional presentations with the possibility of a wide range of special effects such as the building up of complex graphics or the changing of one scene dramatically into another. As a general guideline, the total cost of two Kodak Carousel projectors, long-focus lenses, and a portable AV/amplifier/cross-fade system would be about the same as the cost of a 16 mm projector, but the possibilities for the creative user are virtually limitless. Finally it is also worth noting that twin-projector "cross-fade" presentations may be very effectively transferred to "video", although access to specialized equipment is required to obtain the best results.

TO PURCHASE OR TO PRODUCE?

An increasing range of good AV presentations on conservation issues –
both national and international – is becoming available. Programmes on
threatened species and habitat loss, as well as the broader issues of
population, pollution and diminishing resources, can all be found in
educational AV sales catalogues with prices ranging from as low as UK£3
for the small resource packs to UK£25 for longer presentations complete
with cassettes. Although it may be possible to obtain such programmes on
approval, producers are often somewhat reluctant to risk the possibility of
damage by poor handling. A number of these presentations are reviewed
in the conservation press, and it is usually possible to obtain a good idea of
the content and quality of the materials from such reports.

Sooner or later, however, one may wish to deal with a topic on which no
AV material seems to exist, or to use an approach which differs from the
available presentations. How does one go about producing an AV
programme? What skills are needed? How much will it cost? Limitations of
space only allow mention of a few general guidelines on the subject.
Perhaps the most basic question is "Which comes first – the text or the
pictures?". Experience would suggest that many "live" lectures on
conservation are in fact based on the available slides, the story-line being
developed to suit the pictures in hand. Providing enough material is
available and the presenter well-informed, such presentations are often
very effective and could well form the basis of an "AV" programme.
Several major presentations prepared by the author originated in this
manner. On the whole, however, it is better to prepare a "story-line" first
and then, on the basis of the slide material available, develop the
story-board into a full script. Rarely is it possible to locate all the "ideal"
visuals, but at the same time, excellent slides turn up which were not
anticipated. Modifications may then need to be made to the text to
accommodate them. The soundest procedure is perhaps to first prepare a
written response to the following questions:

1. What is the major objective/message of the proposed AV?
2. What is the target audience? (old/young; literate/illiterate?)
3. Will it be used live (by reading from a prepared script) or using a
   pre-recorded narration? (with music/sound effects?)
4. Are the necessary original colour slides available? If not, will others be
   prepared to loan their material or will it be necessary to obtain them
   from a photo-agency? (and adjust the budget accordingly!)
5. Are the required skills available to prepare the script, select the slides,
   undertake the graphics, record the narration, "mix in" the music and
   sound effects, or will some (perhaps all) of these tasks need to be
   delegated to others? (and how much will this cost?)
6. How many copies are required of the finished presentation?

Some impressive AVs have been prepared by a single individual, but normally substantial additional expertise will be required if the programme is to be fully effective. The answers to the above questions will help in programme planning, to estimate the production costs, and to seek technical assistance/sponsorship as necessary. It is impossible to specify the exact budget required since there are so many variables. One of the most effective and popular presentations prepared by the former WWF/IUCN International Education Project ("Why Conserve Wildlife?") was originated for less than UK£50. The use of all the slides, scripting, graphics, and the narration by Sir Peter Scott were all donated, and the sound mixing was carried out on a domestic stereo tape recorder. In contrast, the most sophisticated presentations prepared recently for twin projectors have had to carry the costs of "bought-in" slides, hired studios, paid narrators, and music copyright fees. It is of course possible to put the whole presentation out to a commercial AV production house, but find your sponsor first! If the decision is taken to tackle the production personally then the most important requirements are probably motivation, the capacity to learn new skills and sheer dogged perseverance! And in case one gets too wrapped up in the technical intricacies of the process, it is wise to get some constructive criticism from others at appropriate stages in the production.

ICCE has in many instances been involved in co-productions with other organizations. Programmes as varied as "Turtles in Danger" (with the Species Survival Commission of IUCN), "Underwater Conservation Code" (with the Marine Conservation Society), "Focus on Otters" (with the Royal Society for Nature Conservation), "Renewable Energy for Today and Tomorrow" (with the National Centre of Alternative Technology), "Desertification – its causes and some solutions" (with UNEP) and "Planning for Survival" (with the Education Commission of IUCN) were all produced in this manner.

ARE AVs EFFECTIVE?

How does one measure success? By the size of the audience, or by the "oohs and aahs" after the performance? By the number of programmes sold or by the solving of conservation problems? Almost 10 years of involvement in AV work suggests that all of the above can be positive indicators. AVs can certainly increase the level of awareness on conservation issues; they can suggest specific action required to tackle conservation problems; they can "motivate" and "enthuse" those who watch them. More than 1000 packs of just one AV programme, "Saving the Whale", have now been distributed to a dozen or more countries and an Icelandic version has been prepared by whale conservation groups for a campaign in that country. "The Mountain Gorilla" – prepared to support the Mountain Gorilla Project in Rwanda and narrated in both Rwandese and French, has

made a major contribution to raising the level of environmental consciousness in that country. More than 300 copies of the programme prepared to
support the WWF Tropical Forest and Primates Campaign ("A Green
Earth or a Dry Desert?") have been widely distributed in English, French,
and Spanish. A "multi-media" pack for children based on the World
Conservation Strategy is in widespread use in British schools and has been
adapted for use in Spain and Belgium (where 6000 copies were distributed
free by one of the large banks). The indications are certainly very positive.

But a final note of caution. AVs are not the "magic answer" to all the
world's conservation problems. They will not prevent the extinction of
species. They will not solve the problems of acid rain. They will not, by
themselves, result in a greater use of renewable energy or save the rain
forest. What they can, indeed will, do, however, is to promote greater
awareness of conservation and the environment, and increase the level of
knowledge and concern. After all, this is the vital prerequisite for informed
debate and appropriate action.

Ecological Information for Non-specialists: an International Case Study

JEANNE DAMLAMIAN and MALCOLM HADLEY

COMMUNICATING RESEARCH RESULTS: FOR WHOM AND HOW?

In the past decade there has been a very marked heightening of awareness to environmental concerns. Coverage by the mass media, together with public and privately sponsored information campaigns at national and international levels, have succeeded in giving the public a sense of the extent, seriousness and urgency of the environmental problems in the world today. This is no small achievement, given the nearly total ignorance, 15 or 20 years ago, of such matters which most people take almost for granted today. And given the difficulty of "competing" with the information being bombarded at those with access to modern mass media.

How have these basic messages about the environment been transmitted? Largely by appealing to people on an emotional level, using striking pictures or graphics intended to make people stop, look, and think. But such an approach, however effective, has limited educational impact, as little or no substantive information is conveyed.

Yet a large body of scientific knowledge about the environment already exists, and research is providing new information all the time. But most of this information is accessible to scientists alone, usually couched in technical language and presented in a way that the layman can neither appreciate nor understand. The need to educate non-specialists about the environment by finding a middle ground of communication – between emotions and technical information – is a major challenge facing scientists and communicators today. The goal is clear, but what we do not know is how.

Ecological research is intended to extend the frontiers of knowledge. But its results also have a practical application outside the academic world. One major user group is those responsible for deciding how natural

385

resources will be used – that very heterogeneous group known as "decision-makers". Also interested is a variety of groups concerned in one way or another with man's interaction with the environment, both locally and in other parts of the world. Educators, environmental groups, local associations and the general public are among such potential users of research results.

Finding the middle ground to allow these diverse audiences to benefit from environmental research means that the results must be "digested", "translated" and "adapted" to their needs. How can scientists ensure that the results of their research are effectively communicated to lay audiences? Unesco's Man and the Biosphere (MAB) Programme is testing one approach to dealing with these questions through its poster exhibit "Ecology in Action".

COMMUNICATION AS PART OF THE RESEARCH PROCESS

MAB is an international programme of research and training designed to produce information for improving land use. Research centres around concrete management problems bringing together whatever disciplines of the natural and social sciences are needed to cover the many facets of the problem at hand, often involving local populations.

Since the underlying goal of MAB research lies in its ultimate application to land use planning and resource management, for a MAB project to fulfil all of its objectives, its results – as well as being diffused through normal scientific channels – need also to be presented in a form which can be understood and used by the "non-specialists" for whom they are also intended.

As MAB field projects began to yield results in the late 1970s, MAB scientists were increasingly interacting with local and national decision-makers, curriculum planners, etc. Scientists generally are not encouraged to consider communication as part of their research function, and not rewarded professionally for their efforts; the knowledge of scientists needs to be articulated with the skills of communication specialists, since neither scientist nor communicator can do it alone; particularly important is transmission of ecological information given its relevance to issues ranging from the day-to-day management of resources, to the content of school curricula and the future of the biosphere itself; communication is not included in determining research budgets and the make-up of project teams.

To help mark the tenth anniversary of the programme the MAB Secretariat was asked to prepare an exhibit which would contribute to a review and evaluation of what had been accomplished within MAB during its first ten years. Rather than prepare an exhibit which would be shown, as most exhibits are, in one place and at one time, the MAB Secretariat, in collaboration with a Paris-based group of communication specialists (Etudes et Planification des Communications), decided to prepare an exhibit which would attempt to reach a very large number of people throughout the world, and which would stimulate further efforts on the part of MAB scientists to communicate research results by providing a high-quality core around which larger exhibits could be built.

The Ecology in Action exhibit (Figure 6, Table 10) consists of 36 colour posters, printed initially in 1000 copies (and later reprinted in 2000 copies) and in three languages (English, French and Spanish). Such a "poster exhibit" has the potential of reaching a greater number of people than almost any medium short of television, radio and other means of mass communication. A book, for example, if mass-produced, may be read or looked at by 40,000 or 50,000 people. A single copy of an exhibit on display for several weeks will be seen by several thousand visitors. Once mounted, an exhibit is "permanently" ready for consultation by the passer-by, unlike a book that has to be opened or a film that has to be shown.

Multiplying an exhibit by a factor of several thousand further increases the number of people involved. When any of the 3000 copies are used several times the impact is even greater. The availability of the MAB exhibit in several languages, and the possibility of easily producing other language versions, are further advantages which increase the usefulness of the exhibit on the international scale. From a cost–benefit perspective the cost per user is very low, especially as the exhibit has been prepared by an international organization on a non-commercial basis.

This multiple-impact approach concentrates scarce funds on communicating the message rather than on the cumbersome and expensive "hardware" (display equipment, etc.) used in traditional-style exhibits, hardware which does not always contribute significantly to getting the message across. The poster form minimizes such costs. Posters can be displayed in a variety of inexpensive and simple ways (from being stuck on the wall to being mounted on cardboard or wooden panels), depending on local resources. Obviously this low-cost approach does not preclude a more elaborate presentation limited only by the imagination of the organizers and the money at their disposal.

MULTILEVEL INFORMATION FOR A VARIETY OF AUDIENCES

Identification of a target audience is a key step in the communication of the results of scientific research. In the planning of Ecology in Action, the idea of concentrating on a single target audience was considered at length but finally eschewed. Rather, it was decided to experiment with an exhibit that could appeal to several audiences and thereby further increase its impact. Such an exhibit could later be adapted to the needs and interests of more restricted audiences by adding complementary components. The target

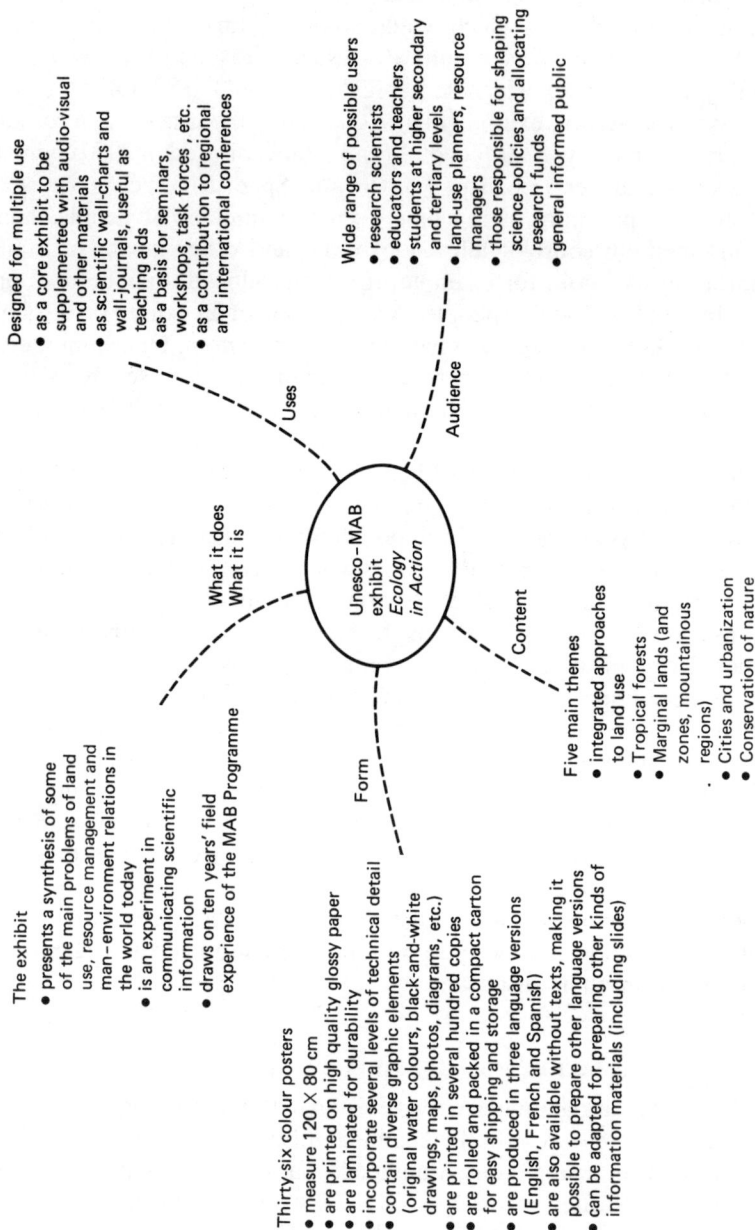

Fig. 6   The "Ecology in Action" exhibit at a glance. From di Castri *et al.*, *Nature & Resources*, 18(2), 1982.

TABLE 10 Ten Design Features of the Unesco Poster Exhibit "Ecology in Action"

1. Root educational and information materials on the results of field research.
2. Seek middle ground between graphics for heightening environmental awareness and ways in which scientists usually report research findings.
3. Look for ways to multiply the impact of synthesized information (e.g. multiple copies, multilevel audiences, adaptability to different uses).
4. Enjoin the efforts of scientists and communication specialists.
5. Present scientific information at different levels of technical detail.
6. Shrink the time delay between generation and application of research information.
7. Seek balance between scientifically proven information and doubts and uncertainties of science.
8. Combine information from social and biological sciences.
9. Take account of diversity of geographical scales, time frames and perceptions in respect to land use problems.
10. Prepare materials which provide a global perspective within which local problems can be placed.

audiences of Ecology in Action thus reflect the heterogeneity of the potential users of the results of environmental research: the informed general public, decision-makers responsible for determining science policy and the allocation of research funds, land use planners and resource managers of various kinds, educators and students at secondary school and tertiary levels, research workers from various disciplines, etc.

To reach these different groups, a "multilevel" or "menu à la carte" approach was adopted; multilevel in terms of the user's interest, scientific knowledge and the time available for viewing the exhibit. These factors are vital to determining receptiveness and the user's ability to understand and absorb the information presented. In practical terms, this approach meant incorporating into the posters different hierarchies of information, more or less detailed, more or less technical, more or less time-consuming to read. Individual viewers can thus make use of the exhibit at a level appropriate to their interests, training and available time.

Resolving the dilemma of how much information to put in each poster was not always easy. A balance had to be struck between presenting small amounts of easily understood information (possibly undermining the scientific impact and use of the posters as teaching aids) and including many more words and details (and thereby running the risk of losing the interest of the decision-makers and the general public). Some aspects of this dilemma are outlined in Table 11.

The time factor was also a difficult hurdle. The way the information has been presented makes it possible for users to obtain something from each poster even in a very short time (30 seconds), while still including the kind and amount of information that can be absorbed only in a longer period (e.g. 30 minutes). The latter is necessary if the posters are to be used as teaching aids.

TABLE 11   The Dilemma of "How Much Information?": Effects of More or Less Text. From di Castri *et al.*, *op. cit.*

Less text	More text
Little information content	Information content relatively high
Tendency to resemble advertising material	Tendency to resemble scientific wallchart or poster lectures
Rapid and direct impact	More effort, more time required to digest information
Short "half-life" (e.g. a few months–1 year)	Longer "half-life" (1–5 years)
Danger of being considered by scientists as too simplistic	Greater chance of capturing interest of scientists
Particularly useful for decision-makers, general public	Less appropriate for communicating with decision-makers, general public
Not particularly useful for teaching	Useful for environmental education and other teaching purposes

The multi-level approach was also reinforced by the need to capture the interest of the various audiences that are likely to be attracted to different styles and forms of visual expressions. Presentation of the results and experience of MAB research for a range of potential users thus called for the use of very diverse visual elements, including: simplification and redrawing of graphics originally presented in highly technical form, use of hard data acquired in field studies to demonstrate general ecological principles, development of new visual representations of certain fundamental concepts underlying MAB research (e.g. human use system, interdisciplinarity, new approaches to conservation, cities viewed as ecological systems), use of photographs contributed by MAB scientists and of maps developed as tools for advancing scientific work. It can thus be said that the Ecology in Action exhibit is indeed "rooted" in MAB research, and as such represents an experimental endeavour to communicate technical research outputs to non-specialists (as opposed to the obviously no less valid approach of developing educational materials on various environmental subjects without basing these materials directly on information acquired in field research).

PUTTING THE EXHIBIT TO USE

The many different ways in which it has already been used would seem to indicate that Ecology in Action is a flexible and adaptable communication tool which can be an effective trigger for further action. And the diversity of those expressing interest in the exhibit can be taken as a sign not only that there is a clear need for such materials, but also that the posters do appeal to a variety of audiences. Among those that have acquired the exhibit are secondary schools, universities, research institutes, environ-

TABLE 12   Sampling of Ways in which the "Ecology in Action" Exhibit
has been Used

Brazil/Portugal: plans to jointly translate posters into Portuguese and to reproduce in multiple copies.

Chile: used to inaugurate refurbished Museum of Natural History in Santiago; preparation of new panels based on MAB field projects – in mountain areas, grazing lands, continental waters.

China: translation of 36 posters into Chinese; preparation of ten new panels on Chinese MAB research; travelling exhibit to seven major cities; plans to put on permanent display at the planned Hangzhou Centre of Man and Environment.

Finland: preparation of slide package based on posters and distribution by MAB National Committee.

France: major 2-month exhibit for general public at Paris City Hall; preparation and printing of 25 new panels on examples and subjects of particular interest to the French public, including some panels based on MAB field projects (both at home and abroad) involving French scientists.

German Democratic Republic: printing of German version of posters envisaged in first quarter of 1985.

India: mounting of several sets of the exhibit and display with locally produced wall-charts in 46 workshop–exhibitions in 14 cities, where viewed by many thousands of school children. Other uses include display in National Museum of Natural History, during Parliamentary Environmental Forum, on World Environment Day.

Indonesia: translation of five posters into Bahasa Indonesia; printing in several thousand copies and distribution to schools envisaged.

Ireland: used as a roving exhibition in conjunction with a national poster competition for school children run by national association of art teachers.

Italy: translation into Italian under way, with printing in one thousand copies foreseen; translation will consist also of "experimental" adaptation of existing texts for schools and preparation of teachers' guide.

Ivory Coast: travelling exhibit to major urban centres; displayed on occasions of meetings of Ministers of Scientific Research (1983) and of MAB Committees (1984) of francophone African countries.

Mexico: displayed during Unesco Week in Mexico; used in conferences and seminars organized by Instituto di Ecologia, INIREB and other tertiary institutions.

Morocco: used in round tables and travelling exhibitions on themes such as "Soils and Development", organized in cooperation with the Centre Culturel Français.

New Zealand: used in training programmes for national parks staff and during the fifteenth Pacific Science Congress.

Nigeria: incorporated in National Science and Technology Fair; used as teaching tool by International Institute of Tropical Agriculture.

Norway: translation of fourteen posters into Norwegian, printing in several hundred copies, and distribution by UN Association of Norway.

Senegal: on permanent display at the Institut des Sciences de l'Environnement; displayed in regional capitals to mark World Environment Day.

Spain: translation of six posters into Catalan, printing in several thousand copies and distribution to all secondary schools in the region; translation of twelve posters into Basque, printing in more than a thousand copies, and distribution to schools in the region.

Sri Lanka: preparation of hand-calligraphed sets of the exhibit in Sinhala and Tamil, loaned to schools by the national authority responsible for Natural Resources, Energy and Science.

Syrian Arab Republic: Arabic translation of text of posters prepared by the Arab Centre for Study of Arid and Dry Lands (ACSAD), located in Damascus (possible ways for publication of Arabic version currently being examined with ALECSO).

cont.

TABLE 12 (*cont.*)

Tunisia: used in events to commemorate la Journée de l'Arbre ("Tree Day"); on display in the ecological museum of Ickheul (biosphere reserve and world heritage site).

USSR: translation of 36 posters into Russian; preparation of fifteen new posters on environmental protection, printed in 60,000 copies and distributed to schools with a teachers' manual; preparation of special exhibits for First Biosphere Reserve Congress (Minsk, September 1983) by the Soviet MAB Committee (concerning the seven biosphere reserves in the USSR) and the Byelorussian MAB Committee (on the Berezinsky biosphere reserve).

United Kingdom: used in displays at Royal Geographical Society in London, Royal Botanic Gardens at Kew, UK United Nations Association Centre, etc.; placed in the libraries of museums such as the British Natural History Museum and Leeds City Museum.

USA: used in conjunction with World Fair in Knoxville, Tennessee; formed part of wider exhibit at the 1984 Summer Olympics in Los Angeles; put on display at environmental education and science centres, zoological gardens, community colleges, National Park visitors' centres.

Zambia: used by the Wildlife Conservation Society of Zambia in seminars and leadership training courses for club leaders and teachers.

---

mental associations, conservation groups, senior citizens' organizations, prisons, municipalities, Unesco Clubs, National Commissions for Unesco, MAB National Committees, learned societies, departments of forestry and land use planning, ministries of education and of science policy planning, museums and international scientific organizations.

In June 1982, posters from the MAB exhibit were widely used in events to commemorate World Environment Day and the tenth anniversary of the Stockholm Conference on the Human Environment, in such countries as Argentina, Australia, Belgium, Chile, Cuba, Ecuador, Malaysia, Malta, Mauritius, Mexico, Nepal, New Zealand, Peru, Senegal, Spain, Singapore. In several countries, including Cameroon, India, Netherlands and Portugal, single copies of the exhibit have been mounted and have been sent on tour from one town to another.

Science museums and botanical gardens in different parts of the world are using all or parts of the exhibit for display. The MAB panels are enriched by the addition of specimens and other materials of interest to their visiting publics. Elsewhere the Unesco exhibit has been incorporated into much larger events, such as the industrial fair Expoquímica 81 in Barcelona, the bicentennial celebration of the founding of the city of Bangkok, and in conjunction with the World Fair and Olympic Games in the United States.

A host of countries are translating or have translated the exhibit into their own languages: Arabic, Chinese, Dutch, Finnish, German, Greek, Hebrew, Indonesian, Polish, Portuguese, Russian, Sinhala, Swahili, Tamil, Thai and others. Some countries (such as Norway and Italy) have arranged for translated versions of the posters to be reproduced in multiple copies for wider distribution, particularly to schools.

The wide interest in using Ecology in Action as a teaching aid in schools is reflected in an initiative in the Region of Catalonia in Spain, where six posters from the exhibit have been translated into Catalan. Five thousand copies of each have been reproduced by the municipality of Barcelona and distributed to secondary schools in the province accompanied by a teachers' guide. A similar effort has been undertaken in the Basque region of Spain. In some cases, such as the Federal Republic of Germany, the posters are being used not only for science teaching but also for language training.

A STIMULUS FOR NEW INITIATIVES

The Ecology in Action exhibit is not expected to meet all the needs of everyone everywhere. This would indeed be impossible given the ecological, cultural and linguistic diversity in different countries throughout the world. In recognition of the inherent limitations of a "universal" approach to communicating ecological information, the exhibit is intended mainly to act as a spur to scientists to take initiatives, if they have not already done so, to communicate their own research results to non-specialist audiences.

To help foster such actions, the exhibit was designed to be used as a core to which other elements can be added: components which address related issues, local examples or research projects, particular audiences, etc. Such additions can take the form of similar posters or panels, audiovisual materials such as films or slide–tape presentations, lectures or discussion sessions, computer simulations, etc.

The fact that the exhibit has been designed in modular form further enhances its adaptability. Each poster can stand on its own, or it can be used as part of a larger module (one of the five sections of the exhibit) or an even larger one (36 posters) to which additional elements can be added. Thus it is possible to apply the core concept not only to the exhibit as a whole, but to each individual poster or each group of posters.

Special panels based on MAB research at the national level have, for example, been produced in Chile, based on field projects in mountain areas, grazing lands and continental waters. In China, too, environmental panels of special national interest were featured in ten panels created to complement the Unesco posters. These panels covered such problems as desertification control, salinization, soil erosion, urban modelling and waste utilization. Efforts for depicting nature conservation were focused on China's three internationally recognized biosphere reserves: Changbaishan in Jilin Province, Wolong in Sichuan, and Dinghushan in Guangdong. The Chinese posters were inspired by local MAB research projects, and their design was the result of close collaboration between scientists, the MAB Committee, and graphic artists attached to the

Museum of Natural History in the capital. An estimated 50,000 people visited the inaugural showing of the Chinese-language version of the Ecology in Action exhibit at Beijing Natural History Museum. Wide television coverage, and articles in the *People's Daily* and the local press, as well as in the *Peking Review* which is widely distributed outside China, have also helped rouse the public's interest in the poster materials, which subsequently travelled to most of China's major cities.

The exhibit has also travelled widely in Ireland. Here, a poster competition for schools was organized in conjunction with the exhibit's visit to some ten cities and towns, following its initial display in Dublin in March 1982. The competition was organized by the Irish Art Teachers' Association and sponsored by the Irish Heritage Trust, with prizes offered for the contribution of different age groups of school children on the theme "Ecology – the Chain of Life".

Inspired in part by Ecology in Action, the Soviet MAB National Committee has produced a set of fifteen posters aimed at school children aged 11–14. The title of the exhibit is "Environmental Protection" and the full-colour posters address either a single ecosystem type found in the USSR (e.g. tundra, steppe, mixed forest) or particular aspects of land use practices (e.g. effect of pesticides on cereal field community, influence of pollution on aquatic systems) or a specific aspect of nature conservation (e.g. protecting and helping bird life). A teachers' manual supplied with the posters provides detailed guidelines on how to explain each poster and stimulate the children's interest and appreciation of their environment.

A final example mentioned here is the work of a group of scientists within the Indonesian Institute of Sciences, who have become increasingly involved in environmental education, as one outlet for scientific information on the Indonesian environment. Pilot schemes have been developed at both formal and non-formal levels. At the formal level, attention has focused on introducing environmental dimensions within the existing school subjects rather than developing separate curricula on environmental issues. At the non-formal level, activities have included writing and drawing contests on environmental issues within children's magazines, contests which attract 700 to 800 entries each (Indonesian MAB National Committee 1984). Some of the winning entries of the drawing and painting contests have been made into picture postcards or used to prepare a series of wallcharts which reproduce a selection of the posters in small format (quarter size), accompanied by a booklet comprising complementary new texts, new graphics, classroom exercises and teachers' questions on the subject matter of the various posters selected.

Another adaptation has been the presentation of the posters in slide form, for use mostly as a teaching tool. Transparencies of the posters for use with overhead projectors have also been prepared by the MAB Secretariat, but for internal use only. In effect, cost precludes the reproduction of anything more than a handful of sets in this form, since the *pro rata* photographic costs involved in the reproduction of transparencies are not greatly reduced with increased production runs.

CONCLUSION

In both its form and content, Ecology in Action is intended to be an experiment, which, like any other, has both successful and less successful aspects. On the positive side, it can be said that the posters have enjoyed an overwhelmingly favourable response and that they have been considered appropriate for use with diverse interest groups, age levels, institutional contexts and cultural settings. It can also be said that one of the basic aims of this exhibit has been largely fulfilled: namely, to produce something which would serve as a stimulus to those in the MAB family and beyond to take further initiatives to communicate research results to non-specialists. Such initiatives have been many and diverse, including translations into local languages, printing other language versions in hundreds of copies, preparation of new posters and panels, slide programmes, teachers' guides, transparencies.

Accompanying these largely positive indications and reactions have been criticisms which are useful in analysing the shortcomings of the exhibit. Positive and negative criticisms will not only help shape immediate follow-up activities, but will enable this MAB effort to attain one of its objectives – that of contributing to the search for more effective ways of communicating the results of ecological research to lay audiences.

Environmental Education and Community Involvement

JAYSHREE MEHTA

During the past decade a growing need has been felt to incorporate environmental considerations into development planning. Environmentally sound development can only be founded on widespread environmental awareness. We have seen a significant development in people's environmental awareness through our work in the Vikram A. Sarabhai Community Science Centre (VASCSC). The Centre has been involved in an environmental education programme for students and the community at large for more than a decade.

All levels of participants, students as well as teachers and the lay public, may find within our core programme interests, degrees of complexity and refinement at whatever quantitative and/or qualitative levels fit their needs and abilities. We believe in using a local backdrop for our activities, and Ahmedabad has its own backdrop, as does any other place. The local scene and community life must be the backdrop for environmental programmes to make them interesting and effective.

VASCSC has two main categories of visitors: children and young adults, and families and teachers. They come to the Centre not only to ask questions but also to use the laboratories and workshops and to visit the exhibits. They have a common scientific interest which makes it easy to increase their environmental awareness and understanding.

Our programmes always have the following elements: problem analysis; practical activity such as experiments or field trips; a demonstration/ presentation; testing and development of a product/result such as public outreach material which will result in greater public awareness and education about some environmental issue. Public participation is emphasized at all stages of our programmes.

We have both urban and rural programmes, and there is an active interchange between them. These programmes include individual and group experiments, exhibits from groups or individuals, publications,

teaching aids, games, slide shows, film shows, educational video programmes and kits generated from programmes.

We have brought out publications and reports based on our work, which
include such titles as: "Environment, the Choice Before Us", "Science,
Environment and the Community", "Environment Awareness in Gujarat". A series of newsletters – EFY (Environment for Young), and the
wallnewspaper "Vignan Drushti" – cover various environmental topics.

The Centre has also produced a series of study kits on subjects such as
birds, ecology at the primary level, food, and trees in the city. Several
participatory exhibits and games have also been developed to stimulate the
educational learning process and foster better understanding of nature.
Such an understanding is the basis for environmental awareness, and from
this awareness comes action, i.e. action to appreciate, understand and
conserve nature.

The Centre has an active visual media programme, producing slide
shows on topics such as living or non-living, trees and pollution. The
Centre has produced more than 40 television films in co-operation with
SITE and the Space Applications Centre, Ahmedabad. Many radio talks
are produced throughout the year, e.g. water, pollution, insects and
conservation.

We have a "do-it-yourself" exhibit area where various models, puzzles
and playthings are displayed, on topics like "Where in the world am I?",
pollution, energy and water. The exhibits are mainly of a participatory
nature. Along with the exhibition we bring out minibooks for visitors to
carry home.

We take some of our exhibits to science fairs. Our programme, "Science
Circus" travelled for 10 days covering five such centres within a distance of
500 km of Gujarat. Other programmes include a very popular live snake
show, and demonstrations on energy resources, smokeless chulhas and
solar gadgets.

The Centre also uses traditional media such as puppetry to communicate
scientific ideas. Two major shows on environment and nutrition have
proved very successful, as have special performing art workshops for
children.

A tremendous educational effort is required to help people understand
the interrelationships between humans and their natural environment. The
programmes described above are effective for the large numbers of visitors
who come to science centres, go to national park sanctuaries or visit
natural areas in and around their towns. Our visitors are already motivated
so an educational input facilitates their understanding and appreciation of
things around them. We have established, and have contacts with, several
local action groups of students, youth and sensitive adults as well as school
nature clubs. These clubs form local action groups which help our
educational efforts. They are effective economically and socially because

they are emotionally attached to local issues and problems. Our media help them to take our message to a wider audience.

Our experience in the rural area has been very interesting. We have found rural people very close to nature, but our work with them requires a very different approach from that with urban audiences. Taking them the right message requires a lot of planning, communication skills and follow-up. Some examples of our efforts in this have been to save the horticultural gardens from a hotel development, to clean the industrial pollution of Kankaria Lake and to clean up the River Sabarmarti, one of India's most polluted rivers. However, in developing countries it is not always easy to decide on such issues, looking only at the "environment" aspect. Many times environmental issues are linked with economic development. Whereas for long-range projects there is time to explain the problem, for urgent action this is not possible.

The Vikram A. Sarabhai Community Science Centre has been very successful in its programme to date, and we need to look at what our future activities should be. We feel that to produce an observable change in society some of our programmes should focus on long-range problems as well as on immediate local concerns.

Environmental Education – the Indian Experience: Non-formal Education

T. N. KHOSHOO

[Parts of Dr Khoshoo's paper have already been quoted in Parts I and III. This section is the latter part of his paper – Eds.]

The present-day programme aimed at increasing environmental education and awareness has primarily helped to convert the converted, and is limited to the wealthier and better-educated through books, films, newspapers, magazines and electronic media. This segment of the population acts both as guardian and as destroyer, as is evident by their per capita consumption of materials and the extent and nature of generation of waste. Even so, this segment has affected decision-making in many countries, particularly with regard to nuclear power, chemical spraying of forest, lead in petrol, hazardous chemicals, etc. Media coverage, though uneven, has helped to enhance public consciousness of special events, and accidents such as Bhopal.

ADULT EDUCATION

Illiteracy is a major impediment to social and economic development of our country, especially because the major part of our population (70 per cent) lives in villages. Although the percentage of literacy has increased from 16.6 (1951) to 36.23 (1981) during 30 years, the number of illiterates has also gone up from 3.7 to 4.2 million between 1951 and 1981. The time has come to slant education towards environmental education, and towards weaker sections of the population like women, scheduled castes, scheduled tribes, tribals, agricultural labourers, slum-dwellers, and residents of drought-prone areas. The neo-literates from these communities will go a long way to spread the environmental message at the grass-roots level. These communities have diverse profiles and use of village gossip

401

(chaupal), puppet shows, audiovisuals and science fairs in such areas would have beneficial effects. Voluntary agencies can also play a distinctive role, using local language, information packs, posters, slides, audio, audio-visuals, camel or bullock cart exhibitions and other material needs to be generated.

RURAL YOUTH AND NON-STUDENT YOUTH

This is a sizeable section of our population which needs to be galvanized into a coherent group. One of the ways to do this is to organize it into a National Conservation Development Corps (NCDC), which should be concerned with environmental regeneration. Even ex-servicemen and other volunteer groups could join this Corps. This effort could be funded under a number of schemes aimed at integrated rural development, anti-poverty schemes and the like, already in operation.

TRIBALS/FOREST DWELLERS

Unfortunately this section of our population is being maligned for many things, like deforestation due to shifting cultivation and consequent loss of top soil. This is due to our own ignorance about tribals and their socioeconomic compulsions to take recourse to shifting cultivation. It must, however, be understood that the dependence of tribals on forests is maximum, and their long-term interest lies in protecting, and not in destroying, forests. Someone has said "Forest to adivasi (tribal) is the same as water to fish". Their whole life, economy, and cultural heritage are intertwined with forests. Furthermore, the forests are the repository of several of our native stocks and primitive cultivars of economic plants, as also of partly domesticated or even wild animals. Although these have very low productivity they possess very valuable genes for life under stress conditions, disease resistance and low resource demand characteristics. These species and varieties are in constant demand from the developed countries. It is very necessary now that a special educational programme be designed based on ethnobiological data from the All India Coordinated Programme of the Department of Environment, started some years ago. Conservation of important plant and animal species and varieties used by tribals is also called for, because of the danger of their replacement by high-yielding varieties. The tribals also need to be educated about the dangers of unrestricted encroachment on forest land. The programmes of education can be taken up by involving their community leaders, women and youth.

ACTIVITIES FOR CHILDREN

This area needs to receive special emphasis for reasons discussed above.

Involvement of children can be ensured through essay competitions for different age groups. Such a competition was conducted by the Department of Environment, Government of India with the help of a voluntary organization, the United School Organization of India, from 1982 onwards in all the 16 official languages recognized by the Union. The results are shown in Table 13. This competition has had a multiplier effect because an average Indian child, before sitting for the competition, usually discusses the subject with his parents, brother, sister, relations, friends and teachers. This is how the message spreads. The cash prizes, together with certificates, are given in each of the 16 languages to those securing the first three positions.

TABLE 13

Year	No. of entries	No. of prize-winning essays	No. of languages
1982	1232	86	12
1983	4176	114	15
1984	8767	158	15
1985	9314	164	16

On-the-spot painting, modelling and poster design contests are conducted for children by the National Museum of Natural History (NMNH), with remarkable results. The NMNH has also involved handicapped children. The prizes include a visit to the nearest National Park along with a parent or a teacher.

ECODEVELOPMENT CAMPS

These camps help to promote ecologically sound rural development by involving youth who have the advantage of knowing the local situations. A set of guidelines has been prepared by the Department of Environment (1984). The main objectives of the programme are:

1. Creating awareness in student and non-student youth about basic ecological principles.
2. Identifying the root causes of ecological problems related to human activities.
3. Taking steps to solve ecological/environmental problems of the locality.
4. Developing a spirit of national integration.

The basic idea of this programme is to inculcate in youth a spirit of learning by doing, a spirit of leadership, and a work ethic and sense of pride.

The activities under this programme include tree-planting operations, like nursery creation, trenching, fencing, seed banks, digging pits, planting, water sampling and testing, cleaning water bodies, health care and energy alternatives.

Emphasis is laid on promotion of alternative energy sources, e.g. biogas, and use of solar energy. Along with several non-governmental organizations, over 50,000 students were involved in 1982–83, which again had a multiplier effect. The example may be given of Dasholi Gram Swarajaya Mandal, who, simply by building a protective stone wall with voluntary labour at Lansi village (Chamoli District, UP), were able to stall-feed all their cattle and solve the fodder problem, as also problems of eco-degradation due to grazing and firewood overuse, both leading to deforestation.

NON-GOVERNMENTAL ORGANIZATIONS

Out of about 187 NGOs, 129 are involved in environmental education and awareness, 56 in Nature Conservation, 47 in Pollution Control, 46 in Afforestation and Social Forestry, 28 in Floristics and Faunal Studies, 11 in Rural Development, 10 each in Wildlife Conservation and Waste Utilization, and 9 in Ecodevelopment. Most of these are educationally orientated activities. NGOs are very important agents of change as far as environmental education is concerned. NGOs also provide a very valuable channel for feedback.

PUBLIC REPRESENTATIVES

India is perhaps the only country which has environmental forums for members of parliament and legislators to discuss environmental problems facing the country. Public representatives have the capability to stimulate public interest and build public opinion. Some of them can be real crusaders for environment. However, they need to be fed with proper information packs and facts and figures about local, national, regional and international environmental issues. Experience has shown that conducted site visits by representatives to ecologically degraded and sensitive areas as also those where curative work is in progress would be most beneficial in creating a visual impact.

TRAINING SENIOR EXECUTIVES/ADMINISTRATORS

These are people who are involved in policy planning and in decision-making. They need to be given a proper perception of environmental issues, otherwise situations with serious environmental repercussions can result. From 1947 to the early 1980s, massive development projects were executed but with no development of pollution control. This created a serious backlog of ecological degradation in land, water and air. If this group of people were sensitized now, then we could ensure curative action on past damage and preventive action for future developmental activities. The Tiwari Committee (1980) recommended the appointment of Environmental Managers/Advisers in each Ministry/Department much in the same manner as Financial Advisers from the Finance Ministry are attached to each organization. This would help to bring environmental concern into development projects at the very inception as also into general governmental functioning.

Regular courses are being arranged by the Administrative Staff College of India (Hyderabad), Indian Institutes of Management, Institutes of Public Administration, etc. The people attending these courses are from government, public and private sector undertakings together with industry at large. Broadly speaking, the courses are of two categories: General Environmental Management and Industry-specific Environmental Management.

RESEARCH AND DEVELOPMENT PROGRAMMES

Solutions to all environmental problems are not yet available. Realizing this, the Department of Environment supports Research and Development activities. The scientific and technical personnel in institutions of higher learning such as universities, Indian Institutes of Technology, colleges, etc., are encouraged to undertake specific projects in the areas of their specialization for seeking solutions to problems in various sectors of environment. The Research and Development Programmes are both in the field of Man and Biosphere as well as basic and applied environmental problems.

ESTABLISHMENT OF CENTRES OF EXCELLENCE

The Department of Environment has established two Centres of Excellence in the country. These centres devote their attention to generating new knowledge and methodology and to training in Tropical Ecology (Bangalore) and Environmental Education (Ahmedabad).

DEVELOPMENT OF TRAINED MANPOWER

Environmental considerations have to play an increasing role in development programmes, and there will be an increasing need for trained personnel at various levels, some of them given below:

Training the Trainers

There is an urgent need to train teachers in the design and implementation of integrated environmental education programmes. The first task would be to develop courses that could be imparted through short-term summer workshops. These components could also be incorporated in training courses for new teachers. Such a training would have a multiplier effect for reaching a larger number of teachers. New educational material in the form of teachers' guide books, hand books, illustrative charts and other teaching aids is also required. NCERT is doing useful work in this direction by arranging refresher courses for in-service training of teachers.

Professionals

Like the school system discussed above, there is also a need for training professionals from various sectors, whose activities have an appreciable impact on environment, e.g. engineers, architects, foresters and personnel engaged in sectors like mining, energy and industries. In brief, all those people who are engaged in assessment and management tasks need such an exposure. There is a need to develop specialized knowledge, advanced skills, techniques and expertise to handle and solve environmental problems, utilization of natural resources and protection and restoration of the quality of environment.

Technical Personnel

Environmental management would also require a large number of technical personnel at the middle level, for analytical, monitoring and abatement jobs. There is also a need to design and develop new instruments that would give accurate results, would be easy to operate and not too costly.

Legal Experts

Since the Bhopal gas leak tragedy there has been a spurt of interest in the legal profession. Environmental law is going to be an increasingly important area. However, legal experts need to have a thorough grounding in scientific and technical aspects of environment before they can argue and help to decide cases in the area of environmental degradation which, like the Bhopal gas leak, involve high technology.

Armed Services

Young officers in all 3 wings – army, air, navy – should be given an environmental education training, as should all probationers.

DEVELOPMENT OF EDUCATIONAL MATERIAL AND TEACHING AIDS

Institutions with expertise in the field of environmental education need to be commissioned to develop educational materials and teaching aids not only for the school system but also for rural illiterate masses of this country. Emphasis would be on preparation of scientifically accurate audio and audiovisual materials, which could be utilized for this purpose, incorporating local examples, materials and experience so as to involve a large number of people. Environmental management education should result in economic benefits to society. Preference should therefore be given to schemes resulting in economic gains out of environmental management and also helping to meet the daily necessities of life for the masses. Equally important is to develop scientifically accurate materials, in popular language, for the media (TV, radio, films, newspapers). At present radio and TV are both urban-based and urban-biased in content, medium and practice. The power of these media is tremendous, and they remain essentially impersonal. The value of the spoken word, particularly in the rural areas, must not be underestimated. In such a situation, a school teacher and a village headman wield considerable influence. In the first instance it is these people who need to be environmentally sensitized. In fact, a correct mix of traditional methods and high technology is needed. Camel/bullock cart exhibitions and modern mobile exhibitions, designed by the Centre for Environmental Education (Ahmedabad) and NMNH (New Delhi) respectively are indeed very useful.

CELEBRATION OF WORLD ENVIRONMENT DAY

World Environment Day is celebrated every year. All the Governments in the States and Union Territories, academic institutions, universities and colleges and a large number of schools and voluntary organizations are encouraged to organize suitable activities on this day with token financial assistance from the Department of Environment. These activities have been growing both in quality and quantity during the past few years. The major activities on this day involve a variety of competitions for children, visits to national parks and sanctuaries, identification and solution of local environmental issues.

NEED FOR INTERNATIONAL COLLABORATION

Collaboration at the international level in this area is very necessary. This could be in the form of exchange of educational material, development of teaching aids, sharing of experience, exchange/training of experts, etc. There have been several international conferences which have highlighted the long-felt need for collaboration in this area. UNEP and Unesco are amongst those international organizations most active. The collaboration is envisaged mostly between NGOs, because it is they who have the requisite field experience.

CONCLUSION

The aim of formal and non-formal environmental education is to widen the base of awareness in India, a country where centuries coexist and which is very diverse in almost everything. Such a mass awareness will lead to location-specific action programmes which must be well thought out and based on scientific and technical knowledge. It would also lead to development that could be sustained on a long-term basis.

The Use of Simulation Games in Environmental Education

ABRAHAM BLUM

ADVANTAGES AND DISADVANTAGES

Playing educational simulation games has proved to be a useful technique in environmental education. This is especially so when educators want to bring out problems in environmental decision-making. The occasions when learners, students or out-of-school youth can make real environmental decisions are rare. The next best setting is in a simulation game.

Like all educational media, simulation games have advantages and disadvantages. Educators try to maximize the advantages and to minimize the disadvantages. Well-planned simulation games have the following advantages: learners are actively involved; they learn while having fun (simulation games can be peak learning experiences); games are easy to understand; learners (players) can be involved in decision-making and problem-solving; complex life situations can be simplified; usually rules can be changed to suit learners' background and the game situation; learning can be cognitive, emotional and ethical.

Some of these advantages can become disadvantages, when the situation is not handled in the right way by the game leader.

All games simplify real-world situations because they cannot cope with the full, fascinating, but alas so complex rules of human life. This can lead to oversimplification. Game leaders should point out this difference between "real life" and simulations, either at the beginning of the game or whenever the first simplified situation occurs.

In some cases learners are not willing to accept a simulation game as realistic enough, and they might suggest a change of rules. This should be possible in a well-planned simulation, and the experienced game leader will adapt the rules in order to explore how this change of rules will affect the game. Changing game rules usually raises a useful discussion on what (in real life) can be changed, what cannot, and why it is so difficult to bring about improvements in the environment.

Usually, environmental games are intentionally value-laden. Probably most teachers who use these games are doing so just because of the built-in message. On the other hand, game leaders can misuse simulations to impress their own values, instead of letting learners clarify their own values, which is possible and preferable.

Simulation games cannot always be played with large groups, but this is also true for other active learning methods, e.g. work in the laboratory, in the workshop or with computers. For most teachers the most serious disadvantage of simulation games is that they are time-consuming, but this is much less of a problem in non-formal education. The need for block planning in itself is not bad, because games thus become peak learning experiences.

HOW TO USE A SIMULATION GAME

Each simulation game has its own rules, but some principles are inherent to most games. The first rule is to play the game by yourself or with colleagues, following the instructions step by step. In most cases the instructions seem to be rather complicated, at least when compared to common card or board games. Only in this way can the rules be mastered and potentialities and difficulties foreseen. With experience, also, mastery in leading and – when advisable – in directing the game will come. Therefore the experience of having played a game oneself before leading a group is important.

When introducing others to the game a similar step-by-step procedure should be used. Don't try to explain all the rules at once. The best way to introduce a simulation game is by explaining the role or assumed role which participants will play in the simulation. Then give the first instructions and let the players execute the step, before you explain the next one.

Long theoretical introductions should be avoided. As with audiovisuals, games should be used and not talked about, at least not at an early stage. The game will speak for itself.

Most games are played in several rounds which repeat themselves. In such a case the first round will be played slowly in order to get to know and understand the moves and rules. The game leader may point out similarities and dissimilarities between the simulated and the real situations, but without slowing the game down too much. Drawing conclusions should be left to the debriefing stage or to participants' initiative.

The closer a simulation game resembles reality, and especially when it is based on a real case study, the more complex the rules become. In such cases only the most important rules should be introduced in the first round, and the rest only when a need arises. Sometimes simulation games use background materials, "law books" which are there for reference whenever a "judicial" question arises, similar to a real-life situation.

Educationally the most important part in playing a simulation game is *debriefing*, at the end of the game. That is the time when the parallels (or missing parallels) between the game and real life can be discussed. The debriefing stage is crucial where participants were expected to take decisions. Now is the time to analyse who made good decisions and why. Usually players are quite ready to explain why they chose a certain alternative, and why they might take a different decision should the same situation arise again.

Debriefing often consists of two parts: emotional and cognitive analysis. In the first part the game leader asks players how they felt during the simulation game. Those who did not have luck, or made wrong decisions, will probably not be too happy. The lucky ones will tell about their enjoyment. Again, parallels to real-life situations can be drawn.

In the cognitive debriefing stage, steps taken by players are critically evaluated. When records of players' moves are kept according to the rules of the game, this part of debriefing can be postponed, but it is always better to have the debriefing session as soon as possible after the simulation exercise.

Once a game leader has had more experience with a simulation game, he can usually improve on his and his group's performance. He will get a feeling for which parts to emphasize, when to intervene and how to do so. The game leader may even try out variations by making small changes in the rules and finding out how these affect the simulated situation.

WHAT MAKES A GAME WORK

It is impossible to summarize in a few paragraphs the rules and experience used by successful developers of simulation games. Good books on simulation gaming and on the development of such games for environmental education are available.* Let me stress only a few central points.

Roles played by participants in the game should be modelled on typical roles people play in the solution of real-life problems. This makes the simulation game valuable as an educational exercise. On the other hand there is nearly always a luck factor, as so often also in real life. This luck

*Blum, A. *et al.* (1975) *End to Hunger – A Simulation Game.* Jerusalem: Ministry of Education and Culture, Curriculum Centre.

Boocock, S. S. and Schild, E. O. (eds) (1968) *Simulation Games in Learning.* Beverly Hills: Sage Publications.

Taylor, J. L. (1983) *Guide on Simulation and Gaming in Environmental Education.* Paris: Unesco.

factor, e.g. in the form of head-down chance cards, gives the simulation its game quality. It introduces surprise and fun into the game. Yet the luck factor should not be so strong as to make it dominant. It should still allow the game to proceed in the planned direction, representing an existing or proposed situation.

In simulation gaming, as in other spheres of life, there is no better master than experience. Try it!

Report of a Workshop on The Use of Games in Environmental Education

PETER FENSHAM

A workshop was devoted to the use of simulation games in environmental education. This approach has been a most useful one for many topics in environmental education and games of various sorts have been developed in a number of countries. The two workshop leaders, Abraham Blum and Peter Fensham, organized about 15 of the participants into three groups to play several rounds of a simulation game. The game concerns decisions about whether or not to spend a society's resources on education or technology or continue its use to maintain the present style of the society. The game also contains elements of chance, showing the role of "luck" or randomness in the overall decision-making process.

The other members of the workshop became observers round the "fish bowl" of the game players, and the two leaders either acted as organizers and facilitators of the games or as commentators to the "spectators" on what was happening.

After two rounds of the game a debriefing session occurred, in which the players were assisted to shed their roles and share the feelings and experiences which the game had produced. They also analysed the extent to which the game gave them a sense of the reality which it was designed to simulate. The spectators and players alike were then encouraged to develop a list of strengths and weaknesses of using simulation games in environmental education.

With a proper appreciation of its limitations this pedagogical approach can do much to assist learners to become aware of the alternatives in environmental planning situations, to learn unknown features of these situations and to experience the emotive tension that is engendered by conflicting situations. While it is not suggested that the game player is experiencing or learning any of these things in the same way that participants in real situations do, simulation games at least provide the opportunity for players to share in the range of aspects concerned, thereby learning more dimensions of environmental education.

3

Emerging Directions in Non-formal Environmental Education: Conclusions of the Environment Workshop

LAURIE WAYBURN

Effective programmes in environmental education have involved a combination of formal and non-formal approaches using a multiplicity of aids and methods. These include practical work on individual or community projects, use of heritage and history, and the use of philosophical, religious and cultural beliefs and customs which promote conservation and environmental protection. Games, audiovisuals, music, dance and drama have also proved effective tools for integrating environmental education in both formal and non-formal learning.

Environmental education is moving out of the schools and into the community at large. It is also moving from concept and theory to practice, demonstrating the interdependence between conservation and development considerations. This can be effectively done through providing positive and feasible alternatives to unsustainable environmental management practices, and encouraging a holistic approach to development issues.

A multi-level environmental education programme which combines a strong grass-roots movement with efforts to influence key decision-makers and also develops public opinion on a large scale was found to be the most effective approach. For all such programmes – school-based, university-based, and community-based – partners can and must be found within the community. Governmental and non-governmental agencies, industry and workers' unions, religious, social, scientific and cultural groups can all become important advocates of the environmental conservation ethic.

On the final day of the Environment workshop the group dealing with non-formal education proposed the following important elements as guidelines for future action:

1. The need to make environmental education both in and outside schools *issue-related* through case studies, *"do-how"-related* through practical projects and *community-related* through use of the children's immediate environment, whether rural or urban.
2. The need for environmentalists *to reach out* to colleagues in other disciplines, professions and groups, both to increase their understanding of environmental issues and to demonstrate that we must all work together as partners in change.
3. The need to *reach into* the resources available within individuals and communities, though art, music, drama, dance and traditional culture, to buld a sense of participation and fulfilment in guiding environmental change.
4. The need to demonstrate how environmental education is a tool for sustainable development as it promotes rational land and resource management.
5. The need to disseminate information about the large bank of innovative educational tools and techniques which are now available in public environmental education campaigns.

Index of Authors and Papers

Paper titles listed below are those on which the conference proceedings were based. The list is by first authors, listed alphabetically. The numbers are those used in the text for reference. Papers which are extensively quoted are given a page reference below. Papers with no page reference were circulated and used at the conference but are not reprinted here. Contributions written after the conference for this volume are not generally listed below.

1. Dr. Michael Atchia 58
   Mauritius Institute of Education
   Reduit
   MAURITIUS

   Concern for environmental improvement: how can it be incorporated into science and technology education for development? A regional answer from Africa

2. Dr. B. D. Atreya 63, 127
   National Council of Education Research and Training
   Sri Aurobindo Marg
   New Delhi 110016
   INDIA

   Science education for the environment — an Indian case study (p. 127)

3. Mrs. Enikö Badacsonyi 56, 57, 70, 183, 213
   Kodály Zoltán Musical General School
   Becsi ut 110
   1034 Budapest
   HUNGARY

   Aesthetics and nature (p. 183)

4. Dr. Albert V. Baez 3, 7, 37, 49, 260
   Chairman Emeritus, IUCN Commission on Education
   58 Greenbrae Boardwalk
   Greenbrae, CA 94904
   USA

   Education and conservation strategy (p. 37)

5. D. K. Banerjee
   School of Environmental Sciences, Jawaharlal Nehru University
   New Mehrauli Road
   New Delhi 110 067
   INDIA

   Special interdisciplinary programme at the School of Environmental Sciences, JNU, New Delhi, India

Leeds LS16 9DU
UNITED KINGDOM

Issue-based education in developing countries (p. 157)

34. Ms. MYRIAM KRASILCHIK   58, 61–62, 64, 101
School of Education
University of São Paulo
R. Itapicuru 817 Apt. 61
Perdizes 05006
São Paulo
BRAZIL

Some problems and perspectives on environmental education in the school (p. 101)

35. STEVEN E. LANDFRIED   67
Social Studies Chairman
Stoughton High School
Stoughton, W1 53589
USA

Video Term Papers become public issue forums

36. DR. GERALD A. LIEBERMAN   75, 189
Chairman, Commission on Education
International Union for Conservation of Nature and Natural Resources
World Wildlife Fund — US
1601 Connecticut Avenue, NW
Washington, DC 20009
USA

The resource management education programme (p. 189)

37. A. LINDSAY and E. H. M. EALEY
Graduate School of Environmental Science
Monash University
Clayton, Victoria, 3186
AUSTRALIA

Brain-washing engineers by a different way of teaching about environment

38. PROFESSOR LEONARDO MALACALZA   295
Department of Ecology
National University of Lujan
CC. 221 (6700)
Lujan
ARGENTINA

The teaching of ecology to students of engineering at the National University of Lujan (p. 295)

39. MRS. JAYSHREE MEHTA   71, 223, 235–236, 349, 397
Vikram A. Sarabhai Community Science Centre
Navrangpura
Ahmedabad 38009
INDIA

(a) Environmental education and community involvement (p. 397)
(b) Interaction of science, technology and society — the way a science centre looks
    at it

Subject Index